ADVANCE PRAISE

"David Ciminello has written a great big rollercoaster of a novel. . . . Read this book! Hilarious and heartbreaking at the same time."

—Fannie Flagg, best-selling author of
Fried Green Tomatoes at the Whistle Stop Cafe

"The brilliant David Ciminello's hilarious and moving novel *The Queen of Steeplechase Park* is a crazy Italian circus with a heart as big as Sicily. I loved Belladonna Marie Donato and her merry band of misfits, outcasts who become chosen family as she makes peace with her family of origin. A glorious Italian American feast! Bravo David!"
—Adriana Trigiani, best-selling author of *The Good Left Undone*

"Ciminello is a master of delicious wordplay. His lusciously cinematic story is a veritable carnival ride culled from his family's kitchen history. *The Queen of Steeplechase Park* is a tasty tale of love, sex, and the holy magic of homemade Italian cooking."
—Blair Fell, author of *The Sign for Home*

"Open your mouth and ready your heart because Belladonna Marie from *The Queen of Steeplechase Park* is about to serve you some unforgettable tales of love and loss, with a side of meatballs. David Ciminello has reanimated Depression-era Coney Island with such vivid and dazzling detail that I wanted to laugh, cry, eat a hot dog, and go for a swim all at once. A phenomenal story of a burlesque queen searching for her lost baby in the glitz, ooze, and hum of sideshows from Brighton to Gravesend. I couldn't put it down."

—Lidia Yuknavitch, author of *Thrust*

"David Ciminello is a writer with an ear for gritty urban rhythms, a love of wordplay, and a gift for making the nostalgic past relevant today. His prose is earthy and incantatory all at once. His novel is a delicious stew—an operatic fan letter to the real-life aunt who inspired the titular character, a paean to the Italian immigrant experience, a quest for a missing child, a family cookbook—and always a comedy heightened by its tragic elements. *The Queen of Steeplechase Park* crackles with the hyper-real comic book energy of a graphic novel, and the recipes are a primer on how to live your best life. Buon appetito! Mangiare bene! Delizioso!"

—Stevan Allred, author of *The Alehouse at the End of the World*

"Meet Belladonna Marie, the force of nature plucked from the historical and culinary passions of David Ciminello. Set in depression-era Coney Island, the novel whips up a bevvy of queer, memorable eccentrics, served with a heaping side of sumptuous language. From Melanzana to Puttana, *The Queen of Steeplechase Park* is a whimsical, gastronomical delight."

—Suzy Vitello, author of *Bitterroot*

THE QUEEN OF STEEPLECHASE PARK

THE QUEEN OF STEEPLECHASE PARK

DAVID CIMINELLO

a novel

FOREST AVENUE PRESS
Portland, Oregon

Library of Congress Cataloging-in-Publication Data

Names: Ciminello, David, 1962– author.
Title: The queen of Steeplechase Park : a novel / David Ciminello.
Description: Portland, Oregon : Forest Avenue Press, 2024. | Summary: "The Queen of Steeplechase Park is the absolutely, positively, practically, almost-true story of infamous burlesque queen and magic meatball maker Belladonna Marie Donato. Pregnant at fifteen after gleefully losing her virginity to pansexual neighborhood strongman Francis Anthony Mozzarelli, she is robbed of her baby by a pack of nefarious nuns and her embittered papa has her sterilized without her consent (legal in 1935). With the help of a besotted Francis and her top-secret meatball recipe, a devastated Bella embarks on a riotous quest through Depression-era Coney Island sideshows, the tawdry world of peek-a-boo striptease routines, a queer mob marriage, and a tasty collection of wisdom-filled recipes to find her lost child, herself, and maybe even true love. It all leads Bella back home, to the scene of her Original Sin, where she boldly faces matters of life and death, questions of forgiveness, and a holy mess only the healing properties of great Italian cooking can fix"-- Provided by publisher.
Identifiers: LCCN 2023050727 | ISBN 9781942436614 (paperback) | ISBN 9781942436621 (epub)
Subjects: LCSH: Donato, Belladonna Marie--Fiction. | LCGFT: Biographical fiction. | Novels.
Classification: LCC PS3603.I45 Q44 2024 | DDC 813/.6--dc23/eng/20231211
LC record available at https://lccn.loc.gov/2023050727

Forest Avenue Press LLC
P.O. Box 80134
Portland, OR 97280
forestavenuepress.com

Printed in the United States
Distributed by Publishers Group West
1 2 3 4 5 6 7 8 9

For Mom, Dad, and Brian

And for Auntie

NO ONE LIKE HER

HAD WILLIAM RANDOLPH HEARST known about her, he would have inked her onto the front pages of his newspapers directly above the banner headlines barking about the war crawling across Europe. Walter Winchell would have broadcast about her on *This Is Your World!* They would have told you how beautiful she was. How men dropped in front of her and howled. How Einstein created a brand-new theory, and how Freud folded his cards after she lit one of his cigars. Hollywood could have made her a great big star. She would have taken Bette Davis and wrung that bug-eyed hambone dry. King Kong would have let go of Fay Wray, dropped that dizzy dame those one hundred and two Empire State stories, just so he could hold her in his gargantuan hand. Glenn Miller would've raised his baton and crooned, "Come on, baby! Front my band! You can swing! I know you can!" Pity was never a song she chose to sing. Her anthems were always "Shoo Shoo Boogie Boo" and "All of Me." When she Coney Island cooch-danced, air-raid sirens rang, Lucky Strikes lit themselves, and palm trees sprouted out of Coney Island's sand. After her Cooking Spirit swooped in, meatballs were never the same. Everyone wanted to taste her tomatoes and dip their bread in her Sunday gravy. Had he met her, David O. Selznick would have ceased his search for his silly Scarlett O'Hara and cast her in a Technicolor epic all her own. Fiddledeedee! Frankly my dears, there was no one like her!

CONEY ISLAND, 1938

SHE STANDS IN FRONT of the roiling Brooklyn sea. Alone. A devastated girl of eighteen. But she is timeless. Ageless. She is a Queen. Almost two years after having lost her baby, not long after losing the love of her life, her gorgeous Jesus-boy, her Hero, her Coney Island King, she rises up from the December sand battered and shivering and weak. Behind her, the amusement park rides sleep, tucked and tarped and snoring. Before the frozen day she had lost her King, death was something she'd only experienced with the messy slaughter of dirty backyard animals. Chickens squawking, goats bleating, pigs screaming. Like her broken heart. Flapping and jerking and bleeding and ready to stop beating. Forever. Her toes touch the frigid water. The starving ocean opens its salty mouth and bears its foamy teeth.

HER NAME

ON THE FIRST DAY of first grade at Saint Anthony's Catholic grammar school in Clifton, New Jersey, in our good Lord's year of 1926, every immigrant student in Sister Mary Cara Malloy's classroom got a good ole U-S-of-A American name.

Elvira became Ellen, Giacomo became Joe, Igor became Eric, Rosaria became Rose, and so on.

"And what is your name, please?" the ruler-wielding nun, an odious old penguin, asked six-year-old Italian factory mouse Belladonna Marie Donato.

Bella's mamma had given her the name Belladonna (beautiful girl) because when she was born she was *so goddamned ugly.* Her papa sometimes called her *gabadost* because she was *so goddamned stubborn* and strong-willed.

She was also fiercely intelligent and incredibly independent.

Full of the guile and charm of a Sicilian folk-tale fox.

She had the fortitude and strength of ten Italian elephants.

She could charm the socks off rocks.

"My name is Belladonna Marie."

"No, it isn't."

"Yes, it is."

The fierce-looking old Irish nun, one of a bitter baker's dozen farmed down from an ancient abbey in Singac, slammed her ruler onto Bella's desk with the force of one of Lucifer's better demons.

The entire class jumped out of their skirts and knickers.

"Young miss, we do not talk back in God's classroom!" The penguin's rheumy eyes traveled up to the fractured ceiling like she was searching for something. "Now, let me see . . ." She tapped her ruler on Bella's desk while squinting up through the cracks. No one was breathing. "BARBARA!" she suddenly screamed. "From now on, in God's classrooms your name will be Barbara Mary!" She extended her skeletal hand and smiled, baring green, tobacco-stained teeth. "Now thank me and kiss Christ's ring."

No one, except maybe Belladonna Marie Donato's papa, was ever able to make Bella do anything.

The little girl crossed her arms. "No!"

"What did you say to me?"

"I said NO!"

The stunned nun's feathers puffed out of her habit. Her beak snapped open. "Barbara Mary, if you do not thank me and kiss Christ's ring this very instant you will be one very sorry little *EYE-talyan* monkey."

"Vaffanculo, vecchio pazzo pinguino irlandese!"

"What did you say to me?"

"FUCK YOU, YOU CRAZY OLD IRISH PENGUIN!"

All twenty-seven students—all the Stevies, the Charlies, the Carols, the Harrys, and the Shellys, bolted to the outskirts of the room and started praying.

"YOU GREASY LITTLE ROACH OF A WOP!"

The old bird's hands flew, but quick as a whip, Bella ducked and plowed into the nun's wool-sheathed shins. Teeth sank, warm blood bled.

"IN THE HOLY NAME OF JESUS CHRIST, LET GO OF ME!"

While the students stomped and cheered, the Italian monkey and the old Irish penguin flailed up one side of the classroom and toppled down the next. They plowed through chairs and flipped desks. They slammed into the blackboard and tumbled out the door. They rolled together like a two-headed, four-armed, four-legged bowling ball down a long, waxed corridor. They bounced down thirty-seven marble stairs, splintered through two more doors, pinwheeled past the school's front offices, and crashed into Reverend Monsignor Teschio's formidable desk.

That's when Bella unlocked her jaw, stood up, spit out a mouthful of wool, and wiped her lips.

"MY NAME IS BELLADONNA MARIE DONATO!" she panted. "AND I AM NOT KISSING ANYTHING!"

HER COOKING SPIRIT

THE DAY BELLA'S SOUL-TORTURED mamma, Lucia Medina Donato, gave birth to her final child, Little Luigi, she threw the steaming baby into Bella's seven-year-old arms. "You have to be the mamma now," she spit. Hair crazing, eyes blazing, she grabbed her daughter by the ears and yanked her close. "I never loved your papa," she hoarsely whispered. "I only ever loved Tino Scarabino. That's it." Then she took a deep breath, stopped talking forever, and never left her bed.

Manolo Antonio Donato, Bella's too-proud papa and the always-tired night watchman at the Robertson Scale factory where the family lived, went his own kind of crazy. He had a smiling scar that started in the right corner of his mouth and sliced up his cheek, but he always looked mean. "Who's gonna cook? What the fuck are we gonna eat?"

"I'm starving!" Bella's big brother, the firstborn, Manolo Antonio Junior, hollered.

"We're hungry too!" Bella's sisters, pretty Concetta Regina

and addle-brained Lucrezia Angelina, screamed. The two girls had tried like hell to cook but they destroyed everything. Chickens met charred ends. Pigs were boiled down to grizzle. Tomatoes never stopped bleeding.

After cursing her life and the world God created, Bella wrapped and plopped her yowling baby brother into a make-shift wooden wagon. She crossed herself, dragged it out of the factory complex and pulled it four long blocks to LoMonico's corner market while singing,

> Lullaby, lullaby, lullaby, ooh,
> Who will I give this baby to?
> Lullaby, lullaby, lullaby, eee,
> I will keep this baby for me . . .

"I gotta make a big pot of tomato gravy for my starving family!" Bella yelled over the infant's wailing as she yanked the wobbling wagon into the store's warm belly.

The owner's giant wife, Big Betty LoMonico, lumbered out from behind the register. She towered over the little girl like a Coney Island elephant lording over a mouse.

"What's your name?"

"Belladonna Marie Donato."

"From the Robertson Scale factory. What's your baby's name?"

"This is my mamma's baby, but she gave him to me. I'm his Bellamamma. His name is Little Luigi."

"Where is your mamma?"

"She's in bed."

"What is she doing there?"

"She's got the great depression."

"What about your papa?"

"He says if I don't make something for my family to eat right away, he's gonna kill me."

Big Betty knew little ones in need of an angel when she

saw them. She lifted the bawling infant out of the wagon and grabbed Bella by the hand. The shock of it made Bella wince. But the little girl's arm tingled in a way it had never tingled before, and she decided she liked it.

"You come with me."

The colossal woman tugged Bella past Big Bud, who was busy butchering behind the meat counter.

"Where are we going?"

She marched her through the crowded store and into a sprawling kitchen, where bright white Jersey sunshine blasted through billowing lace curtains; where a monster stove crouched warm and ready to roar; where a weathered butcher block stood warped and clean; where a vased bouquet of fresh basil rested in the middle of a linened table, lush and inviting; where a Radiola was softly crooning Paul Whiteman's "My Blue Heaven."

Bella never wanted to leave. "You really live here?"

"When was the last time this baby had something in its belly?"

"I don't know."

"Mary, Mother of God, help me. Please."

Muttering the Lord's Prayer, Big Betty rummaged through overstuffed drawers until she found an empty glass bottle and an old rubber nipple. As she boiled them, she poured water into another pot, added unsweetened evaporated milk and Karo Syrup, and snapped a flame on under it. Once the mixture cooled down, she funneled it into the bottle and thrust it into Bella's hand. "Shove the nipple in that baby's mouth and feed him!"

Luigi suckled like a starved calf.

The bottle drained fast.

"Now rub and pat his back!"

While Bella did as she was told, Big Betty gathered several

mason jars of summer-ripened tomatoes, canisters of spices, a softball-sized onion, a ring of garlic, and a rough-edged wedge of Pecorino cheese. After carefully placing the burped baby in a soft pile of dish towels, she clutched her big chest. "Sometimes I have a little trouble breathing," she said. She pinched off a small chunk of the cheese, popped it into her mouth and worked it around. After a moment, she took a deep breath. "There. Now I feel better." With renewed strength, she slammed a thick cutting board onto the kitchen table in front of the basil. "Garlic heads. Always smash them to loosen the skin. Then pop out the cloves." She handed Bella a wooden mallet. "We need at least ten of them."

As Bella got to work, Big Betty poured a heaping glug of Montebologna Olive Oil (*the Olive Oil of Italian Kings!*) into a cauldron-sized pot she had slapped onto the stove. Then she took a healthy swig and patted her bountiful breasts. "Keeps the insides greased. Keeps the old clock ticking."

After frying the garlic cloves and tossing in a pinch of chili flakes, Big Betty had Bella hand crush the tomatoes and throw them into the pot too. Then she grabbed a huge handful of basil from the vase on the table and thrust it into Bella's face. "Take a good, deep sniff," she said. "That's it! Drink it in! Ain't it delicious?"

It made Bella sneeze, but she loved the fragrant spiciness of it.

After they chopped and added the pungent leaves, Big Betty ordered Bella to measure the spices, one at a time, with her hands and toss them in too. Salt. Pepper. Oregano. She didn't tell her how much. But she watched carefully.

"That's it! You got it!" The giant woman gripped Bella's little chin in her big hand and squeezed. "The Cooking Spirit is inside you! Can you feel it?"

The only thing Bella felt was her starving stomach grumbling. "No," she said through squashed lips.

"Don't worry. You will. Believe me," the big woman said as she drizzled a spoonful of honey into the simmering tomato gravy. "My secret ingredient. Don't tell anybody."

"I won't. I promise."

As the tomato gravy sent its Italian perfume into the room, Big Betty plated a fistful of chocolate biscotti. Then she sat Bella at the kitchen table and asked her about her home.

"We live in the caretaker's house at the Robertson Scale factory."

"Tell me about your family."

With a mouthful of chocolate crumbs, Bella gave Big Betty the rundown. "My oldest brother is Manolo Antonio Junior. But we call him Tony. He's ten. He likes boxing. Sometimes he tries to box me."

"Don't let him do that."

"When he does, I grab him by his coglioni and squeeze until he begs for mercy."

"Bravissimo!"

"I also have two sisters. Concetta Regina. We call her Connie. She's very pretty. And Lucrezia Angelina. We call her Lulu. She's stupid. They are nine and six. I will be eight next week."

"I wish you a happy birthday."

"Grazie."

"Prego. When did your mamma get the great depression?"

"Right after she pushed out Little Luigi. She always used to cook and clean," Bella continued. "Now she stays in bed all day and she doesn't speak."

"Not a word?"

"Not nothing."

Big Betty compressed her lips and nodded with a deep

understanding. "Before your mamma got the great depression, was she happy?"

Now Bella compressed her lips.

"Did she teach you how to cook?"

"My mamma never taught me anything."

"What about your papa?"

Memories of Manolo tossing Bella over the waves in the Jersey ocean while her bitter mamma watched from the beach flooded over her.

Papa! Catch me!

He called her his *little tomato*.

This was before Lucia's knife flew. Before Little Luigi came. Before Manolo Donato's tomato garden became his mistress, his only friend, his everything. When he wasn't guarding the factory grounds at night, or asleep on his basement cot when the world was light, he tended his Sicilian tomatoes with a shovel, or a pruner, or a spade. He coddled them and cooed to them. He entered them in every carnival, county fair, and festival contest and usually won first place.

So ripe.

So tasty.

"My papa always makes me wash his feet," Bella whispered to Big Betty.

"What do you mean?"

"I have to do it after he works all night guarding the factory and always after he does his gardening."

In the murky shadows of the living room, Manolo would take a seat on his throne of an armchair like a king. Then Bella would slosh in with a bowl loaded with warm water and place it on the floor. She would kneel in front of his feet, untie and remove his shoes, then peel off his socks to reveal toes cracked and moldy, onioned bunions red and mean.

"So smelly."

Then she would begin washing. She'd done this routine daily since she was three. Never Lulu. Never Connie.

"Only me."

"That's disgusting."

Bella didn't tell Big Betty she sometimes spit in the water before carrying it in, that she sometimes squatted over the bowl and peed.

"My papa hates me."

For a while neither of them said a thing. Then Big Betty LoMonico took little Belladonna Marie Donato's hands in hers. "You listen to me. If the world gets bad. If Manolo Junior tries to box you. If your papa makes you wash his stinking feet. Call upon the holy hands of your Cooking Spirit. The Cooking Spirit will fix it."

Bella wanted to believe the big woman. She really did.

"Can the Cooking Spirit fix the great depression?"

The moment of silence that followed was seismic. It was Vesuvius before the deluge. Tephra and sulfur gasses gathered above their heads.

"The Cooking Spirit can fix anything."

"You mean like the Holy Ghost? Like Jesus?"

"More like a guardian angel. One that will be with you always. Capisce?"

"No. Non capisco."

"Non preoccuparti. Don't worry. You'll understand soon, my little darling."

No one had ever called Bella *darling* before. At first, she wanted to punch the jumbo woman and bite her in her mammoth shins. Then she decided maybe she might hug and kiss her instead.

After the gravy finished cooking, Big Betty dipped her wooden spoon into the pot and gave Bella a taste.

When the sweet tang entered the scrappy little girl's mouth, the floor left her feet. It tasted better than the chocolate biscotti. It tasted better than anything. Her insides swooned, her heart crooned, and she flew all the way up to Heaven.

"Now do you feel the Cooking Spirit?"

"Yes!"

"Of course you do!"

After Bella dropped back down to the floor, Big Betty covered and loaded the pot of tomato gravy into her wobbly wagon along with two pounds of dry spaghetti, the entire wedge of Pecorino cheese, ten tins of White House evaporated milk, and a snoozing Little Luigi.

"Now go and feed the rest of your family!"

Bella wrapped her small arms around the gigantic woman's enormous waist. Then she kissed her pillowy stomach. She wanted to say *I love you*. But she couldn't say those words.

Not yet.

"Come back soon!" Big Betty hollered as she pushed Bella and her wagon out the door of the store. "Next time I'll teach you how to make my big mamma's magic meatballs! Meatballs saved my life once!" the big woman sang. "And someday they're gonna save yours too!"

Big Betty LoMonico's Tomato Gravy

Inherited from Big Betty's big mamma,
Claudia Signorelli.

This recipe carried Bella
in its delicious Italian arms
for her entire life.
It was the Sicilian fuel
that lit the fire that simmered
in her bodacious heart
until the day she died.

(You will have to keep reading for the
magic meatball recipe.)

2 large (half-pound) cans of good quality Italian
   plum tomatoes
3–4 tablespoons of Montebologna Olive Oil
   (*the Olive Oil of Italian Kings!*)
8–10 whole cloves garlic, skinned
a nice pinch or two of red chili flakes
a few dashes of dried oregano
kosher salt, to taste
fresh ground black pepper, to taste
1 teaspoon raw honey
a healthy handful of fresh basil, chopped

1. Separate and skin the garlic cloves. Be sure and
   keep them whole.

2. Place canned tomatoes in a large bowl and use your hands to squash them until smashed real good. Preferably while singing "My Blue Heaven."

3. Put olive oil in a big pot. Take a healthy swig to keep everything ticking properly. Tilt the pot on a flame to create a healthy puddle in its bottom crook and fry cloves until golden. Don't burn them!

4. Right the pot and add red chili flakes and let them sizzle for 30 seconds while muttering the Lord's Prayer.

5. Add hand-crushed tomatoes to the pot.

6. Add dried oregano, salt, black pepper, honey, and stir. Let the holy hands of the Cooking Spirit guide you.

7. Add chopped basil after drinking in the fragrance. Be sure and take a deep sniff.

8. Bring the gravy to a rolling boil while occasionally stirring with a wooden spoon, preferably your mamma's.

9. Lower flame, set lid on pot, and let the gravy simmer for a few hours. Play some cards. Eat some biscotti. Sing a few songs. Dance around the kitchen.

10. When the gravy is done, when it tastes better than candy, thank the Cooking Spirit and serve tossed with your favorite pasta immediately.

11. Buon appetito! Mangiare bene! Stare bene! Delizioso!

THE TASTING

When Manny Donato tasted the tomato gravy Bella wheeled home, he was astounded.

"Who made this?"

"I did."

"Don't you lie to me."

"I'm not lying."

The man was silent for a full minute. Then a small smile played across his lips. "I don't fucking believe this . . ."

Bella thought she was gonna get a sweet kiss.

Her papa's eyes brimmed with tears. He quickly rubbed them away. Then he smacked his stunned daughter to the floor and vanished into his basement sanctuary.

After the rest of the family finished eating (they scraped their plates, they slurped up everything), Bella carried a bowl of gravied spaghetti into her mamma's room. She pulled a chair next to the silent woman's bed and proceeded to feed her with a twirling fork and spoon.

Maybe the Cooking Spirit would swoop in. Maybe her mamma would take a bite and start speaking again.

"I made this with Big Betty LoMonico," Bella proudly whispered. "Do you like it? It's full of the Cooking Spirit."

Lucia took the food into her mouth. She slowly chewed and swallowed without saying a word.

"Don't worry, Mamma," Bella said as she continued to feed the mute woman. "I'm gonna take care of you."

Silence.

"I'm gonna take care of Little Luigi. I'm gonna take care of the whole family. I'm gonna take care of everything."

More silence.

Could be Big Betty was full of shit, pieno di merda, just like everybody.

"Mamma, are you ever gonna talk again? Mamma, why won't you speak to me? Mamma, speak to me! Please!"

SANTA LUCIA

IN THE SICILIAN SEASIDE village of Siracusa in the summer of 1916, men and boys circled Lucia Medina Cicolina like a flock of horny vultures.

They were only after one thing.

"Fly after one of my sisters! You don't want me!" Lucia always used to sing.

She had nine beautiful sisters (much to her doting papa's everlasting dismay).

At first the randy birds swarmed around the other Cicolina girls, but they always flapped back to the one with the corn silk hair and emerald-green eyes.

Lucia Cicolina.

The Sicilian prize.

Some of the suitors offered slaughtered animals as gifts.

A few wrote poems.

Some sang songs.

The handsomest, a mandolin-strumming merchant from Catania by way of Napoli named Manolo Antonio Donato, presented a bushel of the most succulent tomatoes Lucia had ever tasted. While her lips dripped with juice and seeds, he regaled her with tales of a place he called America on the other side of the sea.

He told her America was Paradise.

The Promised Land.

"The streets are paved with gold! The rivers run with milk! The ponds are flooded with honey!"

Lucia laughed at him. "Oh, really?"

"I am going to sail there and plant my tomatoes! I'm going to be rich and raise a great big, happy American family! You'll see!"

He strummed his mandolin and tried to seduce her with a honeyed rendition of "Santa Lucia."

Birds fainted out of the sky.

Goats cried.

The wind sighed.

But Lucia felt nothing.

Not that she didn't try.

One by one, she sniffed and kissed each of her suitors on the lips.

Too salty. Too nasty. Too stinky. Too stiff.

"Soon I will have to choose a suitor for you," Lucia's papa tearfully professed.

"Love is for idiots!" Lucia sneered. "I won't have any of them!"

When true love finally found Lucia Medina Cicolina, it took her completely by surprise.

It happened while she was picking cherries in a crooked tree at sunrise. Reaching for a succulent-looking cluster, her foot slipped, and she dropped into the arms of the most beautiful creature she had ever seen.

A face full of Italian sunshine. Eyes the color of the Sicilian sea.

One kiss was all it took.

Lucia had never tasted anything so sweet.

"Who are you? What's your name?"

"I am Tino Scarabino."

"I am Lucia Medina Cicolina."

Together, they flew down to the ocean and splashed their way into the waves. They fed each other cherries on the beach. They climbed the rocks along the coast and made love in the cliffside caves.

To seal the deal, they danced into Siracusa's only Studio Fotografico hand in hand and had their picture taken, arm in arm, cheek to cheek, hearts beating like two airborne birds waltzing.

Lucia cooked delectable dishes for the two of them to eat.

Fried cassatelle (ravioli-shaped pockets of pizza dough stuffed with fresh ricotta, orange zest, and bits of chocolate), the most delicious timballo di anelletti (a deep pasta pie stuffed with homemade ziti, meat, and cheese), pasta chi sardi (spaghetti with fennel and sardines), and Tino's favorite, pollo al forno (breaded chicken thighs, breasts, and legs braised in a stew of potatoes, onions, and Manolo Donato's succulent tomatoes).

It wasn't long before wicked whispers about the affair swirled around Siracusa. The salacious stories found their way to Lucia's papa, who refused to believe them until he followed his daughter to the ocean one day. When he saw her in the arms of Tino Scarabino, when he witnessed what they were doing, he fainted straightaway.

The next day Tino Scarabino disappeared without a trace. (Island whispers told a tall tale of Tino being tied into a rock-filled sardine sack and tossed to the bottom of the Sicilian sea.)

"How dare you bring such shame upon our family!" Lucia's brokenhearted papa yelled when he found his daughter sobbing in front of the waves. "Tomorrow you will marry Manolo Donato and you will sail away. You are no longer my daughter! You are dead to me!"

The wedding was the most miserable the island had ever seen. Feast-topped tables sadly stretched through the village fruit groves.

Paper lanterns frowned in weeping trees.

The wind died.

The birds stopped singing.

The bride was a despair-filled vessel cinched in satin and lace.

"Look how she cries!"

"Tears of joy!"

"Tears of happiness!"

That night Manolo took what was rightfully his. He pounded into his new wife until she was raw and empty.

The next morning, when their boat set sail, Lucia resolved to jump after Tino into the sea.

But Manolo wouldn't let her out of his sight. While the ship bucked and rocked, he held her in his arms. He held her tight while he strummed his mandolin and sweetly sang,

Santa Lucia! Santa Lucia!

PARADISO AMERICANO

WHEN THE NEWLYWEDS FINALLY arrived at the iron gates (gates like sharp teeth) of the Robertson Scale factory in Clifton, New Jersey, Lucia's feet felt like they were the size of the trunks they were carrying. Her body was ready to collapse. Her heart was broken. Her exhausted belly was already holding their first baby.

"Benvenuti in paradiso! Welcome to Paradise!" Manolo cried.

Lucia glanced up at the belching smokestacks on the other side of the toothy gates. *This place is going to eat me. It's going to chew me to shreds and swallow me, and the world is never going to see me again.* "We are living in a factory?"

"Yes! I am going to be the night watchman!" Manolo proudly proclaimed. "And you are going to cook and clean and raise my great big, happy American family!"

Tucked in the back of the noisy complex, docked on a patch

of dry land, rested a crooked, rambling, ramshackle caretaker's house. From the front, it looked like a long, two-story train car that had lost all of its steam.

"And right there!" Manolo pointed to the barren yard behind it. "I am going to plant my tomatoes! We are going to have the best tomatoes in all of America! We are going to have the best of everything!"

Lucia tried her damnedest to make it a home for them. She scrubbed the splintered floors and took vinegar to the grimy windows. She cooked her way into the crude kitchen.

Manny (as his factory coworkers took to calling him) spent every free minute tilling the ground behind the house and planting his seeds. As his babies sprouted into the free world, he strummed his mandolin and softly sang,

Santa Lucia! Santa Lucia!

Every time he climbed on top of his exhausted wife, she closed her eyes and drifted back to the caves of Sicily, back to the arms of Tino Scarabino.

When a child they christened Manolo Antonio Donato Junior (they called him Tony) punched his way out of his mamma's womb, Manny was so goddamned happy. "This one's a fighter!" he proudly exclaimed. "Just like me!"

Eleven months later beautiful Concetta Regina slid out of Lucia's womb in a puff of Sicilian perfume. The little girl quickly became Manny's favorite. "This one is so beautiful! Just like me! She is my tiny Italian flower. My precious Connie!"

Another twelve months went by, and Belladonna Marie Donato (forever known as Bella) blasted out of her mamma like a circus cannonball on its way to the moon.

"This one is not so pretty," Manny declared after catching the soaring baby. "But her hands are nice and big!" he proudly proclaimed. "She has tomato-picking hands! Just like me!"

As she grew, the little cannonball stormed through life like a chip off her old papa. Always singing. Always dancing. Full of mischief. Incredibly charming.

"Papa! Buy me candy!"

"Papa! Take me to the beach!"

"Papa! Throw me into the air!"

"Papa! Catch me!"

Manny always serenaded his band of scrappy children with his mandolin. He took them on day trips to the Jersey shore. He tossed them over the waves and taught them how to swim.

"Papa! Catch me! Papa! Catch me!"

Lucia tried to be a good mamma.

She really did.

But when her children begged for her love and attention, she slapped their hands away.

She slapped her husband's hands away too.

"I'm finished with your dirty business! No more babies!"

"You will never be finished with me!"

"Ho finito! I'm as finished as finished can be!"

"I bet you'd let me fuck you if I was Tino Scarabino!" Manny sneered while she was butchering a chicken for supper one evening.

They were both surprised when the tip of Lucia's knife grabbed the corner of his mouth and sliced up his right cheek.

As Manny's blood flooded the kitchen the children screamed.

"Papa is dying! Papa is dying!"

It took over sixty stitches to close the gaping wound.

While Manny feverishly healed, Lucia supported the family by setting up shop in the factory lunch stand, selling sautéed sausage and pepper sandwiches to the workers. Sometimes she rolled meatballs and dropped them into the most delicious tomato gravy. Sometimes she fried chicken cutlets until they were tender and crispy.

Bella was the only one who helped her mamma. The little cannonball had a crude knack for cooking, but Lucia didn't have the patience to teach her anything. The little girl worked purely by instinct. Pinching in a little of this, stirring in a little of that. And tasting. Always tasting.

After Manny recovered, he kept his distance from his wife. For weeks he couldn't speak. Once the stitches were yanked out, a hideous scar formed up his right cheek. He buried his mandolin in his garden, and he never sang again. He found solace only in his Sicilian tomatoes. And in his God. He went to church and prayed every day. He prayed for his wife to be docile. He prayed for more babies.

When Saint Anthony's Reverend Monsignor Teschio miraculously presented the parish with a three-year-old orphan, a quiet little girl who had lost her parents in a hideous house fire, Manny volunteered to take her. She came with the name Lucrezia Angelina, but the Donato family called her Lulu.

As the Donato children grew, each of them had a job to do. Tony helped his papa with the gardening. Bella helped with the cooking and washed her papa's stinking feet. Precious Connie helped their mamma with the cleaning. Lulu helped everybody with everything.

While Manny went about his miserable business, the factory workers laughed and snickered. When one of the men asked him if Lucia had cut his balls off after she had sliced his face, Manny downed a bottle of bootlegged whiskey and almost beat the guy into an early grave.

"I don't care if you kill me!" Manny bellowed as he pinned Lucia to their bed and pushed himself into her. "You are my wife! You are my goddamned God-given property!"

While Lucia kicked and screamed, the children pounded on the bedroom door.

"Mamma!"

"Papa!"

"Stop it!"

"Please!"

It seemed to go on forever, the wild grunting and gut-curdling screaming.

After Manny's horrible brutality, Lucia was never the same. For nine long months her belly grew while she floated around her American home like a Sicilian zombie.

"Mio Dio, mio Dio, perché mi hai abbandonato?"

My God, my God, why hast thou forsaken me?

After she gave birth to her final child, a runt of a boy christened Luigi Tommaso (Little Luigi), Lucia never left her bed. She stopped speaking. She turned her head.

"Papa, what happened to Mamma?"

"Papa, we're hungry!"

"Papa, what will we eat?"

Manny dropped to his knees in his tomato garden and wailed like a slaughtered animal. "Che fottuto paradiso mi hai dato?!" he cried up to his God. "What kind of fucking Paradise have you given to me?!"

PENNIES FROM HEAVEN!

DOWNTOWN WAS A RAMBLING bramble of trolley tracks, offices, apartments, and cozy mom-and-pop shops. Coal trucks, milk trucks, and ice trucks trundled from the concrete hearts of Passaic and Clifton and chugged their way through the outlying tree-lined streets harboring one-, two-, and three-family homes.

So sweet.

The kitchen gardens behind those houses saved so many lives.

Every Monday the diaper truck stank by. The coal truck clattered around on Tuesdays. On Wednesdays the milk truck clanked through. The ice truck dropped frozen chunks on Thursdays.

Oak Street (just past the trolley station) was known as the other side of the tracks. Mostly the Poles and the Irish lived among the broken glass and overgrown grass.

Up along Hammond Avenue, Italians hung heavy wheels and stinky logs of provolone and clubs of hard salami in every plate glass grocery store window. For fifteen cents, you could have an award-winning Italian hero, the great Sicilian trophy, in your hands: Genoa salami, provolone, mortadella, capicola, sliced tomatoes, hot peppers, olive oil, shredded lettuce, and vinegar on a seeded roll from Savasta Brothers Bakery.

So tasty.

The Savastas baked across the street from Saint Anthony of Padua Roman Catholic Church.

After confession, after your soul was saved again and again, a quick walk across the street, the snap of a change purse, and for only a nickel you had a long loaf of tit-warming bread cradled in your arms like a precious baby.

A real heart-warmer in winter.

Summertime it was Scarengella's for the best shalollies. Colorful Italian ices. Everything from blueberry to chocolate to the tricolored Neapolitan surprise. You could slowly lick a small and make it last, but why do that when, for an extra penny, you could tongue a large and extend the blast?

Not so fast! Not so fast!

Jews fanned out from Midland Avenue. Dark hardwood floors. Tall, ticking grandfather clocks. Rose-print wallpaper. Fancy rooms where Rachaels and Rosas set linen-covered tables with polished heirloom silverware and cut glass crystal.

Prayers first, then we fast!

At the Erie Railroad Station on Main Avenue, Bella liked to watch the trains come and go.

From there, one could ride all the way to Jersey City. Then it was a short ferry toot-ride to Manhattan for Fame! Fortune! and Infamy!

Was this the train the Great Depression rode in on?

Bella imagined a bearded old man, his facial hair grown to a point that touched the ground. Coal-dark circles under his evil eyes. Long, dirty nails.

She imagined he only traveled at night.

She imagined him crawling into people's homes and ripping the food out of their cupboards while cackling like Bela Lugosi, *Brother, Can You Spare a Dime?*

In bed, nestled between her snoozing sisters, any train whistle Bella heard made her think he was making the rounds.

She imagined him slipping off the train at the small station platform and popping the bulbs out in the streetlamps as he spirited through town.

Only a buttered roll from Lardy's or penny candies from Rowe~Manse Emporium could make Bella forget about him.

Sometimes she would try and outwit him by lifting oranges from Corrado's fruit stand, or by working with a pack of neighborhood kids to trip the coal truck. Together they would drag a ragged tree limb into the street and wait for the rubber tires to trounce over it so they could grab the runaway nuggets and sell them for precious pennies.

THE LITTLE ANGEL
QUEEN OF 1930

EIGHT YARDS OF DELICATELY hand-needled point de Venise lace was used to make her small gown. Her wings were fashioned with white chiffon left over from Big Betty LoMonico's death shroud. (Massive heart attack after sharing Big Mamma's magic meatball recipe.) Her little crown was crafted with pipe cleaners, tiny charms, and jingle bells. The basket she firmly held in her tomato-picking, feet-washing hands was lined with silver satin and filled to the lidded brim with white rose petals.

From her Clifton Savings Bank fire escape perch, eleven stories above the annual feast of San Michele, above the sausage and pepper sandwich stands, vats of frying zeppole, games of chance, the hats and kerchiefs of Italian men and women, the buzz cuts and banana curls of their children, nine-year-old Belladonna Marie Donato could see all of Van Houten Avenue.

S. S. Kresge Five and Dime (a great place for shoplifting);

Bruno's Elbow Room (mafia meetings under smoke-shrouded gambling lamps); Guido's Pizza Pie Palace (sold whole or by the slice); Moglia's Penny Candy, Ice Cream, and Soda Pop Shop (sweater girls rotating on spinning stools); Loprinzi's Gymnasium (where smelly pretty boys made muscles pop and grin); and the neon marquee of the Jewel Box Theater (Saturday-morning cowboy serials, Mickey the Mouse, MGM, Paramount Pictures, Universal, RKO, and *Looney Tunes*). Just off Scales Drive sprawled the Robertson Scale factory (puffing clouds of lung-choking smoke and steam). Resting in one of the long shadows of the factory smokestacks sat Mozzarelli's Star Barbershop (Xavier Patrizio Mozzarelli's American dream: *A Great Haircut Gives a Man Dignity!*).

Not far from all of this Italian bliss rose Saint Anthony of Padua's holy steeple, scratching the mighty balls of Heaven.

The Lord be with you.

And also with you.

Wobbling in the wind next to Bella, Guiseppi Sparza took a stiff nip off his bottle of hooch. With trembling hands, he attached the homemade harness strapped around her torso to a double laundry line that stretched all the way across the street to another pulley soldered to another fire escape precariously rusting off the building that housed Cipolini's Home for Funerals, the death house where Big Betty LoMonico lay in state next to a generous pot of meatballs and tomato gravy. (It had taken ten men and three wailing ladies to pry Bella off the coffin.)

"Silenzio!" Guiseppi yelled. "Silenzio!"

A celebratory fanfare blasted from Dario Scungille's one-man band, and a salad platter of fairy lights (green, white, and red) exploded over everything.

Echoes of *silenzio!* and a few *shut-the-fuck-up!*s from the crowd below brought everything down to a holy hush.

"Close your eyes," Guiseppi whispered into Bella's ear, "and get ready to fly!"

Into the night sky, where the moon had a crazy face.

The Glasgow-grinning face of Coney Island's Steeplechase.

"One! Two! Three!"

Guiseppi gave Bella a rough little shove and she sailed across the line.

Papa! Catch me!

She never felt so alive.

She never felt so free.

Was that the specter of Big Betty LoMonico or Bella's Cooking Spirit flying along beside her?

Bella's soul was soaring.

Lots of *oohs* and *ahhs* from below until her hurtling weight made the rope jump the pulley attached to the bank's fire escape.

The crowd screamed.

Dario flung his instruments and opened his arms wide. "I've got her!" he cried. But just before Bella hit the brave musician's head, Guiseppi Sparza yanked the rope, and Bella was jerked back into oblivion.

A snowstorm of rose petals flew.

"Viva San Michele!" Bella yelled. "Viva San Michele!"

Saint Anthony's dented church bells clanged as petals were caught and wishes were made. Somewhere in the crowd, a turkey-necked old octopus of a woman with a lit Pall Mall toggling between her lips released her ten-year-old son's hand to smack a petal off her head.

"Francis!" the old woman yelled like a Tuscan circus bear as the kid ran. "Francis Anthony Mozzarelli!"

The boy dodged through the applauding crowd, ducked behind a statue of San Michele, and pulled his own cigarette out of his shoe. He ignored his mamma's calls, struck a match, and puffed in solitary bliss until a single white rose petal, like a fat ash from Pompeii, spiraled down in front of his pretty face. He caught it and held it in his fist.

"Viva San Michele," he whispered.

Then he made a secret wish, crossed himself, tossed the petal to the wind, and blew the little Angel Queen of Clifton, New Jersey, a tender kiss.

SAINT FRANCIS

FRANCIS ANTHONY MOZZARELLI WAS the cannoli of his mamma Mary's eye, a torta di mele, her Italian apple pie.

Red Delicious.

Rome Beauty.

Northern Spy.

Like Bella, from the moment he entered the world, he stirred things in people that were better left unstirred.

What a lovely or *sweet* or *darling little girl* was what most people said.

Mio piccolo femminiello, his mamma Mary called him. *My little Caravaggio saint.*

His papa, the nasty old barbershop bookie Xavier Patrizio Mozzarelli, despised his son. He drank and beat the kid regularly, yelling, "See what you made me do!" until the day Mary stepped between them with a gun on the boy's eighth birthday.

"Say goodnight, old man! Your day is done!"

At the tender age of twelve, Francis already had the strut of a tiny tiger in heat. He swung his hips like a dandy little randy bonobo monkey. A pack of Chesterfield's rolled in the short sleeve of his crisp white T, stiff blue jeans cuffed around his ankles, a pair of spit-polished Buster Browns on his feet. He had the face of a mini matinee idol. His aspect was pretty much Rudolph Valentino in *Uncharted Seas*. But the attitude was all Clark Gable in *The Easiest Way*.

At thirteen, the kid loved to light matches, stand behind Old Man Martinelli's garage in the middle of the day, and strike them against the cement wall there. It was especially good in summer when he could watch a hot breeze catch and carry the smoke up past the woodpile. Sometimes he burned bugs with the tip of his lit cig, watched them curl into themselves until they hissed and exploded. Sometimes he let the match he was holding burn down to his skin.

It was a great place to shuck off his clothes with a friend.

He loved to swap a pack of Beech-Nut or Curtiss fruit drops for a playful peek into a buddy's knickers or a quick sniff up a girl's dress. Sugar tempters did little to get pants to drop or a skirt to rise. But chocolate went a long way. Especially a Baby Ruth or a Snickers surprise.

At fourteen, he started working out at Loprinzi's Gymnasium. Pumping iron like a little Strongman. Sweating his body into something Leonardo da Vinci would have pined over. He glowed like one of Saint Anthony's painted saints. Girls (and even boys) followed him around like lost puppies.

"Here comes that gorgeous kid! Here comes Saint Francis!"

When he was a ripe sixteen, the Roman Catholic Arch Diocese of Clifton, New Jersey, commissioned a portrait of the crucified Christ to be painted by artist and community leader Monsignor Teschio. It was the old padre's idea to place the painting above the altar in Saint Anthony's.

It was Mary Mozzarelli's idea to have her son pose as Jesus.

KING OF KINGS

HE COULD SEE THE beginning of tobacco stains on his old mamma's fingers. Thick, efficient hands with nails clipped like a man. She chewed and snapped a wad of Wrigley's as she masterfully handled the clutch, never grinding the gears. Mostly she held the big DeSoto steering wheel at the bottom. A practical all-American car for a practical Italian American woman. The old octopus had the eyes of an eagle, a bird of prey. She always set her hair herself after sanitizing her scalp with Tiger Balm. Not a feather out of place. She didn't like religious icons dangling from her rearview mirror. No plastic Christ magnetized to the dash. She liked to keep things spare.

Especially when she prayed.

Hail Mary, full of grace, the Lord is with thee.

Francis squinted as the sun glinted off the tip of the freshly waxed hood. The blinker click-clacked, click-clacked, the brakes moaned, and they arrived at Saint Anthony's. Car doors creaked open and closed. Chestnuts populated the pavement and grass. Mary kicked them out of the way. *Precious nuts. Ha!* The tops of the trees waved. More nuts fell. The tail of her kerchief flapped behind her. Big, gray clouds spread across a pink sky. Francis thought about Carolina Scarlatto, he thought about rigatoni, he thought about his little queer cock-sucking buddy, Terelli Lombardi. He thought about his seventeenth birthday, only four days away. Terelli had promised something extra special for him on that big day. He could feel the stiff pack of Pall Malls in his pocket pressing against his cannoli.

Is that a gun in your pants? Or are you happy to see me?

Church bells clanged when Mary knocked on the rectory door. She cracked her gum and glanced at her watch. *Come on. Come on.* A chestnut hit the pavement behind her. (Nine inches in the right direction and it would have hit her head.) More wind. Francis looked up. *This is fuckin' ridiculous.*

"Hello!" Mary yelled as she rapped on the stained glass. "HELLO!"

From inside, the snap of a lock. *What the fuck kind of church locks its doors anyways?* Francis adjusted himself as his mamma spit-washed the front of his hair. They both itched for a cigarette. Mary tried not to clock the time again as the old monsignor eased the door open.

"Thank you for coming."

"Yeah, yeah . . ."

Mary pushed Francis in first. The boy was tall. Getting bigger every day. A foot taller than his dead papa, God rest the old fucker's soul.

Bless me, Father. For I have sinned.

Down a long corridor. So spooky for a godly place. But nothing scared Mary. Certainly not anything holy. She was thinking about dinner. Maybe leftover meatballs. Maybe eggplant parmigiana. Maybe rigatoni Bolognese. She settled on spinach-and-ricotta-stuffed manicotti. For dessert, her famous cannoli.

My top-secret recipe.

Angels everywhere. Celestial heads carved out of oak peered down from web-infested corners. Stained glass blondies, angelic youth sporting wings twenty times the size of an eagle's unfurled. Votive candles trapped in cherry glass winked and threw shadows against the dark walls. So dusty. Musty. A dead spider crunched under somebody's foot. *Cleanliness next to godliness? Ha!* Mary followed her son and the old priest.

"This way. This way, please."

The cavernous room the old man led them into was cold. An ice pond of a concrete floor spread to a bank of heavily curtained windows.

The monsignor scraped a cranky torchiere across the cement. Long brass body. Milk glass shade. Powerful bulb. Cord frayed. He snapped it on. Lots of light.

Mary opened her purse. "Mind if I smoke, Reverend Monsignor?"

Without waiting for a response, she struck a match on a window frame (chipped and peeling evergreen paint) that faced the weeded courtyard and the statue of the Blessed Virgin, arms beckoning over an empty birdbath. Tweet, tweet! *Little fuckers. Who has time for crumbs anyways? Birds, that's who.*

Mary found a chair. She sat her ass down and sucked on her cig as she watched her son peel off his shirt. So goddamned beautiful. Her boy didn't have to be told what to do. He was a smart kid. He knew Christ was practically nude. He removed his lucky penny loafers and peeled off his socks too. Then he stripped down to a knitted posing strap. Where the hell did he get that? Monsignor Teschio dropped his paint tubes. The young man was meant for an artist to paint. Meaty thighs. Calves knotted and hard. Taut waist. Stomach lean. Feet Magdalene would have kissed before bathing. Mary crossed herself twice and took a healthy hit off her cig.

"Where do you want me to stand?" Francis asked.

The monsignor was busy pretending to count his brushes.

"Over here?"

The kid had the voice of a man. Always did. Maybe he was an old soul. He came out with the eyes of his dead papa. It gave Mary the shivers the way he looked up at her when he had suckled. The fresher the milk, the sweeter the mozzarella.

"Who's my baby?"

"I am."

"Always and forever?"

"Forever and always."

The canvas the monsignor fussed over was enormous. Enough room for an image to sprawl.

A nice day for hanging the body of Christ.

Mary craved a cup of hot coffee. Seat itching, she stubbed out her cigarette and was up before the first tube of paint was squeezed. The kid could walk home. She had manicotti to stuff and bake. She had cannoli shells to fry and cream.

Francis heard the door slam.

Outside, more chestnuts dropped off the trees.

Inside, Francis slyly smiled at the old priest.

Outside, Mary lit another cigarette.

Inside, Francis begged to be blessed.

Outside, Mary gunned the DeSoto down the block.

Inside, Francis slowly removed his jock.

Outside, Mary stepped hard on the gas.

Inside, Francis made the old priest kiss his ass.

Outside, Mary sped all the way to her house.

Inside, a new King of Kings was crowned.

OLD RAGS AND SHUDDER WILLIES

DURING A PACKED MASS on a humid Sunday in April of 1933 Bella sat sandwiched between her two sisters in one of the rock-hard pews in Saint Anthony's. Manny, Tony, and Luigi (the grammar school nuns had tried like hell to change the seven-year-old's name, but like his Bellamamma, the boy would have none of it) sat lording directly behind them. Their hot breath puffed down the girls' necks as Monsignor Teschio droned on and on. Bella's dress was cemented to the wood, her thighs were glued together with sweat, her intestines were churning, and a burning itch clawed at the base of her back. She tried to take her mind off the pain and the heat by going over a list of favorite recipes taught to her by her old friend, Big Betty:

lasagna Bolognese
baked ziti
spaghetti and meatballs
Italian wedding soup

potato gnocchi

uova da raviolo (the fortune teller's pasta)

seven kinds of tortellini (stuffed with cheese or mushrooms
    or spinach or beef)

When that didn't work, she stared at the painting of the impossibly beautiful young Christ, crucified and floating high on the back wall of the chancel. Her guts gurgled as her eyes wandered around His broad shoulders, as she got lost in the muscles of His arms, and as she counted the rungs in the ladder of His abdomen. She stared so long, the gorgeous painting started to vibrate, and the painted Jesus came to life. He winked and Bella's heart seized. Sweat beaded across her forehead. She got a bad case of the shudder willies. Somewhere in the back of the church a baby shrieked, and the bitching itch at the base of her spine spun into her abdomen and exploded, sending a warm, sticky wetness oozing between her legs. She worked a panicked hand under the waistband of her dress. When it came back her fingers were coated with blood. Holy Christ! She stood straight up.

"I'm dying!" she screamed.

"What's happening?!" Little Luigi yelled.

"Holy shit!" Tony slapped his hands over the boy's eyes. "The bitch is in heat!"

"Get her dirty ass out of here!" Manny ordered his other daughters.

Lulu and Connie hustled their bleeding sister up the aisle, kerchief tails fluttering behind their heads like cotton flames, while the women in the congregation crossed themselves, while the men looked away.

In the balmy narthex the panicked girls used their headcloths and holy water to wash down Bella's quivering legs. Then the three of them burst out of the church and into the blazing day.

"Run! Let's run!"

A trail of shimmering drops of blood glistened on the pavement behind them as they charged all the way down Van Houten Avenue to the Robertson Scale factory. They barreled through the sharp gates and hustled Bella into the house. They charged up the stairs, stripped her fast, and forced her into a lukewarm bath. After a quick scrub, they knotted up some old rags, thrust them between her legs, and packed her into the junk-cloth quilts of their bed.

"Am I gonna die?" Bella asked.

"Don't be stupid," Connie said. "This just means you can have a baby."

"I can't have a baby! I have supper to make!"

"Don't worry!"

"You're not gonna have a baby!"

"We'll take care of supper!"

"We'll take care of everything!"

As soon as Connie and Lulu were gone, a titanic light filled the room and the gorgeous face of Saint Anthony's Jesus appeared. All hazel eyes, pink lips, and white teeth. The color of Christmas in His cheeks.

Hello, my darling Angel Queen!
I'm here to take you all the way to Heaven with me!

A TRUE CONFESSION

As BELLA BLOSSOMED INTO a young woman and her body fell into its improper proper places, her mini pomidori, once-sweet cherries, bloomed into bodacious beefsteaks; her lips plumped nicely; her eyes danced ferociously; and her hips bopped along like bongo drums. When she walked, she sashayed.

And she was so horny.

She was horny every night and every day.

She often found herself alone in Saint Anthony's with her hands between her legs, thinking about fucking Jesus.

"Bless me Father, for I have sinned."

"The Lord be in your heart and upon your lips. What are your sins?"

The voice droning on the other side of the confessional grill belonged to the shaky old monsignor from Sunday mass. The one who liked to watch the grammar school boys shower after football practice. The one who loved to hear them confess about what they did in the privacy of their water closets and on top of their stained mattresses.

"I have dreams about making love with Jesus Christ, Father."

From the other side of the grill, the messy clatter of dropped Rosary beads.

"What exactly do you mean?"

"He comes to me almost every night, and even sometimes during the day. He flies off that painting out there and into my bed and makes holy love to me."

"What did you just say?"

"He mounts me and fills me with His Holy Spirit and takes me all the way to Heaven with Him."

"This is a mortal sin! You're going straight to hell, young lady! When this happens, you should pray right away!"

"I do pray, Father! I pray every night and every day!"

Hell be damned, she prayed for her sweet savior to appear and fill her with His Holy Spirit again and again and again.

WHAT'S MINE IS MINE

CHRISTMAS AT THE ROBERTSON Scale factory in 1935 was bullshit. Bullshit and cold. But downtown's S. S. Kresge Five and Dime during the holidays was a warm escape from the harsh winds of the Great Depression.

While a light snow sifted down outside, Bella strolled around the tinseled aisles and fingered the festive displays. It was like being trapped in a giant tree ornament. Swimming in the red, the gold, the silver, and the green. The tinkling sounds of the holiday echoing. As Bella browsed, a small bottle of Luscious nail polish went up a sleeve. A Drumstick lipstick went between her breasts. A Lady May powder compact (the one Carole Lombard used) was dropped down a boot. And something special from the toy display was snugly tucked under the front of her coat.

When she was finished with her *shopping*, she waddled over to the soda fountain and sat next to her sister Lulu, who was straddling a stool and sipping an ice-cream soda with her nose buried in the latest copy of *Silver Screen* magazine.

"Ain't Clark Gable and Joan Crawford dreamy?"

"Clark Gable's got ears like a goddamned monkey. And Joan Crawford's bowlegged. God, I'm starving."

Bella grabbed her sister's straw and took a greedy sip.

"Hey!" Lulu yanked it back. "What are you gonna make for supper tonight?"

Bella swiped a finger lick off the top of her sister's ice-cream soda. Her Cooking Spirit had been avoiding her lately (but sexy Jesus was with her always). "I don't know. I haven't had time to think about it. I've been too damned busy."

"Will you make your chicken parmigiana tonight? You make the best chicken parmigiana ever! I love all the garlic you use. And the way the mozzarella gets nice and stretchy."

Bella pulled her new lipstick out from between her breasts and made a show of smearing it across her lips. "Okay. Chicken parmigiana it is."

"Can you make the cutlets extra crispy?"

Bella rolled her eyes. "You like your cutlets crispy. Luigi likes them fried light. Tony wants them pounded thin. Connie likes them small. Papa wants them thick. You all drive me fucking crazy." She capped the tube and blew the counter boy a kiss.

Lulu grabbed the lipstick out of Bella's hand. "Hey, where did you get this?"

Bella snatched it back. "Never mind! What's mine is mine!"

"If Papa catches you with that wax all over your lips, he'll knock the lights out of your sockets."

"At least I'll be wearing the right shade of lipstick when he hits me! Hey, I picked out a present for you while I was shopping!" Bella reached under her coat and yanked out a genuine Flirty Eye Princess Beatrix baby doll. Pretty ribboned bonnet and matching nightgown, bowed lips, blushed cheeks, and lashed eyelids that opened and closed when you moved it. Bella ripped the price tag off the doll and tossed it away. "Merry Christmas, dummy!"

Lulu grabbed the doll. "Oh, Bella! Thank you! It's just what I always wanted!" She clutched it to her chest. "My very own baby!"

It warmed Bella to see Lulu so happy. Lulu who was so god-damned sweet. Lulu who never asked anybody for anything.

"Oh! I love it, Bella! And I love you!"

"I love you too. Listen, if it doesn't behave, I can always put it back and steal another one!"

The two girls laughed. Then Lulu froze.

"Hey, why does that man keep looking over here?"

A Dagwood-looking character behind the ornament display smiled and waved.

Bella extracted her new compact from her boot. She popped it open and rolled her eyes. "Oh, that cake-eater! He caught me shopping," she said as she powdered her cheeks. "So, I let him give me a melon squeeze in the employee water closet." She snapped the compact closed and tucked it back down her boot.

Lulu took a sip off her soda. "What's a melon squeeze?"

Bella grabbed her sister's tits.

"Hey! Stop it!"

"He told me he wouldn't rat me out if I let him look up my dress."

"What did you do?"

"I told him I'd let him put his hands over my girdle for a quarter."

"You didn't!"

"I sure did. And for another dime I tickled his little baloney pony. And if you tell me you don't know what that means, I'll squeeze your melons until your gravy bowl screams!"

Bella's Best
Chicken Parmigiana

This was always Bella's best dish.
The one she cooked when comfort was needed.
It was a great Big Betty hug.
Filled with tasty, stretchy, gooey, crispy love.

2 large chicken breasts (from a happy little hen), skinned
    and deboned
2 eggs, beaten
2 cups breadcrumbs (preferably made from a good stale
    Italian bread)
dried basil, to taste
salt and pepper, to taste
½ cup Italian parsley, chopped
1 cup or more of Montebologna Olive Oil (*the Olive Oil of Italian*
    Kings!) for frying
a healthy ball of fresh mozzarella
Pecorino Romano cheese (to be grated)
4 cups homemade tomato gravy (see Betty LoMonico's recipe)

1. After saying a prayer to honor the life of the bird (an Italian
   chef's God-fearing grazie), cut the chicken breasts in half and
   pound evenly to about a quarter-inch thick, nice and thin.
2. Season breadcrumbs with salt, pepper, grated Pecorino
   Romano cheese, and chopped Italian parsley on plate.
3. Beat eggs in dipping bowl (until nice and frothy).
4. Heat olive oil in fry pan (medium flame).
5. Dip each cutlet in egg and then in breadcrumb mixture.
   Coat evenly.

6. Fry seasoned cutlets in a fair amount of olive oil on medium heat until golden brown on each side. No more than a couple of minutes on each side. Do not overcook. Watch for splattering. Otherwise, the oil will jump out and bite you with its fiery teeth. A couple minutes on each side should make the cutlets nice and crispy (just the way Lulu likes them). Drain on paper towels (or an old paper bag or butcher paper).

7. Line a nice-sized baking pan with a fair amount of tomato gravy. (If you don't have a batch of Betty LoMonico's tomato gravy on hand, you can make a quick batch of gravy by hand-smashing a jar or can of plum tomatoes. Add dashes of salt, pepper, and dried basil to taste. Fry some sliced garlic in the oil for the cutlets and add them to the tomatoes.)

8. Place cutlets in pan on top of gravy. Add more gravy over cutlets (don't drown the cutlets).

9. Completely cover gravied cutlets with thin slices of fresh mozzarella.

10. Grate fresh Pecorino over the prepared cutlets.

11. Bake in a preheated 350-degree oven for about 30 minutes or until cheese is golden brown and gravy is bubbling. This is how you will know the cheese will be nice and hot and stretchy. While the parmigiana is baking, hug the oven and tell it how much you love it. Thank it. Bless it. Honor it.

12. Once removed from the oven, let the bubbling chicken parmigiana rest for ten minutes. Then devour it.

13. Buon appetito! Mangiare bene! Stare bene! Delizioso!

BEAUTY AND
THE BEAST

WHEN SPRING FINALLY SPRANG (the same day a new *Looney Tunes*, "I Haven't Got a Hat," starring Porky Pig, premiered at the Jewel Box Theater), gaudy posters bloomed all over Clifton advertising the arrival of a traveling carnival trained in from the Midwest. Thrilling rides, cotton candy, clowns, and a genuine beauty and the beast contest—first prize, a fistful of money and a sparkling crown fit for a queen.

Connie Donato decided to enter with the family's caged canary, Canto.

Bella decided to enter too.

For weeks she fed the backyard pig, a sow she christened Abundantia, everything from pizza scraps and stale cannoli shells to soured milk and moldy potato rinds.

Bella had known the pig since it was born. The runt of a litter of twelve little ham hocks, she saved its weak life by bottle-feeding it herself, burping and singing it to sleep . . .

Lullaby, lullaby, lullaby, ooh,
Who will I give this baby to?
Lullaby, lullaby, lullaby, eee,
I will keep this baby for me . . .

Soon it grew as big and as round as a dirigible. It was as shapely and as wild as Bella herself, often escaping from its garden pen and charging toward freedom.

"Here pig pig pig pig PIG!"

Bella taught the animal tricks by coaxing it with meatball bits. The sow squealed, sat, rolled over, and played dead.

During factory lunch hours, while her night watchman papa soundly slept, Bella shimmied into a plum-colored Jantzen Shouldaire she'd filched from the Girls' Club locker room, slipped on a pair of white pumps snatched from Gelbhart's, smeared on some dime-store-lifted lipstick, tied a rope laced with jingle bells around the big pig's neck, and the two of them ran around the factory grounds practicing their prizewinning runway parade. High-grade pork from squeals to heels. They cantered down alleyways and bounced through clusters of break-time men tossing bocce balls and pitching playing cards and pennies. Long, low whistles and catcalls chased Bella and her prancing pig past the old food stand (closed since Lucia stopped cooking).

"Go girls! Go!"

At fifteen, Belladonna Marie Donato may not have had the face of Jean Harlow, but she had the body of a young bombshell. Hips that swung like church bells. Tits that bounced like bowling balls. Dead were those modesty-gone-mad days of yesteryear! She was her own Gilda. Sadie Thompson. Delilah. Salome. She got past the Durante nose she inherited from her papa with a lipsticked smile that could cream juice out of a stone. Her showstopping days had finally arrived!

Hips bumping, breasts bopping, Bella prodded the leashed

pig with a long stick as they ran. A twig-slap on the pork's ass, and the two of them jiggled like partners running from a storm.

"That's a lot of ham there!"

"Look at them juicy teats!"

"Sa-weeeeeeeeeet meat!"

Bella felt the full power of her sexuality. She felt like a real woman. She felt like a Queen. For the first time in her life, she felt pretty.

"I forbid you to enter that contest!" Manny Donato bellowed when he caught his daughter jogging the sow around the factory grounds.

"If Connie and her stupid bird can enter, why can't I?"

The scar on Manny's right cheek twitched.

"Because you're too *goddamned ugly*!"

"The men at the factory don't think so."

Unlike Bella, Connie had blossomed into a real Italian rose. Emerald eyes like her mamma's, a button of a tip-tilt nose, and lips that formed a perfect bow.

But she wasn't a bombshell.

"I'm gonna enter that contest and win!"

Manny raised his fist and blasted back, "I'm warning you. If you disobey me, I'll knock your teeth into the back of your fucking head!"

THAT'S ALL, FOLKS!

THE SPARKLING PROSCENIUM OF an outdoor operatic gypsy stage spired up against a backdrop of blinking lights, flapping flags, and swirling carnival rides. Standing among the excited crowd in front the footlights of the gaudy affair was the entire Donato family, minus Bella and Lucia. Tony, Luigi, Lulu, and Manny (who had won first place in the Prizewinning Produce Show for his enormous beefsteaks) cheered as Connie and her caged canary Canto joined a line of twenty-seven girls, some with goats, some with roosters, some with cats, some with dogs, and one with a horny saw-toothed donkey.

"Connie's gonna win, Papa!" Luigi hollered through a mouthful of peanuts.

"Where's Bella?" Lulu asked.

"Who the hell cares?" Tony snapped.

As Dario Scungille's one-man band played "God Bless America," the girls and their animals baltered across the stage. The crowd applauded and whistled and cheered as each contestant cantered forward holding or coaxing or dragging her beast. Roosters crowed, goats jumped, and cats hissed.

Connie's canary chirped and flapped its little wings.

"Ladies and gentlemen, we have a last-minute contestant!" the emcee, a real midwestern corn kernel who had trouble pronouncing East Coast names, announced. "Miss Bella Donna Mary *Do-nay-toe* and her three-hundred-and-fifty-pound sow, Abundance!"

"Belladonna Marie Donato!" Bella hollered from the wings. "Sorry!"

As Bella and her enormous pig trotted onto the stage, jingle bells jingling, teats swinging, the crowd hooted and whistled.

"Mamma mia!"

Dario Scungille kicked his instruments into an impromptu tom-tom beat as Bella and her pig bounced around the stage. Abundantia squealed and Bella squealed too. "Howdy, everybody!" she hollered over the brassy fanfare. She waved at the applauding crowd and twirled around in front of the judges: the boy-crazy monsignor from Saint Anthony's; Guiseppi Sparza, who was too old to see; and the carrot-dicked cake-eater from S. S. Kresge. She blew her papa a sweet kiss and smiled like a saint, teeth gleaming, as she gamboled past the judges. Then she sashayed her big beast center stage and meatball-coaxed the animal to roll over, sit, play dead, and speak.

"Papa, look at Bella!" Luigi hollered through a mouthful of cotton candy.

"Son of a bitch!" Manny hissed.

"She's so pretty!" Lulu sniffed.

Dario played a jaunty reprise of "God Bless America" as the girls and their beasts paraded around the stage one last time.

"Bella's gonna win, Papa! I can feel it in my heart!" Luigi cried.

"I'm gonna fucking kill her!" Manny growled.

"Why?"

Bella stood out like a horse in a haystack, but she never felt so beautiful; she never felt so free. She felt like a little Angel Queen again, flying over everything.

Papa! Catch me!

After the judges conferred, the line of girls was narrowed down to four: Connie Donato and her canary Canto, Brunhilda Winklepicker and her snaggle-toothed cat Scarlett O'Hara, Clara Fell and her horny donkey Jackie Boy, and "Bella Donna Mary *Do-nay-toe* and Abundance!"

A drumroll, please.

"And the winner is . . ."

Connie closed her eyes. Brunhilda crossed her fingers. Clara shrieked. And Bella got ready to take her prizewinning bow.

When Connie's name was called, Bella let go of Abundantia's jingle-belled leash and made a run for the judges in a tornado of fury. "Hey, fellas! We had a deal! You promised to vote for me!"

The sow jumped into the crowd and plowed through everyone's legs, the cat went after the canary, and the horny jackass kicked after Abundantia.

Bella was almost swallowed by the ensuing stampede, until a pair of strong hands grabbed her. In the chaos she was quickly lifted and carried to safety.

"Francis!" a gruff-voiced woman somewhere in the crowd called frantically. "Francis Anthony Mozzarelli!"

It all happened so quickly. Before Bella knew it, her feet were planted on the ground.

"Francis!" the gruff voice screamed.

In a swirl of confusion and relief, Bella looked around, but the Hero who had rescued her was nowhere to be seen.

"Francis Anthony Mozzarelli!"

When Bella arrived home, her papa chased her around the house like a rabid racehorse out of its gate. When he finally caught her, he knocked her left cuspid out of her mouth and gave her two black eyes. Then he shot the pig, tossed the carcass into the kitchen, and ordered Bella to cook something delicious with it.

Risi e Bisi con Prosciutto

Risotto was a dish Bella always loved to cook.
She could make it with just about anything.
It required creativity and patience.
She often made it with squash blossoms in spring.
Asparagus and zucchini in summer.
Dried fruits in autumn.
And wild chestnuts and roasted garlic and herbs in winter.
(She never made it with ham after this.)

2 pounds ham meat, cut into quarter-inch bits

3 cups Arborio rice

7 cloves garlic

8 tablespoons unsalted butter

2 large garden leeks, sliced (light green and white parts) and
    thoroughly rinsed

2 cups dry white wine

2 cups fresh peas

Montebologna Olive Oil (*the Olive Oil of Italian Kings!*) for frying

grated zest of two lemons

1 cup (Pecorino) cheese, grated

salt and fresh ground pepper, to taste

fresh basil

12 cups chicken broth

1. In the bottom of a large Dutch oven, sauté the ham meat in olive oil until some of it is nice and crispy. If the pig was a beloved pet, you might shed a tear or two or three, especially if you had entered a genuine beauty and the beast contest together. Thank the animal, honor it, and try not to over salt the pork with your tears.

2. In a separate gravy pot, heat broth and smashed garlic cloves until steaming. Keep warm.

3. Add and melt four tablespoons of butter over medium-high heat in the Dutch oven. Add the leeks and stir until they are soft (3–5 minutes).

4. Add the Arborio rice to the leeks and ham and cook, stirring, until toasted (3–4 minutes).

5. Stir in wine and cook, stirring. Scrape up all brown bits and delicious crispy nubbins stuck to the bottom of pot until absorbed (3–5 minutes). Use a well-seasoned wooden spoon if you are lucky enough to have one.

6. Add six cups of the hot broth to the rice, a cup at a time, stirring constantly, until mostly absorbed (8–10 minutes).

7. Add six more cups of broth to the rice mixture, a cup at a time, stirring constantly, until risotto is tender and thickened (10–12 minutes). Stir with patience.

8. Reduce the heat to low and stir in the peas, cheese, and remaining butter. Add more broth if risotto is too thick.

9. Season with salt and pepper.

10. Top with lemon zest, slivered basil, and more cheese.

11. After a quick prayer for every pig ever killed to eat, serve immediately.

12. Buon appetito! Mangiare bene! Stare bene! Delizioso!

RAGAZZI

THE PUNK END OF autumn that year brought two suitors past the factory gates for Sunday supper. The first to arrive was Dino Montebologna, or Dino the Olive Oil King. His onyx-colored Cadillac 370-D V-12 thundered up Scales Drive, gunned through the pointy gates, growled through the factory grounds, and shot up to the Donato house in a hurricane of mafia hits and shady business deals. The young gangster had taken over the local Elbow Room from the recently deceased Bruno Landini (God rest his fuckin' whacked soul).

"Sassafras! Daddy Warbucks is here!" Luigi hollered as Manny, Tony, Lulu, and Bella spilled onto the front porch.

The slick-looking capo disembarked in a flourish of ankle-length black cashmere and satin spats. He had a beak of a nose, a purple mouth, and the sharp eyes of a suspicious rooster. A tall, barrel-chested goon with the mean mug of a Neapolitan Kong hovered behind him, carrying a jug of Montebologna Olive Oil (*the Olive Oil of Italian Kings!*), a ribboned box of Rowe~Manse Emporium's butter-soft fudge, a black-bow-topped bottle of

Nero d'Avola wine, and a blimp-sized bouquet of long-stemmed bloodred roses swaddled in black bunting.

Manny grabbed Dino's black-gloved hand. "Mr. Montebologna. So good of you to come!" It was seldom anyone saw Manny smile in those days. When he did, the scar on his face tugged into a sneer that kept most people at bay.

The young dandy bowed, but before he could open his plum-colored mouth, an old jalopy of a pickup truck back-fired its way into the front yard. It skidded to a stop an inch from the Cadillac and convulsed, coughing and hacking as the engine expired.

"It's Hopalong Cassidy!" Luigi cried as a lanky cowboy jumped out of the cab and strode up to the front porch. This cock of the walk was tall and skinny, a well-worn Stetson tog-gling on his handsome head, a loaded burlap sack slung over his broad back. (*Just like Santa Claus!* Luigi thought.) Up close, he looked like a real Cracker Jack prize. Cliffside cheekbones under blazing eyes the color of the Azores' skies and legs like pistons powered by long, lean thighs. He tossed the sack to Tony. "Here's a pile of Pink Ladies!" he cried.

Luigi's mouth dropped open. "You really got ladies trapped in that bag?!"

"They're New England apples, kid! Perfect for pies!"

"And applesauce!" Luigi cried.

The cowboy grabbed Manny's hand and pumped. "You must be Mr. Donato, sir! I'm Joe Cabral here all the way from Taunton, Massachusetts. I've come to court your beautiful daughter, Concetta Regina!"

Manny yanked his hand away. "How the hell did a Portagee stunad from Massachusetts come to know my Connie?"

Joe smiled all cowboy wide. "Well, sir, I met your sweet daughter last month when I was down here on a clam run. We shared a cup of joe and a thing called a cannoli at a sweet little place called Rocco's. Then I raced her up to a firing range in Signac. That gal of yours shot like Wild Bill Hickok. She's one saddlebag full of fun!" He swept his hat off his head, jumped off the ground, and howled like a coyote in heat. "Yahoo! Connie, darlin', your Portuguese cowboy is here! Come on out of that house so I can give you a proper greeting!"

The front door popped open, and Connie fluttered onto the porch and floated down the steps in a swirling cloud of store-bought chiffon, her first-place carnival crown sparkling on her pretty head.

Joe grabbed her and spun her around. "You look just like a queen! And you smell good enough to eat!"

"Oh, Joe!" Connie blushed. "Put me down, you crazy fool!"

Lulu and Luigi applauded and cheered.

Bella wanted to spit.

Manny turned to Tony. "Get my fuckin' gun, son."

Dino opened his coat and revealed a little sawed-off number. "Hey, I got one."

With pouting lips and batting eyes, Connie floated over to Manny. "Papa, please let Joe stay. It would mean the world to me."

Manny melted like he always did when faced with the cloying sweetness of his precious Concetta Regina. "Okay. But if that son of a bitch howls again, I'll kill him."

In the dining room, everyone except Bella sat around a table in front of two heaping platters of antipasto: homemade mozzarella, chunks of Pecorino, pickled red peppers, olives, sun-dried tomatoes, and generous shavings of hot salami.

"Everything looks so delicious!" Dino proclaimed as he uncorked his wine and poured a generous taste all around.

"Connie's been working in the kitchen all day," Manny proudly informed him. "She's an incredible cook. The best in the family."

Something dropped in the kitchen.

"Oh no, she isn't," Luigi chimed in. "Bella is!"

Manny grabbed his youngest by the scruff of his neck. "That's enough out of you, guagliò!" He raised a glass of wine in the air. "To Concetta!" he called across the table. "The queen of Robertson Scale factory!"

"To Concetta!" everyone echoed.

In the hot kitchen, Bella pulled a bubbling lasagna out of the oven and slammed it onto the stovetop. She had toiled all morning over the seven-layer masterpiece full of homemade Bolognese and five different cheeses.

"You oughta hear the bullshit that's flyin' around out there," she said as she served her bedridden mamma a mouthwatering slice.

Lucia opened her mouth like a baby bird and Bella shoveled a steaming forkful in. "If those two boys knew the truth, they wouldn't be here for Connie. They'd be here for me."

While Bella bitterly fed her shell of a mamma, the rest of the family wolfed down the antipasti and fired a line of questions at Dino Montebolgna.

"How much olive oil you bring over from Italy in a year?" Manny asked.

"Enough to fill a fleet of ships."

"I bet it's all extra-virgin!" Tony sneered.

"Every last drop of it."

Luigi fired his own line of questions.

"Mr. Boloney, are you really a two-bit gangster like my papa says?"

Manny slammed his fist on the table. "Goddamnit, Luigi! Apologize to Mr. Montebologna!"

The boy turned to Dino. "I'm sorry, Mr. Mountain. How many people have you iced and tossed into the Passaic River?"

"Goddamnit!" Manny yelled.

"Is it true you bumped off Bruno Landini?"

Manny pounded his fist on the table making everyone jump. "One more word out of you, Luigi . . .!"

Dino was the epitome of greasy graciousness, raising a hand and waving the rudeness away. "It's alright, Mr. Donato. Young boys often have busy imaginations."

Tony was next.

"Say, how fast does that snazzy car of yours go?"

"It flies like the wind."

"Can it fly all the way to the moon?"

"It can fly all the way to Heaven."

"When can we get a ride?" asked Luigi.

"After supper. If youse promise to behave."

"Hot dog! I'll be good! I promise!"

Antipasti finished, it was time for the main course. That's when Bella swept into the room carrying a bountiful platter of her steaming lasagna. She was wearing a tight blouse, breasts cinched up to her chin, lips waxed, and cheeks rouged. "Bon appetito, everyone!"

Lulu screamed.

"Wow!" Luigi hollered. "You look like you belong in the movies!"

Tony sniggered. "She looks like a two-bit floozy!"

Manny shot up from his seat. "Go wash that shit off your face!"

"Tell them who made the lasagna, Papa," Bella said without moving.

Luigi crossed himself and dropped his head.

Lulu started to cry.

"Bella, please," Connie begged.

"If you don't wash that crap off your face," Manny yelled, "there's gonna be hell to pay!"

Bella raised the casserole over her head, ready to launch it at him. "Tell them who made the lasagna, Papa . . ."

Now it was Luigi who screamed. He jumped up and spread his arms wide. "No, Bella! Not the lasagna! Please!"

Bella slammed the lasagna on the table, but she went for Dino's empty wine bottle. It sailed like a comet and shattered against the wall next to a crude painting of the Sicilian sea. "I made the lasagna Bolognese!" she screamed. "I made the antipasti! I made everything!" She snatched the crown off Connie's head and slapped it on her own. "*I'M* the real Queen of this house! Not Connie! *ME*! Belladonna Marie!"

Manny kicked back his chair and charged over to his panting daughter.

The two of them stood toe to toe, tails twitching, nostrils blowing steam.

"What are you gonna do, Papa?" Bella yelled. "Hit me and knock out the rest of my teeth?"

Manny swung, but Bella ducked and flew out of the room.

"Wash it all off!" Manny hollered after her. "Or I'll come up there and do it myself!" Then he hiked up his pants and took a heaving seat. "Now, let's fucking eat!"

Queen Belladonna Marie's Lasagna Bolognese

This recipe takes all day.
But the results are always worth it.
The results are always deliciously devastating.

For the Bolognese:

2 tablespoons extra-virgin olive oil

4 tablespoons butter

2 pounds ground beef

1 large onion, finely chopped (about 1½ cups)

2 large carrots, peeled and cut into a quarter-inch dice (about 1 cup)

3 large ribs celery, peeled and cut into a quarter-inch dice (about 1 cup)

4 cloves garlic, finely minced

¼ cup fresh rosemary, finely chopped

¼ cup thyme leaves

large pinch chili flakes

⅛ teaspoon nutmeg

1 (28-ounce) can Italian plum tomatoes, hand-crushed

1½ cups dry red wine (good drinking wine)

1½ cups whole milk

2 cups chicken stock

salt, to taste

fresh ground black pepper, to taste

For the besciamella:

2 tablespoons butter

2 tablespoons flour

2 cloves garlic, finely minced

2 cups whole milk

½ pound whole-milk mozzarella cheese, grated

¼ teaspoon nutmeg, freshly grated

salt and freshly ground black pepper

For the ricotta mixture:

3 cups fresh ricotta

salt and freshly ground black pepper

2 large eggs

¼ cup parsley, minced

For the lasagna:

15 four-by-eight-inch sheets fresh rolled pasta, or 15 pieces
    lasagna noodles from a package, cooked

a mix of grated Pecorino Romano, Locatelli, and Parmigiano-
    Reggiano cheeses (about 2 cups)

3 cups ricotta mixture

Bolognese (3–4 cups or so)

besciamella (2 cups or so)

mozzarella (1 pound), sliced real thin (or grated)

1. When looking to impress a couple of suitors, make a lasagna
    Bolognese! In a Dutch oven or a big pot, heat butter and olive
    oil until butter stops foaming. Add ground beef, breaking
    it up with a wooden spoon, and cook until no longer pink.
    Remove meat, drain grease, and place in bowl. In the pot, add
    carrots, celery, garlic, onion, thyme, rosemary, salt and pep-
    per (to taste), nutmeg, and chili flakes. Cook over medium
    heat, stirring frequently until vegetables are softened.

2.   Mill or break up the plum tomatoes in a bowl with your hand. Add the tomatoes to the sautéed vegetables and stir.

3.   Add the browned meat and stir. Let simmer for a bit.

4.   Add the red wine and stir until most of the liquid evaporates and the alcohol cooks away.

5.   Add the milk and blend. Simmer for a bit, careful not to scorch or burn.

6.   Add the chicken stock and let simmer. Congratulations! You made Bella's Bolognese!

7.   To make the besciamella, heat butter in medium saucepan until foaming subsides (about 1 minute). Add flour and whisk until there's a nutty aroma (about 1 minute). Add garlic. Add milk in steady stream, constantly whisking.

8.   Cook lasagna pasta sheets, drain, and pat dry.

9.   To assemble the lasagna: In large baking dish, add some Bolognese, drizzle with besciamella, and layer with noodles for the base. Then add Bolognese, besciamella, ricotta mixture, grated cheese, and thinly sliced (or grated) mozzarella, and layer with more noodles. Continue this way until you reach the top of the baking dish.

10. Place rimmed baking sheet on lower rack to catch drips. Carefully place lasagna on upper rack and bake in preheated 375-degree oven. Bake until edges start to crisp and top is golden brown (45 minutes to 1 hour). Give yourself a makeover while it bakes. Polish your nails. Rotate the lasagna halfway through baking time.

Admire your handiwork. Pat yourself on the back. Has it started bubbling yet?

11. Remove from oven and allow to sit for 10 minutes. This step requires a lot of patience. Play a round of Italian solitaire.

12. After a quick prayer, slice and serve. Don't let anyone take credit for your hard work. If they do, take a stand. Put a crown on your head and tell them who the true Queen really is.

13. Buon appetito! Mangiare bene! Stare bene! Delizioso!

SCENTS AND SENSIBILITIES

AFTER SUPPER, BELLA SAT in the front porch swing defiantly painting her toenails. Concetta's carnival crown still sparkled on her head, and Dino sat across from her smoking a pungent cigar while his goon leaned against the snazzy Cadillac reading a dog-eared copy of *Sense and Sensibility*.

"You're quite a cook," Dino said, puffing. "Dat lasagna Bolognese was the best I ever ate."

"You should taste my meatballs," Bella said, capping her polish.

"If you was to make me meatballs as good as dat lasagna, I'd hand you the world on a gold plate."

Bella eyed the young capo. "Why do you wanna marry my sister? She can't cook worth a lick."

Dino took a considered hit off his cigar. "I need a sensible wife. One who won't cause me no trouble."

A clucking ruckus sounded from the henhouse out back.

"What are you gonna do about Rodeo Joe?"

"That phony cowboy doesn't love Concetta."

"Do you?"

The young gangster took another considered hit off his stogie. "I don't believe in love."

This intrigued Bella. "Oh yeah? What do you believe in?"

"Loyalty. What do you believe in?"

"Meatballs."

"I hope I get to taste yours someday."

Bella took in the young kingpin's plucked eyebrows, the polished nails, the hair slicked back with perfumed pomade. "I'm never gettin' married," she said. "I don't believe in love either."

Dino chuckled. "If you don't get married, what are you gonna do with your life?"

Before Bella could tell him she was gonna be famous, before she could tell him she was gonna fly all the way to the Glasgow-grinning moon and grab the brass ring, Tony and Luigi popped up on the other side of the porch next to Manny's rosebushes. Between them toggled a disheveled Concetta, hair frazzled, her chicken-shit-stained dress a bit of a mess. The fake cowboy was MIA.

"Hey, can we get a ride in your snazzy car now?" Luigi asked.

As the auto's engine growled around the factory grounds, Bella settled back into the porch swing. She closed her eyes and drifted away to a fairy-tale land full of colorful carnival rides, to ocean waves curling under a cobalt sky, to a young strongman lifting her high, to a moon with the Glasgow-grinning face of Steeplechase, to a brass ring dangling just out of reach, until the pop of a tobacco tin brought her back to reality, to Rodeo Joe leaning against the porch rail, fingering a healthy pinch of chaw into his cheek. "Howdy," he said with a shit-eating grin.

"You were in the henhouse messin' around with my sister."

He picked a piece of straw off one of his sleeves and flicked a clod of mud off a boot. "That's none of your business, sweetie."

"It's a good thing my papa's in the factory guardhouse. If he knew what you were up to with his precious Connie, he'd shoot your balls off."

"I'm not afraid of your papa."

"You're full of shit. I can smell it from here."

The cartoon cowboy spit a stream of tobacco juice into Manny's roses. Then he strode across the porch with the bravado of a young gunslinger, grabbed Bella by her wrists, and yanked her up. He didn't smell like chicken shit. He smelled like the promise of something delicious.

For a thrilling moment Bella thought she was going get her first real kiss. Instead, Joe brought her fingers up to his nose and took a long, deep sniff.

"You know what I smell?" he asked her. "I smell you're nothin' but a silly little virgin who's dyin' for me to take her into that nasty old coop and pop her juicy cherry too."

Bella yanked her hand out of his and smacked him hard across his face. Then she smacked him again and ran into the house.

"Hey!" Joe called after her. "Hey, I'm sorry!"

Upstairs, in the girls' room, Bella wiped the tears from her eyes and sniffed her fingers. Then she pulled the crown off her head and hurled it across the room. Then she undressed, slipped her nightgown on, crawled into bed next to a snoring Lulu, and sniffed her sleeping sister's fingers. Then she settled in and waited for Concetta to arrive so she could sniff her fingers too.

MISS FANCY PANTS

THE FIRST TIME BELLA saw him he was perched like an exotic bird in the middle of the downtown trolley in a white Fauntleroy suit collared with a satin bow tie the size of a summer chrysanthemum. He was a short, slight boy. Maybe about fourteen, Bella guessed. A fuzzy shadow of a mustache bloomed above his upper lip. His eyebrows arched in perfectly plucked half-moons. Two fat shopping bags rested at the toes of his sissy-sock-collared high-button shoes like a pair of obedient poodles. Amazingly, passengers ignored the young Nancy boy with a pound of sugar in his pants, but Bella stared the entire ride down Middleton Avenue. She couldn't take her eyes off him.

The second time she saw him he was perched on a stool at the S. S. Kresge Five and Dime lunch counter gingerly nibbling on a fried baloney burger and sipping a long-strawed, muffin-topped, U-Bet egg cream. This time he was staring at her as she circled the fake jewelry displays, accidentally knocking things to the ground, replacing some of them and pocketing the rest.

"I know what you're doing," he boldly said when she sat three stools away from him and ordered a meatloaf sandwich.

"Excuse me?"

He dramatically sucked on his soda. "You're a thief."

"I don't know what you're talkin' about."

"Oh, yes you do. And you're going to help me with something I need or I'm going to rat on you."

Bella popped off her stool and strode over to him. She pressed her face up to his and kept her voice low. "Listen, Miss Fancy Pants . . ."

"The name is Terelli Lombardi."

"Your name is gonna be mud in a slim second if you don't shut the fuck up."

"Do you know where they send girls like you? To a hideous hoosegow deep in the bowels of godforsaken Pennsylvania to lick grimy floors clean and scrub rancid toilets with a toothbrush."

"Okay, you little asshole. What do you want?"

PARTNERS IN CRIME

STANDING IN FRONT OF the Princess Yarn and Novelties shop, Bella marveled at how small the little son of a bitch really was. The top of his queer head barely reached her chest.

"You want me to steal from in there?" she asked.

"Be careful. The lady who owns the place is a nutty Southern Baptist who doesn't miss a trick."

"Why don't you do it yourself?"

"That old biddy won't let boys into her shop."

"What do you want with a bunch of yarn anyway?"

"WHAT DO YOU CARE?!"

"Okay! Don't spin your panties into a twist!"

Terelli reached into his pocket and pulled out a small piece of paper. "Can you read?"

Bella snatched the paper out of his hand. "Yes, I can read!"

"Make sure the wool is 100 percent cashmere."

"What the hell does that mean?"

"NO BLENDS!"

"OKAY!" Bella thrust the list into her coat pocket. "You better beat it over to the other side of the street while I do this."

"I'm not moving. I want to keep an eye on you."

"Take a hike or I'm not goin' in."

"Don't spin your panties into a twist yourself!" Terelli grabbed a *Herald-News* from Pasquale Bortolini's newsstand. "Be sure and get the right colors!" he called over his shoulder as he skipped across the street. "True navy blue and honeysuckle pink, please!"

A passing boy called him a faggot.

"Fuck you!" Terelli hissed as he skipped past him. "Eat me!"

When Bella stepped into the shop, she was smacked with the cloying scent of Four Roses talcum powder and the itchy stink of ripe old lady. Kodachrome explosions of yarn bouqueted all over the place.

Bella sneezed and a rat terrier of a crone stepped out from behind a busy pattern display. Her face was a powder puff full of wrinkles. Her stiff hair rose off her head like a lacquered pile of purple cotton candy. Around her neck swung a cross big enough to choke the fangs out of Bela Lugosi. "How might I help you, young lady?" she asked with a southern drawl as thick as Grandma's Molasses.

Bella started checking the yarns. "Oh, don't mind me. I'm just browsing."

"Do you knit, young lady?"

"Like the devil."

"What's your favorite stitch?"

Bella found a blue yarn bundle and checked it against Terelli's list. "Oh, I have so many. Is this 100 percent cashmere?"

"Of course. What are y'all gonna make with it?"

"A baby blanket."

"How sweet! Is it for a girl or for a boy?"

Bella smiled. "I don't know." She pointed to her stomach. "It ain't here yet."

The woman placed a claw of a hand on Bella's belly. "My goodness! What a blessing!"

"Yes. The good Lord has really smiled upon me." Bella pushed the woman's hand away. "Can I bother you for a glass of water? My baby's awfully thirsty."

"Why, of course you can!"

After the woman ducked into the back, Bella slipped the bundle of true navy blue into the lining of her coat.

"Here you go, darlin'!"

Bella gulped the water down and burped. "Excuse me."

"Does your baby feel better now?"

"I don't think so."

"What do you mean?"

Bella dropped the glass and grabbed her stomach. "Oh no!"

"What is it?"

"You wouldn't happen to have a slice of cheese or some Ovaltine, would you? The last time I felt like this and didn't have a chocolate drink and some American cheese, my stomach flipped upside down and I almost lost the baby."

"Oh my stars! Well, there's a diner right across the street!"

"I can't move!"

The woman wrung her hands. "I'm sorry, but I can't leave my shop."

Bella clutched her stomach and dropped to the floor. The woman screamed.

Outside, Terelli was about to ditch his newspaper and jump off his post when the old Baptist lady burst out of the shop, flailed across the street, spun past him, and barreled into the diner screaming, "Ovaltine! I need Ovaltine and cheese immediately!"

WHORE'S PARADISE

THE TWO NEW PALS celebrated the heist with a triple-scoop sundae in Bond's Ice Cream Parlor.

"Have you ever been to Coney Island?" Terelli asked Bella.

"No. Have you?"

"Yes. My favorite grandmother has a beautiful house not far from there."

"What's it like?"

"It's simply stunning. Chock-full of amazing antiques."

"What's Coney Island like?"

"Coney Island is a regular Whore's Paradise. They call it *Sin City*."

"Sounds like the perfect place for me."

Terelli opened his newspaper and pointed to an employment ad. "While you were grabbing my yarn, I found this for you . . ."

WANTED: Female dancers
for Coney Island Revue!
Must have fantastic figure. Must be beautiful.

Only ages 18–25 need apply.

No experience necessary.

Telephone: Longacre 5-8847 ASAP

(Lester Feinberg Agency)

"But I'm only fifteen."

"That'll work to your advantage, believe me."

Bella tongued the gap between her teeth. "I don't think I'm pretty enough."

"I can make you gorgeous."

"You can?"

The little dandy ripped the ad out of the paper and thrust it across the table. "Let's go back to the five-and-dime and steal some makeup!"

"I already have a bunch."

"No offense, but whatever you have isn't really working for you."

"Fuck you! What color lipstick and nail polish should we lift?"

"Whore's Paradise!"

PASSAIC PYGMALION

AFTER A SUCCESSFUL BURGLAR'S run through S. S. Kresge, a packed bus ride, two trolley connections, and a long walk down several well-tended streets, Terelli stopped Bella in front of a monster of a Victorian gallantly set back from pristine hedging.

"This is where you live?"

"Home sweet home!" Terelli sang as he skipped up the walkway.

In the imposing entry, an eagle-topped grandfather clock chimed next to a coat of armor holding a long jousting lance.

"Is that thing real?"

"It's from the fifteenth century."

Bella's head spun as she followed her new friend up a broad, center-cut staircase. "How many rooms does this place have?"

"Twenty-four, not including the maid's room."

"You got a maid?"

"I have three."

Bella whistled as they rounded two dark corners and entered a shadowed room the size of an Egyptian tomb. A mastodon of a fireplace hulked across from a canopied bed fit for Marie Antoinette. A fainting couch swooned next to a triple-mirrored vanity that looked like something in a Hollywood movie.

"Alice's room," Terelli whispered as he snapped on a lamp shaded with a stained glass Parisian street scene.

"Who's Alice?"

"My mother."

"You call your mother Alice?"

"What else should I call her?"

"Where is she?"

"She's somewhere out west getting some rest."

"What about your papa? Where's he?"

Terelli pulled Bella over to the vanity. "I haven't seen Dudley since I was three."

Bella ran a hand across the lid of a jewel-topped box. "Everything here is so pretty!"

"Don't steal that. It's a priceless family heirloom," Terelli said as he unpacked their loot:

Tangee red delicious lipstick

Maybelline cover up

Rendezvous face powder

Camille eyeshadow

Starfish false eyelashes

Marvelous Bliss blush

French curlers by Merci Beaucoup

Gayla Hold-Bob bobby pins

Wavy Girl setting gel (for permanent waves and ringlets)

the latest issue of *Silver Screen* magazine

two Hershey bars (one with almonds)

"I'm going to make you look better than Bette Davis in

Dangerous," Terelli proclaimed as he lined everything up on the vanity. "Now, go wash your face and hair in Alice's bath. Then come back and see me."

When Bella returned, Terelli produced a comb and scissors. Once he was done snipping, he grabbed the setting gel, curlers, and bobby pins.

"You've got a great figure," Terelli said.

"Thanks. It's my best asset."

"For now. Have you fucked anyone yet?" Terelli asked as he rolled and pinned.

"No, but I really want to. Have you?"

"More than I care to count."

"Really? Like who?"

"I never kiss and tell."

"Sometimes I dream about fucking Jesus," Bella said.

"I was fucked by Jesus. Three times." Terelli pinned a curler and quickly rolled another. "At least he looks a lot like Christ."

Bella played with a silver brush and comb set on the vanity as Terelli continued to roll and bobby pin. "Do you mind being a degenerate?" she asked.

Terelli pursed his lips and smacked his hands on his hips. "What choice do you think I have?"

"I never met a boy like you."

"Boys like me are few and far between. Except in Hollywood. That town is teeming with inverts."

"You're kidding."

"Clark Gable and Gary Cooper, for starters."

"That's ridiculous! Clark Gable is in love with Joan Crawford! It says so in *Picture Show* magazine."

"Don't believe everything you read. Joan Crawford's in love with Greta Garbo, trust me."

Terelli pinned and patted the final curler. Then he picked up an eyebrow tweezer. "Whatever you do, don't move your head."

Bella flinched. "Ouch! Goddamnit! That hurts!"

"Don't be such a baby."

As Terelli continued plucking, Bella grabbed the vanity and bit her lip to keep from screaming. "Have you ever been in love?" she asked, eyes watering.

"I don't like to tie myself down," Terelli said as he tweezed. "There are too many beautiful boys out there."

"Who's the most beautiful boy you've ever seen?"

"Francis Anthony Mozzarelli."

"Who's that?'

Terelli dropped the tweezers on the vanity, slid a gold-tipped cigarette from a cut glass goblet next to the jeweled box, and lit it like a diner waitress on break. "Francis Anthony Mozzarelli is the most beautiful creature God has ever created." He took a dramatic drag off the butt and exhaled like Tallulah Bankhead in *Faithless*. "He has the eyes of a wolf and the lips of a saint. When I first met him, he was a scrawny little thing. Then I hauled him over to Loprinzi's Gym. Now he's got shoulders like boulders and an ass that makes me want to scream."

"He sounds just like a dream."

"He's a fucking masterpiece."

"Where does he live?"

"He resides with his mamma over on Krueger Place. That old lady is stone-cold crazy. She wants him to become a priest." Terelli tipped the ash off the end of his cigarette and took another hit. "He quit high school and works over at the Charms Candy factory. Shipping and deliveries. He calls me his little bird." Terelli inhaled then blew out a perfect smoke ring. "Tweet! Tweet!"

Bella eyed the half-eaten pack of wild cherry Charms next to the gold ashtray. "Does he like girls?"

"He likes everybody. I've knitted him two scarves, a sweater, a pair of mittens, an oarsman's cap, and a posing strap."

"What's a posing strap?"

"Never mind that." Terelli gently grabbed her chin. "Now for the face." He tamped out his cigarette and with expert hands evenly applied the Maybelline cover up. "Remember, less is more unless you're going to a grand ball or a nighttime soiree."

"How do you know how to do all this?"

"I worked at a beauty parlor in Paterson for a while. Then I worked at Cipolini's Home for Funerals making up the dead."

"You did?"

"I was fired because I made all the corpses look like Jean Harlow. Especially the men. But don't worry. I've branched out since then."

"You know, for a queer boy you got some set of coglioni. You got balls the size of the moon."

"I know. So do you."

The two friends regarded each other. Then Terelli ceremoniously uncapped the tube of Tangee lipstick. "Open your mouth and smile wide. Hey, you've got great teeth!"

"Like a horse. Except for the one that's missing."

"How did that happen?"

"My papa slugged me."

"Why?"

Bella saw the glint of her mamma's blade as it sliced her papa's face.

"Because I entered a beauty and the beast contest with my pig Abundantia."

"Did you win?"

"My older sister and her stinkin' canary did."

Terelli carefully smeared the bright wax on Bella's upper lip. "Your papa sounds like a real jackass prize."

"My papa hates me."

Terelli was uncharacteristically silent for a moment. "My

father hates me too. And so does Alice. She keeps threatening to have me carted off to a place to have the sissy hosed out of me."

"Really?"

"Hold still." Terelli spread the lipstick across Bella's lower lip. "Now, press and spread your lips together, then blow me a devastating kiss."

Bella did as she was told.

"Stunning," Terelli said, congratulating himself. "Simply stunning."

Bella wondered if she was prettier than her sister Concetta. She tried to look at herself in the mirror.

"Not yet!" Terelli admonished.

"My sister, Connie, got herself pregnant," Bella said as Terelli Marvelous Bliss blushed her cheeks. "By a Portagee stunad from Massachusetts who thinks he's a fucking cowboy."

"Just be glad it's not you."

"They're gettin' married and movin' up to Taunton, Massachusetts, next week."

"Poor things."

Terelli dropped the brush and grabbed the Camille eyeshadow.

"Close your eyes for me, please."

One at a time, he shaded her lids, giving her a bit of Garbo mystique. Then he expertly applied the Starfish eyelashes for some Bette Davis batting.

"Perfection," he said when he was finished.

Bella tried to look at herself in the mirror again.

"No peeking, I said! Let's get you dressed first!"

He tugged her into his mother's walk-in closet.

"Jesus! A whole room full of clothes!?"

"Sometimes I get lost in here for days," Terelli said as he tossed her a flutter skirt from Saks Fifth Avenue. He threw her a matching cotton blouse with lavender piping, French hose, and a pair of kitten-heeled pumps.

Bella held up the shoes. "These are a scream!"

"You're going to look better than Joan Bennett in *She Couldn't Take It*."

After Bella finished getting dressed, Terelli removed the curlers and fluff-brushed her hair. Then he pulled her over to the vanity mirrors. "Ta-da!"

Baby bombshell in triptych.

"Is that really me?"

"Another fucking masterpiece."

Bella's eyes filled with tears. "I look like a fairy-tale princess."

"You look like a fucking QUEEN!"

The silence that followed threatened to swallow them both whole. Flashes of their futures burst around them in lightning blasts and upside-down explosions.

Love. Hate. Birth. Pain. Death. Redemption. Forgiveness.

Boom. Boom. Boom. Boom. Boom. Boom. Boom.

Bella's heart filled with an overwhelming sense of something she'd never felt before. "Where's the kitchen in this goddamned place!?"

An hour later the two of them were sitting in front of a plate of Bella's steaming meatballs and tomato gravy.

When he took his first bite, Terelli swooned. "These meatballs are fucking delicious! I've never tasted anything like them!"

"I know."

"How do you make them this good?"

"The holy hands of my Cooking Spirit."

"What the hell does that mean?"

"You wouldn't understand."

"Well, however you do it, these meatballs and your new look are your tickets to fame and fortune." Terelli fork-speared a ball and held it up like a torch. "Watch out, world! Here comes Belladonna Marie, the famous tit-spinning Meatball Queen!"

"I can't believe how beautiful you made me!"

"You're so beautiful you're sure to fuck someone real soon."

"I am?"

"And you want to know something else?"

"Yes!"

"You're going to Coney Island too!"

WANTED: Female dancers
for Coney Island Revue!

Bella caught her smiling reflection in the warped gravy pot on the stove, grimly distorted, a bit alarming.

GOD'S COCK

"JESUS H. FRICKIN' CHRIST, it's fuckin' cold!" Bella yelled. Her breath billowed in front of her as she ran down the icy sidewalk.

"Only three more blocks to the school bus stop! Let's keep running!" Lulu squealed as she struggled to keep up.

Bella blazed along in a lobster-red, fur-trimmed swing coat and matching carmine cloche hat (poked with a couple of rooster feathers) that she had permanently borrowed from Terelli Lombardi's house. Lulu gleefully baltered behind in their mamma's shit-brown hand-me-down. The two of them galloped along until they crashed in front of old man Siano's Christmas crèche.

After quickly crossing herself, Bella ripped off her mittens, dug into her pocket, and pulled out a tube of Tangee lipstick. She generously waxed her lips and blew the wooden baby Christ a kiss. Then she popped open a compact and expertly blushed her cheeks. Then she lined her eyes in the mini mirror before pocketing everything.

"If Papa catches you wearing that stuff again, he'll kill you!"

"Not if that old stronzo can't catch me!" Bella grabbed her sister's hand and the two girls continued running. "My goddamned puchiacha is so cold I'm afraid it'll freeze!" Bella screamed.

"Oh, no! You don't want a frozen puchiacha!"

"Just a hard cazzo!"

The two girls laughed, they hee-hawed, they guffawed as they barreled to the bus stop at the corner of Krueger Place and Gregory Avenue, red faces stinging, snowflakes singing. They huddled in a fit of shivering giggles until across the street, in the parlor window of a two-story white house, a set of Sicilian lace curtains opened and snapped closed.

"Did you see that?"

"I sure did."

Moments later, the front door popped open and a young man with the physique of an Italian stallone and a full head of lush hair stepped out and waved. He was wearing nothing but cuffed blue jeans, a guinea T, a pair of unlaced shoes, and a dandy-looking hand-knitted oarsman's cap.

Bella tossed him a sly Gioconda smile as she waved back.

Lulu slapped her sister's hand down. "What are you doing?"

"I'm sayin' hi."

"Why?"

The young man hop-crunched across the street.

"Now look what you did! He's coming over here!"

Bella licked her teeth as he deftly sidestepped chunks of snow and patches of ice and landed in front of the girls with the ruddy color of Christmas blushing in his Christlike cheeks. Bella had never seen a boy (or man) swing his hips the way this one did.

Holy, holy, holy shit.

"Nice day for a walk," he said and winked.

Up close, his wolfen eyes flashed green with flecks of gold.

He had a strong, square chin and obscenely white teeth. He looked exactly like the Christ painting in Saint Anthony's.

Bella could hear Terelli singing,

Simply stunning!

"You're Francis Anthony Mozzarelli!"

The boy removed the cap from his head and took a deep bow. "Al tuo servizio, mia regina!" He popped back up and smiled handsomely. "How do you know who I am?"

Shoulders like boulders. Biceps popping. Charm bomb exploding. Terelli was right. He was a fucking masterpiece.

"A little birdie told me."

Tweet! Tweet!

"You're Belladonna Marie Donato," Francis said. His lips were pink and wet and devastating.

"How do you know about me?"

Little Angel Queen flying. A single rose petal falling. Carnival Queen fighting. Strong arms lifting.

"All of New Jersey knows about you."

"They do?"

Bella felt like she was dropping out of the sky again.

Papa! Catch me!

"Aren't you freezing out here?" she asked, batting her eyes.

"You want to wait for the bus inside my house? It's nice and warm in there. And I've cooked a big breakfast."

Lulu clutched her sister's arm. "We've already had breakfast," she said. "Besides, the bus is gonna be here any minute, and we can't miss school again."

Bella yanked her arm free. "That goddamned bus is always late. Besides, I didn't eat breakfast," she lied. "And I'm starving. I'm so hungry I can eat a horse."

Francis pawed the ground with his shoe and whinnied uproariously.

Bella squealed.

Lulu screamed.

In the house, the kitchen walls danced with a pattern of bright yellow sunflowers. Fire-licked pots and pans crowded a well-seasoned stove. Above them hung a gold-framed picture of an old woman, beady eyes watching a metal-topped kitchen table where an oval platter teeming with a scramble of caramelized onions, red bell peppers, potatoes, and eggs steamed. Another platter held a pyramid of fresh cannoli, ricotta oozing. The table was set for three.

"Holy crapoli!" Bella cried. "Who did all this?"

Francis picked a set of dumbbells up off the floor and started doing curls. "Me!"

Lulu counted the plates. "You were expecting us to come in here, weren't you?"

"Don't be rude!" Bella pushed her sister aside and grabbed a cannoli. She took a bite. It was almost too sweet, but there was something in it that made Bella's heart sing. What the hell was it?

"My crazy old lady made those!"

"What does she put in the cream?"

"It's a secret recipe. If I tell you, she'll kill me."

Bella took another bite. "Well, whatever it is, it's delicious!"

"It's like sucking on God's cock, isn't it?!"

Bella guffawed.

Lulu backed against the wall next to the kitchen door. "That's disgusting! Where's your crazy old lady?"

"She's at work," the panting young Strongman replied. He was alternating arms with bicep-popping counts of five. "She runs the Star Barbershop over on Market Street."

"What about your papa?" Lulu was unrelenting. "Where's he?"

"My papa's dead. He died when I was eight."

Bella crossed herself and kissed her fist. "I'm so sorry!"

"Me too," Lulu crossed herself. "I'm sorry too." She turned to her sister. "Can we go now? Please?"

"No. I don't want to go."

"Bella, please!"

"Basta!"

Francis dropped the weights and struck a Popeye pose between the two girls. "Feel my muscles!" he exclaimed.

Bella cupped one of his biceps with her hand and squeezed. "My God! It's as hard as a rock!"

"Bella . . ." Lulu tugged on her sister's coat sleeve. "I said I want to leave."

Bella took off her hat and scarf and dropped them onto the table. "Leave! No one's stopping you, dummy!"

"If you make me go out there alone, I'm gonna tell Papa on you!"

"Fuck Papa! And fuck you!"

"FUCK YOU TOO!" Lulu screamed. Then she slapped her mittens over her mouth.

For a moment both girls were stunned.

"Lulu! You cursed!"

All bets were off.

"Well, at least I'm not a goddamned whore!"

"What did you say to me?!"

"YOU'RE A WHORE!"

Bella lunged, but Lulu yanked the door open, jumped out, and slammed it in Bella's face. Then she bounded through the snow like a panicked chicken.

"I'm sorry," Bella said after catching her breath.

"For what?"

"She's not really my sister."

"What do you mean?"

"Never mind."

Francis dropped his weights.

"You're not gonna leave too, are you?"

Bella glanced out the hoarfrosted kitchen window, at the brown smudge of Lulu standing at the bus stop, shoulders shaking. Goddamnit, she was crying. "No. I'm staying."

"Thank you, sweet Jesus!"

Francis helped Bella out of her coat and pulled out a chair for her.

"Mamma mia!" he said as she took a sexy seat.

He straddled the one across from her and lifted the platter of cannoli. "You want another one of these?"

Bella pulled one off the top and took a bite. Then she took another one.

"Christ! I love to watch you eat!"

Francis grabbed one too. He slurped the cream off the end and crunched down. Then he took a magnificent swig off an open bottle of Yoo-hoo, burped like a cartoon monkey, and smiled like a clown.

The two of them laughed, bits of cannoli shell stuck between their teeth, Bella's cuspid gap filled with ricotta cheese. "How come you don't go to school?" she asked.

"I had no use for the crap school tried to shovel at me. It's all a bunch of bullshit. None of it means anything."

Even when he was serious, his face was so stunning it was holy. Francis caught Bella staring at him. "What are you thinking?"

"You look just like the Jesus painting hanging in Saint Anthony's."

The young man's cheeks blushed the color of Christmas again. "That was my crazy old lady's idea. She made me pose for it."

"It's so beautiful."

"It's embarrassing. I hate it."

"I think it's the most beautiful painting I've ever seen."

"I think you're beautiful."

"No, I'm not. Not really."

"Are you kidding? You're a fucking masterpiece."

A bank of wind slapped against the house.

"Bella!" came Lulu's muffled cry.

Christ, Bella thought, *I hope Lulu isn't freezing out there.* She eyed the framed photo of the tough-looking woman hanging above the stove and shivered. "Who's that?" she asked.

"That's my crazy old lady! Mary Mozzarelli! Ain't she something?!"

The eyes in the picture narrowed and the lips curled like an angry dog.

"Bella!" Lulu cried.

"She looks scary," Bella said.

Francis plated a bunch of eggs for his bodacious guest. "She ain't nothin' but an old pussycat. Tell me about your family . . ."

"I have another older sister and an older brother. I also have a little brother. He's my favorite."

"I wish I had brothers and sisters," Francis said as he plated himself some eggs. "Sometimes I get so goddamned lonely it hurts," he admitted as he wolfed down his food. "Someday I'm gonna get married and have a great big fucking family." He grabbed his empty plate, placed his elbows on the table, and licked it clean. He licked it like a wolf in heat.

"Not me." Bella said.

"You don't want to be a mamma?"

"No fucking way."

"Why not?"

"I've been a mamma to my entire fucking family my entire fucking life and I'm fucking done with it." She looked directly into the holy face of the most beautiful boy she had ever seen. "And I'm never getting married."

"Never?"

"Not ever."

A rumble of snow thunder rattled the kitchen windows, threatening to shatter the glass. The picture of Mary growled.

"What's your mamma like?" Francis asked.

Bella fingered her plate of eggs.

"My mamma always sleeps. And she never speaks."

"What do you mean?"

"I don't want to talk about it."

"What about your papa?"

"My papa hates me. He makes me wash his stinking feet."

"That's fucking disgusting."

Francis thought about his old man. "Does your papa ever hit you?"

Bella's tongue felt the gap between her teeth.

"No," she lied.

"My papa used to beat the shit out of me," Francis confessed. "I was my old man's fucking punching bag until the day he died."

The picture of Mary Mozzarelli growled again. The blast of a gunshot echoed over their heads.

"How did he die?"

"I don't remember."

Bella took a bite of her eggs. "I wish my papa would die."

Suddenly Francis jumped to his feet. "Don't say that! Don't ever wish death on anybody!"

Bella was stunned. "I'm sorry."

Francis slowly sat back down. "I think I'm gonna be sick," he whispered into his empty plate.

"Bella!" came Lulu's distant, snow-swaddled cry. "The bus is coming!"

I can make it, Bella thought as the engine's muffled rumble came to a wheezing stop. *I can make it if I run.* She stood up and Francis stood up too. He walked over, put his arms around her, and buried his face in the warm flesh of her neck. He nibbled and licked. Then he slowly kissed his way to her lips. When their tongues met, they danced. Eggs, potatoes, onions, peppers, Yoo-hoo. And delicious remnants of sweet cannoli cream.

Francis caressed Bella's breasts and she moaned. (She wanted to scream.) "I think I better go," she whispered hoarsely.

"Please don't leave. I want to fuck you. Can I fuck you? Please?"

Waves crashing.

Saltwater taffy.

The Glasgow-grinning face of Steeplechase, laughing and cackling.

Mary Mozzarelli growling.

"Okay."

As the bus backfired and farted away, the two of them dropped to the kitchen floor. Is this what her papa did to her mamma? For a horrifying moment Bella was a little girl again, pounding on her mamma's door.

"Stop!' she cried.

Francis was panting. "Are you okay?"

Bella blinked and the violent ghost of her papa slipped away.

"I think so. Yes."

Francis took Bella's face in his warm hands and gave her a soft kiss. "Are you sure you want me to stop?"

"I want you to take me. Take all of me."

Francis quickly wrapped his hands around the bottom of her voluptuous behind and hiked up her dress. Then he slowly (sweetly) peeled down her woolens, exposing her damp (and shivering) bloomers. Then he sniffed between her legs.

Had she bathed that morning? Bella tried to remember.

"My God, you smell delicious," Francis whispered.

Bella farted.

Did he hear it?

With frantic hands, Francis unzipped his jeans. His dick sprang out like a Mars-bound rocket. It was huge! God's cock grinning and dripping.

Oh, holy cannoli!

Here we go!

This is it!

Bella couldn't stop shivering.

"You're shaking."

"I'm cold."

Francis covered her with his whole body. Then he started to thrust himself into her and she screamed. "Stop! Please!"

Francis pulled the tip of his stiff dick out. "I'm sorry! Are you okay?"

"Is it supposed to hurt like this?"

"Only for a minute. I'll go slow. I promise."

"Okay. Go."

He gave her a tender kiss and gently pressed against her again. Then he started rocking his hips and Bella rocked too. The two of them rocked together. They rocked and rubbed and grunted. Then Francis slowly pushed back in. Another sharp sting. Bella's bowels constricted. Her legs melted. She felt like she was swimming in a warm sea. "Jesus, fuck me! Jesus, fuck me!" she hollered.

"I am fucking you! I am fucking you!"

Francis didn't hear his mamma barking.

Bella didn't hear her mamma wailing.

Neither of them heard Terelli Lombardi screaming.

The floor spun. The room turned upside down. Bella couldn't breathe. For a split second, she felt like she was drowning. Then she was floating in honey.

"I'm coming!" Francis hollered as the cream shot out of his cannoli. "I'm coming!" He shuddered and bucked like a bull.

"I'm coming too!" Bella screamed as Francis collapsed on

top of her, panting. "I'm coming too!" The bulbs in all of her sockets blew. Her corpuscles hummed, her veins strummed, her heart drummed. The room filled with a million carnival lights, and she shot all the way to Heaven.

She was a little Angel Queen again.

Flying in the glory of her Lord.

Somewhere over the rainbow.

Bella Belladonna.

Bella bellissima!

Mary Mozzarelli's Secret Cannoli Recipe

Mary Mozzarelli carried
this sweet recipe
all the way to her nasty grave.

For the cannoli shells:

4 cups flour, sifted

3 tablespoons butter, softened

2 egg yolks

2 tablespoons sugar

¼ teaspoon salt

¾ cup dry white wine

1 tablespoon distilled white vinegar

shortening for frying

For the filling:

4 cups whole-milk ricotta cheese (preferably homemade)

1 cup powdered sugar (or less, careful not to make the
filling too sweet)

1 teaspoon pure vanilla extract

1 teaspoon lemon or orange zest

¼ to ½ cup chocolate chips or small chocolate chunks

a pinch of nutmeg, only enough to give the cream a
gentle nutty aftertaste

1. Mix flour, salt, and sugar in bowl. Cut in butter. Add egg yolks and stir with fork. Stir in wine, one tablespoon at a time, until dough sticks together. Stir in vinegar. Form ball with dough and let stand for 30 minutes. Sing a song to your favorite son while you wait. Give him a haircut. But don't introduce him to a priest.

2. Roll out dough almost paper-thin on a well-floured surface. With the rim of a nice-sized (wine) glass (about three to four inches across), cut circles out of dough. With a paring knife, make sure circles are cut all the way through. Wrap each circle of dough around metal cannoli tube, overlapping the ends and pressing to seal. Flare out the edges slightly. Make them pretty.

3. Fry one or two at a time in a kettle or sturdy pot of hot melted shortening (about 360 degrees) for about one minute, turning to brown all sides. Remove from oil and drain on paper towels, seam side down. Cool before removing from tubes. Take a moment or two or three to pray for your enemies.

4. Drain ricotta over cheesecloth. In nice-sized bowl, combine ricotta cheese, powdered sugar, vanilla extract, lemon or orange zest, and nutmeg. Stir in chocolate chunks or chips (be careful not to overmix). Chill for about 30 minutes. Then pipe the ricotta mixture into cooled cannoli shells.

5. Serve immediately with a hot cup of espresso or favorite coffee.

6. Lick and nibble the cannoli as long and as slowly as you can before you crunch into it.

7. When you're finished, see if you don't make crazy love with somebody.

8. Buon appetito! Mangiare bene! Stare bene! Delizioso!

AFTERGLOW

AFTER HE HAD SEX with Bella the first time, Francis Anthony Mozzarelli asked if he could see her completely naked. They were still tangled on the floor of his mamma's kitchen.

"With nothing on?"

"Yeah."

"Nothing at all?"

"Yes. Please."

"Okay."

Bella giggled and rose up in front of him. She pulled her mangled dress (ripped at the arm and torn at the hem) past her hips and down her legs. She stepped out of her papa's old galoshes and her mamma's fat-girl bloomers. Then she undid the metal clasps of the Form-Fit bra strangling her breasts and spread her arms like an angel flying. She towered like a bodacious tree. A young Venus rising out of the sea. A ripe tumble of soft flesh. Glorious pendulums swinging. Starving for everything.

Francis hopped to his knees, crossed himself, and spread his arms wide. "Grazie dolce Gesù!"

Thank you, sweet Jesus!

She was the most spectacular creature he had ever seen.

Holier than anything he had ever poked with his cannoli.

Full of blinding electricity.

For a bundle of heart-shocking moments, he saw wooden horses on golden poles galloping around her, people like seahorses clinging to a monstrous donut swing, the grimacing Glasgow face of Steeplechase smiling, a small room full of glass boxes, each containing a tiny baby.

"Belladonna Marie, what have you done to me?"

He had never felt anything like what he was feeling.

"Can we fuck again? Please?"

They made love five and a half times before noon that day. When they finally finished, the air in the house was thick and heavy with sex. The windows were clouded and slick with its musk and sweat.

After they were done, the two of them sprawled on the linoleum like beached seals.

Suddenly Francis jumped to his feet. He clubbed his chest with his fists and spread his arms like Tarzan. "God, I'm starving! Aren't you starving?"

"Yes!"

Bella jumped up too. They grabbed the food left on the platters and started smashing it into each other's mouths while laughing. They smeared each other's faces with potatoes and eggs. They crushed the remaining cannoli onto each other's heads.

"Let's go outside and play!" Francis hollered.

"Okay!"

They tumbled into the snow like a couple of circus bears,

Francis in Bella's dress, Bella in Francis's T-shirt and jeans. They were little kids again. They lobbed snowballs and rolled around like silly carnival clowns until they got so wet and cold they charged back into the house, where they wrapped themselves in blankets and waited for their joints to thaw, for their teeth to stop chattering.

When the kettle Francis had placed on the stove whistled, he poured the steaming water into a large bowl.

"What are you doing?"

He asked Bella to sit in a chair. Then he gently bathed her feet, caressing them with such tenderness it was overwhelming.

"No one has ever done this for me."

"Someone should do it for you every day. I will. If you'll let me."

After he kissed each of her toes, Bella playfully kicked him to the floor and the two of them made love again.

This time it was completely soft and gentle and slow.

Not an ounce of pain.

No frantic thrusting.

Only tons of pleasure.

The level of bliss was fucking insane.

After they finished, Francis dropped into a deep sleep. He curled up like a baby and snored like a donkey.

"Holy cow!" Bella whispered, standing in front of the open icebox. "There's gotta be at least four pounds of chopped beef in here. And a whole wheel of Locatelli cheese . . ."

She placed the bounty on the table and slammed a large pot on the stove, yanking Francis out of his dreams.

"What are you doin'?"

"I'm makin' you meatballs."

While Bella cooked, she told him the story of her life. She started from the beginning. Her papa tossing her into the sky above the sea. How, after her mamma sliced his cheek, he called Bella ugly and made her wash his stinking feet. Learning how to cook from a neighborhood lady who sent her home with a pocketful of recipes to feed the Donato family. Feeding her goddamned family. Always feeding her fucking family. Entering the carnival contest. Her papa knocking out one of her teeth.

"I was at that carnival. I saw you almost win. I rescued you from the stampede."

"That was you?"

"That was me!"

"Why did you disappear after you saved me?"

Francis suddenly heard the voice of his mamma crack through the air like a whip.

Francis! Francis Anthony Mozzarelli!

"I don't know," Francis said. "I was shy, I guess."

"Do you always disappear?"

"I don't think so."

Bella told him she dreamed about his strong hands for weeks. She told him she dreamed about fucking Jesus.

"I guess you just did."

She told him about wearing angel wings and flying.

"That was you?" Francis said. "The little Angel Queen?"

"That was me! Someday I'm gonna fly the hell out of this place," she said. "I'm gonna fly all the way to the frickin' moon. I'm gonna fly so fast you won't even see me!"

After a feast of the best goddamned meatballs he had ever eaten, Francis crossed himself and kissed his fingers to his lips. "Can I lick the gravy off your tits?"

"Okay."

Bella slathered greasy gravy all over her body. Then she slathered it all over his. Together they rolled around on the floor, lapping and licking until there was nothing left, until the clock struck six.

Francis almost jumped out of his skin. "Oh my God! You gotta get out of here!"

"Why?"

"Because my old lady'll be home soon!"

"I'm not afraid of your old lady. I'm not afraid of anyone."

"She's got a gun."

As the two of them frantically dressed, Francis was filled with an awful kind of horrible dread. An overwhelming sense of loneliness started to creep in. It was deep and wide. It threatened to devour him.

He desperately didn't want Bella to leave.

He wanted to spend as much time as possible with this strange, beautiful girl.

He wanted to stay curled in her arms like a baby.

He wanted to spend the rest of his life swimming in her tomato gravy.

After stealing another kiss, he asked if he could walk her home in the dark and cold, but she pushed him away.

"No," she firmly said.

"Why not?"

She couldn't imagine him walking her past the sharp-toothed gates of the factory where she lived. If he saw the crooked house planted against the back wall, if he met her crazy family, he was sure to hate her. "I don't want you to fall in love with me . . ."

"It's too late."

"Goodbye," Bella said.

When the door closed, the clock on the wall ticked, the leaky faucet dripped.

The entire kitchen looked like a giant tomato had exploded in it.

"Holy shit."

Staring at the sloppy mess, Francis felt more alone than he

ever did. Belladonna Marie Donato was gone, and it felt like she had taken his heart. It felt like she had taken everything.

Well, almost everything.

Perched on the stool next to the door was her red cloche hat, rooster feathers poking the air. Francis fingered the red satin around the brim. He lifted it to his nose and sniffed. Then he carried it upstairs to his room, tucked it into a clean pillowcase, and hid it under his bed. Then he crossed himself and brought his fingers to his lonely lips.

"I will love you forever, Belladonna Marie," he whispered.

Then he crossed himself again, made a secret wish, and blew her a tender kiss.

CALL OF THE WILD

WHILE ON DUTY IN the factory gatehouse night-guarding the factory grounds, not long after Bella met Francis, Manny Donato heard a strange, hair-raising sound. An air-slicing shriek, followed by a hideous howl that blew the cap off his head.

After his scalp settled back down, he listened for several minutes but heard nothing.

Only his own shallow panting.

He shook his head. He must have been imagining things.

Suddenly there it was again. It sounded like a baby screaming.

Manny cleared his desk, grabbing for his Big Beam beacon lamp. He tried to snap it on, but the goddamned thing was dead.

"Jesus, Mary, and Joseph," he whispered.

There it was again! Holy shit! This time it sounded like a couple of tough tomcats wrestling behind the garbage bins. He scrambled for the door of the gatehouse, breaking the window and cutting his hand. The shock of it (the memory of

Lucia's knife slicing his cheek) didn't stop him from stumbling out into a swirling cold and mist. The pavement in front of him glistened with patches of snow and ice. The air hissed.

There it was again!

What was that horrible sound?

An even crazier cry roared from the rear of the factory grounds.

As drops of blood dripped from Manny's wounded hand, he crossed himself and jerked his gun from his holster.

Toggling weapon raised, he forced himself down the long factory alleyways, slipping and tripping all the way to his family's house. He could barely make it out. It loomed like a shrouded ghoul ready to pounce.

Was he losing his mind?

As he felt his way across the yard, another vicious growl sounded. This one capped with a nasty shriek. Manny gripped his gun and stumbled through his fallow garden plot to the low rise of cinderblocks that separated the factory grounds from the train tracks and cow fields.

Suddenly the mist cleared and everything was bathed in a silvery light, all tintyped and glowing, emulsified. Another animal scream and Manny saw, standing in the middle of the frozen fields, a fur-flanked naked thing, half young man, half beast, with the holy face of Christ leering. Was it a monstrous Orcolat? Or the child-snatching Bombasin of Manny's boyhood nightmares? Steam puffed out of its nostrils. Syrupy saliva strings dropped from its sharp teeth. It stood with its clawed arms spread. Its enormous penis was fully erect. It grabbed itself and howled again. Manny was about to raise his weapon and shoot when the back door of the house smacked open and a nightgowned girl burst into the cold night air.

She landed on her bare feet, skipped past the fallow garden, soared over the wall, and jumped into the arms of the horrible thing. The monster swung her around like a rag doll. Then it pushed her on all fours and ripped up her nightgown and mounted her from behind.

The pop of a ripe cherry tomato. Deadly nightshade. Trope of Belladonna Marie Donato! It was Manny's youngest daughter laughing and grinning, eyes bulging, tongue lolling!

"No!" Manny yelled. He wanted to save her, but he couldn't move.

The monster snarled and roared as he thrusted, and Bella roared too. Teeth bared, her own saliva dribbling, she locked eyes with her terrified papa. "Buon appetito! Mangiare bene! Stare bene! Delizioso!" she screamed.

As the beast pounded his cackling daughter, shameful feelings swelled in Manny's pants.

Fury and desire.

Blood and fire.

What the fuck was he thinking?

In a moment of blind disgust, he raised his gun and fired a smoking shot. Then he fired two more. He fired and fired and fired until he woke himself up, face down on his guardhouse desk, his scarred cheek pressed into a puddle of drool and sweat, his dying dick in his sticky fist, his heart drumming through his chest.

BELLA VERSUS THE VOLCANO

SHE NEVER KNEW WHEN he was gonna blow. The cap could have come off at any time.

It could have been the faucet dripping.

It could have been the clock ticking.

It could have been the cat licking.

How long before he would know?

She watched him read the *Herald-News*.

WANTED: Female Dancers
for Coney Island Revue!

She watched him work in the yard tending the animals and sharpening his tools.

She watched him file his pitchfork and grease his long-handled hoe.

She watched him in his garden plot getting the ground ready for his goddamned fucking prizewinning tomatoes.

He doesn't know.

He still doesn't know.

She wanted to tell him. Yell it into the house and watch it ricochet around, knock the pictures off the walls, and blow the mice out of their holes.

I know what it means to be a woman! she wanted to scream. *I have proof! And it's growing inside me!*

How long before he would know?

He must never know.

For four blissful weeks Bella had breakfast with Francis Anthony Mozzarelli almost every morning. She swore Lulu to secrecy and skipped across the street.

At first, when her monthly didn't arrive, she thought nothing of it. Then she started vomiting. Every morning. Then every time she ate.

"Please God, please don't let it be true!" she cried.

She vowed to never see Francis Anthony Mozzarelli again.

She avoided the puzzled boy like the plague.

She ran away from him when she saw him.

"Leave me the fuck alone, Francis Anthony Mozzarelli! Go away!"

But the young man chased and grabbed her. "I love you, Belladonna Marie Donato!"

"I don't love you!"

"How can that be?"

"I'm in love with somebody else!"

"Who is it? I'll kill him!"

Bella grabbed the first name that came into her head. "Terelli Lombardi!"

Francis burst out laughing. "That's ridiculous! Terelli Lombardi doesn't like girls!"

"Well, he does now!"

When the second month breezed by without so much as a tiny stain on Bella's bloomers, her flesh froze.

Francis still hunted her down. Like a hound dog, he followed the scent of her tomato gravy. Then, like a phantom, he appeared. Behind a makeup display in S. S. Kresge. Next to a colorful pile of packaged wool in the yarn shop when she shoplifted for Terelli Lombardi. He appeared in the cow fields behind the factory and howled at night.

"Stop following me!" Bella yelled in the middle of Van Houten Avenue. "Stop standing in the goddamned cow fields! Stop with the fucking howling! If you don't, my papa will shoot your balls off! And if he doesn't, I will! I hate you, Francis Anthony Mozzarelli. And I never want to see you again!"

The look of heartbreak that ravaged the beautiful boy's face was almost more than Bella could bear, but she stuck to her guns. She avoided him like the plague. Walked a different way to school every day.

"Why aren't we taking the bus from Krueger Place?" Lulu complained.

Sitting in remedial math and grammar, Bella found herself staring into space.

"You look different," Terelli Lombardi said one afternoon while the two of them were shoplifting their way through Rowe~Manse Emporium. "You're putting on too much weight."

She had to stop seeing her queer little friend too.

This pained her. But what could she do?

After a while, she stopped going to school. She stopped vomiting, but she couldn't breathe the way she used to. She couldn't sleep.

All she could do was eat and eat and eat.

She cooked like a demon.

Griddled trout.

Plum cakes.

Savory soups.

Sweet stews (pork, chicken, veal, beef).

Long links of hard salami sliced and fried. Spicy.

Tons and tons of homemade cavatelli (each little cradle of pasta about the size of the thing growing in her belly).

After she cooked everything in the house pantry, she ate her way through the jars and buckets and barrels and baskets stored in her papa's basement sanctuary.

Pickled beets and carrots from Manny's summer garden.

Autumn apples from the neighborhood trees.

Whole heads of garlic until she couldn't breathe.

Raw onions until she couldn't see.

"Jesus! You're gettin' as fat as one of Papa's pigs!" Little Luigi screamed.

She took to wearing her red winter coat all day and all night to try and hide what was happening.

She tried like hell to avoid her papa too.

She stayed way out of his way.

"What's for dinner?"

"Fix me a chop."

"Sear me a steak."

"Wash my feet."

"Where the hell is she?"

Predawn hours found her dodging the long ray of light from his Big Beam beacon lamp. She hopped the factory's back wall, stepped over the train tracks, slipped past the weasel packs, crept across the empty cow fields, and tip-toed through the moon-blue streets all the way to Krueger Place.

If she told Francis Anthony Mozzarelli she was carrying his baby, what would he say? Would his mamma shoot her out of her coat?

She could hear the old lady's picture growling.

Too terrified to do anything, she stood shivering at the bus stop for hours, the little cavatelli nestled in her belly.

Two hearts beating.

Both of them calling, begging, praying for Jesus to save them.

She did this every night until, on the first warm day of spring, a knock at the Donatos' front door sent her flying up to the eaves. She was furious that Francis was seeing where she lived. From the girls' bedroom window, she watched the young papa of her blooming baby pick a white rose from one of Manny's prized bushes and take a tender sniff. When he looked up, she snapped the curtains closed.

Did you see that?

I sure did!

She persuaded Luigi to answer the door. It cost her two dirty nickels and an entire homemade ricotta and salami pie.

"Bella told me to tell you she ain't here," Luigi said. "She told me to tell you she hates you and she never wants to see you again."

A single petal from the flower in Francis's hand spiraled down to the porch floor.

Like a fat ash from Pompeii.

"We're not allowed to pick those, you know."

Francis handed Luigi the rose. "Will you tell your sister Francis Anthony Mozzarelli came by? Tell her I have to see her again. Tell her I love her." Luigi had never seen a grown boy cry. "Tell her if she doesn't see me again, I'll die."

When Luigi slammed the door closed, Francis dropped to his knees. He grabbed the hair on his head and clutched the scalloped neck of his guinea T. "Bella!" he screamed. He ripped the shirt open, exposing his gorgeous Jesus nipples. His broken heart was bleeding. "Belladonna Marie! Please don't leave me!"

"He really said he loved me?" Bella asked Luigi when he handed her the plucked flower.

Luigi didn't say anything, but he knew something horrible was happening.

For several weeks he refused to go to school.

Instead, he clung to the tattered hem of his sister's coat. He tried like hell to climb under it until it was time to go to bed. And even then. He started calling her his *Bellamamma* again and helped her with the cooking. He cranked open cans, popped open jars, and chopped vegetables. "I can do it! I can do it!" he always said. He even took over washing their papa's feet for his sister. "Let me," he said when Manny called for Bella.

"Where the fuck is she?"

"Bella's busy."

"Bella's cooking."

"Bella's sick."

"Bella's sleeping."

The first time Luigi washed his papa's feet, he almost fainted. "Jesus! Your frickin' toes stink!"

There was a brief tussle.

"Holy cow! You don't have to clobber me!"

When the truant officer showed up and Luigi was dragged back to school (kicking and screaming), Bella decided the time had come to tell Francis Anthony Mozzarelli she was carrying his baby. She hoped he was still alive.

"Where is he? Is he dead?" Bella asked Mary Mozzarelli when the old woman told Bella he wasn't home anymore.

"Of course he ain't dead."

Bella could smell the old woman's sour tomato gravy. It wafted out of the house loaded with the skunky scent of rotten jealousy.

"I really need to see him." Bella's hand rested over her blooming belly. "It's an emergency."

The old woman smiled like a cat with a stomach full of dead rat. "You think you're the only little whore who rang my bell with a belly full of lies?"

"I'm only tryin' to do what's right."

"Well, you've come to the wrong house. Goodbye."

"Francis!" Bella screamed after the door was slammed in her face. "Francis Anthony Mozzarelli! I'm gonna have your baby!"

The door swung back open, and the old woman raised a glinting pistol. "I'm gonna count to three . . ."

Bella spun in her galoshes and ran like the wind, the old woman's laughter chasing her all the way back through the pointy gates of the Robertson Scale factory.

For days she was unable to get out of bed, every muscle dog-tired, every joint unable to bend.

"Please God, don't let me turn into my mamma," she begged.

As depressed days stumbled into depressed weeks, her body really started changing.

Her breasts swelled like two blowfish.

Her nipples turned purple and pined for something to feed.

She itched in the oddest of places.

Her shoes no longer fit her feet.

Her brain felt like it was melting.

The cavatelli blooming in her belly started talking.

"It won't be long now!" the rotten little thing teased.

The skin on her body prickled. It felt pickled. She couldn't imagine carrying another human being inside her belly.

"I want you to leave," she whispered. "Please leave."

Aren't you falling in love with me?

"No."

Not even a little?

"Nope. Not even the tiniest bit."

Will you ever?

"Not if I can fucking help it."

At night, and especially during the day, she had the strangest dreams. Whales riding enormous swells of salty seas. Giant walls of green, briny broth swelling up to the heavens, reaching to find where God might be.

"Francis Anthony Mozzarelli," she prayed to the ridiculous painting while kneeling in Saint Anthony's. "Francis Anthony Mozzarelli!" she cried to his broad shoulders, to the stars dancing around his beautiful head. "There's a baby growing inside me and it's yours, Francis Anthony Mozzarelli!"

As sloppy spring crested into early summer and Manny Donato's garden started sprouting, petal upon petal opened inside of Bella like a monstrous rose blooming. Her belly was mounding into a volcano. She was churning and bubbling. A musky cloud of fertile perfume wafted out from under her coat as she waddled around the neighborhood. Hot lava rocks. Pumice. Ash. Volcanic gasses. Young men started chasing after her.

(But not Francis.)

First one.

Then four.

Then a dozen.

Then more.

She thought about letting one of them do to her what Francis did. Maybe it would relieve some of the pressure. Kill the baby.

She tried to get rid of the little thing herself by douching with diluted Lysol. She drank large doses of Marchman's castor oil until she hocked like the Italian men that peppered the streets pitching pennies and tossing bocce.

"You're an oily girl!" Guiseppi Sparza slurred after her down Van Houten Avenue one afternoon. "But let me tell you something!" he sloshed. "The guppy uppy inside you won't die! No matter what you do, it'll grow until you explode!"

Bella imagined the little thing blasting out of her like an alien spaceship in one of the Jewel Box Theater's Saturday-morning serials, like a molten cannonball destroying everything.

"Mamma, I'm gonna have a baby," she confessed while bathing Lucia one stormy morning.

Thunder rumbled as Bella grabbed her mamma by the wrist and planted the woman's wet hand on her swollen belly.

Lucia just smiled and stared into oblivion.

"Mamma, say something."

More rain.

More lightning.

The little thing in Bella's belly started dancing.

The volcano was preparing to erupt.

And Bella was drowning.

"Mamma, speak to me. Please . . ."

TELLING THE GOD'S HONEST TRUTH, PART ONE

THE NEXT DAY, ON top of a ragged hill in the Passaic dump, a place Terelli Lombardi told Bella was very special to him, a private place where he could get away from all the horrible bullshit in the world, a place where he wasn't a *fucking faggot* but the king of everything, Bella sat next to her best friend.

"This is one of my favorite spots," Terelli told her. "I often sit here by myself. Sometimes for hours. Hatching grand escape plans and delicious schemes."

"What kind of plans and schemes?"

"Hollywood, for one thing. Maybe I'll go to Tinseltown and break into the movies someday. I can make the stars look even more beautiful, don't you think?"

"Well, you're a real whiz with makeup, that's for sure."

"Or maybe I'll open an antique shop somewhere fun. Like

Coney Island. I was made for that Sin City. Or maybe I'll go to Miami. Florida seems so warm and inviting."

Bits of coal and broken glass winked in the surrounding ash heaps.

"I'll take you with me wherever I go. All you have to do is ask."

"Thank you," Bella said as she grabbed his hand and held it.

For a while neither of them said anything more. Then Terelli spoke. "I have a present for you." He reached into his coat pocket, pulled out a small, meticulously wrapped package, and handed it to Bella. "The apricot paper is from Rowe~Manse Emporium, imported from Paris, France. The satin ribbon too. But I made the gift. Just for you."

Bella slowly untied the bow and opened the paper to reveal the jewel-topped box from Alice's vanity.

"Open it," Terelli said.

Bella lifted the lid. Bundled neatly inside was a knitted pair of butter-yellow baby booties and a matching hat no bigger than Lulu's baby doll's cap. Bella wanted to retch.

"The color is called duckling fuzz," Terelli said. "It's 100 percent cashmere. I had a hell of a time stealing it by myself."

Bella's face puckered, but she wouldn't let herself cry. "How did you know?" The tears started popping out of her eyes.

Terelli grabbed her hand. "Let's get married," he said. "I'll take care of you and your baby. We can live with my grand-mother in Brooklyn until we decide where we want to go. She smells like rotten crab meat. But it's nothing we can't fix. Her house is in a magical neighborhood called Prospect Park South. It's loaded with the most delicious antiques. Compared to Grandmother's house, my house is *nothing*."

Bella kept her eyes trained on a garbage truck as it trundled into the dump. "I can't marry you," she quietly said.

"Why not?"

They both knew why.

Terelli linked his arm through hers. "Are you going to marry the father?"

"I can't."

"Is the father a Negro?"

"No."

"Well, that's something to be thankful for, at least. Who is it?"

The garbage truck squealed to an idling stop. Bella took a deep breath. "Francis Anthony Mozzarelli," she said.

The truck dumped its trash. The crashing sounds of rattling tin cans and shattering glass.

Terelli sprang to his feet. "Liar!" he yelled. "You're lying to me!"

Bella laughed at the absurdity of everything. "Why would I lie?"

"Francis Anthony Mozzarelli is MINE!" Terelli hollered. "I'm his little bird! He loves ME! Not you! ME!"

Bella's eyes narrowed. She sucked in her cheeks. "How could he love you?"

Terelli's eyes narrowed too. "What do you mean?"

"You're an invert! A pervert! A queer! A pansy!"

Terelli's face turned as red as a summer beat. His ears blew steam. For a moment Bella thought he was going to slap her. "You're a despicable person, Belladonna Marie Donato!" he screamed. "You're nothing but a two-bit whore and a god-damned thief. And I never want to see you again! You or your goddamned bastard baby!" He turned on his heels and tripped halfway down the hill until he stopped and whipped around. "AND BY THE WAY, YOUR MEATBALLS ARE FUCKING DISGUSTING!" he hollered. Then he stumbled down the rest of the hill and ran across the dump, kicking up dirt and debris.

"MY MEATBALLS ARE FUCKING DELICIOUS!" Bella

yelled as he disappeared. Then she collapsed. In a fit of rage and anger she started digging. She dug like a hound dog after a bone until her fingers were raw and bleeding, until she couldn't see. She dug until there was a hole big enough to bury the baby cap and booties.

"Fuck you, Terelli Lombardi! Fuck everybody!"

She slammed the knitted things into the jewel-topped box, jammed it into the hole, and clawed the dirt back over it. Then she rose to her feet, stumbled down the hill, and ran all the way to Saint Anthony's.

After a quick prayer in front of the Christ painting, she crossed herself and slipped into a confessional.

"Bless me Father, for I have sinned."

The voice on the other side of the grill was not Monsignor Teschio, thank God. It was young and new.

"The Lord be in your heart and upon your lips. What are your sins?"

"I'm gonna have a baby, Father."

There was a pause.

"How old are you, my child?"

"I'm fifteen."

There was another pause.

"Who's the papa?"

"The boy in the crucifixion painting."

There was another, longer pause.

"How far along are you?"

"Pretty far, I think."

"Have you told your family?"

"Only my silent mamma. I'm afraid when my papa finds out he's gonna kill me."

TELLING THE GOD'S HONEST TRUTH, PART TWO

WHEN BELLA STEPPED THROUGH the sharp iron gates of the Robertson Scale factory holding the young priest's hand, she felt like she was dropping into the belly of Jonah's whale. She felt like she was being swallowed whole. When the two of them walked into the crooked house at the back of the complex, Luigi sprang up from his circle of marbles in front of the warbling radio.

"I only did it that one time!" he cried.

The handsome young priest was kind. "Can you get your papa for us, son?"

"He's sleeping and if I wake him up, he'll club me."

"Get him, Meatball," Bella said.

"Am I in trouble?"

"No."

"I don't believe you."

"GET PAPA NOW! BEFORE I FUCKING KILL YOU!" Bella screamed.

Luigi was up like a shot and he scampered out of the room as the radio blared the obnoxious theme song for *Little Orphan Annie*.

Through the floorboards came Manny's booming voice. "WHO? WHAT? WHERE? WHY?"

This is it, Bella thought. *I'm gonna fuckin' die.*

Orphan Annie's dog Sandy was barking after a bank robber when Luigi marched into the room followed closely by Manny, who was hiking up his pants and smoothing back his hair.

"See! I told you!" Luigi said, pointing. "There he is! But he's not here because of me! I swear!"

The young priest extended a cordial hand. "Mr. Donato, I'm Father Michael from Saint Anthony's."

"The new padre."

"Yes sir."

"What the hell is this about?"

"I'M GONNA HAVE A GODDAMNED FUCKING BABY!" Bella screamed.

A police siren was wailing out of the radio.

Manny stepped over to his daughter. "Who's the papa?" he said evenly.

Bella said nothing.

"Is it you, Padre?"

"I beg your pardon?"

Manny turned back to his daughter. His crooked mouth sneered. "I'm only gonna ask you one more time. Who did this to you?"

Why won't the floor open and swallow me? Where is God when you need him?

"The papa is Jesus," Bella said.

Manny struck her face so hard she hit the rug.

"Leapin' lizards!" Orphan Annie cried as Manny went in for the kill, but Father Michael jumped between them. "Mr. Donato, please!"

A mighty blow cracked against the priest's chin and the holy man went down too.

Luigi grabbed Manny around his legs. "No, Papa! Stop it! Please! Don't kill anybody!"

Father Michael popped up with fists raised. "I warn you, Mr. Donato. I may be a man of the cloth, but I'm fully capable of defending myself!"

Manny kicked Luigi to the wall and swung like a drunken bear, fat paws swiping the air. At first Father Michael respectfully ducked and dodged. Then he swung like a panther, two fast clips, and the tomato king of Robertson Scale factory dropped like a rock.

"Holy cow!" Orphan Annie sang.

"Papa!" Luigi cried, shaking Manny's legs.

Father Michael quickly turned to Bella and extended a steady hand. "You need to come with me," he said calmly.

Luigi yelped as Bella took the young priest's hand.

As they walked out of the house, the little meatball bounded after them. "Hey! Where are you going!" Luigi yelled as Father Michael tucked Bella into the parish car and shut the door. He jumped down the porch steps and pounded on the window. "Bella!" he cried as Father Michael got behind the wheel and started the engine. "Bella!"

Bella mouthed *I love you!* and blew her little brother a kiss.

As the car sped away, Luigi chased after it, arms flapping like a frantic pigeon. "Bella, don't leave me!" he wailed in a swirl of dust and dirt. "Bellamamma! Please!"

RAISING LITTLE LUIGI

FOR THE FIRST YEAR of Little Luigi's life, Bella tugged him around the neighborhood in the old wooden wagon. Only trees, sky, birds, and Bella above. God and Jesus too. But mostly only his favorite sister, floating in the clouds above him like a big, beautiful hot-air balloon.

For the first four years of his life, Bella was the song that sang him to sleep at night.

She was the delicious food in his belly.

She was his light when it was dark.

She was the one who held him when he cried.

She was the sun in his sky.

She was the only mamma he had ever known.

Until Tony, in a boxing mood, broke the news to the boy that Bella wasn't his real mamma.

Luigi didn't believe him.

"What do you mean? Am I an orphan like Lulu?"

"No, dummy."

The boy was confused.

"If Bella's not my mamma, then who . . .?"

When Tony told him his mamma was the silent lady always asleep in the dark, smelly old bedroom off the kitchen, Luigi was horrified.

"That lady's not my mamma . . ."

"She's everyone's mamma. Everyone except Lulu."

"Liar! You're lying to me!"

Luigi spit into his big brother's face. Then he punched him in his nuts and ran away.

Later that afternoon, Bella found Luigi curled up on the henhouse floor, a slingshot in his hand, six of the family's best layers dead.

The blood. The feathers. The severed heads.

"Meatball! What did you do?"

"Is it true what Tony said?"

"What did Tony say?"

Luigi could barely get the words out of his blubbering mouth.

"Fucking Tony," Bella quietly said. "That fucking stunad." She took a deep breath. "Listen to me, Meatball. It's true. That lady in the dark room gave birth to you and to me, we came into this world from between her silent legs, but I am your mamma. I raised you," Bella said. "I made you the boy you are. I made you the man you're gonna be."

She sang "'O sole mio." Then she took him in her arms and held him the way she used to when he was a baby and sang,

> Lullaby, lullaby, lullaby, ooh,
> Who will I give this baby to?
> Lullaby, lullaby, lullaby, eee,
> I will keep this baby for me . . .

When she was finished, she tickle-pinched him and gave him a sweet kiss. "I don't know about you, but I'm really hungry."

Luigi smiled up at his Bellamamma.

All was right with the world again.

"Me too. I'm starving."

Bella gave Luigi a tender bop on the top of his head. "Let's see what my Cooking Spirit has in store for these poor dead chickens."

Little Luigi's Chicken Cacciatore

Bella always made this for her little brother.
She made it for everyone she loved.

2 slaughtered chickens (6 if you have an angry little brother
   with a slingshot and a full henhouse), cleaned, plucked,
   and cut into proper pieces, skin on and bones in (thighs,
   breasts, legs)
2 large (28-ounce) cans of good-quality Italian plum tomatoes
6 sweet bell peppers (use green, red, and yellow if you can),
   cleaned and sliced into quarter- or half-inch-wide strips
1 small sweet onion, diced
5 garlic cloves, whole
1 cup black olives (pitted)
a healthy handful of basil
1 tablespoon oregano
several fresh sprigs of thyme
½ cup red wine
olive oil
flour
salt, to taste
pepper, to taste
chili flakes (always add chili flakes!)

1. After properly cleaning the slaughtered meat, pat the chicken pieces dry, flour each of them, coating them thoroughly (a pinch of salt and a pinch of pepper in the flour really blesses things!).

2. In a large, deep skillet, drizzle plenty of olive oil (take a healthy swig to honor Big Betty LoMonico) and heat the oil over medium heat (until it shimmers like Big Betty's spirit).

3. Add five whole cloves of garlic and fry them until just golden and aromatic. (The sun in your pot, the perfume in your kitchen!)

4. Toss in a healthy pinch of chili flakes and watch them bleed. (Try not to think about Little Luigi and his slingshot run-in with the chickens.)

5. Fry each of the coated chicken pieces on all sides (about 3–4 minutes for each side), until they're a nice, golden color. (Listen to the way the frying chicken makes the oil sputter and cluck. Even dead chickens have something to say.)

6. Once the chicken is fried, crowd it all in the large skillet. Pour in the red wine and braise it on medium-low heat for about 8 minutes. (The aroma will be enough to raise a papa from his basement. It will almost be enough to make a silent mamma speak.)

7. Coat the bottom of large gravy pot with olive oil. (Take another healthy swig to grease your insides, to keep the old timer ticking properly, and say hello to Betty LoMonico when her spirit appears. Give her a hug from Bella.) Tilt the pot on a flame to create a healthy puddle in its bottom crook and fry the remaining five cloves until golden. (You know the routine.)

8. Right the pot on the flame. Throw in a pinch of chili flakes (always add chili flakes!) and watch them bleed. Then add the diced onion and sauté until transparent.

9. Add the thyme sprigs to the pot and add the black olives. Stir it around. (There is magic in thyme spent in just about any dish!)

10. Add the sliced pepper (add a healthy pinch of salt, a healthy pinch of pepper, and the oregano) and stir until peppers are evenly coated and sizzling.

11. Put the plum tomatoes in a large bowl. Break them up with your hands and add them to the pot of cooking peppers. Add a pinch of salt and a pinch of pepper along with the fresh basil. Simmer for 10 minutes or so. (Sing "Santa Lucia" and dance around the kitchen with someone you love until the whole house smells like Italian Heaven.)

12. Place the chicken pieces and all the juices in a deep casserole pan. Pour the pepper and tomato gravy over the chicken, distributing it evenly.

13. Put the uncovered casserole in a 400-degree oven for 1 hour to 1 hour and 15 minutes.

14. Take it out and let it rest for at least 10 minutes.

15. Give someone you love a hug. Brush the tears away from their cheeks if they are crying and tell them you love them more than anything in the world, even more than chicken cacciatore and meatballs. Then eat!

16. Buon appetito! Mangiare bene! Stare bene! Delizioso!

SAINT ANTHONY, SAVE ME

"WE LOST OUR GARDENER last week," Father Michael said as he led Bella through the rectory's ragged yard. Uneven banks of overgrown grass waved away from the two of them as they walked past the crooked birdbath. "He had a heart attack while mowing down the weeds. We just hired a new one. His left leg is lame. He was born with it, but he's as young and as strong as a high school football player."

Bella farted. Lately, she had started regurgitating and burping and passing gas like an old jalopy. "I'm sorry," she said. "I don't know what's wrong with me." Her head throbbed. Her mouth raged. She still tasted blood when she tongued the inside of her cheek.

Father Michael took her hand and led her into the rectory. In the musty vestibule mahogany angels vaulted in high corners.

Jezebel! Bathsheba! Salome!

"I've got to say noon mass soon," he said as he rubbed his

bruised chin. "Not many parishioners during the week, I'm afraid." He lowered his voice and glanced sideways. "Nothing but a bunch of gossipy old ladies. I'm not sure how long we can keep you here," he whispered as their footsteps echoed up a winding set of narrow stone steps. "It will be up to Monsignor Teschio, and I don't know what he'll say. He thinks all young women are streghe malvagie. Evil witches. If he had his way, you'd all be burned at the stake."

Bella remembered the creepy old padre from when she had battled her way through grammar school. He voted against her during the carnival pageant. The old pervert had called her revolting. Now he wandered around the parish like a ghost, always with an altar boy or two or three tethered to his magenta cassock.

On the third floor, in a room the size of a small horse stall, Bella faced a weak-looking cot. It rested under an open window the size of a gravestone.

Father Michael cleared a few cobwebs away and pushed the cracked casement open. "I'll find you some fresh linens and see about procuring you some donated clothes. You'll find the water closet at the end of the hall. Wash up and get some rest. After mass I'll bring you down to the kitchen and introduce you to the old woman who cooks here." He lowered his voice again and made a sour face. "She's Irish. She boils the flavor out of everything."

Bella laughed despite the pain in her cheek.

Father Michael laughed, too, despite the pain in his own kisser. "Can you cook?" he asked.

"Yes. It's what I do best."

"Good. We'll put you to work to earn your keep."

"Okay, Father. Thank you," Bella said.

After Father Michael left, Bella sat on the edge of the cot. At first the silence was deafening. Then she heard voices ringing in the small room. They flew in through the cracked window and started singing,

You're a despicable person, Belladonna Marie Donato!
You're nothing but a two-bit whore and a goddamned thief!
You're just like your mamma! A pain in my ass! A good-for-nothing!
Bellamamma! Why did you leave me?

They sang like a riot of church bells clanging.

Like angels screaming.

To try and drown them out, Bella curled up and wailed until her throat felt like it was shredding. Then she did what she always did when her feelings proved too loud and too furious. She closed her eyes and imagined she was in the garden behind the house at Robertson Scale factory in the heat of tomato season, when the plants rose tall and green, when the ground was soft and warm, when the fruit was ripe and sweet. She imagined Francis standing among the plants, wearing nothing but a crown of thorns. She imagined him kissing and fucking her.

Al tuo servizio, mia regina!

She worked her hands between her legs, massaging herself until she was drenched in sweat, until tomatoes appeared in the air above her bed.

Moiras.

Romas.

Plums.

Beefsteaks.

I will love you forever, Belladonna Marie!

She kept at it, pressing and pushing and panting, until the tomatoes twirled and whirled into a tomato tornado that spun out of control and she screamed, "Saint Anthony, save me!"

THE KITCHEN WITCH

AFTER HE PRESIDED OVER afternoon mass, Father Michael brought Bella down to the rectory kitchen where a stout old woman was standing in front of a woodburning stove fishing potatoes out of a steaming cauldron.

"What in God's name happened to you?" she bellowed when she saw Father Michael's swollen lip and bruised chin.

"It's nothing, Mrs. Concannon."

"It doesn't look like nothin' to me! And who in God's name is she?"

"This is Belladonna Marie Donato, a nice young lady who is going to be staying with us for a while."

The old cook took in Bella's big belly. "Stupid girl," she hissed under her breath. "She doesn't look very nice to me."

"Bella's going to make supper for us this evening," Father Michael said.

The old woman crossed her arms over her ample chest. "Oh, is she really?"

"Yes. She is."

Bella farted.

"The cheek!"

Bella was about to fire another shot when the kitchen door swung open and a rough-looking young man with a wrecked left leg limped in, carrying a small load of chopped wood.

"Angelo," Father Michael said, "This is Belladonna Marie Donato. She will be cooking here for the time being."

The boy dropped the bundle next to the stove and smiled, exposing two chipped front teeth. "Hello, Bella," he said, extending a dirty hand.

Bella smiled too. "Hello yourself," she said.

"Stupid, stupid girl," the old cook snarled.

After Father Michael and Angelo left, Bella crossed herself and called upon the holy hands of her Cooking Spirit. Then she shucked her coat and rolled up her sleeves.

"And what do you think you're gonna be makin', if you don't mind me askin'?"

In the icebox, Bella found a questionable jug of heavy cream, a bunch of limp carrots, a few old onions, a rubbery stalk of celery, and a bloodstained package of some kind of chopped meat.

"You can peel the skins off those potatoes," she instructed Mrs. Concannon.

"I will do no such thing!" The woman planted her ample behind on a rickety stool next to the woodpile. She crossed her arms and watched as Bella expertly diced the carrots and chopped the onions and celery. Once it was all sizzling in the cauldron, she added the chopped meat, the cream, and some wine she filched from the sacristy. As she worked, the awfulness of the day began to drop away. Her fear and sorrow, even her pain, evaporated. She stirred and tasted and stirred some more.

"Delicious!" she announced. "But I think it can use a bit more wine . . ."

"You already put too much in!" Mrs. Concannon hopped off her stool and grabbed the spoon out of Bella's hand. "Here! Let me have a taste!"

"Blow first," Bella instructed.

The woman blew and shoveled a bit of the concoction past her lips.

"Well, what do you think?"

After a moment of stone-cold silence, the old woman lit up like a kid on Christmas morning. "I've never tasted anything like it in me life! What do you call it?"

Bella farted. "Bolognese."

"*Bowl-oh-nazy*," Mrs. Concannon repeated. She took another taste.

"Does it need more wine?"

"It's just right, I think."

"Great! Now we have to make the gnocchi!"

"What is *no-key*, if you please?"

"Italian potato dumplings."

"Well, I'll be . . ."

As the Bolognese simmered, Bella and Mrs. Concannon peeled and grated the cooled potatoes into a large pile of bits. Then Bella added a beaten egg and Mrs. Concannon sifted flour over it.

"It looks just like snow, doesn't it!" Bella said. She used her tomato-picking hands to mix it all together. After gently kneading, she shaped it into a fat log and cut it into four fist-sized pieces.

Working together, the two ladies rolled them into long, thick ropes. Then they cut them into small, inch-sized dumplings.

As the evening church bells clanged, they fingered divots into them.

"Now what do we do?" Mrs. Concannon eagerly asked.

"We boil them and pray."

They plopped the gnocchi into boiling water and after three Hail Marys and one Our Father, the tiny pasta pillows popped to the top of the roiling pot.

"That's it!" Bella announced. "They're finished! We have to scoop them out!"

With a slotted spoon, Bella fished them onto a large platter and coated them with the meat gravy. "Gnocchi alla Bolognese," she sang.

"In English, if you please."

"Little Italian potato dumplings in meat gravy!"

"Might I have a little Irish taste?"

When the sweet tang entered the old woman's mouth, the floor left her feet. Her insides swooned, her heart crooned, and she flew all the way up to the good Lord's Heaven.

"Ain't that somethin'!"

"Holy Mother Mary! It's like a delicious cloud melting in me mouth! Might I have another one, please?"

When the dinner bell rang, the two cooks wrestled the toggling platter into the dining room where Monsignor Teschio reigned. As the old man took his first bite, Father Michael threw Bella a wink. After he swallowed, the old monsignor smiled and addressed the young priest. "Very well. The shameful thing can stay. I want to see what other tricks she has up her sleeves." He leveled his nasty eyes at Mrs. Concannon. "What's the matter with you? Why can't you cook like this?"

The old woman's lips trembled and she raised a shaking hand to her cheek.

"I couldn't have done it without her," Bella said, grabbing Mrs. Concannon's hand.

The monsignor leveled a nasty gaze at Bella. "Did I ask you to speak, Pantàsema?"

"No. And my name is Bella."

The old monsignor's face turned to stone. "You must address me as Reverend Monsignor." He waited.

"My name is Bella, *Reverend Monsignor*."

"You look very familiar to me." He sniffed the air in front of her like a badger. "Let me see your teeth."

Bella opened her mouth.

"You're the girl that crashed through the carnival last year. You're the one that used to bite my nuns when she was a filthy little thing." He motioned her over to the table. "Come closer." He grabbed her hand in his bejeweled fist.

A bubble of gas kicked around in Bella's bowels.

The old man sneered at her, baring fetid teeth. "You must make this for me again," he said. He gave her hand a sharp squeeze, and she released a fart that blasted into the room like a holy roll of thunder.

"Tell me your name again, you rude thing."

"My name is Belladonna Marie Donato," she said. "But you can call me la Strega della Cucina, Reverend Monsignor." She looked directly into the old man's evil eyes. "The Kitchen Witch."

Gnocchi alla Bolognese

If you follow Bella's recipe,
these little Italian clouds
will deliver you straight up to Heaven.

3 large russet potatoes

1 egg, beaten

2 cups unbleached flour

2½ tablespoons kosher (sea) salt

Belladonna Marie Donato's best Bolognese gravy or tomato
gravy or a simple sage butter sauce

freshly ground black pepper, to taste

1. Wash and pierce potatoes with fork, then bake them at 350 degrees for 45 minutes or so.
2. Let the potatoes cool. This would be a good time to make your gravy. A simple tomato ragu, a sage butter sauce with grated cheese, or Bella's hearty Bolognese.
3. Peel the skins off the cooled potatoes.
4. Rice or grate potatoes and loosely spread on a board or sheet pan to let moisture evaporate.
5. Gather the cold potato bits into a mound and make a fertile (receptive-looking) well in the center.
6. Stir in one teaspoon salt and black pepper into a beaten egg and pour the mixture into the well.
7. With both hands, work the potato and egg mixture

together, gradually adding the flour. Knead into a ball of dough. Do not over-knead. Treat it gently, as you would a newborn baby.

8. Lightly dust the dough with flour, flour your hands, and continue kneading until the dough no longer feels sticky (as sticky as Francis's cannoli cream). Form the dough into a ball. Let it rest for a few minutes.

9. Form the ball of dough into a log. Cut the log into six or so equal pieces. Roll each piece into a half-inch-thick rope. Slice ropes into half-inch dumplings. With your thumb or forefinger, press a divot into each of the dumplings. Be gentle with the little pasta babies. Pray to Saint Anthony for salvation. If that doesn't work, say the Rosary.

10. Cook the gnocchi right away in a pot of salted boiling water. The gnocchi are done when they rise to the top. You can pray to pass the short time. Three Hail Marys and one Our Father should do the trick. As soon as they pop to the top of the boiling water, fish them out with a slotted spoon and toss them with a nice gravy, preferably a batch of Bella's delicious homemade Bolognese.

11. Buon appetito! Mangiare bene! Stare bene! Delizioso!

THE QUEEN OF GOD'S KITCHEN

HER FIRST MORNING IN the rectory, Bella was ordered to cook the monsignor's breakfast. After rummaging around the kitchen, she stormed into the old man's office with a plate of dry toast and a cup of black coffee.

The old man was seated behind his big desk. Two beautiful altar boys stood on either side of him like trapped angels.

Heaven, help us! Please!

"Is this all you give me to eat, Strega della Cucina? I am very hungry this morning."

"How do you expect me to cook for you? There's nothing in that kitchen but moldy onions and spoiled cream!"

The old man raised a hand in front of her and waited.

". . . Reverend Monsignor."

A small smile played across the old man's lips. He reached into the parish coffer and tossed a small wad of cash across his desk. "Tell the gardener to stop raking his leaves and drive you to a market for whatever you need."

Into LoMonico's Bella marched, no longer caring to hide what almost everyone (except maybe Francis Anthony Mozzarelli) already knew.

Big Bud was still behind the meat counter, crying over the loss of his big wife, butchering his meat. "Hello, Belladonna Marie Donato! It's so good to see you!"

No time for niceties. No time for memories. No visiting Big Betty's beautiful kitchen. Bella needed to get the job done before she saw any of her family. She was afraid to run into her papa. She would fall to the floor if she saw Little Luigi. What would she do if she saw Francis Anthony Mozzarelli or his old lady?

Hello, Francis. Meet your fucking baby.

"I need a sack of flour, a large tin of olive oil, a rope of garlic, ten cans of plum tomatoes, two dozen eggs, two pounds of fresh ground beef, and a wedge of Pecorino cheese!" she yelled to drown out her wailing feelings.

"What are you gonna make with all of this stuff?" Angelo asked after he loaded the rectory car.

"I'm gonna make a feast fit for Saint Anthony!"

With the engine idling, the two of them wolfed down deli sandwiches Bud had made for them (hard salami, provolone cheese, and a tart vinaigrette packed inside seeded semolina bread). When they finished, Angelo placed a greasy, callused hand on Bella's thigh. When he cupped her left breast, she slapped his hand away.

"Sorry."

"Not here," she said.

As the car sped down Van Houten Avenue, Bella spread her legs and Angelo went to town. She moaned as the car climbed Garret Mountain and swung around Lambert Castle. When they came to a stop in front of a stand of tall pine trees not far from the base of the old stone tower overlooking the old silk mill factories of Paterson, Angelo shifted the car into park. He left the motor running and went in for the whole salami.

Bella wouldn't let him kiss her. She didn't like his teeth. But she let him suck on her exposed breast while he yanked himself out of his soiled pants. His dick was dark. No delicious cannoli, this one. More like a baby eggplant. A purple piccola melanzana. Blue around the head and blazing red at the very tip. Its tiny slit leaked like the lips of a small fish.

"Will you lick it?"

When she wouldn't take him in her mouth he pretended to cry. So she tickled his balls and he was fine. As he pounded himself, breathing hard, steam filled the car. The windows became opaque. When he fired his shot, he kicked the gearstick into drive and the car jumped into the stand of trees.

"Holy shit!" Bella screamed.

"Are you okay?"

"I don't know! I think so!"

"What about the baby?"

"Don't worry. Nothing can kill the goddamned thing."

Back at the rectory, Bella spun a tear-filled tall tale about a drunken man who rammed the car with his truck and sped away. She caterwauled on and on about how she feared for her life and for the life of her bastard baby.

"We're goin' straight to hell," Angelo whispered as they hobbled out of the monsignor's office.

"Are you kiddin' me?" Bella said. "We're already in hell."

After putting the groceries away, she kicked the ratty old shoes off her swollen feet, called upon the holy hands of her Cooking Spirit, crossed herself, and started cooking.

"What are we making today?" Mrs. Concannon asked when she entered the kitchen carrying the day's laundry.

"Polpette e sugo di pomodoro con strozzapreti."

"In English, if you please."

"Meatballs and tomato gravy over priest stranglers."

Bella heard Big Betty sing,

Meatballs saved my life once!

And someday they're gonna save yours too!

After getting a jumbo pot of tomato gravy going, she combined the ingredients for her meatballs. When she was finished mixing, she grabbed a small fistful and rolled a ball the size of one of her papa's cherry tomatoes.

"Make as many of these as you can," she instructed Mrs. Concannon.

As the balls were browned in a skillet and dropped in the bubbling gravy, the intoxicating aroma attracted a couple of nosy parishioners fresh from afternoon mass. Two horsey women, one tall and pinched, the other with hips the size of church bells.

"We heard she was here," the pinched one sneered.

"Look at her!" the hippy one brayed. "Barefoot and big-bellied. Not an ounce of shame."

"What do you have to say for yourself, young lady?"

Before Bella could say anything, Mrs. Concannon flung a pot between the two ladies and dented the wall behind their heads. The nasty creatures flapped out of the kitchen, screaming like turkeys the day before Thanksgiving.

When they were gone, the old woman wiped her hands on her apron. "Now, let's make those priest stranglers!" she said.

They mixed and kneaded a healthy ball of dough. Then they rubbed long, thin strips of pasta between their hands. Then they boiled them and tossed them with the gravied polpette.

When they served the reverend monsignor, they crossed themselves and waited.

After the old man bit into a meatball, he smiled. "This tastes just like Heaven," he said.

That night, clods of dirt hit Bella's window.

When she looked outside, she saw Angelo in the yard standing next to the fig tree, leaning on his mangled leg. His eggplant was out of his pants and he was stroking.

As the moon winked above the branches, Bella flew down to meet him.

Papa! Catch me!

After landing (like a little Angel Queen) in a shower of white rose petals, she made a wish and kissed him. She wouldn't let him fuck her, but she took him in her mouth. When she was finished, he gratefully lifted her nightgown and nipped around her belly. He buried his head between her legs, moist and furry, and lapped and slurped until she felt her skin melt, until her muscles misted, and her bones turned to gravy. Until she felt herself disappear. Until there was nothing left but her baby.

FLOWERS FOR THE QUEEN

As HOT SUMMER DAY sizzled into hot summer day, Bella's belly blossomed into a gargantuan tomato. She felt as big as the late great Abundantia (God rest the beautiful sow's squealing soul).

Walking was hard.

Sleeping all night was impossible.

But eating was easy.

She ate a lot.

When she cooked for the rectory and for herself, her baby had a lot to say.

Chicken cutlets made it stretch its arms.

Soft polenta made it punch and kick.

Tomato gravy made it sing and spin.

Her magic meatballs made it tumble and flip.

After she finished with her cooking for the day, Bella always went into the church to pray.

She kneeled in front of the giant painting of the Francis Christ and crossed herself.

"Francis. Oh, Francis," she prayed. "I'm about to have our baby and I am scared to fucking death. Where will I go once it's born? What will become of my baby? What will become of me? Francis, oh Francis, why hast thou forsaken us?"

When she blimped to the size of a veritable dirigible, a striking boy about Luigi's age with skin the color of copper, celadon eyes, and a smile almost as big as his head showed up and rang the kitchen bell.

"You Miss Bella?"

"Yes."

He presented her with a tree-sized bouquet of long-stemmed bloodred roses swaddled in black bunting.

"These be for you."

"From who?"

A discreet card from Dino Montebologna was nestled in the bunting. His flourished signature and one fancy line:

Will you marry me?

"He can't be serious."

"I believe he is."

"Tell him *no, thank you!* for me, please."

"Okey dokey."

The boy showed up with flowers every Sunday. Bella always gave him a couple of biscotti or walnut and fig cantucci cookies and sent him on his way with the same *no, thank you!* and a packed sack of food for later. Then she started writing little messages for the boy to take back too.

Buy the kid a new pair of shoes, he really needs them.

The next week the boy showed up sporting a shiny pair of black wingtips.

Send me some smart lipstick.

The following week she received twelve tubes of
Maybelline's raging daphne.

When the monsignor got wind of the deliveries (the monsignor got wind of everything), he summoned Bella into his
office. "Strega della Cucina, is Dino Montebologna the father of
your bastard baby?"

"No, Reverend Monsignor."

"Don't you lie to me, Strega."

"I'm not lying to you, Reverend Monsignor."

"Who is it, then?"

"It's Jesus, Reverend Monsignor."

"Blasphemy!" The old man rose from his chair, scaring the two boys standing next to him. "How dare you be
so impertinent!"

"I don't know what that means, Reverend Monsignor."

"It means don't be stupid!"

"If it can happen to Mary, why can't it happen to me,
Reverend Monsignor?"

The old man's face blanched. His eyes rolled into the back of
his head and he collapsed. The two boys gasped.

Bella grabbed the old man's shoulders and shook him.
"Reverend Monsignor! Reverend Monsignor!"

After several panic-stricken minutes, he came to as if nothing had happened. "What are you doing here, Strega?"

"I came to see if you needed anything."

One of the boys giggled.

"What's for supper this evening?"

"Sicilian roast chicken with Tuscan dumplings, Reverend
Monsignor."

"You better get busy."

A CUP OF JOE IN THE GLOAMING

"YOU DIDN'T SAY ANY such thing!" Mrs. Concannon cried as she folded chopped rosemary and plucked thyme into a dumpling batter.

"Yes, I did. And I think it almost killed him," Bella said as she trussed a chicken.

"I wish I could have seen it! I think I would have peed in me bloomers!"

"I nearly did!"

The two ladies clutched each other in a fit of laughter until a persistent rapping on the kitchen window made Bella turn to see a familiar face hovering on the other side of the leaded glass.

"Joe!" she screamed.

Long Joe. Lean Joe. Eager Joe.

The Portuguese cowboy, hatless and smiling a chaw-toothed smile.

In the rectory yard, the two of them sat on a stone bench under a blazing maple tree sipping cups of coffee as the sun set behind the church steeple, making everything glow like it was dipped in eternity.

"Why aren't you up in Massachusetts with Connie and your baby, Joe?"

"We moved back down to Jersey about a month ago. Connie wasn't doing so good up there. And neither was I, to tell you the truth. We're living at the factory now. With your family. Your papa got me a job on one of the assembly lines next to Tony. It really stinks, but it's a steady living. As soon as the day guard leaves, I'm gonna jump over your papa into the gatehouse. Connie's helping Lulu with the cooking."

"How's that going?"

"Everyone holds their nose when they eat."

"How's my mamma?"

"The same. She sleeps all the time and says nothing."

"How's Little Luigi?"

"The five-and-dime caught him stealing last week. Your papa took a belt to him real good. Poor kid hasn't stolen anything since, I don't think."

The church bells clanged.

"Why are you here, Joe?"

"I figured you were gonna need someone to be there for you when the time came. And I figured it might as well be me."

Long Joe. Lean Joe. Sweet Joe.

"I talked to that young priest," he continued. "The one who looks to be about Luigi's age."

"Father Michael?"

"Yeah. What a wet sackcloth he is."

"He's really nice. He was the only friend I had here until I started cooking."

"He made me talk to the old monsignor."

"That man thinks I'm a witch."

"He asked me if I was the papa of your bastard baby."

"What did you say?"

The tips of Joe's ears blushed red. "I said yes."

"Why did you say that, Joe?"

"I don't know. I wanted to protect you, I guess. That old pervert laid into me for a good hour. I never heard so many Bible verses in my entire life. Then he made me get on my knees in front of him and confess all my sins." Joe was quiet for a few minutes. For the first time, Bella noticed his fingernails. It was clear that he bit them. They looked like they were gnawed down to the cuticles.

"Joe, are you okay?"

Joe placed his empty coffee cup on the bench between them. "Connie's pregnant again." He looked at Bella. His blue eyes were hard, the color of the sky just before a storm enters the atmosphere. "I don't want to have another baby with your sister," he confessed. One of his fingers was wedged between his teeth. He placed the other hand on hers, more for his own comfort. "I wish I was havin' your baby with you. I really do."

"I want you to leave."

"What?"

Bella threw her empty coffee cup in the air. "Get the fuck out of here, Joe! Go back to your fucking wife and her fucking babies!"

"Bella, please . . .!"

"GETTHEFUCKOUTOFHEREGETTHEFUCKOUTOF HEREGETTHEFUCKOUTOFHERE!" she screamed until the baby in her belly did a backflip, until her brother-in-law jumped out of the rectory yard and his pickup truck peeled away.

THE FORTUNE
TELLER'S PASTA

TWO WEEKS AFTER SHE was due, to try and forget about the fact
that she was gonna have a fucking baby any day, Bella cooked
like a demon.

"What do you call this?" Mrs. Concannon asked after they
made boiled pieces of pizza dough in portobello gravy.

"Ricetta pizzicotti ai funghi."

"Why, it's nothin' but globs of dough sittin' in a pile of
mushrooms!" the old woman sniffed. Then she took a bite.
"Good Lord up in Heaven!"

When they made casoncelli, little pasta caskets, the old
woman told Bella they were her favorite. "I love things stuffed
with any kind of meat, especially beef."

"Me too," Bella agreed.

After they made scorze di mandorle, pasta seashells coated
with tomatoes and peas, Bella told Mrs. Concannon about her
childhood trips to the Jersey sea. She told her about her papa

tossing her in the air above the waves, her mamma laughing and happy.

"This one I'm not gonna miss after you leave," Mrs. Concannon admitted when they made cavatelli, fork-rolled little cylinders, tossed with broccoli, garlic, chili flakes, and grated cheese. "But I'm sure going to miss you." The old woman reached out and put a quivering hand on Bella's. "I'm gonna miss you and your delicious cookin', me little darlin'."

Not since Big Betty had anyone called Bella *little darling*.

After the two of them made testaroli, Mrs. Concannon taught Bella how to cheat at poker. They drank wine Bella swiped from the sacristy and giggled through several hands.

When Bella taught the Irish woman how to make lasagna bastarde, the old lady became quite sullen. "You know," she admitted quietly. "I had a bastard baby meself."

Bella stopped layering. "You did?"

"Oh, now let me see. It was years and years ago," Mrs. Concannon confessed, barely above a whisper. "I was only about thirteen. Me, a thirteen-year-old girl, if you can believe such a thing. The da's name was James. He went by Jamie. He was only a year or so older than me. He was me first taste of mortal sin. And it was glorious, believe me!"

Bella was afraid to breathe.

"I was a wild thing, just like you. Until me da beat it out of me."

Bella tongued the gap between her teeth.

"As soon as me baby was quick," Mrs. Concannon continued, "I was shipped away just like you. That's how I came to be in America. I'll never forget the long boat ride. The sailing was so many lonely days. After I arrived, me days were even lonelier. Especially after I had me baby and they took him away. I named him William."

"Like William Powell?"

"Yes. But I called him Billy."

"Like the Kid."

"I held him only once. Then I never saw him again. I'll never forget his wee face. It was the most beautiful face I had ever seen." Mrs. Concannon stared into her pudgy hands. "I often wonder where he is." The old woman was lost in her palms for a bit. Then she grabbed Bella's hands in hers. "I'm sorry I called you stupid when I first met you," she said. "You're not stupid at all. You're a wonderful, smart lass. You're a gift from God and don't ever let anyone tell you anything less."

Bella hugged Mrs. Concannon hard and the two of them cried over the lasagna.

"Maybe you can still work here after your baby comes," the old woman whispered in Bella's ear.

"Maybe. We'll see."

That night, when Angelo appeared among the trees, Bella flew down to him again.

"Mangiami! Bevimi! Divorami!"

Eat me! Drink me! Devour me until I disappear again! Please!

The final dish Bella and Mrs. Concannon made together before Bella's own little bastard arrived was uova da raviolo.

"In English, if you please."

"It's called the fortune teller's pasta."

"Fortune-telling is the devil's doing!"

"It's something an angel once taught me," Bella said, remembering the day Big Betty LoMonico showed her how to make the magic pasta. "And now I'm gonna teach you because you've been such an angel to me."

After mixing a big ball of dough, the best friends rolled out two large pasta sheets. They cut sixteen perfect rounds with large canning jars. On eight of them they walloped a healthy dollop of fresh ricotta cheese. Then they nested a bright yellow egg yolk in each, covered them with the remaining pasta pieces, and pinched them closed. After boiling one of them for three minutes, Bella gently ladled it onto a plate and dressed it with melted butter.

"How does it work?" Mrs. Concannon asked.

"Cross yourself and ask the raviolo a question, and when you break it open the answer will be found in the yolk."

"Like readin' gypsy tea leaves?"

"Exactly."

Mrs. Concannon gasped and crossed herself.

"What do you want to know?" Bella asked, handing the old woman a fork.

Mrs. Concannon raised the utensil. She squeezed her eyes closed and crossed herself. "Tell me, oh raviolo," she paused. "Will I ever see me son again?"

When she cut open the pasta, there was only cheese. The yolk was missing!

"I understand," was all Mrs. Concannon said, lips trembling.

Bella said nothing.

"Might we do another one?"

"Yes."

With her fork poised again, Mrs. Concannon crossed herself and closed her eyes. "Tell me, oh raviolo, will Bella be bringin' a baby boy or a baby girl into the good Lord's sin-filled world?" When she cut the pasta open the bright yellow yolk ran in the form of a perfect *B*. "Merciful heavens! You're going to have a boy! Just like me!"

Just then the baby kicked in Bella's belly. Her face crumpled and she started sobbing.

"You're goin' to have a son, me darlin'! Doesn't that make you happy?"

"No! What's gonna happen when he comes out of me?"

Mrs. Concannon grabbed Bella and rocked her. "There, there," she soothed. "It's all goin' to be okay."

"How can it be?"

To comfort them both, the old Irish cook made them the one thing she made best.

"What is it?" Bella asked when Mrs. Concannon handed her a plate.

"A grilled cheese sandwich. I made two. One for me and one for you."

That night cries of "Fuck it out of me! Kill it! I don't want to have this goddamned baby!" brought the old candle-carrying monsignor into the chancel of the church. When he saw Bella and the gardener fucking like demons under the giant portrait of the Francis Christ, he wailed, "Bella!" Then he grabbed his chest and dropped to the floor. This time he stopped breathing.

Outside, a lightning bolt hit the church's bell tower.

Inside, Bella and Angelo jumped to their feet.

Outside, a blast of thunder cracked the sky open.

Inside, Bella's water broke and gushed out of her belly.

Outside, another violent spoke of lightning illuminated everything.

Inside, Bella stood in front of the crucified Francis Christ and spread her arms wide. "HOLY SHIT! THIS IS IT! THE LITTLE BASTARD IS COMING!"

Uova da Raviolo

When Big Betty LoMonico taught
Belladonna Marie Donato this complicated recipe,
she advised her to use its potent power sparingly.

For the basic pasta dough:

3 to 4 cups flour

4 eggs

¼ cup Montebologna Olive Oil (*the Olive Oil of Italian Kings!*)

1–2 tablespoons water (more if needed)

For the raviolo filling:

½ cup grated Pecorino Romano

½ cup fresh ricotta

a pinch of nutmeg

salt and pepper, to taste

7 fresh eggs (six and one for luck)

For the raviolo sauce:

4 tablespoons salted butter

6 fresh sage leaves

1. Make a basic pasta dough by mounding 3½ cups flour in the center of a large wood cutting board. Make a well in the middle of the mound and add the eggs and olive oil. Using a fork, beat together the eggs and oil and begin to incorporate them into the flour. Once the eggs are incorporated, knead the dough until it is firm

but springs back when pinched. Place the ball of dough in a bowl lightly coated with olive oil, cover the bowl with a towel, and let rest in a cool place for 30 minutes. Think about what you want to ask the raviolo. Pick your question carefully.

2. In a bowl, combine the ricotta and grated cheese. Season with salt, pepper, and nutmeg and mix well. Think about your chosen question as you mix. Set aside.

3. Lightly flour the board and knead rested pasta dough for 5 more minutes. Roll the dough into large, thin sheets and cut twelve large circles using a bowl (about six inches wide). Set six aside on a floured surface.

4. In the center of each of the remaining six, place a healthy dollop of the ricotta mixture. With the back of a spoon, hollow out a well in each of the ricotta mounds. Crack six eggs in a large bowl. One at a time, place a yolk in each well. As you do so, silently repeat the question you want to ask over and over again like a prayer. The yolks must remain unbroken. You can coat the edges of the pasta with a tiny bit of water to make sure they remain sealed. Cover each filled circle of pasta with remaining circles of dough and press the edges together.

5. Bring a large pot of water to a boil. Salt the water. Then, one at a time, with a spatula, gently place each raviolo in the water. Boil for 2 minutes. Repeat the question like an incantation, whispering it into the steam.

6. Normally, a raviolo is served in a browned butter sauce. Melt four tablespoons of salted butter with six sage leaves in a large pan or skillet over medium heat. Gently

stir until butter becomes golden without burning. Lower heat to keep warm. When each raviolo is removed from water, place it in the pan and gently spoon butter onto it until lightly coated (2 minutes).

7. Once plated, humbly address the raviolo and clearly state your question. Cross yourself and blow a kiss to Heaven. Then respectfully cut it open and see what it has to say.

8. The raviolo always speaks the truth.

9. Thank the raviolo and enjoy your meal.

10. Buon appetito! Mangiare bene! Stare bene! Delizioso!

WHAT CHILD IS THIS?

A VIOLENT RAIN PUMMELED down as the parish car shot away from the church. The spinning tires were skating on steam. They were screaming.

"Where are you taking me?" Bella cried from the back seat. The pain in her abdomen was excruciating. "Where are we going?" She made a play for the grab strap hanging from the car ceiling but missed as Father Michael swerved around a blind curve, two wheels up, two wheels down. "To the hospital!" he hollered as the wheels of the car bounced on the slick ground. He handled it like an amateur rodeo clown.

"To the hospital?!"

"Someone from your family is meeting us there!"

"My papa?"

Not my papa, please.

"Hail, Mary full of grace!" the young priest prayed.

The car fishtailed and Bella's insides clenched. "Son of a bitch! I think I'm dying!"

"You're not dying! You're just having a baby!"

Another blind curve. Up went the right side of the car, up went Father Michael, up went Bella, up went the baby, but like a banana bird hunkered in its hurricane nest, the little thing hung on. It wanted to tell its mamma not to worry. It wanted to let her know how much it was looking forward to meeting her. It wanted to tell her everything was going to be okay.

"I'll get you there!" Father Michael yelled. "Pray I get you there!"

A blast of thunder boomed and every cell in everyone's body, including the baby's, seized. The little thing took a nose-dive. The spine-twisting pain kicked Bella's legs apart.

"I think it's coming out of me!"

"No! Please! Close your legs and squeeze!"

"I can't! It hurts too much! I swear it's killing me!"

The car suddenly careened from one side of the road to the other, brakes screeching, rubber tires shrieking, baby diving, Bella wailing.

"Hold on!" Father Michael yelled. "Hold on and pray!"

He grabbed the magnetized plastic Christ attached to the dash in front of him and tossed it back to Bella. She caught it and hurled it at his head.

The car swerved and the baby dove again.

"Son of a fucking bitch!"

Father Michael flattened the accelerator to the floorboard and the car sped into the eye of the storm, into a pocket of absolute silence as dark and as deep as eternity.

Father Michael's and Bella's spirits left their bodies. Temporarily. They spun together in a tongue-tied pocket of mute, hair-raising hysteria.

Santa Lucia! Santa Lucia!

When the car popped out the other side of the storm's core, it skidded up to the entrance of Saint Joseph's Hospital, to the figure of a tall man standing under an umbrella, spitting tobacco juice into the pouring rain.

Long Joe, lean Joe, fearless Joe tossed the umbrella and jumped back like a jackrabbit. "Hey, fella!" He pounded on the hood of the car with his fist. "Hey, you crazy fuck!" He ran over to Bella's door, yanked it open, and stuck his head in. "Honey, are you okay?"

"No! I'm dying, Joe!"

"You're not dying. You're having a baby."

"That's what everyone keeps saying!"

He leaned in and scooped her out of the car, and she mooed like a stuck cow.

"Easy does it, sweetheart!"

"Where are we going? Where are you taking me?"

"Into the hospital to have your goddamned baby!"

"Okay!"

He carried her like Errol Flynn carried Olivia de Havilland in *Captain Blood*.

"Son of a bitch!"

"Fuck!"

ROCK-A-BYE YOUR BABY

"I WANT YOU TO push!" A walnut-mugged doctor was in Bella's face. Not an ounce of compassion. Not an inch of grace. "Push, young lady! Push!"

The pain made the hair rise off her head. She tried to move, but her arms were strapped down at her sides and her legs were hoisted apart, feet hitched high. She was completely exposed. The insides of her thighs felt ice-cold. Her spine felt like it was gonna snap in half. Her skull felt like it was gonna explode.

That's when her spirit left her body again and rose to the top of the room.

Papa! Catch me!

"Take a deep breath, hold it in, and really push!" a bullhorn of a nurse hollered like a foghorn in the mist. "Now let the air out of your lungs and yell! That's it!"

From the green, water-stained ceiling, high above everything, Bella could see herself gulping big buckets of air. Each time she did, her body clutched itself and convulsed, every muscle and bone trying to rid itself of the thing she had been carrying for over nine long months. Her hair was wet and wild. A mass of overcooked spaghetti stuck to her head. The stench of her splattering bowels made the nurse curse. Bella's shit was everywhere.

Another nurse, this one a young nun in full habit, appeared. She wiped Bella's brow and cleaned her legs as best she could.

"I don't want to die!" Bella heard herself cry.

"The Lord is holding you in His hands," the young nun soothed.

"Fuck the Lord!"

"Shut up and push!" the doctor yelled. "Push, I said!"

The nun continued to wipe but didn't say another word.

"Francis! Where are you!?" Bella screamed.

Even way up against the ceiling, her spirit could feel the pain. Even way up high, the pain was more than agonizing. It was fucking insane.

"Oh, Christ. Keep her steady."

Had Bella known what was going to happen to her, she never would have followed Francis into his house that cold winter morning. She never would have fucked him.

"I want my mamma!"

"Here comes the little bastard," the doctor said. "It's crowning. I can see the top of its head."

Finally.

The baby.

Bella's soul dropped back into her body. A constellation formed between her skull and the inside of her scalp. Universe upon universe opened, like Russian dolls or nesting cups. Her cooch spit steam and the baby's face appeared.

"Get ready to make the catch!" the doctor yelled.

As if on cue, the little thing Bella-blasted out of his mamma like a circus cannonball on its way to the moon. It hit the doctor squarely in his chest, sending the startled man onto his ass.

"Doctor, are you okay?"

"Jackpot!" the man hollered, holding up what looked like a skinned rabbit, its trunk slathered in a white waxy coating streaked with blood. It looked like something hanging behind Big Bud's butcher case, waiting to be sliced. Eyes closed. Pink arms dangling. A tiny nub of a penis the color of an American Beauty rose. A massively swollen scrotum like a couple of tangelos.

"It's a boy!" the foghorn of a nurse cried.

The raviolo was right!

The young nun crossed herself and sighed, "A boy!"

"Is it alive?"

After the cord was cut and tied, the doctor stuck his finger into the tiny thing's mouth and wormed his digit around. Then he pinched slime away from the pebble-sized nose and smacked its backside hard enough to make even the foghorn nurse flinch.

Nothing happened.

The doctor whacked the little carcass a second time and everyone held their breath.

"Whack it again!"

The doctor did and it opened its mouth and jangled the room with a plaster-cracking cry. Purple and white roared red as the little thing rattled with rage.

"Take him," the doctor said, thrusting the squalling thing at the nun. Then he turned to the foghorn nurse. "Get the girl ready for the next procedure."

As Bella's yowling new baby was bathed, she was properly cleaned and disinfected.

The doctor changed gloves. A new apron was snugged around his body.

A silver tray with an array of long, metal instruments was placed in front of him. One razor-like blade, smaller than the one Bella's mamma used to slice her papa's cheek, gleamed. Others looked like they did more than just cut things.

Bella was suddenly being tossed over a roiling sea.

Papa! Catch me!

The doctor's walnut mug was swimming in front of her face again. "When I place this mask over your mouth and nose, I want you to breathe. Take in deep, steady breaths."

At first Bella's couldn't take in anything. When she tried, she gagged.

"Breathe!" the doctor yelled. "Breathe!"

Sour air ripped up her nose and clawed down her throat. Her heart jumped into her head and pounded like Dario Scungille's bass drum. It felt like it was going to explode.

"That's it!" the doctor yelled. "Breathe deep!"

Somewhere in the room her baby was wailing. An ear-ringing, earthquaking, caterwauling, monstrous sound that grabbed Bella by the throat and rattled her world until all her lights went out.

Recipe for Bilateral Salpingectomy

From *Practical Eugenics and Other Philosophies*
by Dr. Clive Venbratten

rubber gloves

sterile drapes

1 curved surgical blade with handle

2 curved forceps

Metzenbaum scissors

pool sucker

2 abdominal packs

2 clamps

needle

catgut and silk suture material

Foley catheter

1. Receive request from parent or guardian.
2. Paperwork signed.
3. Deliver (healthy?) baby.
4. Scrub up and put on fresh rubber gloves.
5. Fully anesthetize patient.
6. Insert Foley catheter.
7. Scrub skin and surrounding area.
8. Drape patient.
9. Locate point of entry: midline, one fingerbreadth below umbilicus.
10. Proceed with transverse incision. Eight to ten centimeters wide.
11. Dissect through subcutaneous tissue.

12. Identify rectus sheath (a thick, white fibrous tissue). Grasp with two curved forceps. Make small incision in center between forceps. Extend incision laterally with Metzenbaum scissors (be sure not to injure any underlying muscles).

13. With the curved forceps, separate rectus sheath. Gently push down rectus muscles to separate from rectus sheath.

14. With fingers, identify midline and split rectus muscles.

15. Identify peritoneum underneath (appears as a thick, semitransparent membrane).

16. Use moist abdominal packs to carefully mobilize peritoneum and its contents upward and out of surgical field.

17. Identify uterus.

18. Trace and identify fibril ends of tubes and examine ovaries.

19. Clamp each tube, one at a time, with two clamps approximately two centimeters apart. Excise isolated section of each tube.

20. Tie sutures around each end.

21. Release clamps. Check for any bleeding. Ensure sutures do not loosen.

22. Wash pelvic cavity to make sure there are no blood clots. Remove any clots in right and left upper quadrants. Do this by inserting one hand to push bowel away from side walls and gently insert pool sucker above your hand.

23. Upon completing peritoneal washing, make sure there is no bleeding from the stumps. Water should be clear, no blood.

24. Proceed with closure of abdomen. Close and suture sheath. Irrigate, close, and suture subcutaneous layer.

25. Finally, close and suture skin.

26. Apply dressing.

27. Jackpot! Another baby sprung free! Another perfect salpingectomy!

BROADWAY MELODY OF 1936

AFTER THE DELIVERY AND subsequent procedure, Bella—clouded in the haze of a strange journey, fevered, and bleeding—was wheeled into her hospital room and foisted into an iron bed. In and out of consciousness. Hysterical dreams, as choppy as a stormy sea. Her papa tossing her over the caterwauling ocean waves and missing her when she came down. "Papa! Catch me!" Under the salty sea and drowning. "I can't breathe!" Her mamma's depressed wheezing. Little Luigi, a tiny baby again, teething and roaring like the MGM lion. ARS GRATIA ARTIS. Gary Cooper and Clark Gable kissing. Joan Crawford Charleston flailing. Nasty churchwomen flapping around crowded belfries. Nuns pulling ropes and screaming, "Thank me and kiss Christ's ring! Thank me and kiss Christ's ring!" The factory whistle shrieking. The toothy Robertson Scale gates chewing the ass out of the sky. A red river of blood flowing down the aisles of Saint Anthony's. Her brother Tony boxing with a circus bear. Her papa and mamma, young again, tossing meatball beach balls in the air. Mrs. Concannon mixing mountains of dough, forming them into monstrous potatoes. Big Betty LoMonico's sweaty hands inflated like a Macy's parade balloon, like Mickey the Mouse gloves reaching for the moon. Dino Montebologna swimming in a colossal bottle of olive oil like an Italian king. Joe sniffing her fingers and sucking each one. Joe gnawing on his nails and telling her he wishes they were having a son. Was that Joe she heard sitting next to her bed, barking through the fog, "How long has she been out like this? How long has she been in Dreamland?" Was that a kiss she felt on her forehead and Joe telling her not to worry, that he would take care of everything? Francis lifting barbells shaped like cannoli. Swans diving through blazing circus rings. Jesus naked on the cross, sins dangling. Her mamma coming for her stomach with the cheek-slicing blade. "Zing! Went the Strings of My Heart!" Mary Mozzarelli firing a gun the size of a circus cannon. A rocket-sized bullet knocking the fire out of the sun. Terelli curling his own hair with tree trunks, a smoking factory stack dangling from his lips. "Can you dance? You can get a job in Sin City!" WANTED: Female Dancers for Coney Island Revue! A rollicking roller-coaster ride around the Glasgow-grinning moon. Francis Anthony Mozzarelli picking a rose from one of her papa's bushes and presenting it to her before vanishing in an explosion of furious flames. Her baby being yanked out of her bleeding heart. A wolf's lonely cry. "What the hell's going on? Where the fuck am I?" A nervous young man, with the face of Francis, cinched into a bow-tied suit and standing in front of her with a bouquet of brilliant white roses in his shaking hand.

Do you know who I am?

A HERITAGE FROM THE LORD

WHEN SHE FINALLY WOKE, she didn't know where she was. For a moment she thought she was back at the rectory. Then she was sure she was home, at the Robertson Scale factory. A line of stitches across her abdomen itched and burned. Mercurochrome made them scream.

"What happened to me?"

"You just had a baby."

It all came hurtling back.

But did it really happen?

She was weak and empty. Like one of her pots before it was filled with tomato gravy. And she was starving. She inhaled three plates of gray-looking beef melting over mushy noodles and four small bowls of chalky strawberry ice cream.

"Keep eating, young lady!" the young nun from the delivery room encouraged. "You have to regain your strength!"

She did as she was told, then she went back to sleep.

The next morning, after Bella had a long, greasy bowel movement, the young nun reappeared holding a squirming bundle in her arms. "Here he is," she whispered. "He's a regular heritage from the Lord. Would you like to hold him?"

It was true. She had a baby. A wave of nausea like the ones she had experienced during the rocky early days of her pregnancy washed over her and she gagged and coughed.

"No."

The nun ignored her.

"Don't be silly. Of course you do."

The beaming woman gently placed the baby on Bella's chest. "You need to be careful. If he starts to cry, I'll have to take him away. If the others catch me doing this, there'll be holy hell to pay."

Not since Little Luigi had Bella held anything so helpless. So vulnerable.

This is a small part of me. How fucking strange.

Bella's first impulse was to throw the bundle against the wall. He started wriggling around in the wrapped blanket, but his eyes were closed.

"I think he's sleeping," Bella said.

"Count your blessings. This one's a real yeller. A regular Kate Smith when he's hungry."

He had the longest lashes Bella had ever seen. Ruby-colored pimples blotched his cheeks, but the rest of his face looked Flirty Eye Princess Beatrix baby doll perfect. A tiny nose, crusted and wheezing; mini rosebud lips, kiss-ready and glistening. He had big hands. He had Bella's hands.

"Tomato-picking hands. Just like me," Bella whispered.

She reached down and gently touched one of them with her finger. Without opening his eyes, the baby grabbed and squeezed.

"He's so strong," Bella said.

Just like Francis Anthony Mozzarelli.

"He's a regular little strongman, this one is," the beaming nurse whispered.

"Peekaboo, I see you . . ." Bella sang and her tits spit, soaking the front of her hospital gown. When the wet struck the baby, he opened his eyes, flecked gold and green.

Without thinking, Bella pulled the top of her hospital gown open and brought him to her damp breast. When he latched on to the tip of her ripe nipple, the skin jumped off her bones.

"Ouch! He's biting . . ."

"Poke his cheek."

Bella pressed her finger into his pimples and he let go for a second. Then he took the tip of the nipple and a fair amount of the plum-colored skin around it into his little mouth again, mostly with his tongue and lips instead of his gums.

"Bend forward a little bit," the nun coaxed.

The stitches across Bella's abdomen pinched like a son of a bitch.

"That's it," the nun whispered.

When he latched on properly and started sucking, Bella felt the first flush of a release. It was a painful tug at first, almost as painful as her hissing stitches. Then her whole body tingled. Then it was soothing. Then it was pure ecstasy. Her breast felt like it was housing a hive of bees.

Honeybees.

"William," she whispered. "Your name is going to be William Francis Anthony."

William after Mrs. Concannon's long-lost son. Francis Anthony so he will always know who he came from.

"William Francis Anthony is such a nice, sturdy name," the nun said. "You can call him Billy!"

While William Francis Anthony suckled, Bella told him her life story.

She told him about meeting his papa.

"He was prettier than Jesus. He made me feel like a Queen." She told him about her own papa. "He used to be nice but now he's really mean." She told him about her silent mamma. "She used to sing, but then she got the great depression." She told him about her entire family. "They're all crazy. All of them except Little Luigi." She told him about her cooking. She whispered her secret meatball recipe into his little cavatelli ear. "You taste that?" she whispered as he slurped from her buzzing breast. "That's olive oil. Sweet and peppery. Ain't it delicious?" In response his gums massaged her nipple and her whole body turned to cheese. "That's mozzarella." His flecked eyes grabbed hers. "Here comes the Pecorino and Locatelli," she whispered. The baby's cheeks blazed flamingo pink. "That's the cannoli cream your papa fed to me. Those are my meatballs. That's Big Betty's tomato gravy." As he suckled, Bella rocked him and softly sang,

> Lullaby, lullaby, lullaby, ooh,
> Who will I give this baby to?
> Lullaby, lullaby, lullaby, eee,
> I will keep this baby for me . . .

The young nun snuck William into Bella's room every day.

The physical relief Bella felt when he suckled made her feel serene. When he left, she was bereft. The bees in her breasts were furious. They stung. It wasn't until her breasts filled back up and anticipated his tiny lips, cried out for them by hardening and leaking and stinging and singing, that she felt happy again.

As the wound across her belly started to heal, she found it easier to handle him. The stitches had hardened. But they still itched. After they were removed, she almost felt like her old self again.

Everything was falling back into their improper proper places.

She fed and sang to her son three times a day, every day, thinking it was always going to be that way, just the two of them, Madonna and child, completely connected, until another nun, an older one like the one that had tried to change her name when she was a scrappy young thing, swooped in and told her it was time for her to leave.

"What do you mean?"

"You're all better now. You can go home," the old crone said.

Home? To her family?

It wasn't until Bella was packed and sitting with her discharge papers in her hand, that she realized they expected her to leave without William.

Every vein in her body constricted. For several seconds she couldn't see. She couldn't breathe. For a moment her heart stopped beating.

"What about William?"

"Your father arranged for us to take care of him for you."

"What? Why?"

"You're too young to properly look after an infant yourself, young lady."

Bella didn't understand. She had taken good care of Little Luigi when he was a baby. She had dropped him twice and sometimes she forgot to feed him, but he was still alive. He was thriving.

"I'm taking my baby home with me."

The nun cackled. "You poor thing. Don't be silly. You're only sixteen. You don't have a husband. How can you possibly take care of a baby?"

SAINT FRANCIS, SAVE ME!

BELLA SAT ON HER battered suitcase in her red coat in front of the hospital waiting in the cold, the healing wound across her belly tender and itching, her breasts hard as boulders, stuffed with backed-up milk, dribbling and bitching.

Who was coming to get her?

Father Michael? Her papa?

Please, God. Don't let it be my papa.

It wasn't long before the familiar farting of an old truck announced who it was.

"Joe Cabral at your service, milady!" the rodeo Romeo cheerfully hollered as he hopped out of the cab spitting a stream of his disgusting tobacco, all dimple-smiling and self-satisfied. Long Joe, lean Joe, anxious Joe sauntered up to her like the dog-mushing Jack Thornton in *Call of the Wild*.

As soon as he landed in front of her, Bella burst into tears.

"Holy moly! What's all this?"

He tried to get her to stand but she slipped through his grip and collapsed onto the pavement.

"They took my baby, Joe!" she sobbed from the cracked cement. "They told me they would keep him somewhere safe until I was ready to take care of him myself! But I don't know where he is! They won't tell me!"

"Shh, honey," Joe soothed, rubbing her back. Then he went in for the lift. "Let's get you home. Then we'll see about your kid."

With what little strength Bella had, she stopped him. "No! I want my baby! I have to feed him! I haven't fed him since yesterday! He must be starving! He's always hungry! My baby needs me! I need my baby!"

"Okay, okay!" Joe said. He picked her up and carried her over to his truck and tucked her in. "You sit tight," he instructed. "I'll be right back. I promise."

After what felt like forever, Joe finally stepped out of the hospital carrying nothing but an empty baby blanket. When he climbed into the truck and handed it to Bella, her breasts burped and leaked. She started hyperventilating.

"Where is he? Where's my son?"

Joe produced a tiny ID bracelet, six square glass beads, each with a single letter on it.

D-O-N-A-T-O

"What did they do with him?!"

He reached into his glove compartment and pulled out a flask. "Here. Take a swig of this."

The liquid burned Bella's lips.

He told her to take another swallow as he turned the key in the ignition.

Bella grabbed his arm. "Where are we going?"

"To the place where they sent your kid."

As the truck flew down long, ribboning roads past

shingle-patched houses, seedy pubs, and corner markets, Bella wondered if Joe was lying.

"Where are we going?" she repeated. "Where is he?"

"Hang on, kid."

They drove for what seemed like miles. When they finally stopped, Joe pointed to a box of a brick house floating on a small hill rising up from a busy street. Crumbling bricks. Party-hat turrets. It stood bookended by two gnarled trees.

"That's where he is, honey."

An iron sign read:

SAINT FRANCIS OF ASSISI
HOME FOR WAYWARD ORPHANS
AND LOST SOULS

A dented metal lamb rested above the letters.

Was her son in the arms of his papa?

Was this some kind of crazy dream?

Bella didn't understand.

"Come on," Joe said. He eased her out of the truck and coaxed her up the long walk.

Up close, the place was even more menacing. Iron-laced glass front doors fashioned like an ancient set of pearly gates. Dark windows masked with battered gray shades.

Joe pulled the bell handle. No one answered so he tried the knob. It was unlocked, so they pushed in.

The dusky entry hall was as quiet as Christ's tomb. Their shoes squeaked across the pocked floor to a faded statue of the Blessed Virgin. Bella stopped in front of her. "I think I'm gonna faint."

They were interrupted by a tall, pug-faced nun. "Can I help you?"

"We're here to see the Donato baby."

The woman stiffened beneath the folds of her habit. "I'm afraid that won't be possible."

"Why not?"

"Are you the baby's father?"

"Yes, I am." Joe had no problem lying to a nun. "And this here's the baby's mamma and we're not leavin' until we see our son."

The frazzled sister led them into a long, murky room full of mismatched cribs and small beds. On a cot against the wall a grade-school-aged girl sat on her knees clutching a ratty rag-doll. "Are you here to take me home with you?"

"Quiet, Agnes!" the nun hissed.

On another mattress a larger child, maybe seven or maybe six, watched them, his thumb jammed in his mouth.

A toddler crouched next to him started whimpering.

What the hell kind of a place was this?

Finally, in a metal crib tucked in a corner, Bella found William sleeping. Damp lashes closed, hands curled into little fists, his tiny chest softly bellowing.

Bella's heart skipped a beat. Her breasts started belching.

"I wouldn't wake him," the old nun warned. "We have a lot of trouble getting this one to sleep."

Bella's chest was drenched under the wool of her coat. Her tits were screaming.

"His name is William and I'm taking him home with me."

The nun was about to intervene, but Joe stepped between them. "Bella," he whispered with urgency. "If we show up with your baby your papa will toss us all in the street."

"I can't leave him here, Joe. I can't. How can I leave him here?"

"We'll come back and get him when we can. I swear we will," Joe said.

Then came the holy refrain.

"We'll hold him here, in God's care, until you're ready," the nun promised.

NO PLACE LIKE HOME

THE TRIP TO ROBERTSON Scale factory was a silent one. Just the rattles of the truck, the squeaks and moans of its struts.

For a long time, all Bella could see out the window was William's sleeping face.

Then the old neighborhood passed by. The buildings, still huddled together like train cars, once so familiar, looked lost now.

The walls of Saint Anthony's rectory were even more imposing, Dino's Elbow Room seemed to crouch lower than it used to, S. S. Kresge's BIG SALE signs were peeling. The Jewel Box Theater's marquee was empty. LoMonico's corner grocery looked sad and lonely.

The ride down Scales Drive felt like it took half a century.

The imposing entrance gates to the factory looked like a wild animal's sharp teeth.

Rabid and salivating.

"No place like home," Joe said sarcastically. He took the back way around to the house, passing the old lunch stand, all boarded up. When they swung into the yard next to Manny's fallow garden plot, he cut the engine. Unlike the neighborhood, the place looked just the same. Tired and angry.

"Don't worry," Joe said. "I won't let your papa hurt you." To keep from biting his nails, he pulled a pouch of tobacco out of the glove box and packed a wad into his cheek.

Bella dropped away. She felt like she had fallen headfirst into a pond full of a thousand fish swimming in different directions. No matter how hard her heart kicked, she couldn't break the surface.

"I love you, Bella," Joe said.

But she didn't hear him. Being back at the Robertson Scale factory was more than she could bear. Her stomach started convulsing. Her tits were gagging. She was having trouble taking in air.

Joe spit a stream of tobacco juice out the truck window. "You ready to go in there?"

The only soul in the kitchen was Lulu wearing her old nightgown while standing at the table mincing a pile of garlic. When she saw Bella, she dropped the knife (the knife their mamma had used to slice their papa's face) and slapped her hands over her mouth. "My God! You're here!" she cried through her fingers. She grabbed Bella and squeezed. "I thought I would never see you again!"

The scar across Bella's abdomen screamed, but before Bella could tell Lulu she was in pain, Connie swirled in, her infant Shirley squirming in her arms. The little thing was bigger than William. Plump and perfect. Just like Concetta, whose belly was almost as big as Bella's before the delivery.

"Look at you!" Connie teased. "You're so fat! Did you even have your baby?"

Bella eyed the knife Lulu had dropped onto the table. The spirits of Manny and Lucia wrestled within her.

"Come on," Joe said. He gently tugged Connie away. "Let's put our little one to sleep."

Just then the kitchen door banged open and Tony blew in. He slammed his empty factory lunch pail down, threw a glance at his sister, and stomped upstairs without saying a word.

Luigi plowed in next. When he saw Bella, he flung his slingshot and fell to his knees. "Is it really you or am I dreaming?"

Bella crouched down and put her hands on his shoulders to stop him from shaking. "How have you been, Meatball? You've gotten so big! Give your Bellamamma a kiss!"

"No one calls me *Meatball* anymore."

Bella gathered him into her arms and squeezed while he squirmed.

"I grew an entire inch while you were away," Luigi announced. "Papa measured me. Three times. And I built me a real slick kiddie car too. I did it by myself. I found everything I needed in the Passaic dump. By the way, that place is haunted. Papa says I can't take it onto Van Houten Avenue. But I'm gonna wait until he goes to sleep and ride it all the way out of the factory. Did you have your baby?"

"I did."

"Where is it? Is it a boy baby or a girl baby?"

"I had a boy."

"Hot dog! What's his name?"

"His name is William. But I sometimes call him Billy."

"Where is he? Where's Billy?"

"The stork still has him. But he's coming home soon."

"Okey dokey!"

"It's gonna be time for supper soon," Lulu interrupted, hands wringing. "And you know what Papa's like when he wakes up and there ain't any food on the table."

Bella let go of Luigi, who picked up his slingshot, hiked up his pants, and announced he had a rat to kill. "I get a whole nickel for every tail I toss into Papa's garden bucket," he said as he ran out of the room.

"Would you like to help me cook?" Lulu asked Bella. "We can make meatballs and tomato gravy. What do you say?"

"Okay."

For the next hour the two sisters cooked side by side, Bella still in her coat, Lulu in her ratty nightgown.

"It's just like you never left," Lulu said as they dropped the balls into the simmering pot.

When the pasta was done cooking, Bella brought a steaming bowl into her mamma's room.

"Hello, Mamma," Bella said.

Lucia seemed to look right through her daughter.

"Mamma, it's me. It's Bella."

The room looked just the same. And so did Lucia. She was clean, her hair neatly braided. Lulu had done a good job caring for her.

"Mamma, I've missed you."

As Bella fed the silent woman, she told her all about her son.

"He's the most beautiful baby I've ever seen," she whispered. "He looks just like his papa, Francis Anthony Mozzarelli."

Later, at the supper table, Bella sat across from Manny in her red coat. She piled her plate with food and started wolfing it down before they said grace.

Luigi, Joe's old cowboy hat toggling on his head, fought to keep up with his slurping sister.

Manny wouldn't look at his daughter as she stuffed her face. He only concerned himself with the food on his plate.

"Bella's meatballs are so delicious, aren't they, Papa?" Lulu said. "I've really missed them! Haven't you? And the tomato gravy is the sweetest it's ever been."

"You did a really good job with them this time," Connie said. She scraped a bit off her plate and spoon-fed it to her squirming Shirley.

Joe wouldn't take his eyes off Bella while he ate. "It's good to have you home again," he said.

"Yes," Connie echoed. "It really is," she added, like she didn't mean it.

"The tomato plants went crazy all summer," Lulu said. "They practically climbed to the tops of the trees. The corn was so tall and the cabbage was so green. We had a regular field of wild strawberries!"

"Strawberry shortcake!" Luigi hollered. "I wish I could eat it every day!"

"And so much zucchini!" Lulu yammered on like a nervous ninny. "The squash vines ran over the wall and onto the railroad tracks!"

"The railroad crew complained," Luigi informed everyone. "Boy, those old blokes are really mean."

"Christ," Tony said. "Yammer! Yammer! Yammer!"

Lulu ignored him. "I spent the whole summer jarring and preserving. And we had more eggs than we could scramble and fry too. No coddling. No scratching. The chickens pooped them out two and three at a time!"

"I hate tickling those chickens until they shit their little bombs," Luigi complained. "That henhouse is a regular shit farm."

Manny clocked the hat off Luigi's head.

"Yee cripes!" Luigi turned to Bella, his hair standing on end. "Why are you wearin' your coat in the house? It really stinks."

"She smells like a dead skunk," Tony sneered.

"And sour milk!" Luigi added. "Why don't you take it off?"

"Leave her the hell alone!" Joe yelled. He had his fingers between his teeth.

Shirley started howling.

"Now, see what you've done!" Connie screamed. "It's okay, Shirley," she cooed. "It's okay, honey."

Bella's aching breasts started hissing. For the first time since she had arrived, she looked directly into her papa's face. "Papa?" she quietly said. The table went all silent as Bella waited for Manny to look up from his food. "I'm keeping my coat on until my baby comes home," she said directly to him. "I don't care if it's a day, a week, or three. I'm keeping my coat on until my baby comes home to me."

PLEASE, PAPA

THE TOP OF THE bowl was uneven, the lip orange, the foot green. Small hairline fractures webbed across the glaze. A massive tangle of ivy was painted around its belly. In the ivy's center rested a delicate wren's nest containing a tiny blue egg.

Lucia Medina had carried it to America in a musty carpetbag she had tucked in one of her trunks.

It was a special gift, a long-treasured relic she had packed (along with a crude but arresting painting of the Sicilian sea signed by Tino Scarabino, a ribboned lock of Tino's hair, a handwritten recipe, and the photograph Tino and Lucia had taken of the two of them arm in arm and smiling). It was a crazed relic of a lost love. A horrible discovery. A vengeful family.

Bella pulled the delicate bowl out of the dining room sideboard, filled it with steaming water from a whistling teakettle, and placed it on the floor next to Manny's horsehair armchair.

When her papa came in from his long night guarding the factory grounds and sat down, Bella kneeled in front of him. She never thought she would find herself in front of her papa's stinking feet again. She removed his soiled shoes and damp socks.

Slowly he dipped each foot into the warm water. Moldy toes first, then his cracked arches, then the callused heels. "Ahhhhhhhh," he whispered.

Bella looked directly into her papa's eyes and grabbed one of his feet with her hands. She still knew where to press and dig.

"Oh, that's nice," he muttered as he looked away. "That's it. Right there," he whispered. A small smile played on his lips as Bella rubbed. *Please let me have my baby*, her hands begged as she gently massaged her way around his twisted toes. *Please, Papa.* Each small caress was a call for her son. *Papa, please.* Her nipples tingled. She could feel her milk dropping. *Papa, can I have my baby back, please?* One at a time, she pushed into his corroded cuticles. *Can he come home and be with me?* As she massaged the bulbous toe knuckles and kneaded the small bones, her breasts started leaking. *I'll figure out a way to take care of him.* The damp sensation caused her fingers to pinch. Her papa kicked and the water sloshed over the lip of the bowl. *I'll work to support him. I can do it. You won't have to do a thing. You won't even know he's here. I promise.* The water ran around her knees. *He's a good boy,* her hands pressed. *He's beautiful,* she rubbed. *He's the most beautiful creature I've ever seen,* she squeezed. *I want to keep him.* Around the bottom of his ankles, she prodded, *I love him.* More water jumped out of the bowl. *At first, I didn't think I would,* her hands kneaded. *But then I held him and fed him. When his lips kissed my breast, my heart exploded.* The milk from her nipples bled through the wool of her dirty coat, forming two damp stars. A maternal stigmata. *Papa, please let me have my baby. I love him more than anything.*

More than anything, she wanted to keep her son and hold him forever.

Papa. Please.

Manny abruptly yanked his feet out of the bowl. "That's enough," was all he said. He raised himself out of his chair and walked out of the room, leaving Bella on her knees, her breasts spitting. The scar across her belly was bleeding.

MORE TRUE CONFESSIONS

BEHIND SAINT ANTHONY'S ALTAR, the portrait of Francis still hung. The votives below still flickered. The crown of thorns embedded around his head still glowed. His wounds still bled.

"Francis," Bella whispered. "Francis Anthony Mozzarelli, I had our baby. A boy I named William Francis Anthony. But I call him Billy."

Was that a small smile on the painting's face?

A sly Gioconda smile.

"He's beautiful, just like you," Bella continued. "He's a perfect little angel and he eats like a fiend, just like me."

The small smile intensified.

"Some nuns are taking care of him. For a little while. In a terrible place with your name on it. I haven't been to visit him yet," she said. She adjusted her throbbing tits. "I'll bet he's starving."

The pain in Bella's engorged breasts was excruciating. She had to milk herself every day for relief. She usually did it in a warm bath, but sometimes she did it while standing in front of the kitchen sink. She applied hot rags and massaged her bosoms (like she did her papa's stinking feet) until she was able to squirt into the drain. Blessed relief.

Luigi caught her once.

Once she caught her papa watching (both of their scars twitching).

"Francis . . ." Bella prayed in front of the massive portrait. "Oh, Francis Anthony Mozzarelli, save me."

After Bella crossed herself, she slipped into one of the confessionals.

"Bless me, Father, for I have sinned. It has been so long since my last confession."

"Bella!" Father Michael's voice charged through the grill. "Is it really you?"

"Yes."

"I've been so worried about you!"

"I had my baby, Father. They pulled him out of me. At first, I didn't want to see him. But then I held him and fed him. He's the most beautiful baby I have ever seen. Even more beautiful than Little Luigi when my mamma gave him to me. I named him William Francis Anthony. I fed him and sang to him. But then the nuns took him away. They told me they would keep him safe. Until I was able be a good mamma. But, Father, I don't know if I can be. I'm afraid. I do too many bad things." After taking a deep breath, she confessed how on her second day back home she went to the five-and-dime and stole nail polish. And lipstick. And a bottle of lilac perfume. "I stole a pair of rhinestone clip-on earrings too." She confessed she sat at the lunch counter and ate two hot fudge sundaes and a slice of peach pie. "Then I let the soda jerk jerk himself while sucking the milk out of my tits in the employee water closet. He let me leave without paying." She confessed she snuck into the Jewel

Box Theater and sat through *Big Brown Eyes* three times. She confessed a man who looked "exactly like Cary Grant" sat next to her during the afternoon matinee. She confessed she let him slide his hands between her legs. She confessed she loved it. She confessed she loved it so much she went back and did it again and again.

"I'm a good-for-nothing whore, Father. Just like my papa says."

The votives at the base of the Francis Christ flickered, sending long shadows across the church. They reached for the confessional but couldn't get in.

There was a long moment of complete silence. Then Father Michael finally spoke.

"Bella, be strong for yourself and be strong for your son. Be brave. Pray and God will help you find your way."

"I don't think I believe in God anymore."

There was another moment of silence. Then . . .

"Bella, can I confess something to you?"

"Yes. Please."

"Sometimes I lose faith in God myself."

"You do?"

"Yes."

"What about Jesus?"

"I think Jesus was an ordinary man, Bella. Just like me. And His mamma was an extraordinary girl. Just like you."

Bella had a hard time imagining Mary, the mother of Christ, sitting in the balcony of the Jewel Box Theater with a man that looked like Cary Grant. She couldn't imagine Mary on a kitchen floor fucking Francis. She wondered if Mary's papa was mean. If Mary's mamma never said anything. "I think God hates me," she whispered.

"God doesn't hate you. We are all God's children. No matter

who we are. No matter what we do. God loves each and every one of us. God loves your son and God loves you."

"I'm glad it wasn't the monsignor in here, Father. I'm glad it was you."

"The monsignor's gone, Bella. He died the night you had your baby."

"I killed him!"

"You did no such thing. God called him home. The monsignor's at peace."

"Where's Angelo?"

"Angelo's gone too. I think he's somewhere in South Jersey."

"Is Mrs. Concannon still here?"

Bella found the old woman standing in the kitchen in front of bubbling pot of tomato gravy, wooden spoon in hand. A fresh batch of gnocchi was spread across floured towels on the butcher block. "Bella!" she cried when she saw her young friend.

As they hugged, Bella felt something she hadn't felt since she had held her son.

A deep, abiding love.

"Look what I'm making!" Mrs. Concannon proudly proclaimed. "Gnocchi alla Bolognese! Are you hungry?"

"I'm starving!"

The old woman gathered a towel full of the little dumplings and dropped them into a pot of water that was boiling next to the simmering gravy. The two of them prayed until the pasta popped to the top.

"Tell me," Mrs. Concannon said as they ate, "where's your baby?"

Bella told her the whole story. Meeting and fucking Francis Anthony Mozzarelli. The pain of birth. Her papa. The nuns. Everything. She told the old woman she named her son William. "After your boy. And sometimes I call him Billy. Just like you."

"Listen to me, child!" Mrs. Concannon said. "Don't let them do to you what they did to me. You go find your baby's father. Tell him he has a son. Then the two of you go and get your boy. Get William before it's too late! Before something terrible happens and you never see him again! Run!"

THE FIRST DISAPPEARANCE

WHEN BELLA LANDED BACK home, she snatched Connie's Heywood-Wakefield wicker rattan baby pram. She squirted whatever milk was left in her breasts into a jar, capped it, and tucked it into the carriage along with her baby's blanket and bracelet. Then she wheeled her way through the factory gates and ran it all the way to Krueger Place.

What was she going to say when she saw Francis?

What would she do if his mamma answered the door?

When she saw the house, she froze.

It stood gutted and singed on its small plot of land. Most of the windows were boarded up. Long smoke-licks snaked out from them. The mangled second story looked like a black crown.

Do you always disappear?

I don't think so.

"Faulty electrical outlet!" a neighbor lady wrestling trash cans to the curb hollered.

"The boy is in a seminary up north!" another nosy lady yelled from her front porch. "I heard he's studying to be a priest! The mother took off for a small town in Italy, I think!"

"That's not so," another lady called out of her kitchen window. "The boy joined the circus and the mother moved to Seaside Heights, New Jersey!"

Bella quickly wheeled around to the side of the roasted house. She parked the pram and stomped through the overgrown grass loaded with burned debris. It took a few strong yanks to wrench the singed kitchen door open. The room was dark and rancid with the stench of charred wood and rot. When she stepped inside, the mottled floor moaned beneath her feet. The wallpaper was wrecked and peeling. There was a hole in the floor where the icebox used to be. The stove was stained black, the oven door missing, but the picture of Mary was still hanging on the brindled wall, the old woman's beady eyes still peering through the shattered glass, looking insane. Next to the rusted sink rested a single dumbbell. It marked the exact spot where Francis and Bella had made their baby.

Bella crouched down and touched the iron weight.

"Francis . . . oh, Francis," she whispered. "What am I gonna do? Francis . . . oh, Francis. How can I get our baby without you?"

THE SECOND
DISAPPEARANCE

THE WOMAN WHO ANSWERED Terelli's front door looked like a haunted has-been from a Saturday afternoon horror reel. Ash-tipped cigarette in hand, dark circles around bloodshot eyes, pupils soaked with alcohol and other, darker vices.

"Are you Alice?" Bella asked.

"Who the hell are you?" the woman hacked.

"Is Terelli at home?"

"Terelli doesn't live here anymore. He's gone."

Was he in Hollywood? Coney Island? Miami? Or was he locked away somewhere having the sissy hosed out of him?

"Where is he?"

"I sent him away and you're trespassing."

The woman slammed the door in Bella's face.

"What have you done with my friend?!"

"I'm phoning the police!"

Bella kicked the door and stormed down the walk.

When she reached the front gate, she stopped. She pulled the jar of breast milk out the carriage and hurled it against the house, sending a storm of milk and shattered glass everywhere. Then she grabbed the pram's handle and charged down the middle of the street.

She flew all the way to the Passaic County dump and pushed her way to the top of Terelli's hill.

Sweating and out of breath, she dropped to her knees and started digging.

"I'm sorry!" she sobbed as she dug. "I'm so sorry!"

She pawed the ground like a hound. Hands nicked and bleeding, she uncovered the torso of an old baby doll, a mangled fork, a flattened tuna can, the rotted branch of an old Christmas tree. Everything except Terelli Lombardi's handmade baby cap and matching booties. Covered in dirt and ash, she collapsed in a heap. "What am I gonna do?" she sobbed. "How am I gonna save my baby?" Somebody help me! Help me! Please!"

At first the silence was overwhelming. Then the familiar voice of Terelli Lombardi whispered like the wind,

Meatballs! Make your magic meatballs!

Then the voice of Big Betty LoMonico chimed in,

Meatballs saved my life once!

And someday they're gonna save yours too!

With her friends' words ringing in her ears, Bella rose to her feet and raised a defiant fist. "MEATBALLS!" she hollered up to Heaven. "I'LL MAKE MEATBALLS!" she screamed.

ESCAPE FROM GREYSTONE PARK

His first few hours there he was too terrified to move. Shoulders up, head down. He made himself as small as possible, but his eyes were still large and round. He was cold and shivering and starving.

Snickers swirled around him.

"The little invert's in shock."

"It's nothing compared to what's coming."

They shaved his head and strapped him to a metal bed. Bars on the windows. Padlocks on all the doors.

"Do you know why you're here?"

"Because I'm a queer."

To convert the young invert, the doctor began with hypnosis. Fourteen daily sessions of gentle prodding, role-playing, picture-flashing, and subliminal suggestions.

"What is your favorite thing to wear?" the doctor asked after each round.

"A dress with curlers in my hair!"

When multiple sessions proved ineffective, they proceeded with daily doses of hormone therapy. Then a spate of invasive rectal massages to evacuate the prostate, milk it clean so the desire for unnatural intercourse would miraculously leave.

"Kiss me and call me *sweetie*, please!" Terelli hissed every time.

They tried to rinse away his perversion with bladder washings. To restore heterosexual potency, a long, sterilized catheter was inserted through the urethra into his urine pouch. A saline wash was pumped in to sanitize the insides, to get rid of whatever germs were causing the boy's disgusting crimes. After over a dozen unsuccessful attempts of the stringent procedure, they slapped him in solitary and strategized.

"What should we do next?"

"Masturbatory reconditioning?"

"Insulin therapy?"

"Steroids?"

"Chemical castration?"

It was decided they would try a new form of torture they called *electroshock therapy*.

When they wheeled Terelli into the operating room, the air was charged with grisly anticipation.

"If you promise to cooperate, we'll give you a mild sedative to ease the pain," the doctor said.

"Fuck you! Eat me!"

Terelli was slapped on his back on the metal operating table. He was strapped down across his shoulders, chest, waist, and legs.

"Hopefully, if we scramble things up enough, everything will fall back into place the way it's supposed to," the doctor said as sharp clamps were snapped onto Terelli's head.

Three hideous zaps—or *pulses*, the doctor called them—followed by three more. Then another three.

After the first round, Terelli floated away. He spread his wings and flew into the arms of Francis Anthony Mozzarelli. After they kissed, Francis giggled and whispered,

You won't tell anyone about this, will you?

When the prongs were lifted from Terelli's singed and steaming temples and they removed his bite plate, he babbled about being lost in the arms of Christ.

"He found Jesus!" the attending nurse exclaimed.

"It won't be long now," the doctor hissed as they creamed Terelli's blistered skin. "Soon he'll be a normal male!"

"Free of sin!"

"A regular family man!"

"A real stallion!"

Days turned into weeks. Weeks turned into months. Months turned into a year of unrelenting torture and bona fide insanity.

Terelli was drowning in defeat.

The little bird's wings were broken.

His little heart was barely beating.

Once, between electroshock sessions, a woman who looked an awful lot like Mary Mozzarelli appeared in front of him and sheared his head with a buzzing barber's clipper.

A great haircut gives a man dignity!

"Jesus! Save me!" Terelli yelled. But instead of his beloved Francis coming to his rescue (and disappearing afterward), Bella appeared.

Her hair and makeup were done to perfection.

Just like you taught me!

"Bella! You look simply stunning!"

I know, sweetie!

A grass skirt was wrapped around her swinging hips.

A clamshell bra danced over her voluptuous tits. She floated in front of him like some kind of comely sea creature. Like a Hawaiian Island mermaid in a carnival parade. Behind her a giant Ferris wheel spun against a turquoise sky. Roller coasters snaked around the sun. Carousels spun.

"Bella! Where are you?"

I'm in Coney Island, silly!

"Where's Francis? Where's your baby?"

Never mind them! You gotta get the fuck outta here!

Bella sang a bit of "All of Me" as she danced in front of him.

You won't survive what they have planned for you next!

Look what they did to me!

She yanked her grass skirt open. Her belly was on fire, flames blazing.

Save yourself!

"How?"

Spread those little wings of yours and fly
all the way to Whore's Paradise and find me!

"I don't think I can make it all the way to Coney Island. I'm too weak. My wings aren't working!" Terelli screamed.

Do it or die, sweetie!

A SERIOUS PROPOSAL

AFTER BELLA ROSE FROM the wreckage on Terelli's hill in the Passaic dump, she flew back to the house at the Robertson Scale factory. She shucked her smelly coat and the rest of her clothes and gave herself a quick whore's bath. Then she cherry-bombed her lips and Maybelline-blushed her cheeks. She slapped on a swing skirt, a tight cotton blouse, a pair of high-heeled shoes, and a fur-trimmed baby blue car coat of Connie's. Then she hit Van Houten Avenue.

"I'm here to see Dino Montebologna," she announced after she pounded on the back door of his Elbow Room.

A trio of greasy mooks circled her like small pack of Sicilian sandhogs. They whistled and howled and pawed the ground until the familiar voice of Dino Montebologna called out, "Knock it off, you fucking clowns, and show the young lady in!"

The young capo was parked at a corner table sipping espresso and smoking a cigar under a low-hanging gambling lamp. Polished nails, diamond pinky ring, ink-black hair, plucked eyebrows over sharp eyes, fancy barber's pomade. A shiny gun was holstered across his chest. His book-loving goon was stationed next to him, his nose buried in a Bible-thick best-seller. Something called *Gone with the Wind*.

Dino smiled all olive oil greasy. "Well, if it ain't Miss Belladonna Marie Donato! What brings you to my little den of iniquity? You here to finally accept my marriage proposal?"

"I got a proposal for you myself," she said.

The goon stopped reading.

"Oh, yeah?" Dino asked. "And what might dat be?"

"I want you to lend me some money so I can open up a little business."

"What kind of business?"

"I wanna make and sell meatballs."

Dino was intrigued. So was his goon.

"Where you plan on doin' dis meatball sellin'?"

"Back at the factory. I got the keys to the old lunch stand my mamma used to run."

Dino tapped an ash off his stogie. "I know you can cook the crap out of a lasagna Bolognese, but meatballs is different. I once put a bullet in a man for making me a bad meatball."

Bella eyed the pistol strapped to his chest. "My balls'll make you want to kill that man all over again."

"How 'bout you show me what youse can do."

"Now?"

"Hey, Solly!" Dino called to the bald thug behind the bar. "Show the young lady to the kitchen and get her everything she needs."

An hour later Bella appeared with a big bowl of steaming meatballs swimming in her tomato gravy. She placed it under the young capo's nose, along with a napkin and fork and spoon.

The skeptical kingpin lifted the bowl and took a good long sniff. Then he speared a ball and checked its heft. Then he closed

one eye and, with the other one narrowed like a jeweler squinting through a diamond loupe, he assessed. Then he opened his
mouth and took a bite and chewed.

The goon closed *Gone with the Wind*.

The bartender leaned in.

Bella bit her cherry-bombed lip and waited while Dino
swallowed. "Well, are you gonna give me the money or are you
gonna shoot me?"

Dino slammed the table with his fist. Then he stood up.
"Son of a bitch! How much cabbage you gonna need?"

FRIED ITALIAN MEATBALLS AT THE BELLADONNA CAFÉ

WHEN BELLA AND LUIGI plowed into the old factory lunch stand with a pile of buckets and brooms, they saw that under all the dust and grime it was still a serviceable little cooking room. Two griddles and eight burners frosted with ancient splotches of cold grease, a giant double sink, and an icebox big enough to hold a side of beef.

Bella had to take a moment because she remembered helping her mamma chop onions with the knife Lucia had used to slice her husband's cheek. After catching her breath, she handed her brother a mop. "Let's get to work," she said.

"Okey dokey!"

Together the two of them were quite a team, soaping and scrubbing and mopping.

In a corner, under a loose floorboard he kicked up, Luigi found an old cigar box.

"Hey, look at this! A buried treasure!"

In the box was a perfect lock of ash-blond hair tied with lavender ribbon, a slip of aged paper with a recipe for Tino's favorite baked chicken scrawled on it, and an old photograph.

Bella recognized their mamma, so young and beautiful, with her arm around the waist of another young woman who looked like a fairy-tale princess.

"Who are those ladies?" Luigi asked, fingering the picture.

On the back, in Lucia's florid handwriting, were the words *io e Tino*.

Bella suddenly remembered one of the last things her mamma had said the day she stopped speaking.

I never loved your papa. I only ever loved Tino Scarabino.

Bella was stunned.

Zing! Went the blade that sliced their papa's cheek.

Tino was a woman!

"Can I have the picture?" Luigi asked.

"No."

"Can I have the hair?"

Bella quickly pocketed the recipe and buried the box containing the picture and the ribboned lock of hair back in its secret grave.

"Hey!" Luigi cried. "You kept something!"

"Grab a sponge and keep scrubbing!"

With renewed resolve, the two of them washed and polished until the whole place sparkled and gleamed. Then they cranked open twenty cans of tomatoes and got two giant pots of gravy going.

"La famiglia!" Bella said after she gave Luigi a delicious taste.

"La famiglia!" they sang together.

"Meatball time!"

They peeled and chopped and smashed and diced like one of the factory machines.

Together they mixed a huge bowl of fortified meat. Then they argued about ball size. Luigi wanted the balls big. Bella fought for something more discreet. "Do your math," she said. "Use your head. We want them only big enough to fill the rolls, that's it."

While the two of them rolled, they sang the song their wounded papa used to sing.

Santa Lucia! Santa Lucia!

Soon a magical tomato-and-meatball perfume plumed over the entire factory. It wrapped its tomato fingers around everyone and squeezed. It hit their papa over his head. It boxed their brother. It soothed their sleeping mamma. It shook their sisters. It tickled little Shirley. Some say it even raised the dead. By the time the noon whistle blew, a long line of factory workers snaked away from the lunch stand window.

"Step right up! Step right up!" Luigi sang. "Get your delicious meatball submarines!"

Fresh-baked rolls from Savasta Brothers coal-fired bread ovens packed with flavorful meatballs dripping with tomato gravy. For a gooey, stretchy, delicious finish, Bella added slices of fresh mozzarella cheese to each sandwich.

The line moved fast.

More than once, Manny drifted by.

Twice Bella caught his eye.

Both times she smiled and waved.

One elderly man who'd been working at the factory for years took a bite and whispered, "These meatballs are better than Lucia's."

At twenty cents a pop, the golden gondolas really flew.

"Sold out! Come back tomorrow!" Bella yelled when she pulled down the metal shade.

After counting the first day's cash, Bella pressed a crisp simoleon into Luigi's hand.

"Yee cripes!" he cried. "I feel like Daddy Warbucks!"

"What are you gonna do now that you're rich?"

"I'm gonna buy myself a genuine Barlow jackknife and skin a raccoon. Then I'm gonna make myself a coonskin cap. What about you?"

"As soon as I make enough dough," Bella said, chucking the rest of the money into the cigar box under the floorboard, "I'm gonna rescue my baby and fly all the way to the moon!"

WANTED: Female Dancers
for Coney Island Revue!

BELLA'S SWEET LITTLE CANNOLI

EVERY SATURDAY, AFTER A long workday week of selling meatball sandwiches and cooking for her family, Bella took two buses and three trolleys all the way to the Saint Francis of Assisi Home for Wayward Orphans to visit her baby.

She brought along baskets filled with homemade treats for the nuns. Wax-paper-wrapped meatball submarines and mason jars full of homemade pastas swimming in tomato gravy. She dropped the bounty on the table in the communal kitchen and waited for the penguins to swarm in.

"What a bounty!"

"Sinfully delicious!"

"The good Lord is surely smiling upon us!"

While the sisters filled their holy gullets, Bella left to find her son, always tucked safely in his crib.

She liked to give him her finger to grab on to with one of his strong little fists.

"My God, you're gettin' so strong! And so big!"

She wrapped him in his blanket and rocked him and kissed him and sang to him. She pulled crumbled bits of Pecorino from a small sack in her coat pocket and worked them into his finger-sized mouth.

To make sure he knew where he came from.

She never mentioned her trips to the orphanage to anyone.

All during that long, brutal winter business boomed, and she visited her son.

After making payments to Dino and dropping a small percentage into the family till to appease the beast snoozing in the basement below everyone's feet, she stashed the rest in the box buried in the floor of the food stand.

Each day brought her closer to claiming and keeping her baby.

Each day brought the two of them closer to flying away.

Together.

Forever.

Bella and her baby.

She traveled around town, pushing the empty baby pram like a demented circus clown.

Once in a while she parked the carriage in front of what was left of Francis Anthony Mozzarelli's house.

"Where the hell are you, Francis Anthony Mozzarelli?"

She sat on Terelli's hill and thought about her long-lost friend.

"Where the hell are you, Terelli Lombardi?"

Every time she paid a visit to S. S. Kresge, she lifted something new to add to the old suitcase she had stashed under the girls' bed. A polka-dotted blouse. A pencil skirt. A bundle of fancy cotton underwear. She lifted things for her baby too. A bib. A corduroy jacket and matching pants. She stole him a silver rattle from Rowe~Manse.

She watched her sister Connie's belly grow.

She wanted to punch it.

Deflate that fucking dough.

She cooked for her family.

She spoon-fed and bathed her mamma.

To relax and release some steam, she wheeled herself over to the Jewel Box Theater for a little balcony sinning.

Then she ran the carriage over to Saint Anthony's and confessed.

She made glorious meals for Father Michael with Mrs. Concannon.

She sold her meatballs.

She counted her money.

"I've almost got enough for the two of us to run away," she whispered in William's ear while pushing him around the orphanage one early spring day.

She asked the sisters if she could take him to a photo studio so she could have his picture taken.

"Why?"

"So you will always remember him after he leaves."

"What do you mean?"

"The next time I come, I'm taking my baby home with me."

Belladonna Marie Donato's
Eight-Layer Cannoli Cake

If you ever need to thank a gangster,
if you ever need to butter up a bunch of nuns,
if you ever need to cast any kind of culinary spell
over anyone,
make this astonishing Italian castle of a cake!

For the cake batter:

5 cups all-purpose flour

5 teaspoons baking powder

1 teaspoon salt

1½ cups unsalted butter, softened

3 cups sugar

6 large eggs

2 tablespoons fresh orange zest

2 teaspoons vanilla extract

1 teaspoon almond extract

2½ cups milk

For the frosting:

20 ounces fresh full-fat ricotta cheese

16 ounces mascarpone cheese (cream cheese can
    be substituted)

6 cups powdered sugar

1 teaspoon vanilla extract

1 teaspoon almond extract

2 teaspoons fresh orange juice

1 teaspoon ground cinnamon

¼ teaspoon fresh grated nutmeg
½ teaspoon salt
20 ounces small chocolate chips

1. Preheat oven to 350. Butter and flour-dust four nine-inch round baking pans.
2. In large bowl, mix flour, baking powder, and salt together. Think about the first time you fell in love.
3. In another bowl, mix butter and sugar together until fluffy. Think about the first time you had sex.
4. Beat one egg at a time into the butter and sugar. Then beat in vanilla extract, almond extract, and fresh orange zest. Then alternate beating in dry ingredients and milk, a cup or so at a time. Reminisce about all the lovers you have had in your life. All the happiness you shared with each and every one of them.
5. Fill pie pans and bake at 350 degrees for approximately 25 minutes or until a toothpick comes out clean. (Lining the cake pans with parchment paper will aid in removal.) Imagine a beautiful sea waving in all of your precious memories.
6. Cool completely. Then remove, gently, cakes from pans and let continue cooling on wire racks. Brew a pot of coffee. Have a cup with a drop or two of vanilla added, nibble on a few chocolate chips while waiting.
7. Using a dry cheesecloth or a fine strainer, drain ricotta

and mascarpone cheese. Think about the future. Give yourself permission to chase your dreams. List them.

8. In a large mixing bowl, beat together the ricotta and mascarpone (make sure they're cold). Beat in the powdered sugar, vanilla extract, almond extract, orange juice, cinnamon, nutmeg, and salt. Be sure and count your blessings while measuring the ingredients.

9. Carefully cut each of your cooled cakes in half with a serrated knife. Say a prayer each time. Be sure and call upon the holy hands of your Cooking Spirit to help when you do.

10. Place one sliced cake on a cake stand. Frost and sprinkle with chocolate chips. Repeat until all layers are assembled. Once assembled, frost top and sides. Apply a layer of chocolate chips around the sides of the cake. Imagine all your dreams coming true while you are doing this.

11. You can use any extra frosting for decorative piping around the top. Be sure and let someone you love lick the spatula.

12. Buon appetito! Mangiare bene! Stare bene! Delizioso!

THE THIRD DISAPPEARANCE

THE FOLLOWING WEEK BELLA packed a hatbox and snapped her suitcase shut. Then she placed the CLOSED FOREVER sign on the locked lunch stand door and delivered her final payment to Dino Montebologna along with an eight-layer cannoli cake, one of two she had baked.

Each of the layers contained a little taste of her life.

The sweetness of her youth.

Summers at the beach.

Her papa throwing her into the air over the sea.

Her mamma laughing.

Cooking with Big Betty.

Cooking with Luigi.

The first time she met Francis Anthony Mozzarelli.

The two of them fucking.

The birth of her baby.

When she wheeled her carriage into the Elbow Room and

placed the giant confection in front of the young capo, his eyes twinkled like a kid in front of a circus parade.

"What's this?"

She served him a king-sized wedge. "A big slice of Heaven to say thank you."

After his first sweet bite, Dino dropped to one knee and grabbed her hands.

"Belladonna Marie Donato, will you marry me?"

"Stop with your joking."

"I'm fucking serious! Marry me, please!"

Bella laughed as she pulled her hands out of his. "Maybe one day! If you're lucky! Arrivederci!"

At the foundling home, after Bella presented the second cake to the sisters and announced she was there to take her son away, not one of them made a move for the food.

"What's going on? Why aren't you hungry?"

The leader of the bunch, the one Bella and Joe had initially pushed past, stepped forward. "Your son is gone."

"What do you mean?"

The world stopped spinning.

"We found him a wonderful home with a loving family. A proper mother and father. He's going to be very happy." She handed Bella the picture of Billy that was taken at the photo studio and smiled kinda mean. "This is for you. So you will always remember him."

Bella grabbed the photograph. She looked at it. Her baby's face. Alive and happy.

For a split second the entire room disappeared.

"*I'm* his mamma!" Bella yelled. "His home is with *me*!"

One of the other nuns puckered up and started crying.

"Billy!" Bella screamed as she ran into the nursery. "Billy! Your Bellamamma is here!"

She stumbled over to his crib.

Empty.

No blanket.

No pillow.

No mattress.

No Billy.

"WHERE'S MY BABY?!!!"

One by one, the orphans started wailing.

The nuns swooped in.

"Calm down! You're scaring the other children!"

"You fucking lied to me! You told me you would keep him and care for him until I was ready!"

The orphans were bawling.

"I'm fucking ready!"

"Watch your language, young lady. You are in the presence of God. You are in the presence of His children."

"How could you fucking do this to me?" Bella yelled. "I brought you food almost every goddamned day! I baked you a fucking cannoli cake!"

"Lord, have mercy."

"Christ, have mercy."

"Lord, have mercy."

"GIVE ME MY SON! GIVE ME MY BABY!"

"I'm sorry. It's too late. The papers were signed yesterday. He was taken away this morning."

"TAKEN AWAY? WHERE? PAPERS SIGNED? BY WHO?"

GOODNIGHT, SWEETHEART

BELLA HURTLED HOME LIKE a Mars-bound rocket ship. By the time she crashed through the factory gates, the sun was setting over Manny's tomato garden.

"Papa!" she yelled when she blasted into the house. "Lulu? Tony? Connie? Luigi?"

Where was everybody?

Heart pounding, chest heaving, she barreled up to her room. Her suitcase lay splayed, clothes strewn everywhere. Her hatbox was open and emptied across the floor.

She ran to the lunch stand. The front door was busted open. Inside, the loose board was off the floor. The cigar box containing all her hard-earned cash (and Lucia's precious mementos) was gone.

"Papa!" Bella yelled as she charged into the backyard. "Papa!" she hollered when she got to the edge of his blooming garden.

Tomato sprouts poked up from the soil. Green and reaching. Manny was kneeling in the dirt between two rows of the young plants, coaxing and pruning.

Snipping. Snipping.

"Where's my money?! Where's my baby?!" Bella yelled. She grabbed the back of her papa's shirt. "What have you done? I'm his mamma!"

Manny laughed, face twitching, scar yanking. "His mamma?" He stood up, clippers in hand. "What kind of mamma can a whore like you possibly be?"

Bella lunged and Manny batted her arms away.

"You think you can fuck your way around town like a little whore without being punished? Forget about your little baby. He's gone. It's done. You'll never see the little bastard again."

"If you don't tell me where my baby is, I'll fuck until I make another one! I'll fuck and fuck and fuck until I make an entire army of bastard babies!"

"You can fuck all you want, but you'll never be able to make another baby."

He was so close Bella could taste his stinking breath.

"What?"

"After they yanked the little bastard out of you I had you fixed. Like a dog."

"What do you mean?"

"The doctor cut you so you can never have a child again." Manny raised his pruning clippers. "Snip! Snip!"

The second operation.

The tray of gleaming instruments.

All those stitches.

The godless sound that erupted from Bella's wounded belly shrank the sky and quaked the ground. If she had had her mamma's knife in her hand, it would have been curtains for the old man. She grabbed the first sharp thing she could find, his long-handled hoe, and swung.

"Come on!" Manny viciously egged his hysterical daughter on. "You think you can hurt me?"

As Lucia's ancient scream echoed over their heads, Bella aimed for his good cheek. She sliced the air in front of Manny's face, but he jumped back and the clippers flew out of his hand.

"Oh, come, now!" Manny leered. "You can do better than that!"

Bella raised the hoe high, but instead of going after her papa again, she turned and went after his plants.

"What are you doing?!"

She swung and hacked at them. Dirt and tomato stems ripped into the air.

"STOP!" Manny yelled.

When he tried to go after her, she threw the hoe at him. Then she grabbed and yanked and pulled and kicked. Every fucking stem. Every fucking plant. She went after them with every mean thing her papa had ever said to anybody. She went after them with every mean thing her papa had ever done. She went after them with every hand of his that ever flew. She went after them on behalf of her mute mamma. She went after them on behalf of her missing son. She went after them with the undying strength of her broken and battered heart. She went after them with every ounce of anger she carried with her. She went after them with everything she had.

"NO! STOP! PLEASE!"

She was like a human tornado, grabbing and yanking and pulling and ripping until Manny's fist hit the back of her head and she dropped like a rock.

"Goodnight, sweetheart!"

ARRIVEDERCI, ANIMALI!

WHEN BELLA WOKE, THE sun was itching its way into the sky. The birds were chirping, but it was mostly dark outside. It took several minutes for her to figure out where she was. Still in the dirt and debris, curled up among the mangled and crushed tomato plants (her papa's dead babies).

No one had come looking for her. Not even Luigi. Slowly, she pulled herself up. Her head felt sore and heavy. Her knees were scraped and scabbing.

Once she gained her footing, she wobbled through the wreckage and made her way into the house.

The kitchen was quiet. The icebox was snoring. The stove was still dreaming.

Upstairs, in the clawfoot-tubbed bathroom, she peeled off her filthy clothes and quickly bathed.

What was she going to do? Go to bed?

She knew what she had to do.

Fuck them. Fuck all of them.

She found the polka-dotted blouse and matching pencil skirt she had stolen from S. S. Kresge and slipped into them. Then she pulled on a pair of fine hose and stepped into the spiked heels she had lifted too.

After quietly making up her face, she gathered and stuffed what she could into her suitcase (another skirt, a couple of blouses, a sack dress, some underwear).

She cracked open Lulu's piggy bank and balled and tied the $7.26 that fell out (Lulu's life savings) into a clean handkerchief and tucked it into a small rip in the lining of the suitcase along with the picture of her baby and the old dance ad Terelli had given her.

WANTED: Female Dancers

for Coney Island Revue!

In her pink hatbox, she dropped her stash of stolen makeup, a bottle of lilac perfume, and a pair of white church gloves.

She left the clothes she had stolen for her baby in a little heap, along with the engraved rattle.

I guess I won't be needing these.

She couldn't cry. She wouldn't cry. She would never cry again.

So help me, God.

She kissed her sleeping sister. "Sweet dreams, Lulu."

She didn't want to take a chance peeking in on Little Luigi (sound asleep under his homemade coonskin cap).

She creaked back down the stairs and opened her mamma's door. The silent woman was sound asleep. She lifted the woman's rosary beads off the lamp next to the bed and dropped them around her own neck. Then she leaned down and gave her mamma a sweet kiss. "Arrivederci, dolce angelo," she whispered.

After saying goodbye to the kitchen, after hugging the stove and kissing the icebox, she left the house and crossed through the yard. When she got to the devastated garden, she saw what she thought was a ghostly scarecrow.

She stopped cold.

It wasn't her papa, thank God. It was long Joe, lean Joe, lost Joe standing in the middle of the mess, half-dressed.

"Where are you going?"

"I don't know."

"You're lying to me."

"Go back in the house, Joe. Go back to your wife and baby."

"I don't want to. I want to go with you. I want to get the hell out of here too."

"No."

For a tense moment they stood looking at each other.

Bella placed her luggage on the battered ground. Then she grabbed him and kissed him. They shared a long, luscious, Jewel Box Theater movie star kiss. Then she picked up her suitcase and hatbox.

"Hey!" Joe hollered as she walked away. "Hey!"

She tossed her suitcase and hatbox over the factory's back wall. Then she climbed on top of the cinderblocks and spread her arms wide under the ripening sky. "Arrivederci animali!" she cried. Then she blew Joe a kiss and dropped down to the other side.

"Bella!" Joe called after her as she crossed the train tracks. "Bella!" he hollered as she marched across the cow fields. "Bella!" he wailed as she strode toward the sunrise, crisping orange and pink. "BELLA!" he cried as her silhouette shrank and shrank. "BELLAAAAAA!" he howled until, in a burst of eastern brightness, she vanished in one starlike wink.

THE JEWISH CIGAR

WHEN BELLADONNA MARIE DONATO sauntered into Lester Feinberg's midtown Manhattan Vaudeville and Burlesque Agency, he couldn't believe his eyes. He couldn't believe spiked heels could hold up that much young woman.

She had a pair of meaty legs that rose to a set of capacious hips, and the ta-tas that shot out of her chest were barely contained by her red polka-dotted top. For their size, they held up well and pointed directly at Lester, their torpedo-like aim daring him to challenge their bold accusations.

"What can I do for you?"

Bella slapped the ad Lester had placed in the *Herald-News* (WANTED: Female Dancers for Coney Island Revue!) onto his desk and took a seat in one of the two chairs facing him.

The fans were broken. The old vaudeville agent had his jacket off and both sleeves rolled up. He was smoking a cigar to keep cool, yet the buxom piece of Italian candy sitting in front of him hadn't broken a sweat, even after climbing five flights of stairs with a suitcase and pink hatbox in her hands. How old was she under all of that glamour-girl makeup? Sixteen? Seventeen? God, please let her be eighteen. The scent of her was driving him crazy. She smelled like lilac powder mingled with musk, the kind of musk that called to a man the way tuna called to cats. Lester had seen it all, done it all, but he wanted to drop on all fours and beg for a scratch. It was all he could do to pull the soggy cigar out of his mouth.

"What's your name, kid?"

"Belladonna Marie Donato."

"From now on, it's Belladonna Marie."

"Really?"

"You dance?"

"Doesn't everybody?"

Feinberg (as he was known on the circuit) took an even hit off his tightly rolled imitation Havana and exhaled, blowing the smoke in front of Bella's face. She had the astonishing face of a young gypsy Queen. What the hell was she? Spanish? Lithuanian? Italian, maybe? Her lips were full. Her turbulent eyes sparkled. The hair on her head was mischievous and wild. Her tits looked like two circus barrels. The gams went on for miles.

"You bring a bathing suit?"

"What the hell for? I didn't come here to swim."

Lester's nose caught a whiff of heartbreak behind the girl's cheap perfume, and the delicious scent of pain and desperation behind the tough chin.

"What size are you?"

"None of your goddamned business. 38DDD."

"I'm gonna need to see you in a swimsuit."

Lester frantically opened a desk drawer, rifled around, and pulled out a small red bathing costume. It was the color of a vine-ripened tomato.

"Step into the closet and try this on."

"How the hell do you expect me to get into that goddamned thing?"

"You want a job?"

Once in the dark, Bella dropped her skirt, undid her blouse and bra, kicked off her shoes, rolled down her stockings, and peeled down her panties. The wound across her belly suddenly felt tender. It felt like it still had teeth. She tried not to think about her baby as she took a deep breath and squeeeeeeezed the tomato-red suit up and over her tender love bunnies.

Knowing full well what heels did for a woman's carriage and calves, she slipped her spikes back on, tweaked her cheeks, and pinched her nipples hard. She told herself this was just another goddamned beauty and the beast contest. "Heaven, help me," she whispered. She kissed the cross on her mamma's rosary beads, dropped it into her cleavage, crossed herself, took a deep breath, and stepped back into the heavy heat of Feinberg's office.

The horny old gagootz was standing buck naked in front of his desk, stroking his irregularly cut, yam-like, bobbing Brooklyn special.

"You put that goddamned cigar back in its wrapper or I'm gonna dig my heels into your balls so hard you're gonna wish you'd stayed behind that sad excuse of a desk stroking that sorry excuse for a dick!"

Lester swallowed hard. "Can you hula?"

PALM TREES BY AN ENDLESS SEA

As THE BMT TRAIN came to a screeching halt after its long and rollicking ride, the giddy announcer made his final call.

"Last stop, Coney Island! Everybody off!"

The exhausted crowd pushed its way out of the stuffy train and onto the elevated platform, where the air was warm with the scents of sand and sea. Fried clams, vanilla custard, and homemade saltwater taffy.

The pulse of the place was pounding.

Roller coasters rumbled. Carousels careened. Cap guns popped. And people screamed.

Steeplechase Park, Coney Island's glass castle. A castle fit for a Queen.

Luna Park, Coney Island's big, beating heart, with all its swirling fanfare.

Jesus Christ! Bella was really there!

It sounded like a thousand carnivals dancing in the air.

An enormous Ferris wheel spun against a turquoise sky.

Was that Fred Astaire and Ginger Rogers dancing by?

The crowd bumped and pushed.

"Hey doll, are you gonna stand there all day?"

"Toot your caboose!"

"Get the fuck out of our way!"

Bella rode the massive waterfall of people down a steep set of stairs and crested with them across a busy Surf Avenue.

Horns honked.

Tires screeched.

The greasy good smell of grilling meat grabbed her by the hand and yanked her all the way to Nathan's Famous frankfurters and soft drinks stand.

"Give me a frankfurter, please! Make it three! With sauerkraut! And a root beer float with vanilla ice cream!"

"Anything for you, sweetie!"

The Mickey Rooney counter boy swift-served Bella a paper cone brimming with french fried potatoes backed by the hot dogs and drink. "It's all on the house, doll!"

Bella heard Terelli sing,

Welcome to Whore's Paradise! Welcome to Sin City!

She blew the counter boy a kiss and inhaled the food. Then she belched like a hog on its honeymoon, popped open her hatbox, and refreshed her lipstick.

"Which way to the boardwalk?"

"Just follow the troops to the sea!"

Papa! Catch me!

Bella jazz-jiggled and booby-bounced down Jones Walk. She sashayed under the Tornado roller coaster, skirted along Shakey's Clam Shack, and wiggled past Freaks on Parade.

"Christ! Get a load of the ass on that little lass!"

Whistles tooted, bells rang, and barkers sang.

"Step right up! Step right up!"

Sam Tweety's Hawaiian Island Girlie Revue and Peek-a-Booth Theater was right where Feinberg said it would be. It was a small, lightbulb-wreathed building wedged between Stauch's Baths and the Incredible House of Spectacular Oddities, crowned by the Wonder Wheel Ferris wheel spinning up behind it like a giant halo. A tiny strip of an outdoor stage faced a crowded beach and an endless sea.

Papa! Catch me!

In front of a carnival-colored barker's pulpit, a taffy-shaped man leaning on a bamboo cane was tossing cotton candy to a somersaulting monkey.

"You Sam?"

"Excuse me?"

"I'm Belladonna Marie."

The monkey stopped twirling and bared its teeth.

"Talk into my left ear, dolly! The right one is dead!"

"I'm Belladonna Marie! Feinberg sent me!"

"What'd you say?"

"I SAID FEINBERG SENT ME!"

The man hobbled around her like she was a prized cow. He pinched her udders with his eyes, poked at her hooves with the tip of his cane, and growled around her hind shank. "How old are you, sister? Speak up when you talk to me!"

"I'M OLD ENOUGH TO BE STANDIN' HERE!"

"You always this sassy?"

"ONLY WHEN I HAVE TO BE!"

The monkey shrieked.

"Okay, you can show me a little bit of your routine."

Bella dropped her suitcase and hatbox and waggled around the old geezer.

"Jesus Christ! Not here! Get your ass in back with the rest of the whoring Kewpies!"

Down a slim wedge of boardwalk, sandwiched between the

Girlie Revue and the bathhouse, Bella came to a set of patched sheets hanging across a laundry line. On the other side she found a cluster of three tough-looking dames at sea. A portly little gal with a lit cigarette clenched between ragged teeth; a tall, skinny, knock-kneed pretzel of a lady with a lazy eye; and a raisin-skinned biddy with a body like a pulled piece of taffy balancing a beehive hairdo the color of cartoon fire. They were busy adjusting clamshell bras and grass skirts culled from a pile on the ground.

"Howdy!" Bella said as she paraded in.

"Hey, Dolores! Get a load of this bitch!" the beehive cried when Bella stepped in front of them.

The skinny one elbowed the beehive out of the way. "Hey! I thought it was just gonna be the three of us!"

The chubby one, struggling to pull the grass over her sausage rolls, stepped up. "Scrap it, Dolores, and give me a hand with this goddamned thing!"

"Jesus, Agnes! You need to lay off the fudge!"

"Fuck you!"

"What did you fuckin' just say to me?"

As the ladies fought, Bella dropped her suitcase and hatbox. She undid the buttons on her blouse, tugged it past her arms, and tossed it aside. Then she snapped the back of the bra open and really let 'em fly.

The three broads stopped cold.

"Shit."

"Fuck."

"The jig is up."

They watched, dumbfounded, as Bella slowly slid the zipper down the back of her skirt and stepped out of it. "Too hot for undies," she said as she bent over and opened her hatbox. She pulled out a tin of Paris Powder, popped it open, and slapped the puff between her legs. Then she patted it around her ass, under her tits, and all over her face. When she was done, she picked up a set of clamshells and squeezed her powdered breasts into them. Then she grabbed a grass skirt and wrapped it around her waist. "Okay! I'm ready!"

Outside, a lively number kicked out of a set of crackling speakers swinging on a line hanging over the stage.

"Hibiscus Sunset Serenade."

The sheets jerked apart, and Sam and his monkey stepped through. "C'mon girls! Time to dance for some money!!"

"Wait a minute!" Bella said. "What are we supposed to do out there?"

"What did you say?"

"WHAT THE HELL AM I SUPPOSED TO DO OUT THERE?"

"You're gonna do a Hawaiian dance!"

"BUT I AIN'T NEVER BEEN TO HAWAII!"

"Well, you're goin' to Hawaii today!"

"IT DOESN'T LOOK LIKE HAWAII OUT THERE TO ME! HAWAII'S SUPPOSED TO HAVE PALM TREES!"

"Look out at the sand while you're out there dancin', and you'll see fuckin' palm trees!"

"HOW MUCH ARE YOU GONNA PAY ME?"

Sam sliced the air in front of Bella's face with his cane. "Listen dolly, get the hell on the stage out there and shake your ass or hit the fuckin' highway!"

Bella's fingers curled into fists. She was not above going after him the way she went after her papa's fucking plants.

Sam snarled and raised his chin.

"Come on, girls," the beehive quickly said.

The three broads bolted down the alley and mounted the makeshift stage.

"That's it, dolly!" Sam called after Bella as she

hustled after the three flailing dames and jumped under the blinking proscenium.

The monkey clapped and shrieked.

"Step right up! Step right up!"

With the broad expanse of a crowded beach and the shimmering endless ocean unfolding in front of her, everything finally caught up with Bella.

"You better start dancing," the beehive hissed.

At first she followed the other girls, bouncing around like a runaway rubber tire. Then she twisted around like a three-dollar pretzel and struck out on her own, recalling an exotic pose from a South Seas Cruise Line poster she had seen taped to the window of a travel office in Passaic.

"That's it, sweetie! That's it! You got it! You got it!"

As Bella hip-dipped and fanned her lovely hula hands above her head, a small cluster of mooks gathered in front of the stage. A hairy man with his tongue lolling followed the bounce of her clams. A bunch of foreign-looking rats grinned like they were in Heaven. A clutch of young sailors tried to peek up her grass skirt. A boy about Luigi's age pulled a sucker out of his mouth and clapped.

"Step right up! Step right up!" Sam cried. "More girls inside! Visit the girls dancing in private peekaboo booths! Only a dime!"

Steam rose in Bella's pipes and aloha-perked in her hips. Sparks jumped in her eyes, and she cranked into a few low dips. Her lovely hula hands called to the crowd like a guile-filled siren from the South Seas and a shower of nickels and dimes and pennies from Heaven bounced around her feet.

The crowd was throwing money!

"Step right up! Step right up!"

The monkey hopped off Sam's shoulder and collected the

coins in a metal cup. The sailors whistled and slapped each other's butts.

"Step right up! Step right up!"

Suddenly, in the bopping crowd, the beautiful face of Christ appeared.

Bella raised her arms and he raised his too. His eyes flashed gold and green. His smile made church bells sing. He blew Bella a tender kiss. Then he disappeared. Like a lost breath. Like a wailing infant's hot tears.

A HOME AT THE END OF THE WORLD

OVER ON NEPTUNE AVENUE, across from Coney Island Creek, an old two-story sea captain's house porched against a crooked sidewalk like a dry-docked ghost ship. Prominently poised over the front porch steps was an old ship's ornamental figurehead, carved bosom forward under the determined face of a fetching woman with a whittled beard flying from her seafaring chin. Hanging in the front window of the place was a crooked sign . . .

Tenant Wanted

Half Room for Rent

Cook Wanted Too

Inquire Within

Hurry!

The warped front door was slightly ajar. Bella stepped into a long breezeway that sliced through the middle of the muggy house. The only thing besides a threadbare floor runner was a slim hall table with an old ship's bell hanging over a black desk phone.

LOCAL CALLS ONLY!

To her left, an arbor-shaped arch revealed a well-worn par-lor. Faded shades. Frayed couch. Stained floor, boards missing. Wallpaper blossoms faded with age.

To her right, another arch opened to a lazy-looking dining room. A pool-sized table surrounded by a crew of mismatched chairs with a bowl of rotting fruit floating in the middle of it.

Greasy smoke was rapidly filling the air. Food of some kind was burning somewhere.

Bella rang the bell. "HELLO! ANYBODY HOME?"

"Shit! Goddamnit!" someone yelled.

Bella clanged the bell again and a scrawny fireplug of an old man with smoking oven mitts over his hands appeared in the back of the place. He was naked except for a frilly cherry-pat-terned housewife's apron hiked up to his chest. He squinted through the smoke.

"Who's that? Who's there?"

"Are you Chester?"

"Who wants to know?"

"I'm Belladonna Marie. I'm looking for a room. Sam Tweety sent me."

"I'm Chester. I'm the captain of this old ship. You one of Tweety's Sweeties?"

"Hey, something's burning!"

"I know! I'm tryin' to make supper for my crew. So far, I've done nothin' but burn the shit out of a chicken carcass. Can you cook?"

"It's what I do best."

"What can you rustle up?"

"Spaghetti and meatballs. Lasagna Bolognese. Cannoli cake."

"You Italian?"

"Yes."

"Can you make a pizza pie?"

"Can a cat lick its own ass?"

"Hot dog!"

"I can make those too."

The old man shuffled in for a close inspection.

"You afraid of clowns?"

"No."

"Midgets?"

"No."

"Midget clowns?"

"I don't think so."

"What about pinheads?"

"What's a pinhead?"

"A tall man with the head of a child."

"Sounds just like my brother Tony."

"Strongmen?"

"No."

"Fat ladies?"

"No."

"Elephants?"

"No."

"Giant snakes?"

"No."

"You afraid of anything?"

"I'm afraid of babies."

"We ain't got any of those."

"How much you askin' for the room?"

The old man got so close Bella could count the moles on his sagging torso. Tufts of fine white hair, like clouds of spun sugar, puffed off his shoulders.

"It's a half room upstairs in the master suite. The gal already up there goes by the name of Minnie. Her snake is called Hissy. The snake is kinda mean, but Minnie ain't nothin' but sweet. Especially when she gets something delicious to eat. It's ten bucks a week. Seven if you take over the kitchen duties and cook breakfast and supper for me and my little family of side-show freaks. What do you say?"

"How about five dollars a week and the best meatballs you'll ever eat?"

"You got yourself a deal, sweetie!"

Chester extended a mitted hand and the two of them shook vigorously.

"Welcome to your new home at the end of the world, Miss Belladonna Marie! Now, if you'll excuse me, I've got a charred chicken to tend to."

He promptly turned around, exposing his sagging ass, and marched back down the breezeway, swinging his cherries and singing "All of Me!"

MINNIE!

"YOU GOT A GREAT set of bazooms!" Minnie the Fat Lady said when Bella stepped into the suite. "Mine are big too. But it's only because I'm the size of Kalamazoo."

The sumptuous woman smelled like a lavender-wrapped summer peach. She was the largest human being Bella had ever seen. And the most beautiful. Even prettier than Concetta. She looked like a giant pinecone blooming. The folds of her magnificent skin waterfalled down her body like a rush of cascading rock formations spilling all the way to a pair of dainty little feet squeezed into an elegant pair of satin ballet slippers. And there were things Bella couldn't see. Tucked safely under the woman's heavy folds, nestled deep in her perfumed sweat, slept a brother's insistent fingers, an uncle's dirty lips, a father's pushy penis. All those horrific memories eaten but never fully digested, over and over again. Minnie will later confess these gross assignations to Bella and, after a deep breath, Bella will tell Minnie about Manny slugging the tooth out of her skull, the constant beatings, her mamma's knife zinging, and the sterilization after the birth of her kidnapped bastard baby. She will confess she had to wash her papa's stinking feet. Every day. Sometimes twice a day. For years. "On my knees, praying he wouldn't look at me."

After this heartfelt exchange, the two young women will cry. Then they will kiss and hug each other to sleep.

"My name is Minervina Louisa Wichansky. But my friends all call me Minnie."

"I'm Belladonna Marie."

"Oh, that's a pretty name. You new in town?"

"I'm one of Tweety's Sweeties."

"Oh, I know those girls. They're a mean bunch of freaks."

Bella had to agree.

"I used to dance too," Minnie said. "I took fourteen years of ballet. I have trouble staying en pointe now, but I can still do a pretty good grand jeté."

"What the hell's a grand jeté?"

"A giant leap in the air. You wanna pet my snake?"

"Sure. Okay."

The huge woman lifted one of the sweet-smelling folds under her breasts. The reptile in question, as thick as a fairy-tale vine and just as green, was wrapped around her torso. Minnie scratched its slick skin and it started to slither.

"How far does that thing reach?"

"Don't worry. Hissy's harmless. She might curl around your legs at night if I'm not here, maybe slide into your lap for a little canoodling. Go on. Give her a pat. She won't bite."

Bella placed a brave hand on the slinking thing. It was smooth and cold.

"Ain't she something?"

When its head appeared and it flicked its tongue, Bella jumped back and screamed.

The suite was two fair-sized rooms slapped together with

a couple of laundry lines hooked from one corner to the next, strung with unmentionables the size of army blankets. A rainbow of feather boas hung from the ceiling. A small sea of wigs covered the dresser.

"We have a genuine Victrola. We also got a chifforobe and two trunks. We can share them and you can have the sunny side of the room."

To seal the deal, Minnie offered to share a clown too.

"Oui Oui the French Midget. He sleeps in the crawl space under the staircase. He's a rude little thing. But he's good with his tongue, if you know what I mean. He works at the blowhole over at Steeplechase. Lolly the Pinhead squats in the broom closet next to the bathroom. Hero the Strongman is usually in room five. He's a handsome young hunk. The strong and silent type. He goes for days and days without speaking. Still waters run deep. Tons of mystery. He always wears a mask over his eyes. Just like the Lone Ranger. He never takes it off. He even wears it when he sleeps. No one's ever seen his whole face, except maybe Oui Oui, who's in love with him. The big lug comes and goes. Sometimes he's gone for days. Sometimes for weeks and weeks. He disappeared again early this morning. The tiny clown's been howling and crying like a lost puppy."

Minnie's giant speech was christened by a volcanic blast of what sounded like a gargantuan trumpet. It shook the house off its foundation and brought a chunk of plaster down from the ceiling.

"WHAT THE HELL IS THAT?!" Bella screamed.

PEANUT!

"I CALL HER PEANUT because it's what she loves to eat," Chester said the next morning while scrubbing a blackened pot in front of the kitchen sink. He was still naked behind his cherry apron, his prune of a penis still bobbing. "She came to me when my fiancée, Henrietta Maybee the Bearded Lady, vanished on the morning of our wedding day back in 1923." For several seconds the old man was lost in the clouds of his story, eyes tearing. Then he blinked and snapped back to his scrubbing. "That elephant out there saved my life. I saved hers too. She was a big gray mess when she came to me."

Through the lace-curtained kitchen window, Bella could see, floating in a far corner of the yard, a giant Macy's Thanksgiving Day Parade hot air balloon shaped thing.

The sight was astounding.

Chester pushed the scrub brush back into the pot and continued working. "No need to chain the beast. She never wanders too far. Although last week I found her feasting in old man Brower's sunflower patch over on Fourteenth Street. She got into a lot of trouble for that. No peanuts for a whole week."

The elephant brayed.

"What else does she eat?"

"Mostly giant bales of hay. Sometimes grass. If she's feeling anxious, flowers. But peanuts are her absolute favorite. She'll do just about anything for them. There's a tub in the pantry. If she comes to the window, make her do a trick. If she's in a playful mood, she'll twirl a couple of plates. If she's having a bad day, she'll just give her trunk a little shake. If she performs for you, a fistful of nuts will do. Don't give her more than two. If her ears go back, if she gets all uppity and starts stomping her feet, threaten her with a one-way ticket to Kentucky."

Just then a shadow the size of a mountain overtook the room. Everything became early-winter afternoon and a low grumble rumbled as the kitchen window filled with the elephant's entire face. A thick-lashed eye, like the eye of a hurricane, peered in at Bella. For a moment the two girls regarded each other. Then the elephant's long trunk hosed in. It waved around Bella's face and sniffed around her tits. Then it snorted in front of her wounded stomach.

I lost a baby too, the elephant's eye whispered. *He was stolen from me and sold to the Bronx Zoo.*

I can't think about my baby, Bella's eyes whispered back. *If I do, it'll kill me.*

I understand. But don't worry. We'll get through it. We have to.

The big beast shook her head.

"I hear you do tricks," Bella said.

Peanut promptly sat down and raised her front feet.

"What else can you do?"

The elephant raised her colossal bum off the ground and waggled it around.

"That's better than me!"

Bella offered the talented beast a fistful of peanuts. The elephant's long trunk gently scooped them up. *Thank you*, she softly brayed. Then she reeled it back and lumbered away.

Chester raised a freshly scrubbed skillet. "How 'bout rustling up some grub for the rest of us? I'm starving!"

In the moldy old icebox, Bella found half an onion, a couple of puckered peppers, three budding spuds, a bowl of eggs, and an old pile of Nathan's Famous frankfurters.

She crossed herself and called upon the holy hands of her Cooking Spirit. She chopped the ingredients and fried them in the cast-iron pan. Then she beat the eggs and poured them in. When it began to set, she slid it under the oven's broiler.

Minnie was the first to arrive. She greeted Bella with a sweet smile, a tiny half-moon floating in a fleshy sky. Then she floated into the dining room and took a seat on two groaning chairs.

Lolly the Pinhead was next. The head of a sweet child bobbing on the body of a man. He waved when he saw Bella. Then he plopped himself next to the Fat Lady.

Oui Oui the Midget Clown wheeled into the dining room on a unicycle. "Has anyone seen my Hero?" he asked, tears streaming down his cheeks.

Chester (still buck naked, penis still bobbing) danced in with a pile of plates, followed by Bella carrying a sizzling skillet.

"Everybody welcome Miss Belladonna Marie," Chester announced like a ringmaster, "the newest member of our little sideshow family!"

After a round of applause, Bella plated and served. Then she took a seat and surveyed the scene. *If they're all members of a circus sideshow*, she thought to herself, *what does that make me?* Her papa's cruel words echoed in her ears.

What kind of mamma can a whore like you possibly be?

"Let us say grace," she said.

As they linked hands, Chester bobbed, Minnie smiled, Oui Oui's lips trembled, and Lolly giggled.

"Dear God," Bella prayed. "Bless this morning. Bless this frittata. And bless my new family. Amen."

"Amen," they all said.

Outside, Peanut trumpeted.

Bella's Coney Island Frittata

This open-faced Italian omelette
can be made with just about anything.
Disparate, leftover ingredients
can come together
to create a delicious family!

1 medium onion, diced

1 potato, diced

1 roasted red pepper, diced

1 teaspoon salt

pepper

chili flakes

a couple teaspoons of fresh or dry herbs (oregano, basil,
    smoked paprika, etc.)

6 Nathan's Famous frankfurters, cut into coins (if Bella
    were home, this might be salami or ham)

grated or shredded cheese (cheddar or mozzarella)

a couple cloves of garlic, minced

Montebologna Olive Oil (*the Olive Oil of Italian Kings!*)

1 tablespoon butter (more, if needed)

6–8 large eggs, enough to cover the ingredients

grated hard Italian cheese (for gentle crisping)

1. Preheat oven to 400 degrees.
2. On stovetop, over medium heat, melt butter in large
    cast-iron skillet. Add olive oil. Sometimes the art of
    creating something wonderfully delicious consists of

finding some buried treasures in the icebox or pantry. Castaways and leftovers can come together and make something unexpectedly delicious!

3. Cook meat and vegetables in skillet. Start with meat. Sauté until browned a little bit. Use crumbled or coined Italian sausage. You can also dice in hot dogs, bologna, Portuguese linguica, German bratwurst, leftover steak or roasted beef, Taylor Ham, pork roll, or Spam. Pull from the misfits in your icebox or fridge. Anything and everything unique!

4. Remove meat. Add more butter and olive oil, if needed. Sauté vegetables. Begin with longer-cooking ingredients (potatoes, onions, etc.) and end with softer vegetables, until all are cooked through. Potatoes add texture and flavor.

5. Add spices and stir.

6. Add meat to skillet and spread meat and vegetables into an even layer.

7. Spread cheese over top and let it begin to melt. Mozzarella is always great, but a nice sharp cheddar can do more to bind and add flavor.

8. Beat eggs and pour over your meat and vegetable mixture. Tilt skillet to make sure egg mixture is evenly spread and bleeds through the meat and vegetable mixture. Cook on stovetop for a minute or two, until the egg edges begin to set. Here is where it can be beneficial to call upon your Cooking Spirit.

9. Place skillet in middle of oven and bake until eggs are completely set (8–10 minutes). Keep an eye on things. You don't want to overcook it.

10. Grate some Pecorino or another hard Italian cheese over top and place under broiler for a minute or two to gently crisp the top. Again, keep a firm watch on your delicious creation.
11. Let stand and cool for 5 minutes.
12. After a quick prayer thanking the good Lord for all of your blessings, for your home and for your family, however unique, slice and serve immediately.
13. Buon appetito! Mangiare bene! Stare bene! Delizioso!

THE QUEEN OF SIN CITY

BELLA COOKED FOR HER new family and she danced on the boardwalk almost every day. Mostly hula numbers. Sometimes she sang and played the ukulele while whirling around the stage. For a while she was an integral part of Tweety's team, but it wasn't long before she became the main attraction, backed by the other ladies.

Bitter, party of three.

Men from miles around came to see the Belladonna Marie, the Coney Island Hula Queen.

"Where is that Belladonna Marie? Where is she?"

Bella quickly graduated to one of the peekaboo booths inside the theater. Her glass closet was sandwiched between Wilma the Human Wonder Wheel and Tessie the Tornado.

Peekaboo! I see you!

Drop a dime into the slot and watch the velvet curtain lift to reveal . . .

"Our Lady of Steeplechase, Miss Belladonna Marie! The Queen of Sin City!"

Sometimes wearing her tomato-red bathing costume, sometimes sporting a ruffled pair of bloomers and tasseled pasties. Always dancing and singing,

All of Me!

Each coin dropped bought the viewer a sexy surprise.

A dime brought the blow of a lipsticked kiss.

A quarter might inspire the flash of one of her luscious tits.

If a dollar was folded and slipped into the cashbox, the secret door might pop open.

ABSOLUTELY NO TOUCHING!

Unless the customer flashed a sawbuck.

Then all bets were off.

Bella met a regiment of men this way. Steamy encounters that fogged up the glass and blew the top off the place. Some with fudge smudged across their lips. A few with sand still stuck between their toes. Important-looking men in pinstriped suits, hair slicked back with expensive pomade. Paupers who scrimped and saved for a Coney Island holiday. Twice she saw two sailors at the same time. When they kissed each other, she squealed with delight. Even Jimmy Durante and Eddie Cantor waggled their whoopee-makin' frankfurters in front of her.

It's showtime!

Once a musclebound man with a crepe mask over his eyes materialized. He looked like a burly burglar. As Bella danced, he knelt in front of her booth and cried. Then he disappeared as mysteriously as he had arrived.

Cap guns fired. A graveled voice cried . . .

Francis! Francis Anthony Mozzarelli!

She tried like hell to dance and strip her memories away. She performed and fucked to keep her mamma's sharp knife at bay. To forget about her baby and wounded belly. Eight shows a day. Every day except Sunday. That's when she slipped on her white church gloves and ran to the Shrine Church of Our Lady of Solace to confess and pray.

"Bless me, Father, for I have sinned."

"Tell me your sins."

"Father, I'm afraid I'm such a whore . . ."

The attending priest went to see Bella after mass every Wednesday. He dropped church donations into her cashbox for a private trip all the way to Heaven.

"You're not a whore. You're a goddess. You're a Queen."

What did Bella buy herself with her hard-earned Peek-a-Booth money?

At Joy Bell's Lady's Unmentionables, a saucy little lingerie store over on Surf Avenue, she purchased fancy showstopping undergarments.

At L'Antiquaire du Petit Oiseau, a queer little antique shop that had just opened on Mermaid Avenue, she picked up an orange parasol from the nineteenth century.

When she stumbled into that place, the Japanese proprietor, feather duster in hand, was flitting around piles of junk like a hummingbird, bartering and gossiping with his customers and scolding his foulmouthed parrot.

The little ball of green feathers cursed like a sailor on shore leave.

"Fuck you! Come again!"

"Shut your beak, Honeybee!"

"Fuck you! Eat me!"

The bird cursed just like her long-lost friend, Terelli Lombardi.

Tweet! Tweet!

Bella blew a kiss at the feathered little thing. "Say *Bella*! Say *pretty Bella*! Please!"

"Pretty Bella!" the bird screeched. "Bella pretty!"

The shopkeeper gasped. "She never listens to anyone except me! She must really like you!"

"Everyone likes me!" Bella placed the orange parasol next to the register. "I'll take this umbrella, please. I'm gonna use it in my act."

After the shopkeeper rang her up, he asked her what she did for a living.

"I dance and sing."

"Oh! Are you a chorus girl?"

"If you say so!"

"How charming!"

"Pretty Bella!" the bird screeched.

Bella smiled and the shop's proprietor suddenly saw the heartbreak behind the sparkle and bravado in her eyes. He recognized the pain and heard her cries. He knew he had found someone who, like himself, had fought the worst the world had to hurl and survived.

"I have something else for you, I think."

He disappeared in back for a while. While he was gone Bella talked to the parrot. When he reappeared, he presented her with a big, bowed dress box fancier than anything she had ever seen in Rowe~Manse Emporium.

"What's this?"

"Something for you to dance in."

The box contained a Hollywood Made knee-length, tangerine-colored, glass-beaded affair from the roaring twenties. Layers of accordion-crinkled taffeta and sparkling strings.

Not since her missing friend Terelli Lombardi had presented Bella with his mother's jewel-topped box containing his handmade baby cap and booties for her lost son had anyone given her anything so beautiful. It was overwhelming. Her eyes filled with tears of joy and grief.

"This is gorgeous! Is it really for me?"

"Yes, please."

Bella gave the little man a sweet kiss on his cheek. "Thank you!" she said, clutching the dress to her breasts. "I'm gonna wear the hell out of it!"

"It once belonged to me. I used to be professional dancer too."

"You were?"

"Yes. Until it got me locked away."

"Oh. I'm so sorry."

"Not to worry. True love rescued me."

"It did? Where is she? Can I meet her?"

"He's in New Jersey."

"Oh, sorry. *He*, of course."

"He's been there for over a month. His evil mother has a nasty illness in her liver and in her lungs. He is taking care of her. He is very forgiving. Not like me."

"Will she get better, do you think?"

"I hope she dies soon. I miss my lover terribly. I love him like crazy. And he truly loves me." The slight man looked at Bella. "I hope true love finds you too. Maybe it already has. It will when you wear this dress, I think." He winked.

On rainy days and sunny days, too, Bella slipped the orange frock over her head. Then she popped open her matching parasol and floated around the Brooklyn beachside town, blazing up and down the boardwalk like a Jazz-Age Queen. Like human lightning.

Simply stunning!

FRIED ITALIAN MEATBALLS AT BELLADONNA MARIE'S CONEY ISLAND CAFÉ

WHEN BELLA WASN'T DANCING and singing and stripping, she was cooking and feeding her new family. The stove in the Neptune Avenue kitchen was never without a simmering pot of her meatballs and tomato gravy.

Her lasagna Bolognese made Lolly squeal with glee.

Her lobster and crab ravioli made Oui Oui kiss her feet.

Her fettuccini carbonara made Minnie leap.

Her homemade peanut brittle made Peanut trumpet into the trees.

Her cacio e pepe brought Chester to his naked knees.

Her spaghetti and meatballs made the entire house sing, "We love you, Belladonna Marie!"

The delicious perfume of Bella's homemade Italian cooking plucked strangers off the street.

"These meatballs are amazing! They're magical!" was the constant refrain.

Bella proposed opening the house to the public on Sundays.

"We can sell spaghetti and meatball dinners!"

She did it before; she knew she could do it again.

ONLY 75¢! bought a heaping plate of Bella's best, along with unlimited garlic bread, homemade tiramisu, espresso coffee, and almond biscotti.

Tables and chairs were set up throughout the house. Eventually they flooded the yard.

DELICIOUS SPAGHETTI SUPPERS!

FREE ELEPHANT RIDES WITH EVERY MEAL!

Bella had to quit the Peek-a-Booth Theater to keep up with the demand. (Sam cried like a baby.) She was cooking for the public seven nights a week.

The rest of the house quit their boardwalk jobs too. They were thrilled not to be gawked at by hostile crowds, ogling and laughing and heckling.

The winds of change whispered around all of them.

Minnie started dancing again.

Lolly went fishing and crabbing on the Steeplechase Pier.

Oui Oui took up the violin.

Chester threw himself into gardening.

They all helped Bella with the cooking.

Oui Oui ground the meat.

Chester made the breadcrumbs and grated the cheese.

Lolly chopped and diced like crazy.

Minnie assembled the tiramisu and baked the biscotti.

Every night the Coney Island Jamboree played under the fig tree.

After cooking and serving, Bella danced and sang,

All of Me!

Chester built her a makeshift stage. A life-sized saint's grotto laced with twinkling Christmas lights and sparkling grape leaves.

Santa Bella!

Let us pray!

"Ladies and gentlemen!" Chester always announced through a paper megaphone. "May I present to you the star of the evening! Our very own Miss Belladonna Marie! The Meatball Queen of Sin City!"

Peekaboo! I see you!

At the end of every long day, Bella took care of her Coney Island family. She made hot cocoa for Minnie and massaged her aching feet, she patched Oui Oui's little clown costume and socks, she washed and pressed Chester's cherry apron, she hosed down Peanut and made sure the elephant got its hay, and she bubble-bathed Lolly.

"Ouch! Me hurt!" the Pinhead yelled when Bella took an old toothbrush to his ragged fingernails to scrub away the cockle stink. "Tickle! Tickle!" he hollered when she soaped under his arms and shampooed the top of his little head. When she accidentally got soap in his eyes and he screamed and started flailing, Bella gently soothed him into submission and carefully rinsed away the sting. Then she held him to her breast and rocked him. Madonna and child. Taming the wild. The way she used to rock and tame Luigi and Billy.

Lullaby, lullaby, lullaby, ooh,
Who will I give this baby to?
Lullaby, lullaby, lullaby, eee,
I will keep this baby for me . . .

The Pinhead took to calling Bella *mommy*. At first, Bella stopped him from doing this. "Call me Bella," she always corrected him. Then she decided she liked being called mommy.

She often sang Lolly to sleep after giving him a hot bath. Or especially after he woke up screaming from a bad dream.

"Mommy's here. Mommy loves you. Mommy will make it better."

Kissing and tucking the groggy Pinhead into his bed made Bella wonder how her son was doing. She wondered about Little Luigi too. She wondered about the rest of her New Jersey family. Lulu and her motion picture magazines. Connie and her babies. Joe and his anxious misery. Tony and his boxing. Her mamma and her silence. Even her papa and his fucking gardening.

She wondered about Francis Anthony Mozzarelli too.

Where the hell was he?

Was he working in a traveling circus, or was he studying to become a priest?

And where was their lost son?

Who was feeding and bathing William Francis Anthony? Who was tucking him into bed and singing him to sleep?

Bella closed her eyes and prayed. "Dear Lord. Please take care of my baby."

Every night before saying *sweet dreams*, Chester tearfully thanked Bella for taking over the way she did. "It's nice having a young woman's touch around the old place again." He was so moved he brought the old oil painting of his beloved Henrietta Maybee the Bearded Lady, the one Reginald Marsh had painted, down from the attic and hung it in the dining room over a Bauer vase holding a blimp-sized bundle of Dino Montebologna's long-stemmed bloodred roses.

After one of Dino's henchmen had spotted Bella dancing, a bush-sized bouquet along with a fancy card (*Marry me!*) and a bunch of wrapped gifts (lipsticks, powders, sometimes jewelry) arrived once a week.

"Gadzooks!" Minnie said, holding up a string of black pearls. "I ain't never seen clam rocks like these!"

"You're not gonna leave us, are you?" Chester asked, his panicked penis bobbing.

"Not in a million years!" Bella assured him.

To make sure she was always happy, Chester gifted Bella a brand-new bed (tufted feather down tucked into genuine French ticking), a brand-spanking-new Chatham Airloom all-wool blanket, and a fresh set of satin linens from Gimbels in New York City.

It's funny, Bella mused, *what great cooking and a little mothering can get a girl like me.*

It got her almost everything.

Everything except her baby.

A HERO ENTERS OUR STORY

HE STEPPED INTO THE dining room one evening and stood tall in his bright red unitard (as tomato-red as Bella's Jezebel-colored bathing costume). A stockpile of Michelangelo-carved rocks topped with a thick head of long, curly, chestnut-colored locks. He carried himself with the bearing of a triton-wielding Neptune King. He wore a burglar's mask of black crepe over eyes that flashed like fishing lights, intelligent glints of gold and green. A perfect nose. A strong chin. Full lips. White teeth. He smelled like fresh snow falling. Like cannoli cream. Like the air over the cow fields back in Clifton, New Jersey.

Bella's pulse pounded in her veins. The room spun like a carousel.

"Hero!"

Oui Oui hopped off his unicycle and wrapped his tiny arms around the young man's muscular thighs. "You were gone so long I thought I was gonna die! Hero, my Hero!" Oui Oui cried.

The Strongman affectionately patted the little man's head.

Minnie stopped eating.

Lolly rocked with glee.

Chester hugged the young man too. "Welcome home, my boy!"

The young Strongman didn't say a word. He just nodded and took a Heroic seat at the table.

Oui Oui remained glued to his side. "We're having cannelloni stuffed with roasted chicken, pancetta, leeks, and three kinds of Italian cheeses! Isn't that something!? Bella made it!" the little man proclaimed. "Elle cuisine comme un rêve! She cooks like a dream!"

The Strongman's masked eyes met Bella's.

Something electric buzzed down her spine.

"Would you like something to drink?" she asked as she handed him a plate of cannelloni.

"He doesn't like wine," Oui Oui offered. "Get him a Yoo-hoo!"

Everyone watched the Strongman guzzle his chocolate drink and lap up his food. When he finished, he grabbed his plate, placed his elbows on the table, and licked it clean. He licked it like a wolf in heat. Then he locked eyes with Bella, scraped back his chair, and left as silently as he had arrived.

Was Bella awake? Or was she asleep and dreaming?

Why did she suddenly hear her baby wailing?

"Hero!" Oui Oui cried as he scampered after him. "Where are you going? Hero! Wait for me! Please!"

Bella's heart was racing. With trembling hands, she picked up the Strongman's empty plate. In the polished glaze, she didn't see Belladonna Marie the Peek-a-Booth Queen of Sin City. She saw Belladonna Marie Donato, the wounded girl from Clifton, New Jersey.

DREAM WAVES

NOT LONG AFTER HIS furious mamma had set their house on fire, Francis Anthony Mozzarelli thought it was time to leave. Fly the coop. Grow the fuck up. Dive into life's soup.

"Where will you go?" Mary Mozzarelli yelled as he packed up his papa's US Navy duffel bag. "Who will make you meatballs? Who will sing you to sleep?"

A quick routine at the gym to Popeye-pump up his muscles. Then a shave and a shower. Guinea T pressed, cuffed blue jeans crisp, he threw his packed sack into an old, run-down Chevy Superior he won off an amateur gambler and hit the open road.

Windows down, the tar blurring by under a hole in the floorboard, the day's heat flew through the body of the car as he whizzed his way out of New Jersey.

He wanted to feel the air hug his ass. So he undid his belt and yanked his pants down to his knees. Then he grabbed his cannoli. We're really going places now! Across the George Washington Bridge. As the cement crowns of Manhattan's giant buildings poked and chewed at the sky, he pumped hard. He slapped himself against his thigh. Bang, bang, boy. Any way you measure it, a Chevy's ride proves itself again and again! Amen!

He steered around the city's granite behemoths and flew across the Brooklyn Bridge. Then he cruised through the low-riding, brownstoned borough, all the way to the Atlantic Ocean, to the kaleidoscope spectacle cluttering the horizon like a crazy circus clown's dream.

Coney Island by the sea!

Streamers flapping, whiz-bang rockets flying.

He chugged along Stillwell Avenue and parallel parked on Neptune in front of an old pirate ship of a run-down rooming house. He couldn't lock the old jalopy, so he ditched his duffel behind a bush next to the crooked porch and gave in to the bully tug of the ocean's waves. He was starving, but not for a meatball or a bowl of gravied spaghetti. He was panting for some attention. So, after grabbing a slice of pizza pie at Totonno's, he peeled his shirt over his head and went barking down the boardwalk. As he swaggered along, the stares began. Mostly from women, some from men. What are you lookin' at, ya mook! The skirts were never alone. They wandered with a fella or traveled in pretty packs.

"Look at that!" he heard a blousy young broad cry.

"Woof! Woof!" he barked when she sauntered by.

At the end of the boards, he rolled up his pants, kicked off his shoes, jumped down to the hot sand, and did a little dance. Warm bundles of good beach news shot up his legs. What did the headlines say? This just might be the best part of your day! He pinballed his way through the crowd of sunning immigrant sea lions playing cards or snoring under the sun.

At the water's edge, he stripped down to his skivvies and waded in. The slap of the sea against his belly took his breath away.

"Hey, mister! Will you throw me into the air?"

A cherub of a blond girl paddling along like a tiny sea creature and smiling like the sun. His strong hands scooped her up and tossed her and caught her just before she hit the water, again and again and again. She giggled and screeched, flaxen curls grabbing the sun's rays as he threw her above the swelling waves. She reminded him of Bella when she was the little Angel Queen soaring over the Feast of San Michele.

Bella Belladonna! Bella bellissima!

Papa! Catch me!

The girl who grew up to break his heart. The girl who slipped through his strong hands and disappeared.

"Higher!" the little blond girl yelled. "Throw me higher, please!"

More children crabbed in and joined in the fray, and he tossed each one, over and over again.

This would be the next-best part of his day.

After the water brigade broke up, he strode on over to the boardwalk and rode over a dozen rides. The Tumble Bug. The Steeplechase mechanical horse race. The Cyclone. The Virginia Reel. The Tornado. The Thunderbolt. The bumper cars. And a whirl on the Wonder Wheel where, swinging way up high, a dazzling future flashed before his eyes.

ARE YOU A STRONGMAN?

STEP RIGHT UP!

TEST YOUR STRENGTH!

At the high striker, a masked barker caught him and threw a wooden mallet into his hands.

"Hey, Tarzan! Think you're strong enough to ring my bell?"

Bell-ringing was Francis's specialty!

He stepped right up and raised the mallet high. A woman in the crowd clutched her pearls and screamed, "Jesus Christ almighty!"

You got that right!

The hammer flew, the puck shot up the long tower, and the bell clanged.

"Ladies and gentlemen, we have a new Coney Island Strongman!" the barker sang as he tossed Francis a Kewpie doll. "Hey, Samson! You interested in a job? I can make a real Hero out of you!"

Francis lofted the doll to the dame clutching her pearls and bowed away, pocketing the barker's business card.

Was this the best part of his day?

No way.

As the afternoon sun started its slow decline, Francis thought it might be time to find a place to tuck in for the night.

When he got back to his old jalopy parked in front of the frayed house, a sign was hanging in the parlor window.

Cheap Room for Rent

Inquire Within

Hurry!

Oh, holy cannoli! The best part of his day had finally arrived!

THE PHANTOM OF CONEY ISLAND

EVERY TIME BELLA EXPLORED the local terrain, she discovered something new and amazing.

Brooklyn, she found, offered the very best of everything.

The best place to buy vegetables and fruits was a little stand over in Brighton Beach. That's where she got her onions, peppers, and garlic; strawberries and blueberries when in season; and always a pinch on the cheek by stand owner Carlo Pietronini.

When Lolly wasn't fishing off the Steeplechase Pier, it was always Ciro's Seafood for crabs, cockles, shrimp, and every kind of local fish.

"What are you gonna make today, Miss Sin City?"

"Linguini con vongole!"

Major Markets Prime Meats offered the finest cuts of pork, veal, and beef. Jimmy always threw in a little something extra, a couple of soup bones for the crew or some breakfast patties for Minnie.

Often, after a busy morning doing the day's shopping, Bella would pop her orange parasol open and twirl around the Coney parks.

Steeplechase Pavilion, where sunlight blazed through the glass panels, sending solar stars dancing and spinning among the rides.

Or Luna Park with its wild animal exhibits and waterslides.

She was always shadowed on these little outings, or so it seemed.

Sometimes, while kicking her bare feet along the water's edge on the crowded beach, her belly would start wailing, and there he would be.

Hero the Strongman.

Peekaboo! I see you!

Silently bobbing in the waves.

Just out of reach.

Sometimes with Oui Oui.

But mostly alone.

She often caught him staring behind a spinning carousel or peering through clouds of cotton candy.

Once, while she was sitting in the balcony of the Shore Theater during a Shirley Temple double bill, the flickering lights caught his strong silhouette standing in the silver-tinged darkness.

"Why are you following me?"

He never said a thing.

Just like her mamma.

"Why won't you speak to me?!"

It wasn't long before he started appearing in her dreams.

In one of them, he sprouted out of the dirt in the middle of the cow fields behind Robertson Scale factory like one of her papa's tomato plants and started howling.

In another, he held her in his strong arms and asked her to marry him.

In another, he appeared hanging on a cross in Saint Anthony's, holding a baby and singing,

Lullaby, lullaby, lullaby, ooh,
Who will I give this baby to?
Lullaby, lullaby, lullaby, eee,
I will keep this baby for me!

POSTCARDS FROM THE EDGE OF THE WORLD

Dear Little Luigi,

I am living in a wunderland full of magic. A
place where people never go hungry and it
rains candy every day. I've opened a restrant
in a house by the sea. If I send you a train
tiket will you come and live with me?

Love,
Your Bellamamma
2124 Neptune Avenue
Coney Island, New York

Dear Little Luigi,

The rides in Coney Island are so much fun!
There are rides that turn you upside down
but you never fall to the ground. And huge

tops that spin you around and around.
There are even rockets that shoot you into
the sky!

Always and forever your only Bellamamma

Dear Meatball,

I live with a Fat Lady a Strongman a
Pinhead a Midget Clown and a giant elefant
named Peanut. Last week the elefant got
loose. It took three hole bags of nuts and
Hissy the snake to get her back under the
fig tree. For five days she didn't eat. She
told me once she lost her baby. Just like me.
I hope you are catching lots of Indians and
winning all the wars you are fighting. I love
you. I hope you still love me.

Love,
Belladonna Marie

Dear Little Luigi,

Lolly the Pinhead loves my lasagna
Bolognese. He eats a whole tray of it but
he won't eat Minnie the Fat Lady's pignoli
cookies. He says they are too sweet. How
is school? Are you practising your math?
Have you lerned all your times tables? Are
you praying every night? I pray for you
every day. I hope you pray for me too.

Love,
Me

Dear Meatball,

Yesturday I thought I saw you. But it was another little boy with a slingshot. I followed him for ten whole blocks calling your name. When he finally turned around I saw it was Oui Oui the Midget Clown who lives in my house!

p.s. Who is cooking you spaghetti? I hope it is not Lulu!

Love,
Bellamamma

Happy Birthday Luigi! Did you get the Coney Island cap gun I sent to you? How big are you now? The last time I saw you you almost reached my boobies. I bet the next time I see you I will have to call you Big Luigi. HA! HA! Last night everyone swam in the ocean in the dark! It was so much fun! I thought I saw a sea monster. I thought I saw my baby.

Dear Little Luigi,

The Strongman went away yesturday. He looks just like he flew out of one of your comic books. His name is even Hero! He can lift anything even a car but he can't fly. Oui Oui has been crying and crying because Hero went away. Not even my meatballs can make him stop. I hope Hero comes back soon. I think I miss him. I miss you too.

Don't ever forget I love you!

Signed,

Me!

BELLA'S TRIP TO DREAMLAND

ON ONE OF BELLA'S wandering days, while strolling along the boardwalk, she heard a child sobbing. She followed the distressed crying until she found, just inside the Kiddie Land rides, a little boy wearing a smart pair of church pants, a suspendered striped shirt, and a genuine Davy Crockett coonskin cap blubbering behind the Slippery Slides. Without counting the kid's freckles, he looked to be about four or five.

The boy's resemblance to Little Luigi was striking.

"Hey! Are you lost?"

All the boy did was shake his head.

"Where's your mamma?"

The kid started wailing again.

"Holy moly! You sound like a fire alarm!"

Bella reached between her breasts, plucked out a scented hanky, and gently wiped the boy's face. "No need for all these tears!" She tucked the hanky away. "You come with me. We'll find your mamma." She took his hand. "My name is Bella. What's your name?"

The boy just hiccupped.

"You don't have to answer me if you don't want to. I'm used to people not talking. My mamma doesn't speak at all. She hasn't since I was about your size. And now I know a Strongman who won't talk to me either. I think he might've lost his tongue or something. Hey, are you hungry? I'm starving!"

She found an empty table for two at Feltman's and ordered them chili cheese dogs, two knishes, and lemon Nehis. The boy downed everything without saying a word.

"Hey, have you ever been on a Ferris wheel?"

At the Wonder Wheel, the two of them stepped into one of the rocking cages and took a seat. After the door was latched, they circled up into the turquoise sky until they were swinging over the sparkling sea.

Papa! Catch me!

"I can see all the way to New Jersey!" Bella cried.

Way up there, it smelled like rain. The beached people on the strip of sand below looked like an army of ants on a ribbon of sugar, baking.

Bella pointed. "Can you see the palm trees sprouting out of the sand on the beach?"

The boy craned his neck and there they were. Those tropical trees. Waving in the breeze.

Was that the Strongman floating in the waves?

"Hey! What's your favorite holiday?" Bella asked. "I bet it's Christmas!"

The boy shook his head no as they rounded to the bottom and swooped back up again.

"It's Easter!" Bella guessed as their cage rocked to the center of the magnificent wheel and back again.

The boy shook his head no.

"How about Halloween?"

The boy nodded yes.

"Mine too!"

The Wonder Wheel paused, but the weather was spinning. The sky over the ocean was turning dark and cranky.

"Do you have a favorite costume?"

The boy finally opened his mouth. "A tiger," he said. "I love them!"

"Have you ever seen a real tiger?" Bella asked when they jumped off the ride.

"No! Tigers live in the jungle!"

"Not magic tigers!" Bella said, grabbing his hand. "Come with me!"

Samson the Siberian had lost most of his teeth. The few left in his molting mouth were rotten and weak. He was stuck in the back of Luna Park's Ferocious Animal Petting Zoo snoozing the final days of his life away. A battalion of flies dive-bombed around his exhausted body. He wheezed when he breathed. His skin and fur hung on him like an old bedsheet.

"Wow!" the boy said when he first saw the tired beast.

"He used to eat pagan babies in the jungles of Southern Italy," Bella whispered as they stepped inside the crate. It reeked like rancid garbage and gasoline. They held their noses when they approached the panting animal. "But now he only eats Coney Island custard, I think."

The tiger slowly lifted its massive head and yawned, exposing a long, dry tongue and toothless gums pocked with black blisters.

"You can pet him. Go ahead."

The boy hesitated before kneeling in the mud next to the beast and placed a small hand on the mottled stripes.

"Can you feel his ferocious heart beating?" Bella asked as they stroked together.

The tiger's glazed gaze followed the boy's arm.

"Can we go now? He really stinks."

As they walked out of the petting zoo, a nasty wind whipped in from the sea, promising all kinds of storm-filled chaos and electrical tyranny.

The Shoot the Chute was closed. So they raced over to the Steeplechase Pavilion, where they mad dashed over to the El Dorado Carousel, a colossal, three-tiered cannoli cake of a spinning machine tinkling and twinkling like a fairy-tale giant's pipe-organed music box. Under a celestial canopy of hand-painted naked nymphs and cherubs, crowned by a mosaic of glass pieces tossing beams of starlight, Bella and the boy mounted two wooden pigs as large as Abundantia, galloping side by side, spinning in a sea of floating boats and gamboling stallions and tufted Cinderella carriages. They held hands across the swirling floor and laughed until they cried.

Dizzy from the ride, they wobbled over to Chip's Chocolate House and devoured a pile of Dreamland fudge.

As she licked her fingers, Bella drifted away. "It's my birthday today . . ."

"Happy birthday!" the lost boy sang. "Make a wish!"

As Bella crimped her eyes closed and blew Billy a secret kiss, wind whistled through the glass castle, bringing with it the taste of a mean rain and the cry of a faraway baby. "Hey! You want to go to my house and have some spaghetti and cannoli cake?"

"Okay!"

Bella grabbed the boy by his hand and the two of them charged outside and skipped down the boardwalk as ploppy raindrops peppered the sun-dried boards like loose buckshot.

"There he is!" hollered a woman charging toward them with a cop in tow. Her face was a contortion of fear and rage, red and purple and blue, like a toddler's messy finger painting.

"That's him! That's my son!"

Bella and the boy froze.

"Mommy!"

"Yes, sweetie?" Bella said, without thinking.

The frantic woman grabbed the kid and shook him like a rag doll. "Where the hell have you been? And look at what you've done to your pants!" She smacked him across his head, sending his coonskin cap to the ground "You worried me sick!"

"Hey! Don't hit him!" Bella yelled. She picked up the cap, brushed it off, and placed it back on the boy's head. Then she brushed the bits of tiger hay and dirt off the knees of his church pants. "He didn't do anything wrong!" She turned to the cop, a regular spaghetti supper customer named Eugene. "He was lost and he was crying, Gene. I found him and took him on a few rides and got him something to eat."

"I petted a smelly old tiger too!" the boy chimed in. "And I saw palm trees growing out of the beach in front of the sea!"

"*Found* him and took him on a few rides and got him something to *eat*?! PETTED A *TIGER*!" the woman screamed. "How long has he been with you?!" She whirled around and blasted her fury at Officer Eugene. "I want you to arrest this crazy whore for kidnapping!"

The word *whore* cut deep. Almost as deep as the word *mommy*.

"Who are you callin' a whore?! I AM NOT A WHORE!"

They were nose to nose, ready to slap each other silly.

"Well, you look like a whore to me!"

"Girls!" Officer Eugene ran up to the two women and separated them. "Listen, lady," he calmly said to the boy's mother, "you got your kid back in one piece. Why don't get him on home, now. There's a whopper of a storm coming. They're shutting all the parks down."

A ferocious blast of thunder punctuated what the cop said.

"You bet your bottom dollar I'm taking my son home!" the woman yelled as she dragged her boy away. "And it'll be a hot day in Santa Land before I bring him back to this godforsaken place!"

Another colossal clap of thunder boomed, and a heavy rain started to fall.

"Hey!" Bella called after the boy. "Hey, what's your name?"

"Billy!" he called over his shoulder.

The name punched Bella in the gut. "Billy!" she hollered into the squall. "Billy, don't leave me!"

A fierce bank of rain-splattering wind whipped across the boards as the boy and his mamma disappeared.

"Billy!" Bella screamed. "Billy!"

"Hey, Bella, are you okay?" Eugene asked. "You want me to get you home?"

"No! I can't go home!" she hollered. "I've gotta find my baby!" She spun around and started running.

"Bella!"

As the storm thundered in from the sea and the parks emptied, the wind carried Bella all the way to Dr. Couney's famous incubator baby exhibit.

ALL OF THEM ALIVE AND BREATHING!

She gasped when she saw the tiny glass boxes holding live babies not much bigger than Coney Island Kewpies swaddled in tiny glass cases, some sleeping, some crying.

"Billy!"

Bella felt the crack of her papa's hand on her jaw and the stunning pain of her shit-splattering delivery. Her mamma's knife blade closed in. Then she saw her baby's face. She felt him suckling on her mammoth breast. She heard her papa calling her *a whore*. She heard her baby wailing for more.

Peekaboo! I see you!

The desire to have her son back in her arms was overwhelming.

The sudden realization she would never hold him again grabbed Bella by her heart and squeezed.

"William!" she screamed, banging on the window. "Billy!" She bolted over to the door and tried to yank it open. "Billy!" She ran back and pounded on the rain-splattered glass. "Billy!"

Suddenly the phantom figure of Hero the Strongman appeared next to her. Oui Oui was holding his hand.

"Bella! What are you doing?" Oui Oui asked. "A hurricane is coming! We have to get home right away!"

Bella looked at the little clown, her eyes crazed. "I have to find my baby!"

"What baby?"

"My son, William Francis Anthony Mozzarelli!"

The Strongman's face flinched under his mask.

"You had a baby?" Oui Oui asked.

"Yes!"

"When?"

"When I was fifteen, I fucked a boy who looked just like Jesus! He was the most beautiful boy I'd ever seen!"

The Strongman wavered on his feet.

"I fucked him on the floor of his mamma's kitchen! Then God gave me a baby! Then a pack of lying nuns took him and gave him away!"

A bone-splintering rumble of thunder crashed over their heads. A hideous wind wailed in from the ocean. Bella turned and started running again.

"I have to find him!" she yelled as she ran. "I have to find my baby!"

"Bella! Come back!" Oui Oui cried. "Bella!"

Another blast of rain-soaked thunder drowned the thud of Hero hitting the boardwalk. The Strongman lay splayed at Oui

Oui's soggy little feet. The small man screamed and straddled the big brute. He shook the Strongman's shoulders and slapped his slack face.

"Hero! Speak to me! Please!"

The whipping rain ripped the tarps off rides and stirred the ocean into a frenzy.

At the far end of Luna Park an old shack perched on a crude platform rumbled in the wind. A loose billboard splashed with the golden letters TRIP TO DREAMLAND! over its entrance. No one was around when Bella landed in front of it. Another thunderous blast turned the pelting rain to hail and the sign violently flapped about.

Bella heard her baby wailing.

She heard her papa singing,

Santa Lucia! Santa Lucia!

She heard the voice of Francis Anthony Mozzarelli calling,

Belladonna Marie! Come home to me!

"Billy!" Bella screamed.

A hammering wind ripped the sign off the top of the shack and sent it plummeting.

"Bella! Watch out!"

Lights out.

A chorus of ghostly voices bled through the storming darkness.

Here she is!

The birthday girl is here!

Hip! Hip! Hooray!

Through a swirling haze of carnival lights, Bella found herself standing in the middle of the kitchen in the house back at the Robertson Scale factory.

At the stove stood her mamma, Lucia, gravy ladle in hand. She looked like her old self again. She was talking.

"Happy Birthday, Bella! You're just in time for a taste of my tomato gravy!"

Manny was seated at the head of the dining room table, smiling under his mustache.

Luigi was there too. And Joe and Connie and Tony and Lulu!

There was no time to stop and take it all in.

No time to question or to wonder.

"The prodigal daughter has arrived!" Manny cried. "Come give your old man a kiss!" He clutched her face with his garden-callused hands. "I have a birthday surprise for you! Look who I found!"

Sitting at the other end of the table was Francis Anthony Mozzarelli, the color of Christmas in his Christlike cheeks. Standing on his strong lap, bouncing and gurgling, was their son.

"Billy!"

Peekaboo! I see you!

Francis blew Bella a kiss with his beautiful lips.

"Mamma!" Billy cried.

The room started to swim.

"Time to eat!"

Lucia swooped in, balancing an enormous platter of spaghetti and meatballs.

"Buon appetito! Mangiare bene! Stare bene! Delizioso!"

Bella watched as her family ate. Francis, with a napkin bibbed across his broad chest, spoon-fed their baby. Luigi twirled noodles around on his plate. Manny and Lucia fed each other like newlyweds.

"I've missed you! I've missed all of you!"

Suddenly, a tiered cannoli cake the size of Minnie was in front of Bella and everyone was singing "Happy Birthday."

Francis was smiling.

Billy was laughing.

"Make a wish, my little Angel Queen!"

Bella closed her eyes. Then she sucked in her breath and blew. When she opened them, Mary Mozzarelli was standing in front of her holding a gun.

"Arrivederci, puttana!" the old octopus cackled. "Your day is done!"

"No! Not yet!"

A hideous clap of thunder and Mary fired.

Lights out!

Only darkness.

HOME SWEET HOME

WHEN BELLA OPENED HER eyes, a bunch of blurred faces were hovering over her.

"She wake!" Lolly yelled. "Bella not dead!"

Chester and Oui Oui and Minnie chimed in too.

"We were all so worried about you!"

"You slept through your birthday!"

"We ate your cake!"

Bella's head was pounding. A folded damp rag lay across her forehead. She couldn't see straight.

Chester raised one of his hands. "How many fingers am I holding up?"

Bella saw an army of them. "Where am I?"

"Bella home!" Lolly yelled, clapping. "Bella in bed!"

"That horrible hurricane almost ate you alive!" Oui Oui cried. "Hero and I rescued you!"

"Welcome home, Belladonna Marie!"

"Welcome home sweet home!" Lolly sang.

Bella tried to make sense of the faces floating around her bed. "Where's Mamma? Where's Papa? Where's Francis? Where's my baby? Where's my family?"

"Who's Francis?"

"She had a baby?"

"I thought we were her family . . ."

Just then Hero the Strongman appeared. He removed his mask and kneeled beside Bella's bed, taking her hand in his.

The others gasped at the Strongman's unmasked beauty.

"Al tuo servizio mia regina. I love you, my darling Angel Queen."

"Francis?" Bella whispered. "Is it really you?"

He smiled and Bella saw the face of the beautiful boy who had step-crunched across the icy street.

"Yes, Belladonna Marie Donato. It's really me. It's Francis Anthony Mozzarelli."

A Recipe for a Reunion

How will this story ultimately end?
Will this recipe be devoured
and never forgotten?
Stay tuned, my friends!

2 fistfuls of youthful beauty

1 cup raging adolescent hormones

a swirl of immaturity

a healthy pinch of pain

1½ teaspoons of sperm

1 fertile egg

1 pound of confusion

2 pinches of fear

a dash of love

a smidgeon of hate

1 teaspoon of rage

2 cups of dishonesty

1 pint of obsession

½ cup of sudden euphoria

2 tablespoons of hurt feelings

a smattering of old wounds

a sprinkling of jealousy

a complete lack of any true understanding

self-preservation, to taste

1. Combine youthful beauty, raging adolescent hormones, and immaturity.
2. Pour in half of the past pain.
3. Shoot sperm onto fertile egg (preferably while snowing).
4. Blend in confusion and fear (be careful when you do this as it can be overwhelming).
5. Stir in love and hate, alternating.
6. Pour in rage and dishonesty.
7. Split into equal parts and let rest (preferably while it rains), then fold together.
8. Slowly drizzle in obsession.
9. Add and let the sudden euphoria simmer.
10. Whip up hurt feelings.
11. Toss in old wounds.
12. Throw in a dash of jealousy.
13. Combine remaining past pain and lack of any true understanding.
14. Add self-preservation and serve immediately.

CONEY ISLAND ROYALTY

AFTER DAZZLING THE JUDGES with their magnificence, they stood on the contest platform in front of the Steeplechase Pavilion, crowns on their heads, scepters in their hands, and shoulder-anchored royal-purple prize sashes wrapped around their glorious torsos.

"Ladies and gentlemen! I give you the most Beautiful Beach Couple of 1937! The King and Queen of Coney Island! Francis Anthony Mozzarelli and Belladonna Marie!"

Francis with his dazzling mane of hair glowing around his head like a holy halo, his Strongman muscles gleaming.

Bella with her full figure lusciously pinched into her Jezebel-red bathing costume, matching open-toed heels on her feet (she wore those heels on the beach!), victory rolls waving under the crown sparkling on her head, dancing, smile beaming, lips singing,

All of Me!

"Smile and say *cheese*! for the *Brooklyn Daily Eagle*!"

Flashbulbs popped like Hollywood Klieg lights and the crowd went wild. They hooted and hollered. They whistled and cat-called and squealed as the twin trophies sauntered around the Pavilion's sparkling wading pool in form-fitting bathing costumes.

Side by side.

The King and Queen.

Gloriously reunited.

Bella never felt so beautiful.

She never felt so free!

The royal couple celebrated by charging into the Half Moon Hotel's Moorish lobby in their capes and crowns, Francis brandishing his scepter and demanding the best room in the house.

The Coney Island King lifted his Queen and carried her all the way up to the presidential suite. (Thirteen flights! Fuck bad luck!) He kicked the door open, threw her on the bed, and took a Heroic dive.

Bella squealed with delight.

Francis started with her lips. Then he kissed every inch of her until he came upon the scar across her belly. "What's this?"

"It's nothing."

"Did somebody hurt you?"

"It happened when I had our baby."

Francis gently gathered Bella in his strong arms. "Tell me the whole story," he said quietly. "Tell me everything."

After she took a deep breath, Bella told him about how scared she was when her body started changing. She told him about trying to hide what was happening. She told him about the nice young priest who helped her. She told him about the birth. She told him about trying to find him and tell him. She told him about his mamma threatening to shoot her. She told him about how the nuns promised to care for their baby. She told him about how her papa gave their baby away. But she didn't tell him what her papa had the doctors do to her. She was about to, but she felt her mamma's knife blade close in.

When she finished her story, Francis bawled like a baby.

"When we fucked the first time, it was like a dream. I was so goddamned happy," he sobbed. "We had four glorious weeks together. Then you ran away from me. When you said you never wanted to see me again, I didn't understand. My heart broke into a million pieces. Then my house burned down, and my mamma moved us to the beach. When I saw you here in Coney Island, I couldn't believe my eyes. I was afraid to tell you who I was. I thought you would run away again."

Bella cradled him in her arms.

Coney Island Pietà.

The two of them sobbing together.

"I'm going to find our son!" Francis swore. "I promise you! I'll find William Francis Anthony Mozzarelli, if it's the last thing I do! The three of us will be together forever! And we'll have more kids. We'll have a great big fucking family!"

A fear the size of Coney Island grabbed Bella by her scarred stomach and wouldn't let go.

Francis got down on one knee. "Belladonna Marie Donato," he said. "Will you marry me?"

Bella's chest tightened and her throat constricted. She wanted to tell Francis she could never have any more children, but she didn't. Instead, she said, "Yes! Yes, Francis Anthony Mozzarelli, I will marry you!"

Francis clubbed his chest and howled. Then he licked and kissed and tickled and nibbled Bella's whole body. He went in deep. With his tongue. With his soul. With everything.

They blew the roof off the Half Moon Hotel.

They sent it soaring into space.

Then they hit the amusement parks, running like two kids in a grammar school race.

They jumped into the Tunnel of Love and sailed down the slippery slides.

They took in breathtaking circus acts of all kinds.

Horses that dove from the bottom of the sky.

Seals that flipped through rings of fire.

Rockets that shot them higher and higher.

Fireworks exploded over their heads as they ran into the sea.

"I love you, Belladonna Marie Donato!"

"I love you, Francis Anthony Mozzarelli!"

"Don't let go of me!"

"Never let go of me!"

When they finally stumbled back into the house on Neptune Avenue, Bella showed Francis the photograph of their baby.

"This is our son. This is William Francis Anthony Mozzarelli."

Francis stared at the picture for a long time.

"Are you alright?"

"He has your smile."

"He has your eyes."

With tears staining his beautiful cheeks, Francis begged Bella to make him a big pot of meatballs and tomato gravy. "I would crawl back from the dead for one of your meatballs! No one makes meatballs like you! Nobody!"

When the food was ready, he wolfed it down and licked his plate clean. Then, armed with the picture of his son, he tore out of the house. He lifted his old jalopy off its cement blocks and carried it out of the garage. He oiled it and gassed it and cranked it into the street. Then he lifted Oui Oui and popped his little Tonto into the passenger seat.

"Where are you going?!" Bella screamed.

"To find my son! To find William Francis Anthony Mozzarelli!" he hollered as he and Oui Oui tore out of Coney Island.

The two of them raced all the way to the Saint Francis of Assisi Home for Wayward Orphans and raided the place. They sniffed down every lead. They ripped through the records in Clifton City Hall. They even went to the police.

"I'm so close to finding Billy I can feel it," he said when they arrived back in Coney Island without his son. "I can smell him. I can taste him. I can hear his little heart beating."

What would Bella do if Francis found their baby?

Who would she be?

Would she still be a whore?

Would she still be a Queen?

And what if Francis didn't find their son?

Would he still be her King?

How could Bella tell him if he married her, he would never have a great big fucking family?

"I told my old lady we're gettin' married!" Francis exclaimed.

"Is she gonna shoot me?"

He didn't tell Bella that Mary had spit on the ground at his feet and put an Italian curse on their wedding. Instead, he presented her with a ring he had stolen from his mamma's jewelry box.

"Oh, Francis! It's beautiful!" Bella said as he slipped it onto her pinky.

In the dancing sparkles of the tiny diamond, Bella saw the constellation of their lives together.

Birth. Pain. Love. Death.

Boom. Boom. Boom. Boom.

Francis grabbed her and spun her in the air. "I can't wait for us to be married!"

The wedding of the King and Queen of Coney Island was going to be the most magnificent celebration the eastern seaboard had ever seen. Bigger than any San Simeon Hollywood hullabaloo thrown by Marion Davies.

The morning of the big day, Francis jumping-jacked out of bed. "I have a feeling I'm gonna find our baby today!"

Bella's scalp shrank; her heart was thumping through her chest. "You can't! Not today! There's so much to do! You have to help me!"

"I have to follow up on a solid lead! I'll only be a couple of hours! This time I'm gonna find him! I can feel it in my cannoli!"

LOST AND FOUND

THE TABLES IN THE backyard were blanketed with fresh linens and topped with jars full of roses and daisies. It was tough keeping Peanut out of them.

No one noticed how distraught Bella was. No one noticed her hands shaking. No one heard her heart hammering.

Oui Oui saddled the elephant and raked under all the tables.

Lolly strung Christmas lights in the trees.

Chester turned Bella's grotto stage into a mini chapel.

Eddie Cantor was going to sing.

There was even going to be fireworks and a parade.

Minnie baked a magnificent cannoli cake topped with two Kewpie dolls, one in a voluptuous wedding dress, the other in top hat and tails (no mask on its little face).

It was happening. It was really happening.

It was all so overwhelming.

The desire to run grabbed Bella by the legs and almost shook her out the door. To try and calm herself, she called upon the holy hands of the Cooking Spirit to help her boil the crabs,

clean the cockles, and chop the vegetables for the reception dinner's seafood stew.

Twice she found herself wringing her hands.

Once she gagged and almost threw up all over the clams.

To keep herself from collapsing, to keep herself from running away, she focused on making homemade spaghettini and
forced herself to sing,

All of Me!

An invisible chorus sang along with her as she shucked and
boiled and roasted and rolled and chopped and steamed.

Big Betty LoMonico. Mrs. Concannon. Even her silent
mamma.

They were joined by Lulu, Tony, Connie, and Little Luigi.

Even her papa yodeled under the eaves.

A regular riot of ghostly arias rang around the room until
a specter appeared in the back door's window and crooned
her name.

Bella flung a bowl of mussels and screamed.

"Bella!" the ghost hollered. "It's Joe! It's me!"

Lost Joe. Foolish Joe. Scared Joe. Poking his face through the
lace curtains. "Hey, can I come in? There's a giant elephant out
here and it's scaring the shit out of me."

"Joe! How did you find me?"

When Joe entered the kitchen, he dropped the first postcard
Bella had sent to Little Luigi with her address on it onto the
kitchen table.

"Who else knows I'm here?"

"Just me and Luigi."

"Are you sure?"

"Yes." Joe paused and took a deep breath. "Connie had her
second baby."

Bella's scarred gut clenched.

"Now I have two goddamned brats screamin' at me all the

time. Two helpless little brats and a fucking nag of a wife." He took another deep breath. "So I left. I'm finished with the whole goddamned mess!"

"Go home, Joe!" Bella said.

"No!"

The two of them circled the kitchen table, Joe chasing after a ridiculous dream, Bella running away from everything.

"Bella! Stop and listen to me! That's not the only reason I'm here!" Joe spread his arms wide. "I know where your son is!"

"What did you say?"

"I said I found your baby!"

Belladonna Marie's
Stufato di Frutti di Mare

When you are scared and overwhelmed,
when you can't think straight,
when you are racked with anxiety,
when you want to do something stupid
like call off a wedding,
try an extremely complicated recipe.
Lose yourself in your cooking.

1 large onion, diced

1 rib celery, diced

1 fennel bulb, chopped

1 head garlic, minced

2 tablespoons olive oil

1 tablespoon butter

coarse sea salt

fresh ground pepper

chili flakes

1 bay leaf

1 teaspoon dry oregano

1 pound clams, well washed and scrubbed

1 pound mussels, well washed and scrubbed and debearded

1 pound nice whitefish (cod or halibut is great), cut into
    1½-inch pieces, salted and peppered

1 pound peeled and deveined shrimp, salted and peppered

1 nice-sized, cooked crab, cracked into pieces

2 cups good white drinking wine

¼ cup tomato paste

1 (28-ounce) can plum tomatoes, milled or crushed with hands or
    a potato masher

3 cups fish stock or clam juice

1 lemon, sliced into wheels (about a half dozen slices)

½ cup Italian parsley, chopped

spaghettini (or pasta of choice)

grated cheese

1. In a large stockpot (with lid) heat olive oil and butter until it melts and sizzles like a bad memory.

2. Add diced onion, celery, and chopped fennel. Add two teaspoons coarse salt and one teaspoon fresh ground pepper. Sauté on medium-low heat for about 5–7 minutes, until onion softens and becomes so translucent you can see through it without crying.

3. Add minced garlic. Mix and cook for two minutes. Garlic always cures what ails.

4. Add at least a half teaspoon of chili flakes (more if you like it spicy). A kick in the pants, a kick in the ass, or a kick in the gut. All three can feel good. All three can hurt.

5. Add tomato paste and mix well. (Be sure and deglaze the pan.) This will marry all the flavors in the very best way.

6. Add white wine. Simmer long enough to get rid of the alcohol but keep the flavor.

7. Add oregano and bay leaf for a different kind of spice.

8. Crush your can of plum tomatoes (with your hands or with a masher) and add it to the stockpot. Clean the can with a bit of water and add that too. The scent will soothe and calm you.

9. Add clam juice or fish stock, enough to make you want to swim in it.

10. Bring mixture to a boil. Then bring it down to a soft simmer. Cover and simmer on low for at least 30 minutes. Tend to other things while it does this. Tend to your pasta. Tend to your heart. Never mix them together.

11. Taste the gravy. Add salt if necessary. Add more heat (pepper, chili flakes) if need be. You want to elevate the flavor, not kill what you have worked so hard to accomplish.

12. Add lemon slices for a little zing. (Not enough to sting the flavor out of everything.)

13. Stir and simmer the gravy with lid off pot for about 10 minutes to cook down to a nice, stew-like consistency. This is an important step. No skimping.

14. Add whitefish and bring back up to a rolling boil. You want the gravy to invade the seafood, get its blood boiling.

15. Add cracked crab pieces.

16. Add clams and mussels.

17. Cover pot with lid and cook for 5 minutes or until all shellfish open. Discard any clams or mussels that have not opened. These are poison.

18. Add shrimp. Make sure they are clean. No veins. No shells. Only meaty memories of the sea.

19. Cover with lid and cook for another 3 minutes. Contemplate the vastness of the ocean and all its gifts.

20. Add fresh chopped parsley for a final flavor elevation. Take a deep breath and let things settle a bit.

21. Ladle your fish stew over a nice fettucini or spaghetti. Add plenty of grated cheese to marry the earth with the sea.

22. Serve with a nice, warm, crunchy (buttered) Italian bread. This is good for soaking up every last bit, something you will absolutely want to do.

23. Buon appetito! Mangiare bene! Stare bene! Delizioso!

BELLA'S CHOICE

JOE CHEWED HIS FINGERNAILS as he drove. Bella sat beside him in her cooking apron splattered with bits of desiccated seafood and caramelized splotches of grease and tomato gravy. As the truck edged its way through the stop-and-go traffic of New York City, she bit her lip. When they crossed the George Washington Bridge, her hands started sweating. Her stomach tumbled as they trundled through suburban New Jersey.

After sailing through a labyrinth of bucolic streets, they finally landed in a neighborhood that looked as if it had been to the beauty parlor and back. Everything trimmed so neat and lovely. Permanent-curled trees lined sparkling streets. Unblemished lawns freshly trimmed and dusted with poison powder to kill the weeds. Houses all dolled up to please.

Joe parked under a maple's broad canopy and pointed to a respectable-looking little Cape Codder. An adorable mouse of a flouncy-bushed house with a tight yard. Hand-painted picture on a cookie platter sweet.

"He's in there. Your baby's in there."

Periwinkle hydrangeas bomb-blossomed under windows framed with shutters painted evergreen. A fresh-looking American flag flapped next to a wood-framed screen door letting in the humid breeze.

Joe placed a hand on Bella's shaking knee. "You want me to go with you?"

Bella pushed his hand away. The sharp scent of sliced onions, crushed garlic, shellfish, and funky sweat wafted off her like so much sin. Her underarms were soggy. Why hadn't she washed before she left? Why didn't she change into a fresh dress? Put on her church gloves, at least? She twisted the ring Francis had given her around her pinky. "I'm supposed to get married today," she softly said.

"What? You are? To who?"

Without answering, Bella opened the passenger door and stepped out of the truck.

"That's it, sister," Joe whispered as he grabbed a pouch of chewing tobacco off the dash. He packed a fresh pinch of chaw into his cheek to keep from gnawing his fingers. "You go and get your baby."

As Bella strode up the brick walk, the heavy heat pressed against her. It was much hotter in Nutley than it was in Coney Island. No ocean wind to cool down everything. Cicadas' high-pitched clicking sizzled in the air. Everything was hissing. The impulse to turn on her heels and head for the hills was overwhelming. She stopped on the stoop in front of the screen door. Something cakey and delicious was baking. She couldn't see inside. She couldn't see past the screen. She crossed herself and rang the buzzer.

"Just a minute, please!" came a young woman's sugared voice. "I'll be right there!"

It wasn't long before the hourglass shadow of a figure

appeared. "You must be here to pick up the cupcakes for the church bake sale! I'm so sorry. You caught me while I was frosting them. I'm running a little late. Won't you please come in?"

When Bella stepped into the shaded coolness of the house, her heart was hammering. The sun was still burning in her eyes. As they slowly adjusted, lumpy blobs morphed into over-stuffed armchairs and a couple of smart-looking settees. The young woman floated in front of Bella in a yellow tulip dress. She looked as fresh as Myrna Loy in *Double Wedding*. The perfect wife. The perfect mommy. Auburn hair stylishly waved away from an apple-cheeked face, not a wisp out of place. Tender lips smiled all innocence and grace. Kind eyes above a button nose gleamed like one of the angel statues back at Saint Anthony's.

"The cupcakes will only be a few more minutes. I promise," she said sweetly. "I was up all night with my son."

Her son?

"He has such horrible allergies. Can I get you something refreshing to drink? A lemonade? Some iced tea?"

Bella glanced out the screen door. Joe fired a stream of tobacco juice out his truck window. From somewhere in the house, the fitful cry of an infant.

"Oh, no. My son is up."

The veins in Bella's wrists twitched. The world was scrambled. Everything seemed to be moving fast and slow at the same time. "My name is Belladonna Marie Donato . . ." she stammered.

Before she could say anything more, the crying revved up.

"Will you excuse me, please? I'll be right back. I promise."

As the young woman rushed out of the room, the flower patterns on the armchairs bloomed and the gears of an ornate cuckoo clock over the fireplace started grinding. A wooden bird popped out of the carved hut and whistled as the clock struck ten. When it finished its clanging and tweeting, the woman breezed back in holding William Francis Anthony Mozzarelli.

Time stopped.

"William?" Bella whispered. "Billy?"

"His name is Henry," the young woman said. "Henry Charles Dalaster Junior. But I call him *my little Hanky*." She struggled to keep him in her grip. "He's getting so big! He eats like a regular little piglet!"

Bella didn't hear anything the young woman was saying.

It had been over a year since she had seen her son. This boy was so much larger than William. He was about the size of Lulu's Flirty Eye Princess Beatrix baby doll times three. His cheeks were as plump as her papa's prized tomatoes and he had so much hair on his head. He didn't look like a Donato. But his eyes were wolfen and sweet. They were the eyes of Francis Anthony Mozzarelli.

"Can you hold him for me while I box the cupcakes, please?" the young woman begged. "I'll only be a few minutes." She quickly placed Billy in Bella's arms and flitted away like a giant bumblebee.

With the cuckoo clock ticking, with her greasy palms sweating, with her heart reeling, with her underarms stinking, Bella dropped her nose into the tuft of hair on her son's head and took a deep breath. He no longer smelled like grated Pecorino Romano and fresh mozzarella cheese, but it was Billy. She offered him her finger, but he wouldn't grab it. "William Francis Anthony Mozzarelli," she whispered. "It's your mamma. It's me." She kissed him and hugged him, and he threw his head back and flung his arms and kicked his legs and started screaming. "Shh," Bella whispered. "Shhhhhhhh . . ." He squirmed like a cat in a sling and started wailing, but she didn't hear him. She only heard the sharp, cutting words of her papa.

What kind of mamma can
a whore like you possibly be?

She heard Francis Anthony Mozzarelli.

Someday I'm gonna get married
and have a great big fucking family.

As her frantic baby arched his back and tried to kick out of her grip, the interior of the perfect house blurred around her in a panic.

What did she have to offer her crying son? Her life was so messy and ugly.

What did she have to offer Francis Anthony Mozzarelli? Nothing but barren misery.

The baby was screaming.

"Don't worry, Hanky! Mommy's coming!" the young woman called from the sweet-smelling kitchen.

Joe was surprised to see Bella jump out of the house empty-handed.

He watched as she ripped the apron from around her waist and bolted past the truck.

"Bella!" he yelled out his open window. "Hey, Bella!" he hollered and honked as she ran down the middle of the street.

A pretty young woman stepped out of the house with a confused look on her face. She was bouncing a crying baby on her hip and holding a large dessert box in her free hand. "You forgot the cupcakes! Don't you want to take the cupcakes?!"

"Hey, Bella!" Joe yelled as he hammered on his horn. "Bella, where are you going?!"

NEW YORK HERALD-TRIBUNE

Miss Belladonna Marie Donato of Clifton Weds

Simplicity characterized the wedding Friday afternoon of Miss Belladonna Marie Donato of Clifton, New Jersey, and Dino Umberto Montebologna of Naples, Italy.

The ceremony took place at 12:30 p.m. in Saint Anthony of Padua Church at 95 Myrtle Avenue in Passaic. The happy couple was married by parish priest Father Michael Marinetti.

The bride wore a stunning imported Florentine gown of white satin, canton, and lace selected by the groom. She carried a showering bouquet of creeping white campanula bells, pink Mozart roses, and ivy.

A reception dinner of spaghetti and eggplant rollatini was held at Dino's Elbow Room. It was a modest affair in keeping with the simple dignity of the charming ceremony.

An importer of Montebologna Cold-Pressed Italian Olive Oil from his family's European estate, Mr. Montebologna also runs the Here Today Gone Tomorrow Waste Management Company of Passaic County. Mrs. Donato will be a homemaker. The happy couple will make their home in Upper Montclair, New Jersey.

THE HONEYMOON SUITE

SHE RODE IN THE back of Dino's Cadillac in her itchy wedding gown, lace binding, seams pinching. Every so often she found a bit of rice (thrown for fertility) in the folds of the satin.

What have I done?

Her new husband was nestled in the passenger seat in front of her like a shiny beetle. Next to him, his book-reading henchman scowled behind the growling auto's steering wheel.

Speeding through the night.

Bella's flight.

"Hey!" she called up to the front of the car as they shot out of Jersey, "Can you turn the radio on, please?" She desperately needed something to drown out her swirling feelings.

For the next several miles, Bing Crosby's velvet tones crooned them down long, lonesome-looking roads. Then a bunch of other stupid songs softly carried them along.

"This Can't Be Love."

"Turn it up!" Bella demanded.

"Love Is Here to Stay."

"Louder, goddamnit!" Bella hollered.

"You Must Have Been a Beautiful Baby."

No matter how loud the radio sang, Bella could still hear her son crying.

She could still feel him struggling to get out of her arms.

She could still smell that woman's goddamned cupcakes.

The engagement ring Francis had given her hung on her mamma's rosary beads around her neck and burned between her breasts. A garish wedding ring was strangling her finger.

When Bella had arrived at Dino's Elbow Room, after running away from that picture-perfect house in Nutley, she was a zombie, feet aching, hands shaking, heart hardly beating. When she landed in front of the young capo, he ordered his goons to get lost.

"Well, if it ain't the long-lost Meatball Queen of Clifton, New Jersey! To what do I owe dis pleasure?"

"You still want to marry me?"

"But absolutely."

After a quick round of negotiations, Bella was escorted to a spring-bedded room above the bar with a sizable water closet housing a toilet, a free-standing sink, and a clawfoot tub.

Alone in the comfy cell, Bella collapsed in a heap and dropped into an ocean of sleep.

It wasn't long before there was a knock at the door.

Standing in the hall was the boy who had delivered Dino's proposal flowers to the rectory. He smiled his wide smile when he saw Bella. "You're Miss Bella! The girl what got me my new shoes!" He flashed his broad butter-bean smile. "My name is Jerusalem. But you can call me Jerry. Mr. Dino sent me up to look after you and get you whatever you need."

Bella asked him for a Brunswick table radio, a warm loaf of Italian bread, a premium peppered salami, and a waxed wheel of provolone cheese. "Make sure it's good and stinky."

When the kid got back, he drew her a hot bath. Tons of bubbles. While she bathed, he swept the room and steamed her wedding gown.

"This dress sure is beautiful," he said.

"It's old and it reeks," Bella sniffed from within her bubbles. I'm guessin' it belonged to Dino's mamma."

"I expect it didn't."

"What do you mean?"

The boy silently rolled his eyes and kept on with his ironing.

The entire week Bella was above the bar, Dino never visited. Only Jerry showed up with food and magazines, trunks of stylish clothes, the latest makeup, and enough roses to choke a winning racehorse. Once he presented her with a quart-sized bottle of expensive-looking perfume.

Bella gagged when she opened it. "This stuff stinks."

"Parfum de Mystère! It's Mr. Dino's favorite," Jerry informed her.

"Well, he can keep it."

The mafia kingpin also sent a truckload of gifts to the Donato house. Trinkets and frocks for the girls, a genuine all-American punching bag for Tony, expensive linens for Lucia, a set of sterling cap guns for Luigi, and a crate of Sicilian wine for Manny.

The machine-gun wedding took place in the nave of Saint Anthony's.

Clustered on one side of the church was Dino's crew. A crone of a mamma and a bull of a papa fresh in from Italy, along with a boisterous array of aunts, uncles, and cousins. None of them spoke a lick of English, but that didn't stop them from trying to converse with everybody. They were backed by a small pack of two-bit Jersey gangsters. Skinny Scarlatto, Batty Zuko, Vinny the Grim Reaper, and Dino's book-reading goon Melvin the Meat Grinder Marzorati. Perched in a pew behind the gangsters sat little Jerry glued to a tall black man of regal bearing who was pursing his lips under a crisp Homburg hat.

Across the aisle sat the Donato family, minus Bella's mamma, of course. Little Luigi refusing to look at his double-crossing sister and their papa doing the same. Lulu, Tony, and his new German girlfriend—a sour-looking fräulein named Helen—were huddled around Connie, who was busy nursing her squirming new infant, Joanie, long Joe, lean Joe, jealous Joe silently weeping into his toddler Shirley's banana curls and eating his nails, and a lost-looking Mrs. Concannon.

After a quick mass delivered by a confused Father Michael, Bella and Dino hastily exchanged vows. The gaudy ring (fenced in from the diamond district) was slipped onto the bride's finger and Dino gave her a chaste peck on the cheek. When they were pronounced husband and wife, no one made a sound.

Except the portrait of the Francis Christ, which howled and howled and howled.

The reception feast was quick. No band. No dancing. No cake. The unhappy couple barely mingled with guests before zooming off to their honeymoon.

As they barreled down a long, dark Connecticut parkway to their mystery destination, they were accompanied by more swoony ballads and big-band dance tunes.

"Begin the Beguine."

"Bei Mir Bist Du Schoen."

"Thanks for the Memory."

When "Cry, Baby, Cry" popped on, Bella's gut clenched. Her eyes stung. "Change the station?!" she ordered. "I don't like this one!"

"Little White Lies."

"Boo-Hoo."

"If I Didn't Care."

The auto headlamps occasionally illuminated highway signs.

East Lyme.

New London.

Exeter.

Cowesett.

Hillsgrove.

Cranston.

"I gotta pee real bad!" Bella announced.

When they hit Providence, Rhode Island, they peeled into a Texaco station on lower Atwells Avenue.

"Escort my bride to the john," Dino ordered his goon. "I got to see a man about a donut." He pulled a pistol out of his coat, checked the chamber, and stalked off. When he was out of sight, the henchman looked at Bella and scratched his chin. "Let's see about gettin' youse to the toilet, sweetheart."

"I can get there by myself."

"No, youse can't."

In the grimy bathroom, Bella hiked up her satin and ripped down her underpants. After she was finished tinkling, she stood up and looked at herself in the cracked mirror above the stained sink.

Sweat was beading across her forehead. A wave of nausea tumbled up from her gut and she violently threw up. Splatters of eggplant rollatini and partially digested spaghetti dribbled down the front of her wedding gown.

"Youse okay in there?"

"Can you get me my suitcase, please?"

After she quickly changed into a red wool traveling suit with ebony piping, she kicked the wedding gown and veil behind the toilet and flushed before leaving.

Back in the car, Bella and the henchman waited.

"This is some honeymoon," Bella finally said.

"What's the matter? It ain't convivial enough for you?"

"I don't know what that means."

"It means lovely."

"So far, it stinks."

The goon cracked open a thick book.

"What are you readin'?"

"Homer's *The Odyssey*."

"What's it about?"

"A very long journey."

"How does it end?"

"I don't know yet."

"What's your name, anyway?"

A corner of the goon's mouth went up in a smirk full of irony. "My name is Nobody."

"Really?"

The henchman's eyes grabbed hers in the rearview mirror. "It's Melvin. Melvin Marzorati."

Bella laughed.

"What's so funny?"

"You don't look like a Melvin to me. You look more like a fuckin' mook."

"I'd watch it if I was you."

The distant rattle of gunfire clammed them both up.

"What the hell was that?!" Bella asked.

Another violent rash of sniping exploded in the distance. Then a stray bullet pinged the Cadillac's front fender.

"Get the fuck down!" Melvin ordered.

Bella dove to the floor of the car. Moments later the passenger door opened and a leather satchel flew in, followed by Dino clutching a pink pastry box.

"Step on it!" he growled.

Pops and pings ricocheted around them as they fishtailed out of the station and careened onto the highway.

"Stay down!" Dino called back to his new bride. He rolled down his window and fired his gun.

After a high-speed chase through Barrington, Fall River, and New Bedford, Melvin was satisfied.

"We lost 'em, boss."

When the car flew over the Sagamore Bridge into Cape Cod, Bella finally sat up.

"Hey, I'm starving!"

Dino opened the pastry box and handed her a sfogliatella. "Don't make no crumbs."

Sandwich.

Mashpee.

Barnstable.

Yarmouth.

Chatham.

Briny sea air wafted around them as they sped through the outer Cape.

Eastham.

Wellfleet.

Truro.

Melvin killed the headlamps as they rolled up in front of a red neon sign that hissed and blinked THE CRAB TRAP GUEST COTTAGES & SCENIC ACCOMMODATIONS.

They slowly crunched along a small sea of crushed clamshells, past wooden dollhouse huts quaintly marked with names like CONCH SHELL, STARFISH, PORPOISE, SEA TURTLE, NEPTUNE, and MARLIN, until they came to a crawling halt in front of the largest of the lot, the honeymoon suite monikered SEAHORSE.

"Benvenuti nel paradiso in riva al mare! Everybody out!" Dino sang.

"You sure it's safe?" Bella asked.

"Don't worry, Mrs. Montebologna," Melvin assured her. "We wasn't followed."

Standing in front of the cottage door, Dino stared at his new bride.

"Dats a nice outfit youse is wearin'."

"Thanks."

"You want Melvin should carry youse across the threshold?"

"He touches me, I break his neck."

Once inside, the phone was checked and the drapes were yanked closed. Dino ripped open the small leather bag he had tossed into the car in Providence and emptied a pile of rolled bills onto the musty bed.

After the cash was counted and stashed, Dino unpacked a silver-framed photograph of three of the homeliest women Bella had ever seen and set it on the nightstand. Then he grabbed a small suitcase, the pink box of pastries, and bussed his wife on her cheek. "See ya later."

"Where the hell are you goin'?"

"I got to see another man about a donut."

"Now?"

"Don't worry, youse is in capable hands."

As the Cadillac ground away, Bella and her new bodyguard faced each other.

"Ain't you gonna get your own cottage?" Bella asked.

"Nope."

In the moldy bathroom, Bella changed into a form-fitting, peach-colored, bias-cut silk nightie seductively embellished with ecru lace trim that Dino had bought for her. When she boldly stepped back into the room, she found Melvin standing in a pair of black satin pajamas.

The two of them regarded each other for several stiff minutes.

Then Melvin planted himself in an armchair under a reading lamp and cracked open *The Odyssey*.

After crawling into the squeaky bed, Bella glanced at the picture Dino had placed on the nightstand.

"Hey, who are these ugly broads, anyway?"

"They're Dino's sisters."

"He didn't tell me he had any sisters. How come they wasn't at the wedding?"

"They was there."

"I didn't see 'em."

"You wasn't lookin'."

A lighthouse foghorn moaned in the distance.

"Hey, Melvin, can I turn on the radio?"

"Keep it low."

Bella snapped on the bedside Radiola. When the tubes warmed up, she dialed around until she found a station crackling Louis Armstrong and May Alix's "Big Butter and Egg Man." Then she crossed herself and turned off the bedside lamp.

Like a rash of bullets, the past few weeks fired into her head.

She and Francis, winning the king and queen contest.

She and Francis, making love again and again.

The preparations for their Coney Island wedding.

Her baby squirming and screaming.

Running away.

Facing the firing squad in Saint Anthony's.

"Goodnight, Melvin."

"G'night, kid."

LAND'S END

"Big Butter and Egg Man" strummed and horned out of the Cadillac's radio as Dino sped west on Route 6. He sang along with Satchmo, a keen sense of relief washing over him. It was six smooth miles of foggy nighttime breezes all the way to the tip of the Cape, to Paradise at the end of the peninsula, to Land's End.

When the open belfry of Provincetown's Siena-inspired campanile finally peeked through the mist, Dino pressed the pedal to the metal and sailed all the way to the Mobilgas filling station.

The single potty door was marked with whimsical wooden sea creatures. Two triton-wielding mermen, frolicking. Dino ducked in with his suitcase and after fifteen minutes of fingers fumbling, wig fluffing, fabric smoothing, seam straightening, and face painting, he high-heeled out a fabulous woman dolled to the nines and ready for anything.

It was a slow car-crawl down Commercial Street to Captain Jack's Wharf, a string of mismatched fishing shacks slapped together on a dock that jutted out over the bay. Old ship lanterns swung over salty boards, a tin piano clanked, cocktail glasses clinked, and giddy shrieks and throaty laughter tinkled in the air like so much sea spray.

Among a colorful cluster of gaudy ladies bunched around the front shack's card table were Ginger Robbers (aka Skinny Scarlatto), Barbara Scamwyck (aka Vinnie the Grim Reaper), and Greta Go Boom (aka Batty Zuko).

When Miss Olive Oil (aka Dino Montebologna) entered swinging her pink pastry box, they hugged and kissed like a clutch of silly sorority sisters.

"Oh, you bitch! You brought us cannoli!"

The ladies quickly crunched into the pastries.

"This is gonna kill my figure!"

"Honey, that sure was one gorgeous wedding!"

"Thanks for inviting us, sweetie!"

"Your bride was simply ravishing!"

"I want that vintage dress she wore for myself, darling!"

"Clam up and deal me in, you silly queens."

After ten raucous rounds of poker and almost as many cranberry daiquiris, the girls linked arms and gamboled down Commercial Street on their way to Cesco's Italian Restaurant for chicken parmigiana and spaghetti.

Heels clacking.

Handbags swinging.

All of them singing "A Pretty Girl Is Like a Melody."

A MAMMA'S LOVE IS EVERYTHING

WHEN FRANCIS ANTHONY MOZZARELLI realized Bella had left him, he dropped to his knees. He pounded his chest and yanked the hair out of his beautiful head. Then he spun around like a lost dog, sniffing and digging and yelping.

Chester was beside himself too. "Oh no! Not another runaway bride!" he cried.

"Where she go? Where she hide?" Lolly wept.

"A cartoon cowboy appeared and swept her away!" Minnie informed everybody.

"What do you mean?"

"Was it a kidnapping?"

They fanned out and bloodhound-searched the entire town. They scoured the boardwalk, under and above.

Francis kicked open the Peek-a-Booths one at a time and snapped the lights on in the Tunnel of Love.

They checked around the carousels and behind every horse in the Steeplechase mechanical horse race.

They swept through every fun house and scoured every animal cage.

"Belladonna Marie! Where are you?!" Francis cried. "Belladonna Marie, come home to me!"

The fresh spaghettini hanging from the kitchen ceiling dried and dropped. The seafood stew congealed and turned into slop. The wedding cake collapsed. The reception flowers died. The lights in the trees winked out one at a time.

"We gotta try and get things back to normal around here," Chester calmly said. He gave Francis an elephantine sedative and gently tucked the sobbing Hero into bed.

Oui Oui wouldn't leave his sleeping buddy's side. The tiny man kneeled at the foot of his Hero's bed and prayed. "Jesus! Bring Bella home to my Hero! Please!"

When Francis finally opened his eyes, he wouldn't eat. He wouldn't drink. He just stared into the ether, sobbing and muttering, "Belladonna Marie. Come home to me . . ."

As the former Strongman began to waste away, the worst was feared.

That's when a tough-looking woman with a lit Pall Mall clenched between her teeth pulled up to the house in a growling DeSoto with Jersey plates.

"I'm here for Francis Anthony Mozzarelli!"

When she landed in his room, she confronted the trembling cluster of sideshow performers. "What the fuck have you freaks done to my son?"

As Oui Oui screamed, the furious old octopus lifted Francis out of bed. With the wailing midget wrapped around her legs, she carried her son down to her car and swaddled him into the passenger seat. She pulled out a gun and fired into the trees, scattering everybody. Then she peeled away chased by Oui Oui and the rest of Francis Anthony Mozzarelli's Coney Island family.

In her cottage in Seaside Heights, Mary propped Francis in a chair. She opened her traveling barber bag, plugged in her clippers, and buzzed his head.

"A great haircut gives a man dignity," she muttered, a fresh cigarette clenched between her teeth.

After clipping his beautiful curls to the floor, she gently tucked him into his boyhood bed. "Don't worry," she soothed. "Mamma's gonna take care of her baby. Mamma's gonna take care of everything."

> *Lullaby, lullaby, lullaby, ooh,*
> *Who will I give this baby to?*
> *Lullaby, lullaby, lullaby, eee,*
> *I will keep this baby for me . . .*

"Belladonna Marie!" Francis screamed. "Come home to me!"

MEANWHILE, BACK AT THE CRAB TRAP (SEA PERILS AND DEFEAT)

WHEN BELLA WOKE IN the musty cottage on Cape Cod, the moon was still pushing its silver light into the room. She was still alone in the squeaky bed and Melvin was still snoring in his chair, his big book still open in his lap, his gun on the table next to him. The radio was still softly playing, "They Can't Take That Away from Me."

Under the romantic warbling, Bella thought she heard her name. She sat up and switched the radio off. As the tubes died, there it was again. A tortured howl.

Belladonna Marie! Come home to me!

"Francis?"

The call was coming from somewhere outside . . .

Belladonna Marie! Come home to me!

Bella slowly eased herself out of bed. She padded past Melvin and cracked open the creaky door.

Dino's car still wasn't there.

She listened.

There it was again!

Belladonna Marie! Come home to me!

The call was coming from behind the cottage. From somewhere out near the sea.

Bella ran around to the back of the honeymoon suite, where the broad expanse of a moon-kissed beach spread to a rough and tumbling ocean.

Belladonna Marie! Come home to me!

Suddenly Bella saw, standing at the water's edge, a familiar silhouette. It raised its arms in a classic Strongman pose. Then it turned and dove in.

"Francis!" Bella bolted across the sand.

Belladonna Marie! Come home to me!

This time the mournful wail was followed by the distressed cry of a baby bouncing across the waves. Then Bella saw him, swimming away from her, lapping along like a little puppy.

"Billy?!"

Belladonna Marie! Come home to me!

Bella ran into the sea, but before she was able to charge through the shallows, she was brutally grabbed by a strong pair of hands and reeled back onto the sand.

"You crazy bitch!" Melvin hollered. "What the fuck are youse doin'?!"

Bella's arms flailed. "My baby! I've got to get my baby!" She was hysterical, punching and kicking and screaming. "Francis! Francis is calling me!"

Melvin shook her hard and brutally slapped her across the

face. Then he scooped her into his arms and carried her back to the Crab Trap.

In the cottage's bathroom, he threw her into the shower, cranked on the cold water, and gave her a good dousing until she collapsed, exhausted and sobbing. After he pulled her out, he stripped her, rubbed her shivering body down with a clean towel, and threw her into bed. He collapsed back into his chair and took a few minutes to steady his breathing. Then he opened *The Odyssey*.

"So, surrender to sleep at last," he read out loud. "What a misery, keeping watch through the night . . ."

As dawn crept into the room, Dino's Cadillac rolled across the Crab Trap's parking lot. He slithered into the cottage like the Shadow and quietly dropped his suitcase on the musty carpet. Then he padded over to a snoring Melvin and eased *The Odyssey* out of big brute's hands. For a moment he looked at his sleeping wife. Even in repose she looked like a bombshell pinup.

"I wish I could be dat beautiful," he sighed.

After scrubbing his face and brushing his teeth, he dropped a flannel nightshirt over his head and crawled into the bed. "Goodnight, Belladonna Montebologna. Sweet dreams," he whispered. Then he settled onto his pillow and promptly fell asleep (dreaming the outrageously gaudy dreams of a Provincetown drag queen).

As Dino and Melvin snored in unison, Bella's eyes fluttered open. For a moment she wasn't sure where she was. She heard ocean waves lapping in the distance. Was she in Coney Island? Was running away and her marriage to Dino all just a crazy dream? For a second her heart swelled with hope. Then she looked over at the man snoring next to her.

"Francis Anthony Mozzarelli," she hoarsely whispered into the darkness, "please forgive me."

THE LITTLE QUEEN
OF PROSPECT
PARK SOUTH

IF YOU TOOK CONEY Island Avenue north from Brighton Beach, just before you hit Prospect Park's sheep-filled greens, you would encounter an esplanade of ravishing beauty. A six-block-long portion of Albemarle Road backboned by a running island of gracious grass and grandfather trees.

Stately homes, mansions really, spread their skirts and lounged on both sides of the splendid street like gentile Southern ladies fanning themselves in Yankee territory.

One with Doric columns and webbed leaded windows.

Another with mysterious passageways tucked in its silver-spooned linings.

Another with fat turrets wrapped in miter-cut shingles and dormers nested like sugar roses blooming off an Easter cake.

The grandest of them all was a long-porched wonder of

regal intelligence and good breeding staunchly standing on the corner of Albemarle and Argyle.

Distinguished. Great bones. But in desperate need of weeding. The old place was sun-bleached and frayed. Its turrets pinched and bleeding.

Built in 1899 by dye merchant Alfred E. Cooke for his wife Amelia, the old thing was originally constructed to stand free from any undesirable elements in society.

That all changed the day a wounded young man dressed in a starched nurse's uniform and another young man wrapped in a stiff doctor's coat arrived.

"Grandma!" the nurse called up to the buckling eaves. "It's your favorite grandson! It's Terelli Lombardi and his darling companion, Daiju Sato!"

The ancient woman who opened the warped door was stooped and barely breathing. When she realized the strange little nurse was her treasured grandson, she screamed with glee.

"My sweet little bird! You've flown home to me!"

Terelli had spent entire summers with his adoring grandmother for most of his childhood, until his father Dudley drifted away and Alice started guzzling gin like a tramp on a holiday. He found such solace behind the old lady's diamond-cut shingles. The two of them spent their days roller-skating around Coney Island, inhaling buckets of buttered popcorn in movie palaces, and knitting.

Terelli was eight when he told his grandmother he loved a boy the way Greta Garbo loved John Gilbert. When he asked her if she thought there was something wrong with him, the old woman looked her grandson directly in his queer little face. "Any man that claims to be all man, or any woman who thinks she's all woman, is full of horseshit. There's nothing wrong with you. You're perfect."

When Terelli and Daiju crossed the threshold after their harrowing escape from the home for the insane, the stench of spoiled crab meat, bunion cream, and animal feces was overwhelming. The house was packed with mice and cats and fleas, wormy antiques, and ancient dust-swaddled tchotchkes. Oil lamps with delicate hand-painted bases and fogged glass shades finely etched with Gibson girls puffing on long cigarettes. Music boxes from the nineteenth century (one with metal bees buzzing along the bells) tinkling Tchaikovsky. A collection of late eighteenth-century parasols even more disarming. Fainting couches with hand-stitched velvet cushions, three bearskin rugs, and a stuffed lion roaring on its haunches.

It was a gay boy's fever dream.

So full of glorious possibilities.

Terelli and Daiju immediately went about cleaning and polishing.

"What are we going to do with all of these treasures?" Daiju wondered. "There are so many!"

"We can open a little shop in Coney Island with all the pieces we don't keep!" Terelli exclaimed. "We'll call it L'Antiquaire du Petit Oiseau! We'll make a small fortune! More than enough for the upkeep! More than enough to eat!"

When the authorities showed up, the two escapees hid under a trapdoor beneath the living room's Persian rug.

"I haven't seen my grandson in years," Terelli's grandmother said. "I won't have anything to do with that goddamned little pansy!"

"Sorry to disturb you, madam . . ."

"Did you just call me a madam? Do I look like an old whore to you?"

"No, ma'am."

"Get lost before I phone Washington. I'll have you know I'm

personal friends with Franklin D. Roosevelt. I went to school with his mother. Horrible woman."

Giggling under the floorboards, Terelli never felt so safe. He never felt so happy. He kissed his traveling companion. "We're finally free!"

The little bird's wings were finally healing.

Back at Greystone Park, he had been pummeled down to cashing in all of his chips when Daiju Sato was hauled in. The two immediately bonded in auto repair class. While replacing a set of squeaky brakes, they concocted a plan for their escape. Terelli felt bad tying up the old nurse and stripping her of her uniform, but he relished clubbing the nasty doctor.

Once they settled into their new home, Terelli's grandmother gave her favorite grandson and his darling Daiju free rein.

Terelli hired an army of brawny workmen to repair and paint the place. One of them looked so much like Francis Anthony Mozzarelli. It made Terelli shiver the way the studly young man worked without his shirt on, his paint-splattered muscles popping under the Brooklyn sun.

The boys quickly brought the old mansion back to life, christening it Dojo Lombardi.

It wasn't long before they opened their little antique shop in a sweet little storefront on Coney Island's Mermaid Avenue.

To celebrate, Daiju gifted Terelli with a squawking parrot they named Honeybee.

"A sweet little bird for my sweet little bird!"

Tweet! Tweet!

When Terelli wasn't treasure hunting for the shop or taking care of his ailing grandmother, he was teaching his parrot to curse like a sailor on shore leave.

"Shithead! Fuck you! Eat me!"

He tugged an old Radio Flyer in and out of estate sales and

strolled along the Brooklyn beaches. He did this to maintain his newfound sanity. As he ambled along, he often thought about Belladonna Marie Donato and Francis Anthony Mozzarelli. He wondered about their baby. Were they all together? Were they in Sin City? He considered looking for them. But the old hurt and pain welled up and he decided against it.

He ignored Bella's clarion calls to find her, but she still came to him in his dreams. She was always dancing and singing and cooking. Any visions of Francis were always cloudy. He never saw their baby.

The antique shop did fantastic business. Daiju was the front of the house proprietor, keeping a trained eye on things, while Terelli tugged his wagon around with his foulmouthed parrot flapping about him.

"Fuck you! Eat me! Fuck you! Eat me!"

THE SEARCH FOR SIGNS OF BELLA'S NEW LIFE

NOT LONG AFTER ARRIVING in Brooklyn, Terelli's grandmother passed away. Of course the funeral, held in Dojo Lombardi's parlor, was extremely tasteful. An open coffin prominently on display. Of course Terelli made up the corpse. He artfully assigned her all the glamour of Gail Patrick in *Death Takes a Holiday*. "Another fucking masterpiece," he whispered while kneeling in front of the fancy casket.

The mourning crowd was discreet. Mostly locals. A string quartet played as a posse of beautiful young men passed hors d'oeuvres on antique silver trays. They marched around the house like a clutch of dazzling Broadway chorus boys on parade.

Terelli's grandmother left the gargantuan house to her favorite grandson and his Japanese companion. As soon as the corpse was interred in the family crypt in the Green-Wood Cemetery, Terelli and Daiju opened the house to a small bundle of boarders:

A closeted salesman named Wade Wentrell from Zelienople, Pennsylvania, who sold Miracle Brooms and Carpet Sweepers. When he was home, he always dusted and swept the place.

A single gal named Trudy Fairweather from Bangor, Maine, who was studying to be an opera singer. When she practiced her arias, it drove the parrot fucking crazy.

"FUCK YOU! EAT ME! FUCK YOU! EAT ME!" it shrieked.

A beautiful young man from Nebraska named Jack Getch who modeled hats and underwear. Terelli was his primary photographer.

"Smile and say *Terelli*, darling!"

With income from the new housemates and the antique shop, Terelli went on a spending spree. He traded in his grandmother's old Model T for a brand-new 1937 Buick Special the color of buttered Cream of Wheat. With the assistance of his luxurious new automobile, he went on a number of day trips. The time he spent in Prospect Park was nothing but bliss. Until the day a desperate call came from his mother, sick and dying in Passaic.

"Don't listen to that evil lady! It's a trap!" Daiju insisted.

His heart tugged by the umbilical undertow of ailing Alice's fucked-up love, Terelli threw on the nurse's uniform, tossed a packed suitcase into the back of his Buick, and drove all the way out to New Jersey.

He found her prostrate in bed, looking like an ancient skeleton, hopped up on goofballs and painkillers.

"Terelli," she barely whispered, "can you ever forgive me?"

"Yes, Alice."

"I love you, son."

"I love you too, Mommy."

Like a good little Florence Nightingale, Terelli tended to his mommy during her final days. Nursed by her queer son's undying love, she hung on well past the diagnosed several weeks she supposedly had left. When she finally wheezed her final breath, Terelli gave the old witch a tender kiss. "I loved you so much," he whispered. Then he clapped his hands together and yelled, "Bon voyage, you old bitch!"

On his way out of town he parked in front of Francis Anthony Mozzarelli's fire-licked house.

He idled in front of Loprinzi's Gymnasium.

After driving past the Robertson Scale factory, he swung over to the Passaic dump.

Perched on top of his hill, he recalled the last time he was there. He had said so many rotten and hurtful things to Belladonna Marie, his Meatball Queen. It brought tears of sorrow and regret to his eyes. Crying on their old ash heap, his heart brimming with the joy of forgiving his dead mommy, an overwhelming desire to see Bella flooded over him.

Fly all the way to Whore's Paradise and find me!

After racing back to Brooklyn and reuniting with his beloved and their cursing parrot, he scoured Coney Island. The dance halls. The stages.

He hovered around Sam Tweety's Hawaiian Island Girlie Revue and Peek-a-Booth Theater, watching the girls shake their hips and tits.

The deaf old carnival barker was tight-lipped. The whores in the back were all new. Bella was gone, they insisted. "She left Coney Island several weeks ago," one of them confessed. "No one knows where she is."

Twice Terelli thought he caught the scent of Bella's tomato gravy. But after sniffing around Coney Island Creek, it brought him to a dead end, to an empty beach.

"Where the hell are you, Belladonna Marie?" he hollered across the cursing waves.

LITTLE ITALY
IN NEW JERSEY

As DINO MONTEBOLOGNA'S EBONY Cadillac zoomed back to New Jersey from honeymoonland, Bella sat wedged between two new steamer trunks. She had been on her stinkin' honeymoon for over a goddamned week. Five long days stuck in the Crab Trap with Melvin guarding. Then three more perched in a suite at the top of the Waldorf Astoria Hotel in New York City.

Caged like a stinkin' canary.

Every day Dino had to see a man about a donut. And every night he disappeared until the wee hours of dawn, leaving Bella alone with Melvin, who did nothing but read. The humorless henchman had finished *The Odyssey* and was plowing through a Bible-sized book called *War and Peace*.

To amuse herself, Bella continuously ordered room service. Steak Diane, chicken à la king, ice-cream sundaes, and bottle after bottle of the best champagne.

"Hey, Melvin. Why do you read so many goddamned books?" she slurred while slicing through a medium-rare filet.

"I learn things."

"What kindsa things?"

The big guy shrugged. "I find out what goes on in other parts of the world. What it might be like to spear a whale, or fight in a duel, or fuck the living daylights out of a saucy maid."

"You wanna fuck me?"

"I don't think so."

"Whysnot?"

"'Cause if I do, your husband'll kill me."

"It'll be worth it, believe youse and me."

"No fuck is worth gettin' iced over."

"I used to be known as Queen of Sin City."

"I don't care if you was known as the fuckin' queen of Italy, I'm keepin' my paws to myself. And if I was you, I'd do the same thing."

Twice during their little Manhattan holiday, Dino took Bella shopping. They spent two whirlwind days trunking through the designer showrooms of Fifth Avenue, where a parade of models displayed the latest fashions from Paris, France. They hit the garment district and the shipping docks on the lower Hudson. Dino knew an awful lot about women's fashion.

"Dat's the wrong color. Do you have it in a sapphire blue?"

"Dis is too close to last season's cut. I thought hems were a lot shorter dis year . . ."

If he didn't like an outfit, he dismissed it with a curt wave of his manicured hand. If he loved something, he bounced up and down like a jack-in-the-box in front of a dancing band. He made Bella try on an enormous variety of gowns and shoes, even wigs and lingerie. Once he draped a charcoal-gray cinema suit in front of himself and insisted the color was simply stunning.

Two large steamer trunks full of the latest fashions and accessories were packed into the Cadillac.

"You're gonna live in a castle fit for royalty!" Dino hollered as they sped along Upper Mountain Avenue in Montclair, New Jersey.

Coney Island flashbulbs popped in front of Bella, and she saw the beautiful face of Francis Anthony Mozzarelli smiling, a crown of thorns around his handsome head.

"Home sweet home!" Dino sang as they cruised up a winding driveway to a stonemason's wet dream. A palazzo built with imported travertine. Square bell towers and boxed turrets peaked in the Garden State sky. Iron-cased windows with diamond-shaped panes winked. Sprays of dense ivy crawled up smokeless chimneys.

"I call it *Piccola Italia!*" Dino proudly proclaimed. "It's my very own Little Italy. And now it's yours, too, my Queen!"

Bella heard Francis Anthony Mozzarelli howling.

As they braked into a wide porte cochere, a tall, middle-aged black man in a stiff butler's uniform regally stepped out of the servants' entrance to greet them.

"Dis is my main man, Sweet Jim," Dino said.

The formal-looking fellow pursed his lips and glared.

"Jim runs the whole show here," Dino informed Bella. "Anything you need, you just ask him."

"Boy! Get them bags and trunks!" Sweet Jim called and Jerry, Bella's little guardian angel from her stay above the Elbow Room, popped out of the house. He was pinched into a formal pallbearer's suit and smiling.

"Hello, Missus!"

"Hello, Jerry!" Bella cried.

The sprightly kid scampered to the back of the car and started unloading.

"We got giant clams from the Cape!" Dino sang. "They're called *co-hogs*. Ain't dat name hilarious?"

"Boy!" Sweet Jim hollered. "Drop them bags and get them pig clams in the kitchen!"

Dino and Bella, led by Sweet Jim, marched around to the front of the mansion with Melvin following. When Bella stepped into the grand foyer, her mouth dropped open.

Towering walls covered with oversized paintings of dramatic Venetian scenes swirled around her. A wide waterfall of a grand staircase tumbled down from a stained glass window the size of a barn door. Not a saint or angel in flight. The rainbow-colored glass depicted a bare-chested warrior saddled on a brutish stallion rearing against a voluptuous sky.

"It looks like somethin' out of a picture show in here," Bella said as Jim toured them through the mansion's bare ballroom. It was big enough for a couple of Coney Island's carousels to spin around in. Under a cluster of crystal chandeliers, a sea of polished parquet spread to an empty bandstand.

Then came the solarium. Fat ceramic pots filled with full-figured trees and naked statues of men, some posed alone, some wrestling together, a couple pissing water into shimmering pools stocked full of the biggest goldfish Bella had ever seen.

"Jesus!" she said when they entered the enormous restaurant-style kitchen. Two griddled stoves and a long center island with three sinks.

"Jesus had nothin' to do with it," Sweet Jim muttered under his breath.

"Dis is all for you, Belladonna Marie Montebologna!" Dino proclaimed. "You're the mistress of Piccola Italia now!"

Sweet Jim audibly cleared his throat and Jerry chuckled as he dragged one of the steamer trunks across the kitchen floor.

"What is you makin' us for dinner?" Dino asked Bella.

"How about Sicilian stuffed quahogs?"

"Boy!" Sweet Jim called to Jerry. "You best start scrubbin' them big clackers clean!"

The rest of the place felt like it took forever to travel through. Room after room cluttered with an angry array of massive antiques. Hand-carved sideboards (wolf heads baring teeth), piecrust-shaped wine tables (claws for feet), and harvest-colored Tiffany lamps (crows and ravens flying).

"What if I get lost?" Bella asked as they passed through a well-stocked library.

"Ring one of the call buzzers," Dino said. "Sweet Jim or Jerusalem will find you."

"Maybe so," Sweet Jim muttered under his sweet breath. "Maybe not."

After padding through a confusing maze of second-story hallways, they entered a satin-walled tunnel of pocket-sized rooms. Tufted jewel boxes stuffed with an array of feminine things. Lamps embedded with colorful glass beads. Marble-topped tables with dainty paws for feet.

"Dis is all yours!" Dino proclaimed.

"My God!" Bella exclaimed.

"God had nothin' to do with it," Sweet Jim hissed with disdain.

In the first room, sheer pink curtains billowed in next to a Parisian vanity much grander than Alice Lombardi's dressing table.

In the second room, they were greeted by a storm cloud of a canopy bed the size of a carnival tent, caped in bloodred velvet drapes, and a chifforobe as big as Peanut the elephant.

"Show her the powder room, Jim!"

Sweet Jim narrowed his eyes considerably. "Yes, Mr. Dino."

The regal houseman pushed open a set of French doors to reveal a sea of blue and white tile weaving to an ocean-sized bathtub big enough to drown a Queen.

"Why don't youse take a bubble bath," Dino said. "I've got to see a man about a donut."

"You eat a lot of donuts," Bella said.

"You don't know the half of it," Sweet Jim muttered. "How do you take your water?" he asked Bella, after Dino and Melvin left. "Ice-cold like the Hudson in January? Or scalding like the devil's sea?"

SICILIAN STUFFED QUAHOGS IN LITTLE ITALY

AFTER A LUXURIOUS BUBBLE bath, Bella slipped into a blush satin marabou-trimmed waterfall robe and rang the buzzer next to her bed. It wasn't long before Jerry showed up and escorted her down to the kitchen where the marble counters were packed with fresh loaves of Italian bread, baskets full of fresh vegetables, a sack of flour, a bowl of eggs, a case of white wine, a wreath of garlic, and a sixty-pound round of Pecorino cheese.

The boy dragged the tubbed quahogs and a snaked wheel of hot Italian sausage out of the mammoth icebox. "What else can I get you, Missus?"

"What kind of pots does this place have?"

"What kind you need?"

Together they piled the quahogs in an ocean-deep lobster pot, covered them with white wine, and turned up a flame.

"Do you live here, Jerry?" Bella asked.

"I do now," the kid responded. "Sweet Jim lives here too."

"Sweet Jim ain't so sweet to me."

"Oh, he just be jealous is all."

"Jealous? Of what?"

"Before you came along, he was the lady of the house."

"How can that be?"

"Let's get cookin'."

Jerry knew all the tricks of the trade. How to pop a garlic clove out of its skin, how to hold a matchstick between his teeth so he wouldn't cry while chopping an onion, and how to wave a knife over the pepperoncini to properly exorcise them of evil spirits before scraping out the seeds.

Bella was duly impressed.

"I can cook anything!" the boy proudly proclaimed. "I can make fried chicken with Peabody gravy. I can roast a ham like it's nobody's business. I can candy myself some yams, bake ash cakes, boil rice and peas, and roast a whole lamb for company. I can even make chopped suey."

"Who taught you how to cook?"

"My mamma taught me before the good Lord took her away."

"I'm sorry you lost your mamma, Jerry."

"Oh, it's okay. She was a mean old thing. She'd whip the word of the Lord into my wicked little ass as soon as look at me. She made me memorize the entire Bible."

"Every page?"

"The whole goddamned thing. If I was good, she would love me up and hug me hard. Especially after she found the bottom of a whisky bottle. If she drank enough, she'd give me a peck on my lips and tell me I was a prince. Did your mamma teach you how to cook too?" Jerry asked Bella.

"My mamma lives in her bed and never says a word."

Sharp knife flying.

Lucia screaming.

As the Piccola Italia kitchen filled with the briny seaside steam of clams opening, salty memories flooded back to Bella like ocean swells cresting.

Her papa laughing and throwing her over the sea.

Her mamma laughing and crying.

The hunger of the Great Depression.

Cooking for her family.

"I miss my mamma," Bella wistfully said.

"I miss my mamma too. How about we start stuffin' some of them clams?"

Bella's Sicilian Stuffed Quahogs

This delicious recipe carried Bella
through many a stormy sea.

12 large quahog clams

4 cups dry white wine

2 bay leaves

1 pound hot Italian sausage meat, uncased

1 medium onion, diced

2 celery stalks, chopped

2 red bell peppers, chopped

6 tablespoons butter

¼ cup olive oil

⅓ cup Italian parsley, chopped

1 large loaf of Italian bread, roughly torn into one-inch bits

Montebologna (or the very best) Olive Oil

salt and pepper, to taste

chili flakes

grated Parmesan cheese

paprika

1. Scrub the quahogs to remove any dirt or sand. Feel
    the meat of their memories while you hold them in
    your hands.
2. Place them in large pot. Cover with wine and water
    (about two inches above clackers) and add bay leaves.

Bring to a boil and let simmer until the giant mollusks open (5–10 minutes). As they open and release their memories of their time in the sea, think about your own precious memories.

3. Remove quahogs and let cool. (If you come across a clam that didn't open, toss it. It's poison.) Strain and reserve the broth. It is full of the clam's history. Here is where most of the flavor is. Most of our flavor comes from our memories. Celebrate the good ones. Discard the bad ones.

4. Remove the cooked clam meat from the shells and roughly chop it. Separate and rinse the shell halves, then set them aside as you rinse and separate your memories.

5. In a large skillet, pour in some Montebologna Olive Oil and brown the uncased sausage meat. Think about the foods your mamma or someone you love used to make. Think about your mamma or someone you love laughing and singing.

6. Remove the cooked sausage. Add butter to pan and sauté the diced peppers, onions, and celery until soft. Add the cooked sausage meat. Bella's mamma used to make her own sausages. She used to grind the meat, spice it, and sing while she cranked out the spicy links.

7. Place the ripped pieces of Italian bread into large bowl. Add the cooked sausage and vegetable mixture, the chopped clam meat, the parsley, and the grated cheese. Add salt, pepper, and chili flakes to taste and combine. Moisten with strained broth. You can do miraculous things with leftover bread. Bread soaked and souped

and crumbed got many people through the worst of the Great Depression. A delicious bread soup or savory stuffing can always put a smile on any face.

8. Pack stuffing into the empty clamshells. Sprinkle paprika over tops. Place a small pat of butter on each one. Butter makes the clams extra flavorful and extra crispy. Bella had a clear memory of her mamma telling her butter on anything was everything. Buttered sandwiches of ham, lamb, or roast beef were the bee's knees.

9. Place shells on baking sheet. Wave a knife over them to ward away any bad memories or demon spirits. Cross yourself and slide the packed clams into the oven to bake at 350 degrees, until tops are nice and toasty (15–20 minutes). Things that are crunchy and crispy and packed full of flavor always offer the best memories.

10. Think about your mamma or someone who loved you like a mamma while you cook and eat. Think about the good times. Celebrate your maternal history.

11. Buon appetito! Mangiare bene! Stare bene! Delizioso!

BELLA'S WELL OF LONELINESS

WANDERING FROM ROOM TO room in Piccola Italia, taking bubble baths, reading movie magazines, and cooking meals fit for an Italian King and his Queen was a goddamned lonely business.

Day after lonely day, week after lonely week.

"How come you never try and fuck me?" Bella asked Dino one evening while the two of them sipped martini-glassed hooch in front of the living room's blazing fireplace. Melvin was sitting behind them, his face buried in a dog-eared copy of *The Great Gatsby*.

"I had a long day. I'm bushed," was all Dino said. He gave Bella a chaste peck on the cheek.

"You want me to come to bed with you?" Bella asked.

"Nah. You finish your drink. I don't let no one in my room. Ever. I like my privacy."

"What's wrong with you? Why won't you fuck me? Do you even like girls? Are you fucking Melvin?"

"Hey!" Melvin hollered.

Dino stared at Bella. Was he even breathing? His face took on the color of a ripe cherry. "Another fuckin' word out of you and I'll set those fabulous gams of yours in two blocks of cement and drop you into the Passaic River," was all he said. Then he stormed out of the room.

"I guess I must have struck a nerve," Bella whispered.

Melvin rose up from his chair. "If I was you, I'd apologize for that."

"I'm sorry."

"Not to me."

The goon closed his book and stalked out of the room too.

Later that night, while Bella was trapped in a cluster of fitful dreams (her Coney Island family surrounding her and singing "All of Me," Francis holding their baby, her papa climbing on top of her screaming mamma, her mamma's knife blade zinging), a secret panel in her room slid open and a hulking figure stalked over to her bed.

"Bella!" the figure whispered. It shook her until her eyes snapped open. Then a callused hand quickly muffled her scream. "Shh! It's me. It's Melvin."

"What are you doin' here?" Bella spit through his fingers. "Are you gonna kill me?"

"I'm here to make love to you, if you'll have me."

He tenderly gathered her into his arms and devoured her lips with his tough mouth. His tongue tasted like danger and delinquency. "I've been wantin' to do this since the night I rescued you from the sea," he whispered. "That night I knew my mind would never romp again like the mind of God unless I had you. So I waited, listening for a moment longer to the tuning fork that had been struck upon a star. Ever since then it's been like . . ."

"Oh, for Christ's sake! Shut up and fuck me!"

The big beast knew exactly what to do. He was rough when

Bella wanted it. Tender when she needed him to be. He ravished her with surprising gentility. Then he took her with the
unbridled force of a Coney Island hurricane.

"Francis! Oh, Francis!" Bella yelled when the two of them
came together.

"Who's Francis?" Melvin asked as he lay next to her, sticky
and panting.

Without warning, Bella burst into tears. Her entire body
shook with sorrow and grief.

Melvin tenderly took her in his warm arms. "Don't cry,
Bella," he gently whispered. "I think I love you."

Bella wiped her cheeks. "Oh, for fuck's sake."

The next day a maid showed up. A fast-moving Jamaican
woman who zipped around from room to room, smoking and
cursing and dragging an Electrolux the size of a small dinosaur
that sucked the dust off of everything.

Melvin slid through Bella's secret panels most nights, but
after a while Dino and Melvin were never around. There was
always a donut meeting or two or three. If they were gone for
more than a day or a week, they took Sweet Jim with them.

"I want to go too!" Bella always complained.

"You stay put until we get back," Dino would always say.

"This is bullshit," Bella said to Jerry every time the Cadillac
rumbled away.

"It sure is," the boy always said.

During those long, lost, and lonely days, Bella and Jerry
cooked everything from oxtail stew to osso buco. They cooked
as a team, but Bella always ate alone at the mile-long dining
room table, ringing a buzzer to get her plate cleared, wine
poured, or dessert delivered. During one of those isolated
meals, Bella asked Jerry to sit with her.

"I can't do that, Missus."

"Why not?"

"'Cause I be the help."

"That's bullshit."

"It sure is."

After an early supper one lonely evening, Bella dolled herself up and wandered down to Bloomfield Avenue, to the Wellmont Theater, to take in *Snow White and the Seven Dwarfs*. When the colorful little men popped across the silver screen mining and marching and singing, Bella had to bite the inside of her cheek to keep from crying. She missed Oui Oui and Lolly and Minnie terribly. She missed Chester and Peanut too. And she missed Francis Anthony Mozzarelli. She missed Francis like crazy. When the Prince kissed Snow White awake, Bella's well of loneliness exploded and she sobbed into the greasy bottom of her empty popcorn box. She wailed in her velvet seat. Then she slapped herself in the face, yanked herself up, and whistled her way back to Dino Montebologna's Little Italy.

The next morning, after a solitary breakfast, Bella rang the buzzer.

"Hey, Jerry. Mr. Dino won't be back until late. What say you and me go on a little adventure today . . ."

"Okay!"

After getting all dolled up and raiding the cookie jars for hidden rolls of dough, they entered the mansion's eight-car garage.

"We got us a 1932 Pontiac roadster, a Buick Y-Job, a Chevrolet Confederate BA four-door sedan, a Plymouth, a Cadillac V16 Madame X cabriolet, a regular ole Ford, and a Duesenberg Model J that hasn't got any roof on top of it."

"Let's take that one."

"You know how to drive, Missus?"

"How hard can it possibly be?"

After a few false starts and several gear-grinding jumps, the two of them trundled down the winding driveway and took to the open road.

"Arrivederci, animali!" Bella hollered as they whizzed down Upper Mountain Avenue.

"Where we goin', Missus?!" Jerry asked.

"Have you ever been to New York City?" Bella yelled over the roaring engine.

"No!" Jerry yelled back.

"Well, you're in for a real treat!"

As they revved onto Route 46 East, the two of them yodeled along with songs dancing out of the radio.

"Satan Takes a Holiday."

"You Must Have Been a Beautiful Baby."

"Drivin' is easy!" Bella cried into the wind.

They zipped along like two Baum characters flying all the way to the Emerald City.

With the craggy Manhattan skyline looming across the Hudson, they corkscrewed down through a tollbooth and slipped into the mouth of the Lincoln Tunnel. The loud whoosh as they careened through the cement tube was like one long amusement park ride.

"Can we do that again?" Jerry asked when they popped out the other side.

"On the way home!" Bella hollered over horns honking, brakes squealing, and engines zooming. She double-parked the Duesenberg in Herald Square and bopped into Macy's, Jerry marching behind. The boy marveled at how many things Bella could stuff between her breasts and up her dress while they browsed around the loaded glass cases and well-appointed mannequins.

Bella bought Jerry a sharp-looking little-man suit and a snazzy pair of Buster Brown shoes.

For herself, she grabbed a pagoda-sleeved cape coat with leg-o'-mutton shoulders.

When the salesman at Tiffany's playfully pinned a

diamond-studded brooch over Bella's left breast, Jerry squealed, "I think Mr. Dino would want you to have that."

"Let's go to Bloomingdale's and Saks Fifth Avenue!"

They were like two kids on a tear.

After a thrilling morning of shopping (and shoplifting), they cruised down to Joe Stanziani's on West Fourth Street for mountain-sized plates of spaghetti.

"Your meatballs are better than these," Jerry assessed. "And this pasta ain't homemade."

After inhaling hot fudge shortcake and apple whips in Schrafft's, they cruised around Central Park and stopped in to see the park zoo's penguins.

"The one that's trying to fly looks just like Mr. Dino!" Bella exclaimed.

"I think you should leave Mr. Dino and marry me!" Jerry proclaimed.

On the way home they stopped at the Milk Barn in Wayne, New Jersey, for coconut ice cream smothered in caramel and rainbow jimmies. Then they hit Nagel's Candy Barn for chocolate-covered caramel turtles, Mary Janes, and jelly beans. Bella instructed the clerk to pack and gift wrap a one-pound box of nonpareils.

"Where we goin' now?" Jerry asked when they flew past their exit on Route 46.

Bella kept her eyes trained on the road. "We got one final stop to make before we head back to Piccola Italia . . ."

WELCOME TO CLIFTON, NEW JERSEY!

Down Van Houten Avenue the Duesenberg careened, until it took a hard left onto Scales Drive.

Papa! Catch me!

The car came to a skidding halt, its nose juddering in front of the fearsome factory gates.

"What kind of place is this?" Jerry asked Bella.

"It's where I grew up."

"Really?"

The surprised face of long Joe, lean Joe, sad Joe let them through. As Bella drove along the narrow alleys, she smiled and waved.

Of course the lunch stand was still closed.

But the factory machines were still humming.

The smokestacks were still coughing and spewing.

At the caretaker's house, Bella's bumper bit into one of her papa's rosebushes, sending a rash of bees into the trees. As Jerry watched, she grabbed the wrapped box of chocolates and left the car. "You wait here for me."

Before her feet hit the porch steps, the front door swung open and Manny Donato stepped out of the house. He looked like a hobo. Gaunt and disheveled. He was a pale imitation of the old beast.

"I came home to see my mamma!" Bella hollered. "I brought her favorite chocolates!"

"Get the hell out of here," Manny said. "This ain't your home anymore. You're dead."

The windows of the house filled with the faces of the rest of her family, masked by old lace, like the ghosts of Christmas past.

"I want to see Mamma!"

"Go back to your crooked life. You're Dino Montebologna's problem now. You're his whore of a wife."

"I want so see my mamma!"

Manny stepped back inside and shut the door.

The fuzzy faces behind the curtains disappeared.

"MAMMA!" Bella screamed. She dropped the gift wrapped box of chocolates and collapsed on top of it, bellowing, "I WANT TO SEE MY MAMMA! PLEASE!"

Jerry jumped out of the car and ran over to his mistress. "Missus, get up!"

"MAMMA!" Bella screamed.

"Missus! Let's get out of here! Please!"

Jerry lifted Bella and guided her back to the car. After tucking her into the passenger seat, he ran back to the crushed box of chocolates. He picked it up and cautiously placed it on one of the porch steps. Then he quickly scampered back to the car, hopped behind the wheel, keyed the engine, and floored them away.

They got as far as LoMonico's market before they were pulled over by a motorcycle-roaring police officer.

"How old are you, boy?" the officer asked when he stood next to the car.

"Thirty-three."

"Do you have a license?"

Bella snapped out of her stupor for a sane second. "He doesn't need a license," she said. "He's with me."

"And what's your name, young lady?"

"Belladonna Marie Dona—Montebologna. Belladonna Montebologna."

The officer's face blanched. "Did you say M-Montebologna?"

"I sure did."

The engine of the car growled as it rested.

"Any relation to D-Dino M-Montebologna?"

"I'm his whore of a wife."

The cop's face dropped. "I'm awfully sorry, M-Mrs. M-M-Montebologna," he sputtered. "Would you like a p-personal escort to wherever it is you're going?"

Before Bella could say anything, Jerry spoke up. "No, sir. We was just on our way over to a church to pray."

The officer tipped his hat. "Well, you two have a blessed day."

TELLING THE GOD'S HONEST TRUTH, PART THREE

IN THE HUMBLE HEART of Saint Anthony's, Bella and Jerry sat in front of the painting of the Francis Christ, sharing a bag of jelly beans.

The boy popped one in his mouth and looked up at the striking young savior, gorgeous and glowing. "Before my mamma flew up to Heaven, she told me if you was real quiet and listened carefully, you could hear Jesus speakin'. I always thought it was her drinkin'. But then one day I heard Him too."

"What did He say?"

"He said not everything is what you see." The boy glanced up at the portrait. "My mamma told me Jesus was black like me."

"How could that be?"

"She said Jesus is everything."

"He used to be everything to me."

"What do you mean?"

As Bella clutched the pinky ring hanging on her mamma's rosary beads, she told Jerry the story of meeting Francis Anthony Mozzarelli. She told him about their baby. She told him about Coney Island. She told him about Hero the Strongman. She told him about being crowned King and Queen. She told him about how she and Francis were supposed to get married. She told him about how she ran away from her marriage and her baby.

Jerry thoughtfully sucked on a cherry-flavored jelly bean. "Do you love your Francis?"

"Yes."

"Do you love your baby?"

"More than anything."

"Then why did you leave them?"

"I was scared, I guess."

"What was you so scared of?"

"The truth."

"What truth?"

"The truth that I'm not good enough."

"Good enough for what?"

Bella looked up at Francis. "When I had my son in my arms, I felt so ashamed."

"What was you ashamed of?"

"Everything. Lying and sinning mostly."

"The Bible says Jesus died for our sins."

"What if our sins are really bad, Jerry?"

"My mamma said Jesus will forgive anything. All you have to do is ask."

Bella looked up at the portrait of the crucified Christ, at Francis. She could see his heart beating. She could hear him howling.

Belladonna Marie! Come home to me!

"Did you hear that?" Bella asked Jerry.

"I sure did."

"What do you think it means?"

"If I was you, I'd run back to your Francis King and tell him you're sorry. Tell him you made a terrible mistake. Tell him you love him. Ask him to forgive you. Then you two go and get your baby."

"I can't do that," Bella said.

"Why not?"

"I'm married to Mr. Dino now."

Jerry grabbed a fistful of jelly beans. "Oh, you can get outta that easy."

"What do you mean?"

IN THE CLOSET

"THIS HERE BE MR. Dino and Mr. Jim's bedroom," Jerry said as he slipped a hairpin Bella gave him into the keyhole of a red patent leather door at the end of long hall in the east wing of Piccola Italia.

"Dino and Jim share a bedroom?"

Once they were inside, the boy ran over to a set of heavy damask drapes and tugged them apart. Late-afternoon light spilled into the room, illuminating a bed shrouded in purple satin and mounded with an array of gaudy pillows.

On the wall opposite the bed hung a life-sized portrait of two ugly women framed by a wall of leather-bound books. The hound-faced ladies were standing side by side and holding hands. They had more makeup on their faces than a couple of jail-bound boardwalk floozies.

"That's Miss Olive Oil and Miss Lena Horny!" Jerry announced.

"Who the hell are they?"

"I'd look real close, if I was you."

There was something regally striking about the sour set of the black woman's painted lips. The eyes of the white dame contained a dangerously familiar intensity. "Wait a minute," Bella said.

The boy parked himself on an elaborate high-backed Renaissance chair and clasped his hands behind his head. "Sometimes when the whole house is empty, I sneak on in here and pretend I rule the world. Sometimes I just come on in here to read. I'm about halfway through them books. But this ain't all of what I wanted to show you."

"It ain't?"

The boy hopped off his throne, dragged it over to the wall of bookshelves, climbed onto the velvet seat cushion, reached up high, and tugged on a leather-bound volume of *Little Women*. The huge portrait slowly slid open with the slippery ease of a sneaky speakeasy panel, revealing a showgirl's tricked-out closet the size of a Paris boutique.

"Holy shit!"

"You said it!"

"What is all this?" Bella said, stepping into the blazing cave.

"Ain't nobody ever supposed to go in here," Jerry whispered as he followed.

It was ten times the size of Alice Lombardi's closet. It was like stepping into the dressing room of a Ziegfeld queen. Bella felt like she was standing in the middle of a gumball machine. Racks of dazzling dresses dripping with sparkling beads and baubles, tons of marabou in Technicolor orange, red, yellow, pink, and green. On a long shelf crowning the gowns rested a long line of wig-topped dummy heads sporting every style and color imaginable. Blond, brunette, black, and auburn. On the floor, below the dangling hems, stood enough heels to shoe a line of Rockettes. Close-toed, open-toed, high and low. Some buckled, some laced, some bowed.

Way at the end of the closet sat a mirrored makeup table riddled with a gaudy display of lipsticks, blushes, powders, and perfumes.

Beyond all the razzle-dazzle, an archway opened to reveal a master bath as pink as a summertime petunia.

Bella could hear Terelli Lombardi tweeting,

Simply stunning!

Bella walked over to the vanity and picked up a used tube of Marvelous pink satin lipstick. "Hey! This one belongs to me! I've been lookin' for this for weeks!" She turned to Jerry. "That fuckin' rat fink!"

A PRETTY GIRL

LATER THAT EVENING, AFTER Dino and Melvin and Jim waltzed into the mansion, Bella served them a glorious meal of her best eggplant parmigiana ("Nobody makes better eggplant parm!" Dino cried. "I'd kill anyone who tried!"). When supper was over, Bella brought the young capo upstairs alone. She led him through his secret bedroom suite and marched him into his secret closet.

In a flash the capo pulled the gun he always carried from the holster under his jacket and leveled it at his nosy wife. "I'll make you sorry you didn't mind your own fuckin' business!" he sneered. "I'm gonna fuck you up! I'm gonna fuck you up real good!"

Bella's blood stopped flowing for a second. She wished she had her mamma's cheek-slicing knife. "What are you gonna do? Shoot me and dump me in the Passaic River?"

"Yeah!"

"You think that's gonna make all this go away? Look at

you! Miss All Slick with your rose deliveries and your marriage proposals! You think you're so tough with your guns and your donut meetings! You're nothing but a slippery little bitch who doesn't know how to dress and wear makeup!"

Dino's face flinched. "I gave you everything."

"You gave me NOTHING!"

"I rescued you from a bullshit life!"

"Only heroes rescue people, Dino! And you're no hero, believe me! You married me and kept me locked up in this god-damned Piccola Italia like a fuckin' fairy-tale princess under false pretenses! Well, let me tell you somethin', *Miss Olive Oil!* I am no princess. I'M A FUCKIN' QUEEN! A REAL QUEEN! NOT A GODDAMNED SISSY!"

Bella waited for the mobster to blast a hole through her heart. Instead, he collapsed onto the stool in front of the dressing table and started sniveling. "All my life I wanted to be pretty," he blubbered. "Ever since I was a little boy back in Italy. I wanted to be pretty. Just like you. I still do," he sniffled. Then he got real quiet. Then he silently nodded to himself. "Tell Jim I'm sorry. Tell him I love him. Tell him goodbye." Dino raised the gun to his temple and cocked the trigger.

"NO! DINO! DON'T DO IT! I CAN MAKE YOU PRETTY!" Bella screamed.

For a second Dino's entire body tensed. Then he looked up at her, eyes wet and expectant. "What do youse mean?"

"I can make you beautiful, if you let me." Bella took a deep breath and held out her hand. "Be a good girl and give me the gun."

The wrecked man did as he was told.

"Go take a bath," she ordered. "Clean yourself up real good and give your face a nice, close shave. Then come back and see me right away."

As the water in the bathroom ran and steam billowed into the closet, Bella emptied the gun's chamber and tossed the bullets behind the kick line of shoes.

When Dino returned all bath-puppy-wet, Bella sat him in front of the makeup table.

"Now face me and close your eyes," she said.

With hands that shook a little, she expertly spread Maybelline Sheer Beauty over his forehead, down his nose, and around his mouth and cheeks.

"Dat feels good."

"No talking. Remember, less is more," she advised. "Unless you're going to a nighttime soiree or a fancy ball," she added as she blended. "Once you have a good base, then you can start contouring."

"Where did you learn how to do dis?"

"A little birdie taught me."

Tweet! Tweet!

With steady hands, she picked up a contour brush and compact and worked on giving Dino a Dietrich nose. Then she shaded under his cheekbones for some Hepburn haughtiness. Then she Harlow-plucked his eyebrows.

"Ouch!"

"Don't be such a goddamned baby."

"Hey! I don't let nobody talk to me dat way!"

"Shut the fuck up. I need to concentrate."

"Sorry."

With a Swan Stick grease pencil, Bella shaped and thickened Dino's eyebrows for some much-needed Crawford nastiness. Then she blushed his cheeks for a little Lombard freshness. "Always go easy on this stuff. You don't want to look like a Coney Island clown." She found her tube of pink satin lipstick in the pile on the table and uncapped it.

"I stole dat from you," Dino confessed. "I thought it was too dainty for your face."

"Bold colors can sometimes be off-putting. But sometimes they're just what a girl needs. Open wide," Bella instructed. She generously spread the wax over his lips and made him smack them together. Then she popped the lid off a jar of Vaseline. "This'll give your smile an extra nice sheen."

"Thank you."

"You look better than Joan Bennett in *She Couldn't Take It*."

"Can I see?"

"No!" Bella scolded. "Now close your eyes. I ain't finished yet."

She expertly glued on a set of Star Glow fake lashes and used the grease pencil to delicately line his eyes. Then, with a tiny eyeshadow brush, she gave his lids a bit of Garbo shade and mystery. "Always use two colors from the same family," she said. "I'm using Maybelline's ashcake and smoky mountain."

When she was finished, she popped open the Evening in Paris powder tin and lightly dusted his whole face. Then she picked the grease pencil back up and beauty-mark-dotted the tender jowl of his left cheek. "Another fucking masterpiece," she whispered. *Thank you, Terelli Lombardi.* "Now, let's pick out a hairdo and dress."

"Can I wear the cobalt Elsa Schiaparelli we picked up in New York City?"

"That'll go real nice with the blond bob you got in there."

"And my Aris Allen black satin T-strap d'Orsay dance shoes."

Ten minutes later Dino stood in front of a full-length mirror. The woman staring back at him was the most beautiful creature he had ever seen. "Holy shit!" he exclaimed. "I'm beautiful!"

"You're simply stunning!"

He started to cry.

Bella was immediately at his side, waving a handkerchief. "Don't do that! You'll ruin your makeup!"

When Dino was done dabbing, he took Bella's hands in his, tears of gratitude standing in his star-lashed eyes. "How can I ever repay you?"

ARRIVEDERCI PER SEMPRE, MIEI CARI!

As THE DUESENBERG IDLED in the porte cochere, Bella said her goodbyes. First she gave Melvin a tender kiss. "I'm gonna miss you," she whispered.

The goon leaned in and kissed her cheek. "Parting is all we know of Heaven and all we need of Hell," he whispered back.

"I don't get it."

"It's from Emily Dickinson."

"I don't know her."

"Please don't leave me, Bella," Dino said when she hugged him. He was sporting a little beaded cocktail number under a Slim Jenny car coat and an auburn upswing. His makeup was done to perfection. "I love youse with all of my cold, cruel heart," he said.

"I will only ever love Francis Anthony Mozzarelli," Bella replied. "That's it." She took off her vulgar wedding ring and slid it onto her husband's manicured finger. "Don't forget about the annulment."

"I'll phone the pope first thing in the morning."

Bella looked at Dino's beautiful face. He looked relaxed and happy. She was happy too.

"I lied when I said you gave me nothing," she said. "You gave me an awful lot, my friend. You loaned me money so I could make my magic meatballs. You gave me dozens of beautiful roses and wonderful gifts. And when I had nowhere to go, you took me in." Bella gave him a lipsticked kiss on his beauty-marked cheek. Then she blended it into his blush. "Thank you," she said. "And thanks for the swell car too!"

Dino's eyes welled up. "If you ever need anything else, anything at all, you know who to call."

"I do, Olive!"

Dino started to cry.

"Stop that!" Bella gave him a final hug. "You'll be okay without me. Just remember, less is more." She gave his hand a firm squeeze. "Be good to Lena Horny. She really loves you."

"I know."

"And be good to little Jerry." Bella grabbed the faux-fur lapel of Dino's car coat. "If you lay a hand on that kid, I'll hunt you down like a dirty whore and fuck you up real good." She tossed Melvin a big wink. "That's from Belladonna Marie Donato!"

"Where you goin', Missus?" Jerry asked Bella as she planted a kiss on the top of his head.

Bella crouched down in front of the kid. "Are you gonna be okay without me?"

The boy flashed her his butter-bean smile. "Don't you worry, Missus. You ain't seen the last of ole Jerry."

After Bella got into her snazzy new car, she blew Dino, Melvin, and Jerry a big kiss.

The three of them waved goodbye.

As the Duesenberg swooped down the long driveway, Bella tasted the truth for the first time in her life, and it tasted fucking delizioso!

"Arrivederci per sempre, miei cari!" she cried as the car raced along Upper Mountain Avenue. "Francis Anthony Mozzarelli, here I come!" she hollered into the wind as she barreled toward the only real home she had ever known.

Bella's Best Eggplant Parmigiana

Dino Montebologna's favorite dish.
(Melvin Marzorati loved it too.)

3–4 luscious eggplants, each roughly the size of a ticking time
    bomb (or a small baby); they must be a deep purple with a
    glossy sheen and firm (they should make a nice drummy
    sound when you flick them with your thumb)

2 (maybe more) cups homemade breadcrumbs, well seasoned to
    taste (don't be stingy but don't overdo it) with grated Pecorino
    cheese, salt, pepper, garlic powder, chopped fresh Italian
    parsley, dried oregano, dried basil, and chili flakes

fresh whole-milk mozzarella (at least 2 balls), grated

2 farm-fresh eggs

1–2 cups flour

1 cup (maybe more) olive oil

1 cup fresh grated Pecorino cheese

salt and pepper to taste

4 cups homemade tomato gravy (see Big Betty LoMonico's Tomato
    Gravy recipe)

1. Wash and cut off tops and bottoms off your eggplants. Then,
with a potato peeler, slice stripes of skin off, top to bottom.
Slice your eggplants longways. Make slices about a half-inch
thick (no more). Salt and place the slices in a colander to drain
for about an hour. This will bleed any bitterness out of the
slices. It will tenderize and coax the most flavor. Salt works
many miracles here.

2. Heat Big Betty's tomato gravy and set it aside.

3. In three pie plates, set up your dipping station, one with your eggs, beaten well (add ¼ cup water, salt, and pepper); one with flour; and one with your seasoned breadcrumbs. This is the Italian trifecta for frying.

4. Gently rinse and pat dry your eggplant slices. Treat them like you would treat a baby.

5. Heat a generous amount of olive oil in a twelve- to fourteen-inch fry pan on medium heat. Be careful not to overheat or burn the oil. It should be shimmering. Like a lost dream.

6. One at a time, dredge your slices in the flour (shake off excess), then dip them in the egg mixture until evenly coated, then coat evenly with the breadcrumbs, then place them in heated oil. Fry about 2–3 minutes per side, until nice and golden and crisp. When slices are completely fried, place on plated paper towels to absorb some of the grease. Once all of your eggplant slices are fried, ready a ten-by-ten-inch, three-inch-deep casserole dish by coating the bottom with a ladleful of tomato gravy. Lay as many slices as might fit in the dish in a single layer. Cover slices with tomato gravy. Then liberally sprinkle with shredded mozzarella and top with grated cheese. Repeat until you reach the top of the casserole. After a final coating of Big Betty's tomato gravy, cover generously with grated mozzarella cheese and grated pecorino cheese. This will make the top nice and crispy!

7. Bake in a preheated 400-degree oven, covered with foil, for 30 minutes.
8. After 30 minutes, remove foil. Cover the top layer with cheeses and bake for another 10–15 minutes, until top is golden and the casserole is bubbling.
9. Let casserole rest for 10 minutes, then serve while it is still steaming. There is nothing more comforting than a great eggplant parmigiana. Properly made, your eggplant parmigiana will taste like home. It will taste like family.
10. Buon appetito! Mangiare bene! Stare bene! Delizioso!

FORTES FORTUNA IUVAT

FROM THE DAY FRANCIS Anthony Mozzarelli was yanked out from between his mamma's hairy legs, he was like a tender dogwood that had to be carefully watered. By the time he was eight, he was as pretty, as strong, and as fresh as a summer rose blooming.

He was a regular little charm bomb.

"Ain't he fuckin' beautiful?!" Mary Mozzarelli cried to anyone who would listen.

His papa, Xavier Patrizio Mozzarelli, the neighborhood's best barber, called him *ragazzo debole*.

Weak boy.

Then he beat Francis to a pulp to try and toughen the kid up. Especially when the old man was drunk. "You're too close to your fucking mamma!" he yelled as his fists flew, drawing blood. "That old woman's a crazy-assed octopus!" he warned his son. "She's tryin' to strangle the manhood out of you! I won't let her do it!"

Xavier Patrizio brutally beat his boy the night his wife shot the old man dead. The last thing he said before the bullet slugged into his head was, "No son of mine is gonna be a fucking faggot!"

After Mary's husband "disappeared," she took over his Star Barbershop. The old *Octopus vulgaris* slithered in and literally cleaned the shit out of the place. She lined the tonic bottles from tallest to shortest, polished the chrome on all the chairs, and swept every stray hair into the street.

She hung a hand-painted sign over the shop mirror:

A GREAT HAIRCUT GIVES A MAN DIGNITY

She always kept a pot of meatballs simmering in tomato gravy on the old coal-eating stove. She charged a quarter for a shave, fifty cents for a cut, and sixty for both. For an extra dime, she threw in a mugful of meatballs swimming in tomato gravy.

On Mondays, when the shop was closed, she packed a traveling barber bag and clipped the patients at the state mental hospital.

She was not completely without empathy.

Want a great cut and shave? Go see Mary Mozzarelli!

Neighborhood wiseguys lined up. They shrugged into the shop scompigliati and bopped out gleaming with virilità.

Mary loved cutting men's hair. Especially her beautiful son's.

As he grew, Francis tried to be tough. But he had no friends. Only the little Nancy boy his mamma despised.

Terelli Lombardi.

Little Bird, Francis called him.

Tweet! Tweet!

"Stay away from that fucking invert," Mary warned. "Don't make me get my gun, son."

Despite Mary's warning, Francis let Terelli take him under his sissy wing.

"I'm gonna make a real Hero out of you, you'll see."

The little bird taught Francis how to maximize what the good Lord had already given him.

It started with a solid regimen of push-ups and sit-ups. Then a steady routine of lifting rocks and bricks. Then cinderblocks and automobile bumpers.

"How many push-ups did you do today?" Terelli asked when they met to work on hair greasing. "Your mamma's pomade stinks!" He advised him what to wear. "Only T-shirts and blue jeans!" And taught him proper hygiene. "Always wash your dick after working out," the little bird informed him. "And always after you pee. And especially after fucking."

Francis couldn't wait to fuck.

"If you insist upon poking your penis into girls, stop cuffing your jeans," Terelli said. "Keep your thumbs hooked in your belt loops and strut when you walk. No swishing," he insisted. "Walk like your mamma. I'll bet that woman's got a massive cannoli dangling between her hairy legs!"

Francis liked cuffing his pants. He was powerfully proud of the way his hips swung like church bells when he walked around. No one sauntered along like Francis Anthony Mozzarelli. He swung and strutted like he didn't have a care in the goddamned world. Like he owned the entire universe.

No one owned him.

Except maybe his crazy old octopus of a mamma.

"Well, I tried!" Terelli cried.

The little bird took Francis to the Montauk Theater in downtown Passaic and showed him Clark Gable. "You see the way that man carries himself."

"Like a gangster," Francis whispered in the movie-toned dark.

"Like a man on a masculine mission," Terelli whispered back.

Even though Francis was fascinated by the way Clark charmed Carole Lombard and manhandled Joan Crawford and Constance Bennett, he was unconvinced. For his part, he taught Terelli how to cheat at cards, win at marbles, and toss a mean bocce ball.

They practiced smoking and drinking and occasionally kissing.

"It's called *Frenching*," Terelli declared when Francis jumped back after tasting his little bird's tongue. "Trust me! The girls will love it!" Terelli insisted.

They did.

And it always led to other delicious things.

Arrivederci, virginity!

Hello, virility!

For the budding young stud's thirteenth birthday, Terelli gave Francis a whopping French kiss and a new pair of penny loafers with dimes wedged into them.

"When you find a coin, stick it in heads-up, make a wish, and think of me," the little bird teased. "Tweet! Tweet!"

When Francis turned fourteen, Terelli introduced him to Loprinzi's Gymnasium.

The sign over the door read:

FORTES FORTUNA IUVAT

"That means fortune favors the brave," Terelli informed his beautiful friend as they entered the masculine heat of the musky place.

A large oil painting of a nude Lorenzo Loprinzi hung on the wall above the front desk.

No fig leaf, only his hands artfully fisted in front of his cannoli.

"Lorenzo was my first love," Terelli whispered with moon-eyed reverence.

Arms akimbo, back arched, the oil-painted strongman's

abdomen was a slab of symmetrical rocks, his legs were as thick as tree trunks, his biceps baseball-popped out of his arms.

"He wrestles cows to the ground for extra exercise," Terelli whispered. "He lifts sheep over his head. He tosses full-grown pigs the way most men toss basketballs."

Francis regarded the painting with stark admiration. "I want to be strong just like him."

Terelli lit a cigarette. "Fortune favors the brave, my pretty friend!"

By the time Francis turned fifteen, he worked out every day. He could bench-press twice his weight without grunting.

"You call that a sit-up?" Terelli barked like an army drill sergeant. "Keep those knees together, soldier!"

By Francis's sixteenth birthday, he had sprouted from a pretty-boy Popeye wannabe into a young Tarzan. His ass alone was breathtaking.

"Simply stunning," Terelli whispered when they kissed.

The little bird knitted him a loincloth and three jockstraps to work out in.

"Simply stunning!"

Francis fucked girls like a steam train piston. He fucked his way through Passaic and Clifton like a runaway locomotive on a funny honeymoon.

Terelli Lombardi was seething with jealousy. "I want you to stop seeing other women."

"What do you mean?"

"I love you, Francis Anthony Mozzarelli. Doesn't that mean anything?"

"Listen, Little Bird," Francis calmly said. "I don't think I need to practice with you anymore."

"Practice?! Is that all I mean to you?! I thought you loved me!"

Francis laughed. "Love you? I don't love anybody."

"Except yourself! You fucking beast!"

After a moment of careful consideration, Francis did what he thought best. "I don't want to see you anymore, my little friend."

"Are you breaking up with me?

"How can I break up with you?! We were never together!"

"Fuck you, Francis Anthony Mozzarelli. I hope you die someday soon!" And with that the little bird flew away.

Standing in front of the long oval mirror on the back of his bedroom door with his dick and balls snugged into one of his little buddy's knitted jocks, Francis raised his arms like Lorenzo Loprinzi. He studied his new physique. The plates in his chest were raised like a suit of armor, his waist was taut and slim, his biceps danced like baseballs when he curled them.

"FranCIS! FranCIS Anthony MozzarELLI!"

Mary Mozzarelli called him to the kitchen table every morning for a Strongman's breakfast of a slab of crisped bacon and a half dozen fried eggs.

They sat at the table together with crowns of garlic around their heads (to honor the dead).

"You're so good to me, Ma," Francis always said.

"Who's my baby?" Mary always responded.

"I am."

"Forever and always?"

"Always and forever!"

The old cephalopod loved to clean her son's cage. She blew away the sand and debris with her siphon, searching the floor for dirty underwear and socks (and knitted jocks). She squeezed through small spaces, trailing her long, pliant arms behind her as she dusted and stripped and refreshed his mattress. At night, she eased his bedroom door open and floated in to watch her gorgeous son sleep.

"Mamma, what are you doing . . .?" Francis whispered as he tumbled through bundles of mixed-up dreams.

A little angel flying.

Fucking the daylights out of an old priest.

Pounding the virginity out of neighborhood girls.

Frenching and fucking Terelli Lombardi.

Hearts expanding.

Muscles growing.

Helping his mamma get rid of his papa's dead body after she killed the old man.

"Careful. Don't wake him," Mary had whispered as they dragged the deadweight down the back porch steps and into the grape arbor.

"What happened to Papa?"

"He's dreamin' sweet dreams," Mary said as she dug her husband's grave.

"But he's bleeding! He's not breathing!"

"That ain't blood! It's tomato gravy!"

The next day a crow the size of a small rooster landed on the fresh grave and sat there for three weeks without moving a feather.

"Shoo, Bisso Galeto!"

It spooked the hell out of Mary the way it just laughed at her. So she shot it.

"FranCIS! FranCIS AnthONY MozzarELLI! Come help your mamma pick grapes!"

"FranCIS! FranCIS AnthONY MozzarELLI! Where the hell were you all day yesterday?"

Over time, Francis had trouble keeping his mamma, that slippery old octopus, from wrapping her eight arms around him. He felt like she was trying to squeeze him to death. Polpo femmina. Eyes never missing a trick. Toes the color of the ocean.

Blood copper-rich. Three hearts beating. One monstrous brain. Always obsessed. Always calculating. Always suffocating.

"Who's your best girl?"

"Gypsy Rose Lee!"

"Wrong answer!"

"You are?"

"Bingo! And don't you ever fuckin' forget it!"

"Never ever."

"Your mamma is stone-cold crazy," Terelli used to like to say. Francis missed his little friend. He missed laughing and feeling gay.

"FranCIS! FranCIS AnthONY MozzarELLI!" his mamma called after crisping his bacon and frying his eggs.

Francis knew he had to get away.

FORTES FORTUNA IUVAT

Fortune favors the brave!

At seventeen, he diligently began to plan his escape.

He quit school and got a job at the Charms Candy Factory in shipping and deliveries.

He squirreled his hard-earned cash and thought about nothing but leaving.

He thought about it every second of every day.

While he ate his old lady's greasy meals, while he pumped iron, while he chased neighborhood skirts and delivered his Charms. Even while he masturbated.

Late one evening, while he was pounding his cannoli in front of his bedroom mirror, he didn't hear the door to his room creak open. How long had she been standing there? Watching.

"Ma! Jesus Christ!"

"What the hell are you doin'?"

"It itches."

"Well, stop touchin' it!"

Once a year, a Midwestern carnival trained into town. Francis loved to watch the strongest strongmen in the world, masks over their eyes, lift giant iron balloons into the twinkling sky.

The bravest of the brave!

They were real heroes!

"I want to be just like them!"

FORTES FORTUNA IUVAT

His fortune unfurled in front of him.

The day he turned eighteen, he was packed and ready to leave, but then he met and fucked the best girl in the world, the love of his life, that bombastic and bodacious girl from the Robertson Scale factory.

The day they fucked was the first time he really made love to another human being. The sky cracked open, his world turned upside down, and his heart crooned. It made him want to hold her in his strong arms and fly them all the way to the moon, until the day she told him she never wanted to see him again.

When Francis's crazy mamma got wind of what was happening, when she got a visit from the man-eating puttana and smelled the whore's ripening baby, she set fire to the fucking house and dragged her brokenhearted son away.

"Mamma will take care of her baby. Mamma will take care of everything."

"Bella!" Francis cried in the bed his mamma tucked him into after she rescued him from Coney Island. She was so happy to feed him again, to nurse him back to health and happiness, to have him home with her where he belonged.

> *Lullaby, lullaby, lullaby, ooh,*
> *Who will I give this baby to?*
> *Lullaby, lullaby, lullaby, eee,*
> *I will keep this baby for me . . .*

In his stupor of pain and grief Francis heard Bella singing, *All of Me!*

He felt her tender kisses.

"Take me! Take all of me!" he heard her holler in ecstasy.

He tasted her meatballs. He licked her tomato gravy.

"Who's my baby?" his mamma whispered as she wrapped her tentacles around him and squeezed.

FORTES FORTUNA IUVAT

Fortune favors the brave!

"BELLADONNA MARIE, COME HOME TO ME!" Francis screamed.

HOME IS WHERE
THE HEART IS

WHEN BELLA PULLED UP in front of the old captain's house on
Neptune Avenue, she couldn't believe her eyes. She couldn't
believe it was the same place she had left behind.

Posts splintered, glass broken, shutters hanging,
shingles missing.

The ornamental figurehead poised over the front porch
looked sad and exhausted.

The heart of the house was no longer beating.

As always, the warped front door was open, but the long
breezeway was cold and dank.

"Hello?" Bella called into the musty abyss.

A gruff woman's voice whirled in from the back like a nasty
spirit growling in the wind.

"Who's that? Who's there?"

"It's Bella! It's me!"

A tall lady in a daisied housedress with what appeared to be a beard on her face emerged from the end of the tunneled hall. "How can I help you?"

"I'm Belladonna Marie. I used to live here. Who are you?"

"I'm Henrietta," the woman said, stepping forward with the grace of a professional ballet dancer. "But you can call me Henry."

Bella's heart skipped a beat when she heard the name Henry. It made her think of Billy. "You're Henrietta Maybee the Bearded Lady!"

"Yes. That's me . . ."

"Where is everybody?" Bella asked while shaking the woman's hand. "Where's Chester?"

"The old man's outside. I left him sitting in his chair in front of the elephant's grave."

"Peanut is dead?"

"Yes. The big beast passed away yesterday. I'm afraid the old sea captain's not far behind."

Bella charged through the wreckage of the kitchen where a circle of flies danced above the stove. The sink was piled high with crusty dishes. "Chester?" she called as she made her way across the ragged yard.

She found the old man sitting between the birdless weeping willow and the figless fig tree. Hunched and swaddled in one of his elephant's wool blankets, chin down, he looked like Elvin the Bat Boy or Antoinette the Ant Lady. His skin was the color of old earwax. He had no hair on his veined head. Across from him, a pile of freshly dug dirt rose up next to an elephant-sized mound. Between them was an open hole the length and width of the old man.

"Chester!"

"Bella?" he lifted his bald head and squinted. "Is it really you?"

Of course he was naked under the blanket. His chest was

concave. His eyes were sunken. There was no spark left in the old sparkplug of a man.

"Yes. It's me. Oh, my sweet Chester! I'm so sorry about Peanut."

The old man reeked of grief and decay, but he was smiling. "It's good to see you, Belladonna Marie. Where have you been, my dear? It feels like you've been gone for half a century."

Bella pulled the elephant blanket up over his bony shoulders. "Chester, when was the last time you had something to eat?"

"Eat? I don't eat anymore. I'm being eaten alive, sweetie. The monster of death is feasting within me. Oh, Bella, he's got such sharp teeth. When he first appeared, he only nibbled at my toes a bit. Then he started taking Peanut-sized bites. Now he swallows whole chunks of me without chewing." The old man's chin dropped back down to his ribs. "I'm dying."

He was so light, Bella had no trouble carrying the trembling man into the house.

In the dust-filled living room, she gently tucked him into the frowning couch and gave his scaly head a warm kiss. "Who else is here?" she asked Henrietta.

"It's only Chester and me."

"What about Minnie and Oui Oui and Lolly?"

"They all made a clean break for the southern circus train as soon as summer ended."

"What about Hero? What about Francis?"

"I don't know no Hero. Or anybody called Francis."

With Henrietta's help, Bella set up Chester's bed just off the kitchen. She found an old canister of pastina and a mauled slab of butter. She popped a pot of water on the stove and matched a flame.

After bathing the old man (his skin swirled around his bones like a dead chicken's), Bella tucked him into some fresh bedding. As she spoon-fed him the buttery pasta, his frail ribcage bellowed and wheezed. Every dozen notes or so, he stopped breathing for a moment. Then he coughed and continued eating. When he took in all his expiring body could handle, he nodded off to sleep.

"Chester?" Bella softly said. "Do you know where Hero is?"

The old elephant trainer's eyes fluttered open. "Hero . . . my boy . . . he was always like a son to me . . ."

"What do you mean *was*? Where is he?"

"Hero is . . . gone."

"Gone? What do you mean gone?"

"A little devil of a woman . . . she took him soon after you vanished. I don't know . . . where . . . he . . . is. But I can hear him howling. I hear him crying for . . . you. You must let him know you're here. Let him . . . know . . . you are home . . . and he will . . . come back. I know . . . he will. He could never stay away from you."

"How can I reach him?"

"Make . . . your . . . meat . . . balls," Chester sputtered. "He loved . . . your meatballs so." With a final burst of energy, the old man smiled a radiant smile. Then he closed his eyes and permanently drifted out to sea.

Henrietta sobbed as they carried the body out of the house.

As they lowered Chester into his fresh grave, a crazy wind kicked up leaves and debris and the whole world turned gray. The fig and the willow trees bucked and swayed. Thunder rumbled and a light rain rashed down as Bella shoveled the pile of loose dirt back into the ground.

Once the ground was patted down, Henrietta marked both graves with two slabs of flat stone upon which she scrawled,

HERE SNORES CHESTER
THE OLD SEA CAPTAIN'S SWEET SOUL
IS FINALLY BOBBING OUT TO SEA

HERE TRUMPETS OUR BELOVED
PEANUT
FINALLY FREE

As the storm closed in, Bella sent her to Major Markets Prime Meats with cash and a long list of ingredients.

The wind started to rage and a wild rain fell as Bella cleaned the kitchen.

When Henrietta returned with the goods, Bella immediately called upon the holy helping hands of her Cooking Spirit.

"Francis!" she hollered as she fried garlic and milled tomatoes. "Francis! Oh, Francis!" she sang up to the heavens as she mixed ground beef with eggs, parsley, garlic, and grated cheese. "Francis, my Hero!" she hollered as she rolled the balls, fried them, and dropped them into a big pot of her burbling tomato gravy. "Francis Anthony Mozzarelli," she chanted. "Come home to me!"

Bella's pleas went up with the savory scent of her meatballs like flares over a shipwreck.

Meatballs saved my life once!

And someday they're gonna save yours too!

The heart of the house started beating again.

The radio snapped on and started playing,

All of Me!

In Mary Mozzarelli's house in Seaside Heights, Francis sat bolt upright in his boyhood bed. "Bella . . ." he whispered.

Francis Anthony Mozzarelli! Come home to me!

Behind the old house in Coney Island, an enormous bolt of lightning struck the ground between Peanut's and Chester's graves.

The radio in the living room stopped playing.

All the bulbs in the house exploded.

The lid sailed off the tomato gravy.

The world was pitch-dark.

Henrietta ran to a window. "The whole town is dead! It's a blackout!" she cried.

Bella lit a couple of hurricane lamps and purposefully stirred her meatballs.

As the gravy simmered for a few hours, she coolly cleaned the house. Then she serenely set the kitchen table for three.

"Who's coming?" Henrietta asked.

"You'll see."

As the world squalled and howled around them, Bella and Henrietta sat at the kitchen table in front of a bundle of flickering candles and waited.

"I'm scared," Henrietta whispered. "Hurricane season is over!" she sobbed. "This shouldn't be happening!"

"There's nothing to be afraid of."

Suddenly there was a rough pounding on the front door.

Henrietta dove into the broom closet, slammed it closed, and tried desperately to lock it. "Don't answer it!" she cried.

"Who is it?" Bella yelled.

"It's me!" came the strong reply. "It's Francis Anthony Mozzarelli!"

Bella ran down the breezeway and pulled open the door.

Another murderous bolt of lightning turned night into day and illuminated the recovered figure of Bella's Hero, her Coney Island King, Francis Anthony Mozzarelli in all his glory.

"Francis! Oh, Francis! You've come home to me!"

When their lips locked, they tasted each other's pain. They tasted their undying love for each other. They tasted everything.

"What's happening?!" Henrietta screamed behind the closed closet door.

The radio snapped back on and started playing "Happy Days Are Here Again."

"What's happening out there?" Henrietta frantically called from her hiding place.

As Francis and Bella continued kissing, the entire town of Coney Island sprang to life. Every heart in Luna Park electrified, the mechanical horses jumped out of their Steeplechase gates, the boardwalk roller coasters flew off their tracks, the carousels spun, the Wonder Wheel whirled, fireworks lit up the night sky, the illuminated moon took on the Glasgow-grinning face of Steeplechase and it started singing,

All of Me!

Belladonna Marie Donato's Magic Meatball Recipe

Inherited from Big Betty LoMonico,
who inherited it from
her big mamma Claudia Signorelli.

Especially useful
if you need to conjure
or resurrect someone.

Good for any miracle you may need.

2 pounds fresh ground beef (the better the beef, the better
the balls)
2 eggs, beaten
1½ cups breadcrumbs (preferably from a good Italian bread)
1 cup grated Pecorino Romano or Parmesan cheese
3–4 garlic cloves, minced (Bella was generous with this)
½ cup Italian parsley, chopped
¼ cup fresh milk
a fair amount of quality olive oil, for frying
a nice big pot of tomato gravy (Big Betty LoMonico's recipe)

1. Place all the ingredients in a large bowl (preferably one
    that has tremendous sentimental value). Throw in your
    deepest desires. Toss in your heart's dream. Add a pinch
    of passion. Remember to breathe.
2. Mix all ingredients together in a bowl with hands. Honor
    all of your cooking ancestors while you do. Call upon
    the holy hands of your Cooking Spirit to assist you. Give

voice to your desires and dreams while you work. Ask God and the universe for what you need.

3. Form meat mixture into one- to one-and-a-half-inch (golf-sized) balls. Sing a favorite song or two while you do. (Bella highly recommends "All of Me.")

4. Fry the balls in a pan of extra-virgin olive oil heated on medium heat (test it with a small bit of meat, it should sizzle nicely). Turn the balls gently to brown all sides. Blow a kiss to your mamma and to Belladonna Marie Donato while they sear, locking in all that delicious flavor, all your hopes, your desires, your needs, and your dreams.

5. Drop the fried balls into a big pot of tomato gravy (see Big Betty LoMonico's recipe) and let simmer for at least an hour. Take some time to dance around the kitchen while the magic happens.

6. When the meatballs and gravy are finished cooking, thank your Cooking Spirit, thank Big Betty, and thank Belladonna Marie Donato.

7. Eat a nice, big bowlful or serve them with your favorite pasta topped with grated fragrant pecorino or a nice, sharp Locatelli cheese. Then wait for your prayers to be answered and for all of your dreams to come true!

8. Buon appetito! Mangiare bene! Stare bene! Delizioso!

I HAVE SOMETHING TO TELL YOU

IN THE KITCHEN THE next morning, Francis found Bella at the stove, cracking eggs into a large skillet. Coffee blurped on the stove as he took a seat. When she brought the food to the table, she kissed him and sat down across from him.

"I have something to tell you," she said.

Francis listened as Bella told him what she couldn't tell him back at the Half Moon Hotel after they were crowned King and Queen. She closed her eyes and tried to keep her mamma's blade at bay while she recounted what her papa had the doctor do to her after she brought their son into the world.

"The scar under your belly?"

"Yes."

"Son of a bitch!" Francis wailed and bawled like a baby.

"I have something else to tell you," Bella said.

As Francis sobbed into her breast, she told him about Joe

showing up the morning of their wedding day. She told him about Joe taking her to see their baby. She told him about how she held their son in her arms. About how she almost didn't recognize him. About his pretty life. The perfect house. The sweet woman and her sweet-smelling cupcakes. "I heard my papa call me a whore. I felt dirty and disgusting. I thought, *What kind of mamma can I possibly be*?" She told him about leaving their son and running away. "I couldn't come back to Coney Island and face you. I had to leave you. I had to leave everybody." She told him about her marriage to Dino (she left out Dino's cross-dressing and fucking Melvin Marzorati). "I thought if I ran far enough away, all my crazy thoughts and feelings would disappear. But they didn't. They followed me. They chased me down and wrestled me to the ground. They almost killed me. Francis. Oh, Francis. Can you ever forgive me?"

Francis took a deep, Heroic breath. Then he cradled Bella in his arms. "Of course I forgive you, my Queen. I love you, Bella. I always have. I always will." He hugged her and kissed her. "It's all over now. We're alive. And we're together," he said. Then he leveled a strong gaze at her. "I have something to tell you too."

"What is it, my King?"

"We're gonna go and get our son. And the three of us are gonna be a happy fucking family. Together. Forever."

Amen.

A DREAM IS A WISH YOUR HEART MAKES

When Bella and Francis pulled up in front of the house in Nutley, New Jersey, they both saw the SOLD sign spiked in the overgrown grass at the same time. The windows of the little Cape Codder were shaded. The awnings and screen door were missing. The bushes looked like they were teased into oblivion. Everything was in desperate need of a good trimming.

"They're gone!" Bella cried.

Francis busted open the front door and sniffed around the house. "He was in here. I can smell him!"

"I can smell him too," Bella whispered.

They learned the name of the family, but they couldn't find out where the couple had moved. None of the neighbors were able to help. Not the realtors. Not the government. Not God. Not anyone.

But that didn't stop them.

They didn't eat.

They didn't sleep.

They had to find their baby.

Even Joe helped. He showed up in his truck and he and Francis drove from lead to lead like the Hardy Boys in *Hunting for Hidden Gold*, flashlights clenched between their teeth. They traveled all over North Jersey.

As they hunted for his son, Francis and Bella renovated the old captain's house in Coney Island. Chester had provided a generous endowment for Henrietta. He also left a large stash of cash and the house to Hero, *who has been like a son to me.*

"This will be our home! Forever!" Francis cried.

He and Bella worked side by side, turning the place into a beautiful nest for their little family.

After painting Chester's master suite, they installed a brand-new Orthoflex mattress set. Bella lovingly made up the fresh bed with the satin sheets Chester had gifted her.

"Thank you, Captain!"

For the living room, they purchased an electric-blue horse-hair couch and matching burgundy armchairs.

They offered Henrietta the Strongman's old room, but she left to join the southern circus train.

"Now that Chester is gone, there's nothing left for me here," she told them.

In Bella and Minnie's old suite, they papered the walls with a circus print of clowns tumbling like Oui Oui. They wheeled in a new crib and dresser and raided the Coney Island games of chance for a zoo of stuffed animals. They filled the drawers with toddler clothes.

In the kitchen, they papered the walls with a fresh pattern of crosshatched cherries. Bella hung festive curtains Lulu made for them. White lace trimmed with plastic fruits that clacked against each other when the ocean breezes rustled in. Francis yanked out the old icebox and installed a brand-new Crosley Shelvador with more usable space, faster freezing, and quick-release ice cube trays. A brand-spanking-new, Cooking Spirit–friendly Wedgewood Estate stove was delivered and hooked up. After cinching in a new sink, they mopped and waxed the new Kentile linoleum until it was buffed and shining.

When the two of them were done with their nesting, Bella cooked a glorious meal of homemade spaghetti and meatballs and chicken parmigiana.

After they finished eating, Francis filled a teakettle. He slapped it on the stove, snapped on a flame, and grabbed a bowl from the breakfront in the dining room. Then he sat Bella in one of the horsehair chairs and removed her shoes. When the water was properly warmed up, he gently poured it over her feet. Then he washed them. Tenderly. A Coney Island King honoring his Steeplechase Queen. After he lovingly kissed each toe, he pecked his way up her legs and ravished her whole body.

"I will love you forever, my little Angel Queen!"

They did nothing but have sex and eat and sleep for an entire week.

On the seventh day, Bella retrieved the recipe she had snatched from her mamma's hidden cigar box, called upon her Cooking Spirit, and cooked Tino Scarabino's favorite dish, a delectable tomato-topped casserole of breaded chicken pieces baked over stewing potatoes and onions.

After the oven timer rang, Francis and Bella drove the casserole all the way to the house at the Robertson Scale factory in Clifton, New Jersey. When they walked into the kitchen, Bella's papa stood up.

"What the hell are you doing here?"

"You must be Bella's old man!" Francis said.

It was the wild monster from Manny's nightmares! The bombastic Orcolat! The old man's cheek scar twitched uncontrollably as he backed away.

"Who the hell are you?" Manny's voice was hoarse and thin.

"I'm Francis Anthony Mozzarelli!"

"This is the papa of my baby!" Bella declared to her entire family. "He loves me! And I love him!"

"I thought the baby's papa was Jesus," Luigi said.

"He is," Lulu whispered.

Francis Anthony Mozzarelli stepped up to Manolo Antonio Donato. "We're gonna find our son, sir. The grandson you gave away. We're gonna find him and we're gonna be a happy family."

The two bulls stood toe to toe, Hero the Strongman and Manolo Antonio Donato.

"It's your fucking funeral, guaglio," Manny sneered. "You can have the whore if you want her. But don't expect me to give you my blessing."

With all the strength Francis could muster, he hauled off and clocked Manny across his scarred kisser and the old man hit the floor.

"That's for what you did to your daughter, you fucking son of a bitch! That's *my* blessing!"

"Papa!" Little Luigi cried.

The boy ran to make sure his papa was still breathing.

"He's just knocked out," Francis said. "He'll be alright."

As Luigi and Lulu tended to their papa, who was slowly coming to, Tony stepped up to Francis and punched his boxing gloves together. "That was some left hook! How long have you been boxing?"

Luigi ran over to Bella and grabbed her hand. "Bellamamma, I have something to show you," he whispered.

The boy pulled Bella into the dining room. He dragged a chair over to the sideboard, climbed on top of it, and removed Tino Scarabino's painting of the Sicilian sea from the wall. Behind it was a hole the size of shoebox. He reached deep inside it and pulled out the old lunch stand cigar box. Then he jumped back down to the floor and presented it to his sister.

"It's all here. The picture of the pretty ladies, the hair, and every cent you made selling your meatballs. I took it because I didn't want you to leave. I'm sorry."

"Thank you, Meatball."

"You're welcome, Bellamamma."

"I love you, Meatball."

"I love you too."

After bringing Francis into Lucia's room and introducing him, Bella fed her mute mamma the baked chicken. As she forked the food into the woman's mouth, she told her the incredible story of her adventures in Coney Island, her marriage to Dino, and her glorious reunion with Francis Anthony Mozzarelli.

After her last bite, the old woman's eyes filled with tears, and she spoke for the first time in over ten years. "Do you love him?" she hoarsely croaked.

"Mamma! You spoke!"

Bella hadn't heard her mamma utter a word since she was seven. She was flying over jeweled waves again, catching the sun with her hands.

"Yes," Bella said through tears of joy. "I love him."

"Does he love you?" Lucia whispered.

"He washes my feet."

Lucia smiled. "Tino used to do that for me."

Bella took the rosary beads from around her neck and placed them back where they belonged. Then she placed the old photograph of Lucia and Tino in her mamma's hand. "I love you, Mamma," she said.

"Where's the lock of hair?" the woman asked before she went all silent again.

At the dining room table, Luigi, his old homemade coonskin cap on his head, sat between Bella and Francis. Lulu beamed across from them. Next to Lulu sat Tony.

"Hat off at the table," Manny said to his coonskin-capped son.

Joe, who couldn't stop smiling, plated some chicken for his oldest daughter, Shirley. "Aunt Bella made this for us," he said. "Isn't it delicious?"

Connie, who was busy breastfeeding their new baby, a second little girl they named Joan, looked at Bella and said, "It's good to have you home again. I mean it."

Manny was stone-cold silent, but the rest of the family was full of so many questions.

"Did you really live in Coney Island?"

"Did you get to eat all the cotton candy you wanted?"

"Tell us about the elephant again!"

As soon as he finished eating, Manny got up to leave.

"Wait a minute, Mr. Donato." Francis stood up and faced the old man. "In front of you, in front of the whole family, I would like to formally ask your daughter to marry me."

Connie gasped.

Joe dropped his face in his hands.

Lulu yelped with glee.

Luigi cheered. "Holy moly!"

All Manny said was, "She's already married."

"That's all been taken care of, sir. She's as free as a bird."

Francis walked over to Bella and dropped to one knee.

"I'm gonna do it right this time."

He reached into his pocket, pulled out a small jewel box, opened it, and presented her with a fat (almost vulgar) diamond ring.

Connie gasped again.

Lulu screamed.

"Holy cow!" Luigi cried. "Look at the size of that thing! It's bigger than my biggest aggie!"

Bella's legs turned to jelly. She was having trouble breathing. The scar across her abdomen clenched and screamed. It all seemed too good to be true. She could see Lucia's knife glinting. Ocean water was rising. Was she having another fever dream? Was Mary Mozzarelli going to appear and gun her down? Was she going to wake up dead or drowning in the sea?

"Belladonna Marie Donato," Francis said, beaming. "In front of God and your whole goddamned family, Belladonna Marie Donato, will you marry me? Can we be a happy family?"

The Donato family watched as Bella's entire life reeled away from her at breakneck speed.

Papa! Catch me!

She was up in the air, flying above the ocean, flying in Heaven.

When she landed in front of Francis, her hands were in his. A beautiful smile was playing on his holy lips.

"Yes, Francis Anthony Mozzarelli! I will marry you! I will marry you and we will be a happy family."

Everyone applauded and cheered. Everyone except Manny Donato, who walked out of the room and disappeared.

Lucia Cicolina's
Sicilian Baked Chicken

Tino Scarabino's favorite dish.

Delicious enough to
break someone's heart-sworn silence.

2 large bone-in chicken breasts

2 nice-sized russet potatoes

1 large sweet onion

1 egg

dash of milk (or water), for the egg when scrambled

1 can plum tomatoes

plain breadcrumbs

salt

pepper

red chili flakes

fresh-grated pecorino cheese

fresh Italian parsley

dried oregano

dried basil

garlic powder

olive oil

1 tablespoon butter

1. Prepare chicken by taking off the skin and any small stray bones (such as rib bone bits). Think about a long-lost love, one that broke your heart, while you do this.

2. Prepare breadcrumb mixture, enough to coat both breasts

well (at least a full cup or so), by adding garlic powder, dried oregano, dried basil, chopped fresh parsley, chili flakes, grated cheese to taste, a healthy pinch of salt, and several grinds of pepper. Revisit the love of your life while you do this.

3. Beat one egg, adding a dash of milk (or water), some salt, and pepper. Remember everything lovely about your lost lover while you do this.

4. Wash and peel the potatoes, then cut them into long quarters. Continue to think about the wonderful love you left behind.

5. Slice the onion into thick rounds and cut them in half. Blow your lost lover a kiss. Try not to cry while you do this. (Hold an unlit match between your teeth to keep from crying.)

6. Place potatoes and onion in bowl. Drizzle them with olive oil. Add spices (oregano, basil, salt, pepper, chili flakes, garlic powder, and fresh parsley to taste). Mix and place in a casserole dish. Revisit the first time you and the love of your life made love while you do this.

7. Dip chicken breasts in egg mixture one at a time, then coat them with the breadcrumb mixture. While you do this, imagine making love to the love of your life all over again. As you go through the next several steps of this recipe, do it like you are making love for the first time again.

8. Place breasts, meat side up, over potatoes and onions.

9. Open can of plum tomatoes. Pull out whole tomatoes, reserving the juice for later.

10. Crush with hands and gently place all over top of chicken.

11. Sprinkle the top with salt, pepper, oregano, and basil, and drizzle with a little olive oil.

12. Dot the top with some butter.

13. Carefully pour liquid from tomato can down the insides of casserole dish so it rests in the bottom. Add a half cup of water or so too. Enough so that when you tilt the casserole, you can see some of the juice.

14. Place lid on top. Your casserole dish should be large and deep enough so that when you place the lid, it covers everything (you must close it completely).

15. Bake in the middle of a preheated oven at 350 or 375 degrees for an hour and a half to two hours. Let your broken heart rest while it cooks.

16. Take the lid off and bake for another 15–20 minutes. Liquid should be bubbling up around chicken. The top should be browned a bit. Check on it. Watch it. Don't overcook it.

17. After you slide it out of the oven, let sit for at least 10 minutes. Hold your broken heart in your hands.

18. Serve to family and loved ones. Share all of your broken-hearted memories and aching feelings along with it and watch as a miraculous healing happens!

19. Buon appetito! Mangiare bene! Stare bene! Delizioso!

A BIG BANG THEORY

FOUR DAYS AFTER HER only son announced he was going to marry the love of his life and they were going to find their bastard baby and be a happy family, Mary Mozzarelli sat on the edge of his abandoned bed in Seaside Heights like a sack of rotten sea urchins and bitterly sucked down the last of her unfiltered Pall Malls. Ever since the day Francis had hit her with the horrible news, burning tobacco had been her only form of nourishment.

"I love her, Mamma! I'm so goddamned happy!" he had said.

After he handed her the wedding invitation, Mary slapped him. She hit him so hard he dropped to the floor and the specter of her dead husband swooped in and applauded.

"See what you made me do!" Mary yelled.

"Mamma!"

"You're lucky I didn't shoot your balls off! I should have killed that dirty little whore when I had the chance! If you marry her, I'll kill YOU! I swear I will!"

"Mamma! Please!"

"I love you, Francis! Nobody will ever love you like I do! NOBODY! YOU'RE MY BABY!"

When she said this, Francis laughed uproariously. He spit into her face. Then he grabbed her and shook her like a broken gumball machine. "What the fuck do you know about love, old woman?! You don't fuckin' know what love is! You never did!"

The last thing Francis said to his devastated mamma before leaving her forever was, "If anything ever happens to Bella, I'll fucking kill you and bury you back in the goddamned grape arbor next to my papa!"

Sitting in her son's room with the crumpled wedding invitation in her trembling hands, with the ashes from her cigarette dropping onto an old pair of Francis's penny loafers, scuffed and penniless, Mary Mozzarelli stared at the nautical-patterned wallpaper in front of her.

The little boats frolicking in the waves looked like they were sailing away.

On top of the tall dresser opposite the bed, anchored among the dust balls, was a half-empty bottle of Carino! (*Italian Toilet Water for Men*). Next to the Carino! was a woman's red cloche hat with a couple of rooster feathers poking out of it. *Where the hell did this come from?* A photo clipped from the *Brooklyn Daily Eagle* capturing the Queen and King of Coney Island was tucked in the satin band around the brim.

Mary snatched the picture. She stared at the defiant face floating next to her son's, the victory rolls of voluptuous hair, the vulgar bathing costume, the dancing eyes, the disgusting tits, and the full, painted Gioconda lips, smiling and mocking the old woman.

"Puttana!" Mary cried.

With eagle-eyed precision, she scanned the rest of her son's belongings. The snow globe from Coney Island Francis's papa had bought for him, an ashtray full of subway tokens, and an old rabbit's foot. For good luck.

"Son of a bitch!"

Mary shook the globe and waited for the flakes to settle. Then she slipped the clipped photo into the pocket of her ratty old snowflake-peppered flannel nightgown, placed the cloche hat on her head (uneasy is the head that wears the Queen's crown), marched into her room, and reached into the very back of her closet. There, smothered in an old flour sack, was her gun and a box of greased bullets. She grabbed the bundle and reached in deep. For a hair-raising moment, she felt the full weight of her former marriage in her hand. She dropped the gun and the box of bullets into her handbag, yanked on a pair of her dead husband's old galoshes, grabbed her purse, and left the house without putting on a coat.

After packing an old crate of empty seltzer bottles into the trunk of her car, she rattled all the way to the Ocean County dump. How she got there she didn't know. Alone between the piles of rubbish and refuse, she lined the bottles up on a wobbly old sawhorse. She loaded the gun, stepped seven paces away, turned, and started firing. She obliterated a rusted tin can. She perforated a warped bald tire multiple times. She nicked the hide of a dump cat. She even mauled a rat. She hit everything except what she was aiming at. She had lost her goddamned touch. In a fit, she hurled the gun and empty bullet box into a pile of trash. Then she stormed back to her car.

After a twenty-minute drive, she pulled up in front of Bandini's Meats & Produce in Toms River. From where she idled, she could see the bins of vegetables through the broad plate glass window. Everything looked pretty good. She cut the engine and left the car. As she trudged into the store, the wind almost slapped the hat off her head.

"Fucking whore," she hissed.

The eggplants were big and bulbous, a deep purple, almost black. Real melanzana. She picked two, squeezed and thumped them under the watchful eyes of Edoardo and Generosa Bandini. Who was this old Italian woman in nothing but a nightgown, a crazy church hat ("Look at those goddamned rooster feathers! My mother had one like that!"), and factory galoshes, muttering to herself, "Fucking whore! Fucking whore! Fucking whore!" while picking through their vegetables, thumping and pinching and tossing?

At least the basil was big and leafy. Trucked in from California, the small sign said.

"Big fuckin' deal," Mary spit.

She grabbed a medium onion and five healthy heads of garlic.

After inspecting the day-old bread and slamming it onto the counter like a baseball bat, she had them grind a pound and a half into crumbs. The Parmesan she would grate herself, at home.

"Gimme a quarter-pound wedge," she said. "Without the rind. No monkey business."

She also demanded a pound and a half of fresh ricotta, and a half pound of imported mozzarella di bufala.

She threw four one-pound cans of San Marzano whole plum tomatoes and one industrial-sized tin of Montebologna Olive Oil into her cart. She was sure she could do better than the sweet Italian sausage displayed in Generosa's refrigerated case, but the clock was ticking.

As she was being rung up, she had Generosa toss in a carton of unfiltered Pall Malls.

Edoardo loaded the loose items into an empty banana box and helped her to her car.

Mary was silent. No goodbye. No tip.

Back in the familiar warmth of her Seaside kitchen, she lit a cigarette and unpacked her groceries, taking care to place the empty box on the floor next to the door. With Bella's hat still perched on her head, with the picture of the whore still in the pocket of her nightgown, she diced an onion. She peeled and minced the garlic. She milled the canned tomatoes. In a deep pot, she sautéed the onions and garlic in a liberal helping of olive oil. She added salt, fresh ground pepper, dried oregano, and stirred with a wooden spoon. After adding the tomatoes, she pan-browned the sweet, uncircumcised sausages, giving them a good sear, and threw them into the gravy and stirred some more. She tasted as she stirred but she was off her game. Her anger made her lose her touch. She couldn't really taste anything.

Even so, the walls of the house hummed with appreciation. Somewhere angels sang a gentle refrain of "Mille cherubini in coro."

With the angels serenading, Mary coddled one of the giant eggplants. She held it like a baby. She cooed to it and tickled it under its chin. Then she gently placed it on her cutting board, grabbed a large butcher knife out of its block, tested it with her left thumb, and patted the photo of the whore in her pocket. Then she wacked the head off the piccolo bambino melanzana and ripped the blade across its belly.

After breading and frying the cutlets she'd sliced, she layered them into two deep lasagna pans along with the gravy and the grated mozzarella cheese. Then she slid them into the oven at three hundred and fifty degrees.

While the eggplant parm baked, she washed and set her hair, she ate a healthy slice of chocolate cake, and drew herself a nice, bubbly bath.

Outside, a light snow began to fall from the sky.

Fresh out of the tub, she moisturized and dabbed a bit of

Carino! behind her left ear. She selected a respectable church dress the color of a bare Christmas tree. Then she retrieved the clipping of her son and the puttana from her nightgown and dropped it into her handbag.

One pan of eggplant she covered and placed in the empty banana box by the door, along with a container of extra gravy, a dining setup, and a small shaker of grated Locatelli cheese. The other pan she doled into meal-sized portions and packed them into the icebox for later.

In the mudroom, she yanked her husband's old galoshes over her church shoes. This time she put on a coat. After all, she didn't want to appear crazy.

Snow swirled as her old DeSoto slid along the North Jersey streets.

A ghostly crow the size of a small rooster followed it.

Mary gripped the wheel and proceeded through the fury of flakes at a steady pace. It was the first snow of the season and it was sticking, but she would get where she was going.

She had no choice.

The entrance to Melvin's Elbow Room was on Van Houten Avenue, but Mary went around back to the black metal door next to a set of dumpsters. She ignored the stern warning on the sign and knocked twice. It slowly swung open to reveal a striking green-eyed black boy with teeth like Italian beans.

"I'm here to see the boss," said Mary, cradling the big banana box in her arms.

"What's the password?"

"I got homemade eggplant parmigiana."

Melvin the Meat Grinder Marzorati was sitting at the corner card table thumbing through *The Complete Works of William Shakespeare* when Jerry marched in trailing the determined visitor. No need for introductions. It was the old broad who gave the neighborhood men their greasy haircuts, shaved their faces, fed them stiff meatballs, and plied them with cheap limoncello for bits of information.

"To what do I owe this pleasure, barber lady?" Melvin said.

Mary looked the new capo square in the eye and brought her voice down to the level of conspiracy. "My sainted husband and I helped you fellas run numbers out of the Star Barbershop for years and never asked for a thing."

Melvin held her gaze with no expression.

Neither of them blinked.

"Now I'd like to call in a favor," Mary continued. "For all of my hard work and for my undying loyalty."

"What's in the box?"

"A little somethin' I whipped up to sweeten the deal."

Mary placed the warm bounty on the table in front of him. She unpacked it, unpacked the dining setup, and plated him a generous helping. Then she placed the clipped photo of the puttana and her son in front of the plate.

Melvin picked up the clipping and took a good long look at it. "So dis is Francis," he said to himself. He dropped the clipping and leveled a stern gaze at Mary. "Plenty and peace breeds cowards; hardness ever of hardiness is mother."

"What the fuck did you just say to me?"

"Why don't you tell me what this is all about."

Mary pointed to the picture on the table. "That puttana married your boss and now he's gone. Disappeared. Probably pushin' up daisies or sleepin' with the fishes, maybe . . ."

"He's comfortably retired."

Melvin and Jerry both knew Olive and Lena were merrily swinging their purses together somewhere happy and gay. Provincetown or Key West. Or some other rainbowed place.

Mary smirked. "Rumor has it that puttana stripped your old boss of his manhood."

When Mary saw Melvin's face flinch, she knew she hit pay-dirt. But the immediate flash of anger in the new capo's eyes made her tug in her reel a bit. She shrugged. "It's just a theory," she said matter-of-factly. "That means it's probably just idle gossip."

"I know what the fuck the word *theory* means."

Mary leaned in and whispered, "From what I hear, that puttana broke your heart too. Some of my customers said she ruined you."

Now Melvin shrugged like none of it meant anything. But it did. "Most friendship is feigning, most loving mere folly."

"That feigning bitch is cursed, is what she is!" Mary screamed. "And now she thinks she's gonna marry my mamma-loving son! My Francis!"

Melvin calmly took a bite of the eggplant parmigiana. Then he started crying. As he chewed and sobbed, Mary splayed all her cards on the table. "If you don't kill her, I will."

After the old woman was brusquely shown the door, Melvin spit the eggplant out. "This shit is fuckin' disgustin'," he said as he wiped the tears off his face. He had Jerry toss the rest of the casserole in the garbage. Then Melvin threw Bella's picture in after it and went back to his reading.

The next night Mary's phone rang. The gruff voice on the other end assured her that come the following morning, she'd wake up a happy woman. After wrapping her hair in toilet paper and netting it, she popped the cork off a bottle of champagne, lit a Pall Mall, and raised a toast to her son. Then she climbed into her cranky bed, said a quick prayer, and blew God a grateful kiss.

The explosion that rocked Seaside Heights went down in history as the biggest in the tri-state area (until the Passaic County gas main break of 1963). The flaming hole left in the ground where Mary's house had been was almost big enough to swallow a battleship. As billowing smoke smiled into the night sky, Jerry charged away from the scene of the crime. He sprinted under a large umbrella as bits of eggplant, gravy-crusted shingles, a singed rabbit's foot, a splintered wooden spoon, and several pinches of Mary (tentacles, curlers, a singed cigarette) rained across northern New Jersey.

Bella's flaming hat sailed all the way to Coney Island.

THE BIG DAY

Francis Anthony Mozzarelli and
Belladonna Marie Donato
request the honor of your presence
at their wedding ceremony.

November 14, 1938, at eleven o'clock in the morning.

Saint Anthony of Padua Roman Catholic Church
101-103 Myrtle Avenue
Passaic, New Jersey

Reception to follow at Melvin's Elbow Room
759 Van Houten Avenue
Clifton, New Jersey

After Francis curbed his old jalopy, he briskly strode down Myrtle Avenue. He wasn't thinking about the epic fight he had with his mamma before he left the old woman for good. He wasn't thinking about walking out on her while she wailed his name. He was blissfully unaware that the night before his big day she was violently blown to smithereens.

"Fuck her!" he sang into the cold air. "Fuck that old lady! I never want to see her again!"

The only thing Francis was thinking about was how he was going to tell Belladonna Marie he had finally found their son.

Thanks to a perfume-scented card tucked in a bushy bouquet of fist-sized bloodred roses delivered to the house in Coney Island right after Bella had left for Saint Anthony's.

Dear Bella,

Congratulations upon your pending nuptials.
Here is a little gift to complete your loving family.
You can find your son at the following address:

Mr. and Mrs. Henry Charles Dalaster
1 Cherry Lane
Union City, New Jersey

Best wishes to you and your family always,
Dino "Olive Oil" Montebologna

The sweet-smelling envelope had been sealed with a lipsticked kiss.

"It's all over now!" Francis cried through tears of joy. "We're together! And we're going to be a happy family! Forever!"

As he hustled along the slick sidewalk with the enveloped card clutched in his hand, the clouds above his head turned an ominous gunmetal gray. A glassy snow started swirling down from Heaven. Chilly gusts of wind were blowing. Some autos slowed down to a safe crawl. Others didn't slow down at all. Northern cardinals, tufted titmice, blue jays, and black-capped chickadees raced through the gales to find shelter among the shivering branches of freezing trees. A ghostly-looking black crow the size of a small rooster darted across the white sky.

At the intersection of Main and Oak, an elderly woman wrapped in a wool cloak and carrying a bloated sack of groceries slipped off the curb, but Francis was quick to catch her.

"My Hero!" she said.

She didn't know the half of it.

Francis offered to walk her to her door and gallantly escorted her into her doilied apartment.

"Thank you, young man! What a nice boy you are! Your mamma must be so proud!"

Francis didn't say a thing. He just smiled politely.

The woman insisted on thrusting a dollar bill into his gloved hand. Then she inspected him more closely. She took in his Brylcreemed hair. His bow tie. His sweet lips. His dancing eyes. The color of Christmas in his Christlike cheeks.

"Look at you all dolled up! You look so handsome and so happy!"

"I'm gettin' married today!" Francis said.

"Oh! Congratulations!"

Francis waved Dino's note. "And I found my son too!"

The old woman looked confused. "Oh, that's nice! Good for you!" She thrust another dollar bill into his gloved hand. "For the lucky bride!" she cooed.

Francis gave her a sweet kiss on the cheek. "Thank you, Mamma," he said without thinking.

"Oh, you're gonna make me blush! You have a marvelous wedding!" the lady trilled as he hurried out the door. "And have a wonderful life!" she shouted down the hall after him. "And you be careful out there!"

"Fortes fortuna iuvat!" Francis hollered back to her.

Outside, the frozen pavement was gathering snow. Across the street a couple of rambunctious boys were scraping together handfuls of the stuff and lobbing snowballs at each other.

Francis was thwacked on the back of the head, but he didn't care that it fucked up his hair.

Someday I'm gonna throw snowballs with my son! he thought to himself.

He imagined the two of them Nash Park sledding together in winter weather.

Working out at Loprinzi's Gymnasium.

And playing summer catch in a park in Brooklyn.

"We're gonna do all the things my papa and I never did! I'm gonna teach my son how to be a Hero, just like me! I'm gonna be the best papa the world has ever seen!"

Three blocks away, a snot-freezing wind blew open the doors of Saint Anthony's.

Inside the church sacristy, Bella adjusted her crown and veil.

"What was that noise, Father?"

"It was the good Lord sending His blessing."

Just then a large crow flew in, settled into the holy rafters, and cawed frantically.

Outside, Francis was floating at the corner of Myrtle and Monroe. It was so cold he couldn't feel his hands in his gloves. Where were his feet? He clutched the enveloped card he was holding, looked up at the blustering sky, and thanked God for his great fortune. When he kissed his fingers and made the sign of the cross, the wind snatched the lipstick-stained envelope out of his hand. Without thinking, without looking, he frantically stumbled after it.

It happened so goddamned fast.

In a horrible hair-raising instant, bus number 65, the very same bus that was supposed to take Bella and Lulu to school the morning Bella met Francis, braked and sledded on a pond-sized patch of black ice.

The panicked driver trying to control the out-of-control metal behemoth was sure he saw the face of Jesus, jaw square, a look of horror and surprise in His holy hazel eyes, before it was smacked down to the ground.

"Holy Mother of Christ!"

The young Strongman was tough. An enormously impressive pile of Michelangelo marble. But when the bus juddered over him and spun, every passenger felt the sure-footed Firestone Tires smash and crush him.

The winter birds stopped tweeting.

The crow stopped cawing.

Angels stopped singing.

For a split second, even God stopped breathing.

In the relative warmth of Saint Anthony of Padua church, Bella's heart dropped, and she fainted onto the floor of the sacristy.

COME TO ME, MY MELANCHOLY BABY

AS FRANCIS'S SPLATTERED AND shattered remains were being lifted off the snow-covered street, Father Michael was leaning over Bella in Saint Anthony's sacristy. He removed her sparkling crown and veil and rapidly fanned her face.

"Bella! Bella! Are you okay?!"

Her eyes fluttered open. "Francis . . . where's . . . Francis?"

"He'll be here soon," the young priest soothed. He placed a sacramental chalice filled with sour wine to her trembling lips. "Here, drink some of this."

Bella took a shaky sip.

"Take another swallow. That's it . . ."

Once Bella was fully back in her body, she shuddered and suffered a blast of confusion and paralyzing dismay. "I'm scared, Father," she said as she tried to collect her senses.

"What are you afraid of, my child?"

"I'm terrified I'm gonna run away again. Something strange

is happening. I can feel the wings sprouting out of me."

After taking a moment to think, Father Michael told Bella the story of how he became a priest. "Being in the church meant everything to me. I gave up my layman's life. My family was so proud. I studied so hard. I couldn't wait to serve a congregation. But when the time came for my ordination, I had some serious doubts. As I was about to take my vows, I couldn't open my mouth. I fainted like you just did," he said. "And then I saw God standing over me. I asked Him what I should do, and He spoke just three words."

"What did He say?"

"Fortes fortuna iuvat." Father Michael took Bella's hand in his. "Do you know what that means?"

Bella smiled and saw Francis standing over her. He was waving. He blew her a tender kiss. A tsunami-sized wave of nausea suddenly washed over her like a pound of boiled spaghetti draining. The overwhelming desire to run away reared its ugly head again.

"Fortune favors the brave," she said as she trembled.

"Don't worry, Bella. God and I are here for you."

With or without the Lord, the two of them waited for Francis in the church for hours. Even after Bella's family and Mrs. Concannon left, they waited and waited.

"Of course that stinkin' stunad's not gonna show up," Manny had said before he walked out. "No one wants to marry a whore. Especially in God's house."

Bella and Father Michael waited until the sun disappeared behind the church bell tower, until the candles at the base of the Christ painting burned down.

When the bells in the tower tolled seven times, a stammering police officer came in and told them that the snowstorm had killed Francis Anthony Mozzarelli.

Bella laughed.

Even when she saw his mangled body on the table at the morgue, she refused to believe it was true.

"That's not him," she insisted. "He would never have flown to Heaven without me." She laughed again. She laughed uproariously. Then she dropped to the floor and started screaming. She threw herself onto the ravaged corpse and howled like an Italian widow at a Sicilian funeral. "Take me with you!" she screamed. "Francis Anthony Mozzarelli! Take me with you! Please!"

MAMMA, CAN YOU HEAR ME?

THE ONE PERSON BELLA needed more than anyone after Francis was buried, after the cold ground devoured him, even more than her silent mamma, was her too-proud papa.

Papa! Catch me!

She needed Manolo Antonio Donato to hold her and tell her everything was going to be okay.

She didn't want the papa who beat her and kicked her while she begged for mercy.

She didn't want that papa.

Not the one who slaughtered pigs as punishment.

Not the one who butchered her belly and gave her baby away.

Not the one who called her *a whore* and *a disgrace*.

Her heart beat back to the sweet papa who tossed her in the air over the ocean waves.

Papa! Catch me!

Her heart howled back to the sun-kissed afternoons her papa was busy in his garden, tilling, pruning, plucking, and crooning along with his old wind-up Victrola,

All of Me!

Her heart danced back to the time she caught him waltzing among his prizewinning tomatoes, chin to the sun, having some fun. Who was that in his arms? Was it a ghost? Or was it Santa Lucia?

Papa, Can You Hear Me?

For days, Bella wandered around the house in Coney Island, clutching one of Francis's shirts. She hugged it and bawled like a baby. She wailed from the bottom of her wounded belly. She sat in front of their rotting wedding cake.

Across from her sat the ghost of Francis.

Behind him appeared the specter of another young man in a bow-tied suit, a bouquet of brilliant white roses in one hand, a suitcase in the other. A visitation from the future . . .

Do you know who I am?

The young man's resemblance to Francis was striking.

Halos wreathed both their heads as they shimmered in front of her.

They were smiling.

"Can you forgive me?" Bella asked both of them. "Can you ever forgive me?"

For what?

"For everything."

She ignored the house phone ringing.

She ignored the knocking on the windows.

"Bella!" Joe called from the front porch. "Are you in there?"

"Bella!" Lulu yelled at the kitchen door.

Hurry! The bus is coming!

Even Father Michael showed up to try and see if she was okay.

Upstairs, in her baby's nursery, Bella stood over the empty crib. She lifted one of the toy animals and held it to her breast.

It's all over now! We're alive! And we're together!

And we're going to be a family!

Bella collapsed onto the floor of the nursery. She wailed and sobbed and screamed until her grief made her throat bleed, until she was unable to utter another sound.

Mamma, can you hear me?

Recipe for a Great Depression

This is an extremely dangerous recipe.
Often passed down
from generation to generation,
it is one that needs to be handled
with ladles of
unconditional love,
empathy,
and understanding.

1 cup horrible thoughts (when profound sorrow is added,
  these will multiply like fleas)
1 swirling gallon of supreme sadness
6 tablespoons of searing self-doubt (more if needed)
a pound or three of paralyzing grief
a flurry of ghostly memories
a mass of confusion
1 cement sack full of overwhelming exhaustion
buckets and buckets full of never-ending darkness

1. Let the mind dwell only on horrible things.
2. Marinate in self-doubt and paralyzing grief.
3. Give yourself over to swirling sadness. Completely.
4. Avoid all people except ghosts. Absolutely no human beings.
5. Draw all the curtains. Close all the blinds.
6. No eating.
7. No drinking.

8. Only sleep.
9. Give in to overwhelming exhaustion (until your whole body feels hard and heavy).
10. Give yourself over to never-ending darkness until you can't see or breathe.
11. Lose your ability to speak.
12. Let go of any will to live.
13. Only think about dying.
14. Barricade yourself in the house.
15. Never leave.

THE RESCUE, PART ONE

Coney Island in winter was its own kind of wonderland. The skeletal gray of early December hung over the snoozing carnival like a death shroud, but it was still alive. Its hibernating heart was still beating, keeping its frozen spirit flying and singing. Gulls still screeched. ("Where is everybody? Where is everybody?") They still searched and pecked for scraps along the boards, but all they found were orphan nails and loose splinters. The endless ocean jelly-waved along the shoreline of the vast beach, empty except for the occasional upside-down Coke bottle, broken shell, or ripped candy wrapper flapping in the stiff breeze. Who was that walking on the hard sand? A queer little man, bundled against the elements, pulling an old Radio Flyer wagon loaded with tinkling antiques, a frantic green dot of an exotic bird flapping around his head.

At the venerable old house on Neptune Avenue, the hall phone rang off the hook for weeks and weeks. Occasionally someone rapped at a door or window. Panicked family and friends still came from as far away as New Jersey.

"Hello!"

"Anybody home?"

"Bella!?"

"Is she even in there?"

"I don't think so . . ."

But she was.

In bed.

Not dreaming.

Not speaking.

Just like her mamma.

Mute and depressed.

And waiting.

For her body to stop breathing.

For her Coney Island heart to stop beating.

Ocean waves of sorrow and grief lapped at the stale sheets.

An impatient ghost hung over everything.

Swirling around and whispering . . .

Belladonna Marie! Come home to me!

Dino's vased roses on the entry table were long dead, the stems bowed down, the blooms dry and brown.

The wedding cake on the kitchen table was moldy and crumbling.

Spiders spun webs.

Other bugs were scuttling.

The mice were having a field day.

On a particularly frigid morning, as the wind made the tough siding of the old captain's house curse and scream, a familiar old pickup truck coughed up to the front steps and hacked to an abrupt stop under the bearded figurehead. A lanky young man sporting a toggling cowboy hat and a boy in a ratty coonskin cap with a monster of a slingshot poking out of his back pocket hopped out. They climbed onto the front porch and peered inside. They knocked and yelled, but the wind drowned them out. Their noses pressed against the windows, marking and fogging the dirty glass.

"Bella!"

"I don't see anybody. Do you?"

After conferring with each other, the two partners ambled around back.

"Bella!" Joe yelled as he rapped on the back door window, the same one he had appeared in when he was last in Coney Island.

"Take your fingers out of your goddamn mouth and break the glass!" Little Luigi cried.

"What?"

"Break the fuckin' glass! Hurry up! It's freezin' out here! Oh, never mind! I'll do it!"

A rock the size of a baseball plowed through, taking one of the lace curtains with it, scattering the mice.

"Hey! You got great aim, kid! That's some slingshot!"

"I've only done this about a million times. Reach in and grab the lock," Luigi instructed.

"I don't want to get cut . . ."

"Jesus! Do I have to do everything?" The boy's hand poked through.

"Watch it, kid!"

"Stop being such a lady!"

The door popped open and the two of them stumbled in, losing their hats as they tumbled onto the linoleum.

"Bella!?"

"Jesus! Get the hell off me!"

The place was a rancid mess, everything dangerously askew and hushed over with dust and cobwebs.

The mice were back, gnawing at what was left of the cake.

"Holy cannoli!"

"Bella!?"

The two of them kicked through the debris as they ran from room to room. They bounded upstairs. They charged in and out of doors until Luigi found her face up in her bed.

"She's in here! Jesus! She stinks!"

"Is she alive? Is she breathing!?"

She was wrapped in a pale veil of silence, her face ashen, her lips chapped and barely wheezing.

"Holy shit!" Joe hollered. "She's returning to her mamma's skin!"

"She's not dead, is she?!" Luigi screamed.

After making sure Bella was still alive, after Joe slapped her face three times, the two rescuers went about making the place fit for human habitation.

As Joe cleaned Bella's room, Luigi tended to the kitchen, where he found the icebox empty, the cupboards bare.

"Christ! She must be starving!"

Once the bathtub was scrubbed and loaded with warm, soapy water, Joe gently lifted Bella out of the fetid bed. The mattress tried to grab her back. But Joe wouldn't let it. Long Joe, lean Joe, sobbing Joe cradled and carried Bella to the tub and slowly lowered her into the suds, carefully cupping the back of her head with his hand.

The way Bella used to cradle Billy's head when she fed her sweet son.

The way Francis used to cradle her heart.

The way he still did.

"Easy does it. That's it," Joe whispered.

Bella's throat let out a small "whoooooo . . ." as her body submerged, but her eyes were still vacant and glazed over.

"Bella," Joe whispered. "It's me. Joe."

Tiny lights, like little love votives, sparked in each of her pupils. A dim flicker of something far away. Jesus stars blinking. Bella's soul winking.

"Francis?" Bella croaked.

"No. It's Joe."

Luigi was standing in the doorway, a feather duster in one hand, an apron of Bella's tied around his waist. "Is she really as bad as Mamma?"

"It's too early to tell."

"Is she talking?"

"Yes!"

"Thank you, sweet Jesus! Now we gotta get her to eat! We gotta get her strong again so she stops dying!"

After they tucked Bella into her freshened bed, Luigi gave Joe a list of things to get at the local market. He reached into his pocket, pulled out a fat wallet, and peeled off a handful of fresh bills.

Joe was astounded. "Where in God's poor world did you get all of that cash, Luigi?"

"Never mind. I got me a job."

"What kind of job?"

"Hey! I ain't no rat! We gotta feed my sister to keep her from dying!"

As Joe's truck tore away from the house, Luigi filled a pitcher with water under the kitchen faucet. He grabbed a glass, ran back upstairs, and scraped a chair next to Bella's bed. He made her take slow sips and told her stories to keep her mind alert, to keep her thoughts nice and busy.

Francis was with them, watching.

"Guess what Lulu did yesterday?" Luigi said as he patiently held the glass to his favorite sister's trembling lips. "She told Papa she hated him. She found herself a boyfriend. Can you believe it? Some pancake-flipping stunad from Hackensack. Papa caught them on top of each other on the floor of the henhouse. He chased them all the way to Saint Anthony's! He beat the shit out of the dumb pancake flipper and knocked out two of Lulu's teeth. (The old knife blade was still zinging!) Right there in the church, with a couple of nuns screaming! There was blood all over the sacristy. Lulu didn't speak to Papa for three whole weeks. Mostly because she couldn't because her mouth was so goddamned swollen. She looked just like Papa's old jackass. Tony called her *Hee Haw* and wouldn't stop laughing for ten whole days."

Something poked Luigi on the back of his neck. The rambling boy batted it away, but it kept returning. Like an errant fly. It was so goddamned annoying.

Go home! Leave her to me!

"About a month ago Mamma got really sick," Luigi continued. "She had a really bad fever. She soaked her whole bed. Papa took over washing and feeding her. I never saw him so upset. He stopped yelling at everybody. I think I heard him crying."

Mamma, Bella wanted to say. But she couldn't. Not yet.

"Papa's hands started shaking the other day. Concetta noticed it right away. She has to pour his wine for him at supper. He can hardly get the glass to his mouth on his own. The doctor said it's a nervous condition. He said we have to be real quiet around Papa, which is really hard for me." Luigi poured more water into the glass and gently tipped it into Bella's mouth. "Tony took over guarding the factory at night. Joe still guards it during the day. Connie takes Papa for long walks. I keep as quiet as I can, and I do all the cooking for everybody. I cook real good. Even Papa gobbles up everything I make."

Papa! Catch me!

Mamma, can you hear me?

"I got a secret job to help bring in some money," Luigi whispered. It was like he was trapped in Saint Anthony's confessional. Only he wasn't lying. He checked over both of his shoulders to see if anybody was listening. "I've been delivering packages and things for Melvin Marzorati," he said with a sly smile. "Lately I've taken on some pretty big jobs. One of their boys got a promotion after making an extra-special delivery a couple of weeks ago. So I've been working a lot lately. The bigger the package and the farther I go, the more money I get. I usually get a dollar. Sometimes I get three! Once I got a crisp ten-spot! And once I got a whole twenty! Yesterday I went all the way into New York City. All on my own. Jesus, that place is big. It's fuckin' gigantic! And loud too! I couldn't hear myself fuckin' think. I've never seen or heard anything like it. I want to live there some day. Do you think that's crazy?"

Of course, Bella didn't answer.

"What do you want for Christmas this year?" Luigi asked his nearly catatonic sister.

"Francis," Bella whispered. "Billy . . ."

But Luigi didn't hear her. "By the way, I don't believe in Santa Claus anymore," he said as he placed the glass of water on the floor. He found a hairbrush on the crowded dresser and gently brushed his sister's hair while singing the lullaby she used to sing to him when he was her tiny meatball . . .

> Lullaby, lullaby, lullaby, ooh,
> Who will I give this baby to?
> Lullaby, lullaby, lullaby, eee,
> I will keep this baby for me . . .

"I had me a steady sweetheart up until yesterday," Luigi said as he brushed his sister's hair. "Hinda Kaminski is her name. She was nice and all, but she didn't like that I needed to see other girls. Papa said he didn't like that she was a little Polack from Passaic. And a Jewess to boot. He said Poles are stinking thieves and Jews eat babies. I don't really believe any of that. Do you?"

"Billy . . . my baby."

"Yesterday Hinda told me she loves me," Luigi confessed. "She wanted me to say it back to her. But I clammed up. I didn't say nothin'."

"Francis . . . Oh, Francis . . ."

"Boy, was she sore about that. She told me if I didn't say it back, she was gonna die . . ."

Francis was howling.

The sea was calling.

". . . but she's still alive." Luigi dramatically rolled his eyes. "I'm swearin' off dames, at least for a little while." He grabbed his sister's hand. "Bellamamma," he whispered. "Please don't die. Please don't leave me."

A bank of wind rocked the house and Luigi's heart hit the ceiling. After a moment, the broken back door flew open and Joe plowed in with a couple of brimming grocery sacks.

Luigi hopped off his chair and ran down to the kitchen.

"It's about time!" he hollered as he grabbed the bags. "Hey! Where's my change?"

"There wasn't any."

"Don't be a chump! Drop the leftover cabbage on the table! Don't make me twist your stinkin' arm!"

After Joe emptied his pockets, he didn't waste any time running back upstairs to tend to Bella.

As Luigi unpacked the groceries, something that sounded like the wind whispered in his ear . . .

Make meatballs!

But he ignored it.

To fortify his sister, Luigi had thought about fixing sautéed calf's liver with caramelized onions and plenty of garlic, but he hated liver. The smell of it cooking or on a plate made him gag. Seriously. Even when Bella made it, he would clothespin his nose and refuse to eat. So instead he settled on his favorite dish of all time. Steak pizzaiola. He loved it more than his genuine Roy Rogers pistol, even more than his slingshot and his homemade coonskin cap. If he could've, he would have eaten it all day, every day. He always made it for himself. He made it for everyone. (After all, it was the favorite campfire dish of Italian cowboys!) Like his favorite sister, Luigi adored cooking. Not only had he taken over making all the meals for the entire Donato family after Bella left and Lulu gave up, but he also fed the entire Robertson Scale crew.

"La famiglia!"

He created banquets that fed a sea of neighborhood families and friends.

"Just like Bella!" they all swooned.

He even cooked at the rectory for penance.

He rolled and pinched and stuffed and cut and boiled and tossed a mouthwatering array of homemade pasta dishes that rivaled Bella's pregnant stay, that rivaled absolutely everything she ever made.

He delivered wagonloads of food to Melvin's Elbow Room.

"You cook just like your sister," Melvin sniffed.

He baked pastries at Easter and cookies for Christmas.

After he finished organizing the groceries in the Coney Island kitchen, he riffled around in the pot cabinets until he found a deep, Bella-seasoned, hubcap-sized skillet. He matched the new Wedgewood stove and slammed the pan onto the burner. Once the olive oil started shimmering, he salted and peppered and seared three fat-marbled steaks. Bella preferred to use tenderloin, but Luigi used any part of the beast.

"Beef is beef."

He removed the seared meat from the pan and threw in smashed garlic gloves and a Bella-sized pinch of fresh oregano. The rich scent made the walls of the house moo.

It made Bella moo too.

In a big-bellied pot, he parboiled the plum tomatoes. Then he skinned them, cut them in half, shucked out the seeds, and coarsely chopped them.

He sliced mushrooms and showered them into the smoking skillet, where they sizzled and screamed.

He dropped in a fat pat of butter, flurried in some salt, and wooden-spatula-grabbed the bits of caramelized steak fond as he sautéed. He sprinkled in chopped peppers and cooked them down. Then he plopped in a whole mess of minced garlic. He glugged in some white wine (he snuck a little swig) and stirred and mixed. He let the swirling concoction simmer down. Then he dashed in some dry oregano and let it drown. Then he poured in his tomato concasse. He pinched in some red chili flakes and squirted in a healthy stream of balsamic vinegar. Once the gravy was gently bubbling, he snuggled the seared steaks back into the pan. Then he took a discriminating taste.

"La famiglia! Delizioso!" he sang.

As he spooned the gravy over the braising steaks, Joe came into the kitchen.

"Luigi, do you believe in ghosts?" Joe asked the busy boy.

Luigi immediately remembered the strange pokes against his neck in Bella's room. The windy call for meatballs.

"Maybe. Why?"

"I think I just saw one standing at the foot of Bella's bed."

"What did it look like?"

"It looked like Francis Anthony Mozzarelli."

"Holy shit! He's come to snatch her away! We gotta feed her quick! Before it's too late!"

Into Bella's room the two of them squeezed, slowly in case any angry spirits were armed and waiting.

"Sit her up!" Luigi ordered. "Hurry!"

Joe did as he was told.

"Careful! She's not one of Lulu's goddamned baby dolls!"

When Bella caught a strong whiff of Luigi's world-famous steak pizzaiola, her eyes fluttered open. Joe held her steady as Luigi cut the steak into tiny bite-sized pieces and slowly fork-fed his heartbroken sister.

"Chew, Bella! Chew!" Luigi said.

And she did.

Tiny bites at first. Then she wolfed down the food like one of Bostock's lions.

For the next several days, Luigi continued cooking and force-feeding his sister. When he was tired, Joe took over. They worked in shifts like one of Robertson Scale factory's well-oiled machines.

The ghost of Francis watched Bella lick the soup and stew bowls clean and scrape the pasta off the plates.

After a week of them feeding Bella just about everything Luigi knew how to cook, the color was back in Bella's face. She was talking and singing nonstop. They couldn't get her to shut the fuck up. She was even hula dancing around the bed before going back to sleep.

"She's almost back to her old self!" Joe proclaimed.

Luigi wasn't so sure. He knew his sister better than anyone. Twice he caught her standing alone in the middle of the baby's room, singing,

> Lullaby, lullaby, lullaby, ooh,
> Who will I give this baby to?
> Lullaby, lullaby, lullaby, eee,
> I will keep this baby for me . . .

Later one afternoon, while Bella was napping and Joe was fawning next to her, Luigi cleared all the baby gear out of the house. He tossed the little outfits, the baby blankets, and the stuffed animals into Coney Island Creek. After rolling the crib under the boardwalk, he decided to have a snoop around. He peeked under the giant halo of the Wonder Wheel. He gazed up at the behemoth and heard his sister's voice slicing through the bitter winter wind. It was chock-full of happy taffy, magic, and meatball optimism. It was singing to him.

He spent the rest of the day wandering through the shuttered parks like a lost boy. He poked through the snoring rides. He lifted tarps. He broke into the fun house. At the far end of Luna Park, he found himself standing in front of an old shack perched on a crude platform. Over the entrance hung a billboard splashed with the words TRIP TO DREAMLAND! in golden letters. As he looked up at the sign, an enormous crack of thunder popped in the silver sky like a rifle shot over his head. Frozen rain began to plop down like ice. A wicked wind like sharp fangs sliced. Luigi had to hold on to his coonskin cap. He held on for dear life. Laughter and voices seemed to be whispering from deep inside the old shack. There was joyful singing. Luigi could smell pasta pie. He heard his papa calling everyone to supper. He heard Bella and Lulu fighting. He heard Concetta and Joe trying to get little Shirley and Joanie to stop crying.

The specter of Francis appeared and hovered over Luigi's coonskinned head.

It's time for you to go home now, kid! Go inside!

Enter Dreamland! Say goodbye!

"No!"

Manny's call came from deep within the vortex of the tiny old building.

LUIGI!

More voices wafted out, swirling all the way from the Robertson Scale factory.

Hip! Hip! Hooray!

Come on in!

The same Dreamland that had snatched Bella away for a

while threatened to inhale Little Luigi. The tug on his racing heart was wicked powerful (the grip was almost violent). He found himself being pulled and pushed as if by strong forces.

All hands on deck!

Heave ho, here we go!

Francis howled,

Go home!

"NO!" Luigi dug his heels into the ground. He bouldered himself down. "YOU CAN'T FUCKING MAKE ME!" He pulled his slingshot out of his pocket, picked up a small, sharp rock, and took aim. "I'M NOT GOING IN! I'M STAYING IN CONEY ISLAND! I'M HERE TO PROTECT MY BELLAMAMMA! I'M GONNA TAKE CARE OF MY SISTER! I DON'T CARE HOW STRONG YOU ARE! I'M STRONGER!"

GO HOME, I SAID!

"NO!!"

While Luigi heroically resisted being sucked down the Dreamland rabbit hole, Joe was back at the old captain's house, telling Bella stories to keep her company. He sat next to her bed and held her hand in his.

"Sometimes I go fishing or clamming alone," he said. "I drive all the way up to the Cape and stay for days. I stay in a shaky little shack in the dunes and live off the sand and sea. I run a boat across the waves where it's nice and quiet and I can hear myself think. When I'm there I don't have a care in the world. No crying babies. No nagging Concetta. Christ almighty! Being out at sea makes me so goddamned happy!"

It was Joe's very own trip to Dreamland.

Long Joe. Lean Joe. Lonely Joe.

Biting his nails and bobbing in the waves alone.

His shoulders started shaking uncontrollably. A finger was in his mouth. He was crying.

"I'm so goddamned unhappy, Bella. I don't know what to

do. Should I abandon my family? I love them, but I can't keep doing this . . ."

"Come here," Bella whispered like she was back in her Peek-a-Booth. "Come to Mamma . . ."

Without letting go of Bella's hand, Joe crawled into her bed. At first, he held her like a lamb, but she was having none of that.

"I want you to fuck me," she quietly said.

"Really?"

"Yes. Fuck me hard. Ride me like the cowboy you've always wanted to be."

Joe couldn't believe he was about to fuck the goddess of his dreams, the young woman he was convinced he loved. Miss Belladonna Marie! The Meatball Queen of Sin City!

Joe wasn't able to contain his excitement. He was shaking so hard he almost shook the bed off its frame.

The whole house vibrated.

The sky above the roof swayed.

The ground beneath the foundation quaked.

The gravestones in the yard gyrated.

Chester and Peanut spun in their graves.

When he mounted and entered her, Bella grabbed his back and clawed like a wild jungle cat. "Francis! Oh, Francis!" she screamed. "Fuck me, Francis Anthony Mozzarelli! Fuck me! Please!"

"I'm not Francis Anthony Mozzarelli. I'm Joe Cabral. It's me, Joe . . ."

"Francis . . ."

"No, Joe!"

"For Christ's sake! Shut up and fuck the living daylights out of me!"

A frenzied cloud of jealousy stormed around the bed.

The walls rumbled.

The floorboards grumbled.

The ceiling raged over their heads.

Get the hell out of my wedding bed!

After Joe emptied his smoking gun and scraped off every bit of Bella's flavorful fond, he gathered the exhausted young woman into his trembling arms.

"I love you, Bella," he whispered. "I love you so much."

Bella sighed. "Well, I don't love you. I never have and I never will. Not the way you need me to. I will always only love Francis Anthony Mozzarelli. That's it."

Joe seemed to accept what she said. "Concetta's pregnant again," he whispered as he drifted off to Dreamland. "We're hoping for a boy this time. A little Joe Junior to join Shirley and Joanie . . ."

Bella's first impulse was to slug him with all her restored strength. But deep down, deep in the deepest depths of her Sicilian soma, she didn't care. "Fuck me again," was all she said.

When Luigi arrived home (cold and wet and exhausted), his slingshot broken, his coonskin cap missing, he found the door to Bella's room closed and locked.

"Bella? Joe?"

The boy curled up on the floor outside his sister's bedroom door. He turtled into himself and sucked on his thumb (he hadn't done this since he was extremely young). He sucked and silently listened to bedsprings squeaking, to the muffled groans and heavy sighing. A few whoops, a couple of yelps, and then Bella was screaming. Was Joe fucking or hurting her? Luigi jumped up. He was ready to pound on the door. He was going to shoulder his way in, kick it down like Rhett Butler in *Gone with the Wind*. But then he heard his sister laughing. She laughed uproariously. Then it got real quiet again. Then he heard her moan and yowl. Then she started singing "All of Me."

Francis whispered in Luigi's ear,

That cowboy is fucking my beloved.

If he keeps it up, I'm gonna fuck him myself!
I'm gonna fuck him up until he joins me in Heaven!

The next day Bella was out of bed and singing. She started cooking again.

Chicken parmigiana.

Rigatoni Bolognese.

She even made a Sicilian timballo the size of a trashcan lid. A gargantuan pasta pie as deep as the endless Coney Island sea filled with diced hard-boiled eggs, chopped salami, three kinds of cheese, mini meatballs, cooked homemade ziti, and tomato gravy.

"You better stop messing around with my sister," Luigi said to Joe across the dinner table as the three of them ate. "Or I'm gonna tell Concetta. And you're gonna lose everything."

Joe was silent as he chewed. "Okay," he finally said.

"Okey dokey."

The next day a shalolly-purple Plymouth roared up to the house and honked. When Bella, Joe, and Luigi stepped out onto the rickety porch, a smiling boy about Luigi's age hopped out of driver's side door and waved. "Howdy, Missus!"

"Hello, Jerry!"

The kid opened the driver's side back door and a well-appointed, high-heeled Italian lady stepped out looking like a crazy Technicolor movie queen. She was carrying a blimp-sized bouquet of long-stemmed bloodred roses swaddled in black bunting. The kid scampered around to the passenger side back door. He yanked it open and a regal-looking woman sashaying with the elaborate gele of a Nigerian princess on her head, slithered out of the auto and elegantly tossed a marabou boa around her imperious neck. "So this is Coney Island," she hissed. She set her eyelash-batting eyes squarely on Joe. "Where can I get me one of them Nathan's Famous frankfurters I've been hearin' so much tell about?"

Joe's Portuguese wiener shrunk in his jeans.

"Me too," the Italian lady said, presenting Bella with the enormous bouquet. "I'm famished beyond belief."

"Lena! Olive!" Bella cried.

Luigi suspiciously narrowed his eyes. "You look really familiar to me," he said to the Italian woman.

"This is Miss Olive Oil and Miss Lena Horny," Bella said. "Two dear friends of mine."

To Luigi, the two gaudy ladies looked like exotic picture-book birds, fanning rare plumage.

"I gave you a ride in my car once, kid," Olive said.

"I don't think so," Luigi countered. "I'd remember you if you did."

An unbelievable glint of recognition suddenly sparked in Joe's eyes. "Hey, wait a minute!"

Olive took an aggressive step in Joe's direction. "You got somethin' you want say to me, cowboy?"

Joe felt himself shrink in his pants again. He swallowed hard. "No, ma'am," he said.

Around the dining room table, they all sat surrounded by over a dozen bush-sized rose bouquets.

Bella served a platter of pan-grilled frankfurters along with her special Italian relish and a high pile of Sicilian potato salad.

"Christ, you can even make questionable meat byproducts taste like Heaven," Olive said. "God, I miss your cookin'."

"I sure do miss it too," Jerry chimed in.

"Me too," Lena insisted.

"Well," Bella smiled. "You know where I am!"

"We sure do!"

While they all devoured the food, Lena leaned over to Bella. "I need to have a word with you." She placed her manicured hand over Bella's. "Listen to me, child. I lost me a man once just like you. He was the love of my life. His name was Hercules . . ."

"I thought Olive was . . ."

Lena smiled all bittersweet. "Hercules was my very own Hero. Olive is my white knight. Don't you worry, child. Someday a loving knight is gonna find you too."

"I'm afraid my knight has come and gone," Bella said without an ounce of emotion.

Luigi was still trying to make sense of everything. "Hey, who are these people anyway?"

Joe cuffed him across his head. "Don't be rude."

"Yee cripes! You don't have to club me!"

Bella looked around the table. It wasn't that long ago that she had first served her Coney Island family a delicious frittata she and her Cooking Spirit had cobbled together from stuff she had found in the old icebox. Chester. Minnie. Lolly. Oui Oui. Where were they all now? Dead or scattered to the carnival winds? She tried not to think about them, but she couldn't help but see all of their faces again.

Lolly smiling.

Minnie giggling.

Oui Oui balancing on his unicycle.

Chester naked and twirling his spaghetti.

She saw Francis blowing her kisses.

After the new crew finished crunching their cannoli and sipping their espresso, Olive announced it was time for them to leave.

"I got to see a man about a donut!"

"Come back anytime," Bella said when they all surrounded the Plymouth.

Olive took Bella's hand. "I just wanted to make sure youse was okay."

Bella gave Olive a tender kiss on her cheek. "I'm fine. Really, I am. Thank you, sweetie."

"I hope you still go after your baby."

For a prophetic instant, the startling image of a beautiful young man who bore a striking resemblance to Francis flashed between them.

Bella didn't say anything back. She just stared at Olive blankly.

Olive gave Bella's hand a squeeze. "You'll do it when you're ready."

"Nice job on your makeup," Bella said. "What color is that lipstick you're wearin'?"

"Pretty Girl pink."

"It suits you to a T."

Olive's eyes misted. "Remember, if you ever need anything, anything at all, all you have to do is ask." She opened her beaded purse, pulled out a small lavender card, and thrust it into Bella's hand. "So you'll always know how to find me. I love you, Bella."

"Thank you," Bella said. "I love you too."

The two of them embraced until Lena coughed loudly and smacked her hands on her hips. "Can we go now, please?"

After Jerry gallantly escorted the gaudy ladies back into their car, he bowed and gave Bella a sweet nod. "I'll be seein' you later, Missus!" Then he got behind the wheel of the purple automobile and the three of them peeled away.

Joe looked Bella square in the eyes. "How do you know those dames?"

Bella tossed him her sly Gioconda smile. "Not too long ago they rescued me. Then I rescued them."

Joe watched the Plymouth disappear down Neptune Avenue. "What do you mean?"

"Heroes come in all shapes and sizes," Bella said. Then she took Joe and Luigi by their hands. "I think it's time for both of you to go too."

Luigi dropped to the street and started moaning. "No! We can't let the ghost have you!"

"What ghost?"

But Bella knew.

"Don't worry, Luigi. We'll come back real soon," Joe reassured the boy. He was reassuring himself too. Then he tried to reassure Bella. "I mean it," he said.

The Portuguese cowboy hoisted Luigi to his feet, but the boy was unsteady. It was clear he was getting ready to fight, but Joe firmly told him they had to go home. They couldn't keep playing hooky.

"Why not?" the boy sassed back. "Concetta's fine without you. And those goddamn penguins at Saint Anthony's grammar school won't miss me. I know how to do all my stinkin' times tables. I know my science. And I can fuckin' read."

Joe cuffed the kid across the head again. "You watch your mouth!"

"Okay! Okay! You don't have to fuckin' hit me! Jeez Louise!"

"You want another smack?"

"That's enough, you two!" Bella walked over to her little brother. She crouched down and put her hands on his shaking shoulders.

"We can't go!" Luigi blubbered. "What if you get sick again?"

"I won't get sick again."

"I don't want you to die."

"I won't die. I promise."

"You promised me something once before, you know. You promised me you wouldn't ever leave without taking me. And you lied."

"I'm sorry."

"How do I know you're not lyin' again?"

Bella gave Luigi a sloppy lip-smack on his cheek. Then she

tenderly placed a hand on the lipstick stain. "La famiglia?" she whispered.

"La famiglia," he said. Then he threw his arms around his sister, buried his face in her neck, and started sobbing. When he finally wound down, Bella cupped his chin in her hand. "I want you to stop working for Melvin Marzorati," she said.

"I make a lot of dough workin' for him!"

"That cabbage ain't clean."

"I don't know what you mean . . ."

"You know exactly what I mean, Meatball. Do it for me. Please."

"Oh, hell. Okay." A sly smile suddenly spread across the boy's face. "I promise."

"C'mon, kid." Joe tugged Luigi. "Let's go."

"Okay! Okay! Gee whiz! Stop grabbin' and maulin' me!"

Bella watched as Joe's truck farted away. She stood on the porch for a long time after it disappeared. Then she heard the wind howl and whisper her name.

Little Luigi's World-Famous Steak Pizzaiola

Satisfying and fortifying!
This recipe can rescue anyone from anything!

2–4 nice steaks (Bella liked to use tenderloin or some other
    nice cut of steak)

3–4 tablespoons of Montebologna Olive Oil

1 red bell pepper and / or a few green Italian frying peppers,
    diced (any peppers will do)

10–12 garden plum tomatoes (or any good fresh, ripe
    tomatoes), stemmed and with cores removed

8–10 ounces baby bella or crimini mushrooms, cleaned
    and sliced

8–10 whole cloves garlic, skinned and minced

1 cup good white wine

a nice pinch or two or three of red chili flakes

a few dashes of dried oregano

a few pinches of fresh oregano

kosher salt, to taste

fresh ground black pepper, to taste

a healthy handful of fresh basil, chopped

butter

a fresh ball of mozzarella (optional)

sliced Italian bread (also optional)

1. Prepare a bowl of ice water. Then get a nice big pot of
    water boiling. Use a sharp knife to core your tomatoes and

score an X on the bottom. Blanch your tomatoes (cook them for about 10–30 seconds; the riper the tomatoes, the less time they will need). Fish them out and shock them in the ice water. As soon as the tomatoes are cool enough to handle, remove from the ice water and peel off the skin. (It will come off so easy!) Cut the tomatoes in half and remove all the seeds. Then chop the tomatoes nicely. Set aside in a bowl.

2. Pound your tenderloin to the desired thickness and generously season with salt and pepper. You can use any cut of steak for this recipe (a marbled ribeye, NY strip, top sirloin, even T-bone—but never flank). Bella preferred the buttery tenderness of tenderloin, but Little Luigi used whatever was handy. "Beef is beef!" the little chef always liked to say.

3. Place your skillet on high heat with a little olive oil in it. (Take a healthy swig to keep everything ticking properly.) Make sure the skillet is very hot; the oil must be shimmering. Place the steaks in the pan and sear them on each side (about 2 minutes per side), enough to brown them but not long enough to overcook the insides. Add a few pats of butter while you do this. Then remove the steaks and set aside.

4. Throw your sliced mushrooms, along with a nice chunk of butter and a healthy pinch of salt (to bring out the mushroom's water), into the steak-seasoned skillet. Bring the flame down to medium. Pinch in your chili flakes (to taste). Grind in some fresh pepper. Pinch in your fresh oregano. Sauté for 5–6 minutes, until the mushrooms are golden and the caramelized steak fond

(and crispy bits) are pulled off the pan. The fond holds a tremendous amount of flavor.

5. Toss in the chopped peppers, stir, and cook for 2 minutes or so (soften them slightly, you don't want them soggy).

6. Add the crushed garlic. Continue to sauté for a full minute. Do not brown the garlic.

7. Add the wine. (Luigi says, "Be sure and sneak a sip or two!") Raise the heat up to medium high. Cook for about 3 minutes. Pinch in some dry oregano. Cook your mixture down until almost all of the liquid has evaporated.

8. When the wine in the mixture is kind of low, add the fresh chopped tomatoes. Stir them in and bring the mixture back up to a simmer. Add a healthy handful of chopped fresh basil. Simmer for 3–5 minutes.

9. Add a tiny splash of balsamic. This sweetens and balances the acidity. Stir and simmer for another minute or so, then add more chopped fresh oregano.

10. Give your mixture a taste and adjust your seasoning. More salt? Another pinch of chili flakes?

11. Reintroduce your steaks to the pan and cook until they arrive at your desired doneness. Bella liked them nice and rare. Luigi always cooked his beef until it was medium. You can test the steaks by pressing your thumb into them. Squishy for rare. Soft for medium. Firm for well-cooked.

12. You can toast or grill a nice slice or two or three of good Italian bread and place them on a plate. Top them with thin slices of fresh mozzarella. Then top them with your steak pizzaiola! This is the way Luigi loved to do it!

13. Buon appetito! Mangiare bene! Stare bene! Delizioso!

LA RISURREZIONE FALLITA

As soon as Bella walked back into the house on Neptune Avenue, she slammed a big-bellied pot onto the Wedgewood stove and snapped a flame on under it. Then she cranked open a couple cans of premium plum tomatoes.

Meatballs saved my life once!

And someday they're gonna save yours too!

She had conjured Francis Anthony Mozzarelli once before. She was certain she could do it again.

I would crawl back from the dead for one of your meatballs!

They're a part of me!

After all, Bella reasoned to herself, *Jesus was raised from the dead . . .*

She closed her eyes and prayed, "Francis! Oh! Francis!"

She called upon the holy hands of her Cooking Spirit as she mixed and rolled and fried a pile of meatballs.

"Francis! Oh, Francis!" she sang as she sent them swimming in an ocean of her tomato gravy. "Francis! Oh, Francis! Come home to me!"

As the balls and gravy simmered, she set the kitchen table for two with the good china from the dining room breakfront (the fine stuff Chester had mail-ordered from Kalamazoo for his ill-fated wedding to Henrietta Maybee) and a couple of crystal champagne glasses (boardwalk prizes Chester had also procured for his runaway bride).

Bella grabbed the sliver candlestick holders, poked them with candles, and lit them. Then she ran upstairs, opened the trunk at the foot of her bed, and pulled out her wedding dress. The one she was supposed to wear to marry Francis.

Instead of wailing into the white lace, she stripped down to nothing and stepped into the elaborate gown. She fastened it as much as she could. Then she slid into the white stockings, snapped the ruffled garters around her thighs, jammed her feet into the silver satin shoes, and placed the bejeweled crown and veil on her head.

Once dressed, she waltzed back down to the kitchen and did a little hula routine around the flickering table (she could hear Francis laughing; she could see his Jesus face smiling). She spooned steaming meatballs onto the plates, popped and poured two glasses of her wedding champagne, and sat down and waited for . . .

"Francis! Oh, Francis!"

To return from the grave.

She waited and waited.

I will love you forever, Belladonna Marie!

She waited and waited and waited.

"I will love you forever, Francis Anthony Mozzarelli!"

She waited for a resurrection that never came.

"Fine!" she hollered up to Heaven. "If you won't come to me, I'll come to you!"

Without blowing out the candles, without turning off the flame under the pot of bubbling meatballs and tomato gravy, she did what she always did.

She danced out the door of the house and flew away.

FRANCIS! OH, FRANCIS! (THE RESCUE, PART TWO)

As Bella runs through Coney Island, the old oceanside town stands shuttered against the icy cold of a frostbitten mid-December. A light snow starts falling, dusting everything in a blanket of frozen precipitation.

Falling and swirling and covering.

Enough to make the world look like some sort of circus Heaven.

Freezing seagulls and pigeons huddle together under overhangs, heads tucked beneath shivering wings, all guttural grunts and ruffled complaints.

They clap and stamp and ha-ha-ha whistle into the frigid gales like fussing old men and cranky old women.

Of course Nathan's is open, Christmas lights twinkle.

Coney Island Santa faces wink and blink. The sharp scent of meat being grilled into tasty submission is Bella's only greeting.

She charges past the old hot dog stand and the tarp-covered cars of the freezing Tornado.

Stalwart oceanfront buildings stand huddled along the boardwalk like a long row of chattering teeth. Sinister puddles of frozen frost gather at their feet. Sam Tweety's Hawaiian Island Girlie Revue and Peek-a-Booth Theater is snugly boarded for a long winter's sleep.

No palm trees are sprouting out of the abandoned beach. No hips are flinging. No island maidens are singing. Only Santa Bella, devastated daughter of silent Santa Lucia Medina Cicolina and mean Manolo Antonio Donato, is standing at the edge of the boards in full bridal regalia, wailing and billowing.

High in the sky behind her, a noxious cloud of black smoke plumes across the white (white like a stiff sheet of blank paper) Coney Island sky.

Is that the Glasgow-grinning face of Steeplechase cackling way up high?

Not too far away, the house on Neptune Avenue is engulfed in flames. The fire that had started in the kitchen after Bella burst out the back door viciously licks its way up from the tomato-gravy-stained stove to the shingles screaming around the calescent chimney.

As distant fire truck bells clang and sirens sing, Bella jumps down onto the broad expanse of the cold sand, empty except for the faraway figure of a little man bundled against the elements and pulling a wagon loaded with tinkling antiques. A tiny green dot is circling above him, flapping and squawking, "Fuck you! Eat me! Fuck you! Eat me!"

Standing in front of the endless sea, Bella kicks off her silver wedding shoes. Her stockings rip and shred on broken clamshells, sea glass, and sharp pebbles as she mindlessly makes her way to the water's edge. The big, gray Atlantic yawns in front of her, as vast as the sky above her head, alive and breathing.

Unlike Francis.

The ocean is eternal.

Its hibernating heart is beating.

Gelid waves crawl to Bella's numbing feet, then slowly slide away.

On the hard wet surface of the soaked sand, she looks down at her toes poking through her ripped stockings, each nail painted plum passion.

Francis had once bathed and kissed each and every one of those toes. He had made them curl with undying pleasure.

I will love you forever, my darling Angel Queen!

Now Francis is dead.

And Bella is determined to follow him up to Heaven.

As the ocean opens its wintry mouth and waits, the frantic wind whips the crown and veil off of Bella's head. They roll down the beach like a sparkling tumbleweed and whack the little man with the wagon.

"What the fuck is that crazy girl doing?"

In a blind fury, Bella rips herself out of the wedding gown. She tears off the ruffled garters. She peels off the shredded stockings and tugs her panties down.

This is her last striptease routine.

Her showstopping grand finale.

Peekaboo! I see you!

Bella crosses herself. She kisses the ring Francis had placed on her finger and steps into the starving sea.

The little man down the beach drops the handle of his wagon. "Hey!" he yells. "Hey!"

The biting salt water strangles Bella's ankles; it latches on to them with its sharp teeth, sending shocks of searing pain up her legs. Like razorblades, scraping. As she steps in up to her knees, it knocks the breath and prayers right out of her shaking tits. A pushy wave tumbles in and laps at her pubic hair, then her scarred belly. Before Bella knows it, she is in up to her shivering shoulders. Almost unable to move. Eyes wide. Heart clenching.

The little man abandons his loaded wagon and races toward her. Vibrant bits of magenta kimono peek out from under his flapping overcoat as he stumbles across the sand. "Hey! Lady! What the fuck are you doing?!" he screams. "Hey!"

"Hey! What the fuck! What the fuck! Hey!" a parrot coptering above his head echo-screeches.

The glacial water surges and lobs around Bella's neck, smacking her in the mouth, icing her lips and teeth. It blasts down her throat in frozen fits until she's choking. When she goes completely under, her hair laces out behind her like a flat of frozen seaweed.

As the current drags her down, as the greedy undertow grabs her by her painted toes and tugs and tugs (the way it once tugged the doomed *Titanic*), Bella sinks.

The little man hops up and down at the water's edge, yelling deliriously.

The parrot flaps back and forth above him, squawking hysterically.

Occasionally something scrapes at Bella's legs and grabs at her feet. The starving waves force her under the water, then above it, then under again. Her body is burning cold and weightless. She wants to float away, to let go, so she pushes and kicks. Farther and farther out, away from the loss of her baby, away from the death of Francis, away from the world, away from everything.

In the briny darkness, the murky wetness, Bella opens her eyes and sees a fabulous house full of singing and dancing. Spaghetti and meatballs. Joy and the spirit of forgiveness. She sees a young man strikingly similar to Francis, eyes flecked gold and green, the color of Christmas in his Christlike cheeks. He floats in front of her, wearing a bow-tied suit and holding a bouquet of brilliant white roses and a suitcase.

You're my mother, I believe.

Billy?

Yes, it's me.

Then the boy vanishes. Only blackness. Then everything blanches electric-white like the night Francis came back to her.

Then nothing.

Then Lucia's blade closes in.

Then a new Dreamland appears.

There is the Glasgow-grinning face of Steeplechase grimacing.

There is the scarred face of her angry papa yelling.

There is the silence of her depressed mamma roaring.

There is the stunning face of Francis Anthony Mozzarelli howling.

Hello my darling Angel Queen!

I'm here to take you all the way to Heaven with me!

Somewhere in the turgid depths, a baby is wailing. Francis is singing,

Belladonna Marie! Come home to me!

"No!" Bella roars into the depths. "I don't want to die!" The briny water blasts down her throat and into her lungs. "I don't want to die! I want to find our son!"

Suddenly the voice of Big Betty LoMonico sings,

Call upon the holy hands of your Cooking Spirit!

The Cooking Spirit can fix anything!

Without warning, Bella's whole body is violently seized, as if by an enormous pair of hands.

I love you, Francis Anthony Mozzarelli!

I love you and I'm sorry!

The water around her starts to swirl.

I love you too, Belladonna Marie Donato.
I will never forget you, my darling Angel Queen!

A Cyclonic rumble, lustier than the one that quaked below Vesuvius, suddenly erupts and Bella explodes out of the sea like a Coney Island cannon clown. The little Angel Queen is flying. Venus is rising. No need for her papa or anyone else to catch her.

She is soaring all on her own.

She never felt so alive.

She never felt so free.

"Watch out!" the little man on the beach screams.

With the ferocious airborne force of a sparkling carnival comet, the Queen of Steeplechase Park arcs over the parrot flapping around the little man's head and slap-lands on the beach like a dead seal. Pale white and bloated blue. Is it really the woman who walked into the squalling sea? Or is it a dead fairy-tale mermaid?

Is this some sort of crazy dream?

The little man runs up to the inert body and peers into the slack face. It's the most beautiful face he has ever seen.

How could this possibly be?

"Oh my God! Belladonna Marie Donato!"

"Pretty Bella!" the parrot squawks. "Bella pretty!"

It had been a long time since Terelli Lombardi had seen his old friend, but there was no mistaking who it was.

There still was no one like her.

"Oh, holy Jesus Christ!" Terelli screams. "Bella, what the hell have you done?" He throttles her. Nothing. In a blind panic, he listens at her lips. "My God! She isn't breathing!" He throttles her again. "Honeybee, she isn't breathing!" he desperately calls up to the hovering parrot. "God in Heaven, help me!"

Terelli grabs Bella's frozen ankles and tugs her away from the greedy ocean. He elevates her chin and tilts back her head. Then he pinches her nose closed and gives her all of his breath.

He clasps his fingers together and, with the heel of one hand, presses between her breasts and pumps her chest. He pushes air into her frozen mouth and pumps again and again and again until a forceful stream of seawater blasts out from between her purple lips and hoses him in his left eye.

"Ouch! Goddamnit!"

"Goddamnit! Pretty Bella! Bella pretty! Goddamnit!"

Bella chokes and coughs. She gasps and heaves. The world in front of her spins all vague and wobbly. Terelli removes his overcoat. He wraps it tight around her and vigorously rubs her entire body. As she begins to warm up, she is able to see the blur of a familiar face juddering in front of her. A little older. A little wiser. Smiling and glowing. With chattering teeth, she tries to say his name . . .

"Ter . . . Terrrr . . .?"

There's a catch in Terelli's throat. He wants to cry but he won't. Not yet. "Yes, Bella! It's me! It's your old friend Terelli Lombardi!"

"Am I dead? Am I in Heaven?"

"You're alive! You're in Coney Island!"

Bella tries to raise herself up from the icy sand, but she can't. "Wha-what are you doing here?"

"Of course I'm in Sin City, darling! Where else would Terelli Lombardi be?"

Bella tries to sit up again, arms akimbo, head toggling. Her eyes are watering. Tears are streaming.

"Oh Terelli, I'm sorry. I'm so so sorry!"

"Stay still and try and breathe! Can you breathe for me?!"

The sky above them turns furious. Dark, cracked and veined with slivers of silver lightning. Blasts of snow thunder crawl across the roiling sea like war bombs dropping. The angry air is choking on smoke and ash from the house burning over on Neptune Avenue. Just then a single white rose petal, like a fat ash from Pompeii, spirals down from the sky and lands on the beach at Bella's feet.

"Francis . . . d-dead . . ." Bella sputters and coughs and spits. As Terelli takes in what she has just said, her pallor slowly blends from purple to a splotchy shade of paradise pink. "Francis in H-Heaven. Our b-baby . . . g-gone . . . t-taken . . . away . . . f-from m-me . . ."

Sirens are roaring.

Terelli looks into Bella's beautiful face. The two of them regard each other. For a moment, they rest in the wonder of their lucky reunion.

They rest in everything that came before.

They rest in everything yet to come.

Love. Hate. Birth. Pain. Death. Redemption. Forgiveness.

Boom! Boom! Boom! Boom! Boom! Boom! Boom!

Terelli giggles the way he used to. "You know, you could really use another one of my makeovers."

Despite the freezing pain, Bella laughs along with him. "F-fuck you!" she sputters. Then she smiles and he smiles too. "I love you, T-Terelli L-Lombardi," she hiccups.

Terelli gathers her in his arms. "I love you too, Belladonna Marie Donato. I always have and I always will."

The two old friends burst into tears of joy and happiness as the parrot circles above them . . .

"Bella! Terelli! Terelli! Bella!"

Two old friends.

Together again.

Two old friends.

Ready to win in the end.

THE QUEEN OF STEEPLECHASE PARK

SHE RISES UP FROM the Coney Island beach like a phoenix, luminous angel wings spreading. Who the hell is she? Standing in the sand in a tomato-red bathing costume and matching open-toe high-heeled shoes. A bodacious Botticelli Venus. 34, 29, 38DDD. "Here she is, ladies and gentlemen! The Queen of Sin City!" Hands on hips. Bare shoulders catching the sun's popping glints. She wears her first-place purple sash well. Can you see the sparkling crown blazing on her glorious head? That saint's golden halo framing her beautiful Italian face? Brighter than the Virgin Mary on a heavenly holiday. A cherry-bombed Gioconda smile full of gusto and guile. Lovely hula hands with nails painted the color of Whore's Paradise. One hand holding up a giant bowl brimming with her world-famous spaghetti and magic meatballs swimming in a stunning tomato gravy. She grabs life by the clams. The world is her oyster. And she shucks the holy balls out of it. She is as big and as broad as the universe. Not even the ocean could contain her in the end. Her favorite songs are "Shoo Shoo Boogie Boo" and "All of Me." A big-band swing of her prizewinning can, and it is the dawn of a brand-new day. One that crowns her a legendary woman. A mythic warrior. A glorious Queen. The Queen of Steeplechase Park. For all of eternity.

Belladonna Marie Donato, Coney Island, 1943.
The handwritten caption on the back of the photo reads:

Me!

ABOUT THE AUTHOR

DAVID CIMINELLO is a Lambda Literary Fellow and the proud recipient of a Table 4 Writers Foundation Grant. His fiction has appeared in the Lambda Award-winning anthology *Portland Queer: Tales of the Rose City, Nailed Magazine,* and in fine artist Stephen O'Donnell's *The Untold Gaze.* His work has also been published in the literary journal *Lumina* and the online anthology *Underwater New York.* His original screenplay *Bruno,* an Academy Nicholl Fellowships in Screenwriting finalist, was made into a motion picture directed by Shirley MacLaine. He holds a bachelor of fine arts degree in acting from The Catholic University of America and a master's degree in fiction from Sarah Lawrence College. David and his husband, photographer and podcast artist Brian Delaney, currently reside in Portland, Oregon.

One Writer's Recipe of Thanks

Served with an abundance of humble gratitude and
deep-hearted appreciation.

1 germ of bodacious inspiration
1 large cohort of enormously talented and patient
     fellow writers
several heaping scoops of tough love and unbridled honesty
     from mentors and teachers
1 healthy handful of invaluable encouragement and support
2 dashes of unconditional love
1 ingenious and incomparable publishing team
1 delicious Cherry

1. Take 1 germ of bodacious inspiration and whip it into
    a series of raucous, fun-filled stories, rough around the
    edges. Thank you, Auntie.

2. Spend approximately twenty years writing and sharing
    and revising and stewing and simmering and revising
    and sharing and stewing and revising pieces with an
    incredible cohort, a literary community of enormously
    talented and extremely patient fellow writers: Patricia
    Kullberg, Blair Fell, Desmond Everest, Lynn Bey, Rebecca
    Koffman, Helen Beum, Kathleen Concannon, The Henry
    Writers, Kathleen Lane, Robert Hill, Elizabeth Scott,
    Steve Arndt, Dian Greenwood, the Dangerous Writers,
    Domi J. Shoemaker, Colin Farstad, Jessica Wallin Mace,
    Stacia Brown, Nicki Pombier, Jonathan Callahan, Eric

Maroney, Yael Schonfeld Abel, Laurel Franklin, Nicole Jean Turner, Cooper Lee Bombardier, ER Anderson, the J. J. Writers, Daniel Elder, Rosanna Nafziger, Cassondra Bird Combs, and Jonathan Scarboro.

3. Engage with the expertise of several important mentors and teachers, ones that nurture and promote the individual voice with heaping scoops of tough love and unbridled honesty. Thank you for your deep wisdom and generous guidance, Tom Spanbauer, Lidia Yuknavitch, Carla M. Trujillo, Ernesto Mestre-Reed, David Biespiel, Mary LaChapelle, and Lucy Rosenthal.

4. Fold in the invaluable support and encouragement of special organizations, friends, and family. I will forever be indebted to the Table 4 Writers Foundation, the Lambda Literary Foundation, the Provincetown Fine Arts Center, Adriana Trigiani, Fannie Flagg, Suzy Vitello, Stevan Allred, Vito Ciminello and Jean Ciminello, Keith Ciminello, John F. Delaney Jr. and Dolores Delaney, Lynn Ciminello, Paul Ciminello, Linda Garofalo, Andrea Veras Lima, Joan DeIntinis, Barbara Cronin Harrington, Dina Williams, Stephen O'Donnell, Lani Scozzari, Vivian Taylor, Nancy Agabian, Lisa Schroeder, Colleen Mendola, Elaine Howell, and Jeffery Mallory.

5. Always rely on the dashes of unconditional love that stir into your life and sustain you. With my whole heart I want to thank my mother and father, Shirley B. Ciminello and David E. Ciminello, for gifting me the freedom and courage to be myself and for nurturing my Writing Spirit. I will always love you.

6. Be sure and hand everything over to an ingenious and incomparable publishing team. This book would not be the book it is, were it not for the indelible guidance of the Queen of independent presses Laura Stanfill, writer, editor, and publisher extraordinaire. Deep appreciation to my incredible copyeditor Gina Walter. And awe-filled gallons of gratitude to the peerless Gigi Little for bringing Bella to such beautiful cover-life. Thank you to the entire team at Forest Avenue Press.

7. Top it all with a delicious Cherry. A very special thank you to my angel and my forever-love, Brian Delaney, the best husband (and discerning reader) a man could ever hope for.

THE QUEEN OF
STEEPLECHASE PARK

DAVID CIMINELLO

a novel

READERS' GUIDE

BOOK CLUB QUESTIONS

1. While *The Queen of Steeplechase Park* is loosely based on a true story and rooted in reality, there are moments of fabulism, where something seemingly impossible and magical happens. Can you name a few of them?

2. Appetite is a major theme in the novel. Which characters go after what they want? How does the author use joyful sexual encounters and delicious meals to propel the story? Are there consequences to indulging these desires? How about rewards? What do these outcomes say about the historical period?

3. What are some of the ways *The Queen of Steeplechase Park* celebrates queerness?

4. How do the characters challenge our ideas of gender and sexuality, particularly within the historical context of the 1930s? How do you think these characters would do in today's world?

5. Consider the author's use of the Great Depression to describe clinical depression. What are some of the similarities and differences between Bella's grief at the end of the novel and her mamma's?

6. Is food a character in this book? Why or why not?

7. What are some other books that feature food and food preparation? Have you read any of them? If so, how is *The Queen of Steeplechase Park* similar or different?

8. What other books, TV shows, or movies take place in Coney Island? Have you seen or read any?

9. In what ways is *The Queen of Steeplechase Park* a novel of immigration and the Italian American experience in New Jersey? How much research do you think the author did?

10. The chapter titles often reference books and movies from other eras. What are some examples of this technique? How does the inclusion of modern references impact your reading of the book as *historical*?

11. How do the recipes function in the text? Were there any that surprised or delighted you?

12. Is Bella a feminist in your opinion? Why or why not?

13. Even though she's been separated from her baby, Bella takes care of a number of characters in the novel—*mothers* them, especially Little Luigi. Who does Bella mother? Who mothers Bella?

14. What are the three disappearances? Name all three. How does the story shift around these?

15. What does the phrase "Fortes Fortuna Iuvat" mean? When does it first appear in the story? Is this a novel about bravery and courage? Why or why not?

16. Bella's relationship with Terelli Lombardi changes throughout the novel. What are some of their similarities as characters? Their differences?

17. How does the theme of forgiveness play out? Which characters forgive? Which are forgiven?

18. Are there examples of bullying in *The Queen of Steeplechase Park*? If so, how do characters succumb or overcome this kind of adversity? Who are the victims? The survivors?

19. How is the theme of *la famiglia* represented in the book? What does the story have to say about family dynamics—Italian and immigrant families, in particular? How do families hurt and harm each other? How do they love and support each other?

20. Bella faces an internal conflict about being a mother. What is this conflict rooted in? Is it resolved?

21. Is the ending a happy one? A sad one? Somewhere in between? What do you imagine is next for Bella?

FOREST
AVENUE
PRESS